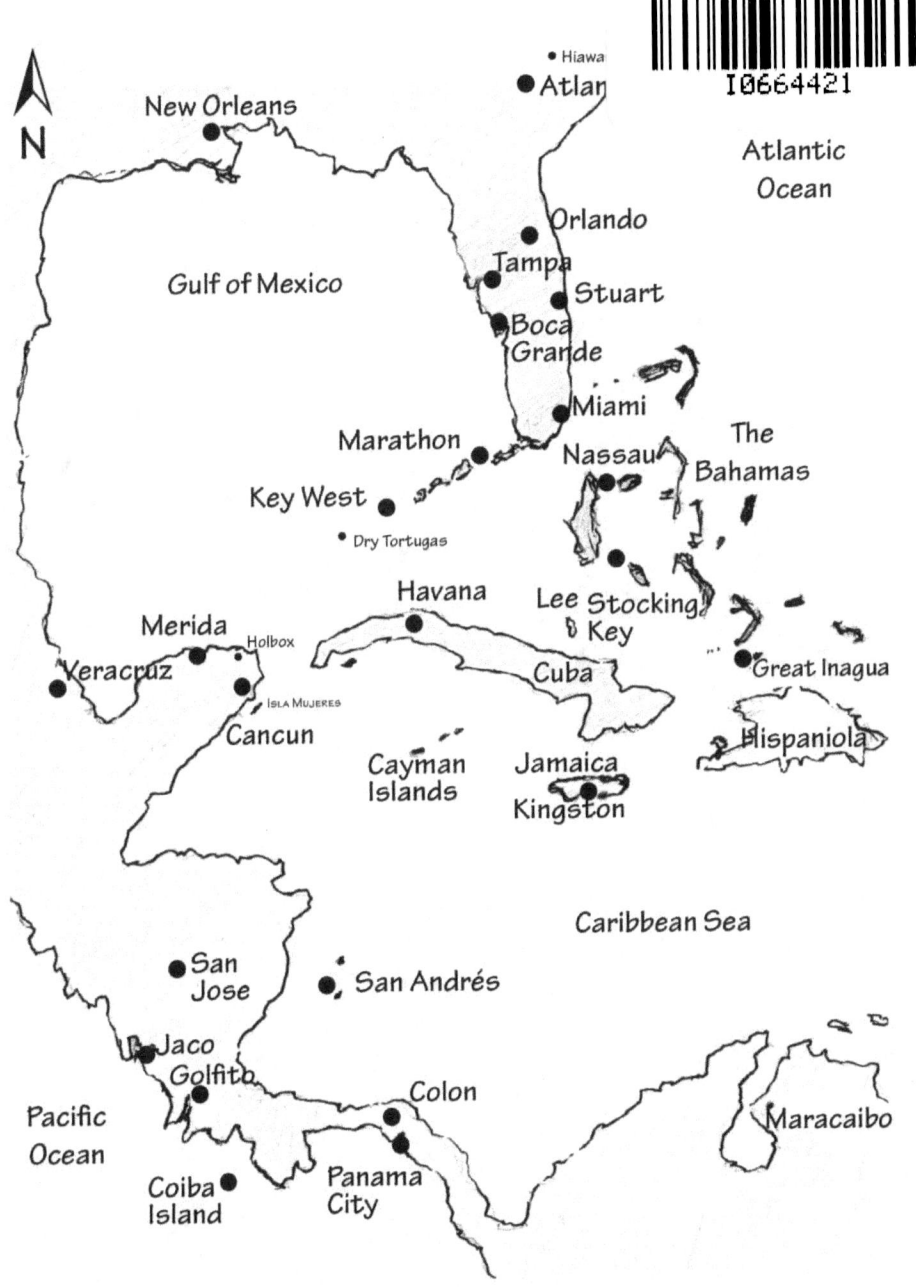

N

New Orleans

Gulf of Mexico

• Hiawa

Atlan

Atlantic
Ocean

Orlando

Tampa

Stuart

Boca
Grande

Miami

Marathon

Nassau

The
Bahamas

Key West

• Dry Tortugas

Havana

Lee Stocking
Key

Merida

Holbox

Cuba

Great Inagua

Veracruz

Isla Mujeres

Cancun

Cayman
Islands

Jamaica

Hispaniola

Kingston

Caribbean Sea

San
Jose

San Andrés

Jaco

Golfito

Colon

Maracaibo

Pacific
Ocean

Coiba
Island

Panama
City

Author's Note :
You might consider tracking the plot with
Google Earth to enhance your reading experience.

COSTA RICAN REPRISE

BY

NATIONAL AWARD WINNING AUTHOR

WILLIAM VALENTINE

This book is a work of fiction. Names, characters, places, and incidents are the product of the author's imagination or are used fictitiously. Any resemblance to actual events, locales, or persons living or dead, is coincidental.

Published by Shutterplank Publishing LLC
6800 Gulfport Boulevard, Suite 107
South Pasadena, Florida 33707

Cover design by Marcelo D. Sanchez

Cover photo with the permission of Jose Eduardo Chaves—owner of JOSE'S CROCODILE RIVER TOURS, Tarcoles, Costa Rica.

Printed in the United States of America

ISBN: 978-098947-54-3-3

OTHER NOVELS by William Valentine:

SALT CREEK JUSTICE ......

THE 2014 INDIE EXCELLENCE BOOK AWARDS, 1st PLACE, CRIME FICTION

THE 2014 NEXT GENERATION INDIE BOOK AWARDS, 1st PLACE, REGIONAL FICTION

THE INDIE BOOK OF THE DAY, MARCH, 13th, 2014

DEDICATION

IT'S STILL ... *SLIM*

THANK YOU

To my crack crew of eagle-eyed editors who kept me on track: Andy Arnold, Jim Byrne, Marshall Craig, Debbie Hayden, Dean Karikas, Lee Obenshain, Harvey Partridge and Glenda Shakespeare ...... **Also**, to my fishing and hunting buddies (*you know who you are*) who I have traveled half way around the world with in small boats and planes ...... **And**, for the first time, to my readers who encouraged me to write this sequel to SALT CREEK JUSTICE.

PROLOGUE

Almost two years to the day have elapsed since Seth Stone, in SALT CREEK JUSTICE, snatched his younger brother Beau from certain death in Costa Rica. The brothers then staged a spectacular explosion aboard the 54 foot Bertram sportfish, *CHICA*, to eliminate all the evidence ... or so they thought until now...The explosion, fire, and subsequent sinking of *CHICA*, in Herradura Bay, convinced the Tampa Mafia that the unidentified captain and their stolen millions were gone forever. Mafia Don "No Nose" Cipriano had his minions continue to search, unsuccessfully, for the turncoat Fernandez brothers, who owned the Bertram. They had reportedly departed the *CHICA* a week earlier in Panama and had vanished. The saga reconvenes on a crocodile infested river in the Central Pacific Coast region of Costa Rica.

CHAPTER ONE

Jose Eduardo Chaves eased out of his tour boat and stood knee deep in the river bank's soft mud. He moved carefully towards a 25 foot crocodile that was sunning himself at the river's edge. Jose had been hand feeding him and several other giant crocs daily for the last four years. Because of this obviously dangerous and spectacular feat, performed three times daily, Jose and his Tarcoles River Tour had become world famous. Half of a plucked chicken dangled from Jose's right hand. He concentrated intently on the huge crocodile as he slogged through the mud, one step at a time, until he was standing three feet in front of its huge snout. Jose waved the rancid chicken as close as he dared to the croc's nostrils, and the croc slowly opened his eyes. He held the chicken up a little higher. The croc stirred and moved slowly forward. Jose took a backward step and held the chicken up as high as he could. The croc opened his immense jaws, lunged, and snapped at the chicken. Jose pulled the chicken back and deftly moved out of harm's way.

His patrons in the tour boat gasped out loud from the edge of their seats, while they snapped pictures non-stop. The sight of the giant croc's menacing teeth and prehistoric spiked hide sent chills up and down their spines. They were wet with sweat caused by the tropical heat, humidity, and their own nervous energy. The rising tide only heightened the smell of salt water and the river's pungent mud on each tourist's already overloaded senses.

Jose held the chicken out at arm's length again, and the croc reared up with its mouth wide open. He dropped the chicken into the croc's gaping jaws and the croc slammed them shut. Jose calmly turned and slogged his way back to the boat. The croc moved slowly toward the tour boat, which was only ten feet away, then stopped. For a fleeting moment, the patrons feared for their own safety. Jose climbed back into the boat to a cheering and very relieved audience. He acknowledged his still unbelieving patrons with a smile, a tip of his hat, and a genuine … "Thank you."

As he pulled the boat back into the river, he noticed a large snag of fallen trees near the opposite river bank. What caught his eye was a large piece of gray flotsam that was jammed between several of the large tree branches. He made a mental note to come back to check it out closer after he dropped off his passengers on this, his third and last tour of the day.

He turned his head around and could still see the Highway 34 Bridge that crossed the river less than a kilometer behind him. The 50 foot high bridge carried all the traffic from San Jose to Jaco, Quepos, and Golfito on the southern Pacific coast of Costa Rica. The bridge approaches were still crowded with parked tour buses, and the center of the bridge was filled with tourists taking pictures and feeding the congregation of giant crocodiles below. Enterprising locals sold the tourists fish to hurl at the hungry crocs waiting beneath the bridge.

As they made their way back down the river, Jose picked up his microphone and told his patrons, "Costa Rica is experiencing a severe drought. We're almost two months into the summer rainy season, and so far it has rained very little. The river is only half as wide as it should be at this time of year."

"Has it ever been lower than this?" asked a woman in the front of the boat.

"I've lived in Tarcoles all of my 35 years, and I can't remember the river ever being this low," answered Jose.

The scarcity of water exposed vast mudflats and random piles of fallen tree trunks, more than Jose had ever seen before. There were still plenty of parrots, macaws, egrets, spoonbills, hawks, and herons for the tourists to see, but the iguanas and the Jesu Christo lizards, so named because they could walk on the water, were hard to find. The white-faced monkeys, who could be enticed to jump into the boat for a free banana, anteaters, kingfishers, and bats, were harder to see as the dense, green, jungles edge was twice the distance from the water as usual. The glib Jose carefully pointed out the river's flora and fauna as he piloted the tour boat up and down the river basin, "Notice on your right, our wild banana trees. They're starting to brown up around their edges from the lack of rain."

One of the tourists asked, "Jose, are the wild bananas edible?"

He laughed and replied, "No, the fruit is 90% seeds and only the birds and monkeys like them."

Jose pulled the boat into the mouth of a small estuary where some mangroves were still close to the water and cut the engine. "We may see some monkeys here if they're feeding." He made some strange monkey noises, and the tourists heard a rustling in the branches. Within a minute three or four furry little faces peered down through the leaves.

"Stay still ... while I peel this banana and put some pieces on the foredeck," said Jose. "They may jump down."

Two minutes later the monkeys took turns leaping down for the banana pieces. They took their time eating them and checked out the tourists taking their pictures. Then they were gone as quickly as they appeared.

The only thing that the drought made easier was finding the stars of the tour, the 15 to 25 foot crocodiles that inhabited the lower parts of the Tarcoles River. Normally, there were 25 crocs per square kilometer--2500 crocs on the entire river--but the drought condensed them into the remaining water. The mudflats on both sides were littered with them, and the river water teemed with those that were feeding.

Jose had become prosperous, had put a second tour boat in service, and trained three employees how to recognize which crocs to feed.

Most of Jose's tour patrons came from the Pacific cruise ships that made Puerto Caldera, in Punteranas, one of their destinations. He advertised his tour with the cruise ship lines, Trip Advisor, all the area hotels, and the major hotels in San Jose. There was also a steady stream of patrons from the Jaco hotels and the Los Suenos Resort and Marina. He also maintained a booth on the Paseo de los Turistas, a palm lined beach road with wall to wall bars and restaurants, between the cruise port and Punteranas. Many native "Josefinos", down from San Jose for a weekend at the beach, also drove over to watch the death-defying crocodile feeding.

Jose delivered his tourists back to the tour dock in Tarcoles. He shook hands with each one of them as they departed the boat, and they were generous when they stuffed their dollars into the tip box that was fastened to a piling up on the dock. Most of them were still visibly shaken by what they had just seen. After the tourists departed, Jose enlisted Pepe, one of his employees, to ride back up towards the bridge with him so they could check out the flotsam in the snag.

As he rode back up the river he wished that the government would start to clean up the Tarcoles River. The tourists that he ferried everyday were mesmerized by the vibrant jungle foliage, the abundant, colorful, tropical birds, the troops of frenetic monkeys swinging thru the trees, and the huge number of giant crocodiles. But Jose knew that the river was slowly dying. It was being polluted by the sewage and industrial waste of 50% of Costa Rica's population as the river flowed from the heavily populated central valley west of San Jose into the Gulf of Nicoya.

Jose spotted the tree snag where he saw the flotsam and eased the tour boat up into the mud beside it. He and Pepe waded thru the mud and started to pull small branches and muddy debris off the large object that was stuck between the large diameter tree trunks.

"Well, look at that … it's one of those rubber inflatable dinghies the American boaters use … but, with no air in it."

"It must have holes in it, *Jefe*."

"Pepe, splash some water on the hull sides to wash the mud off. I want to see the rest of the numbers and brand markings at each end of the tubes!"

"Ok, *Jefe*."

Pepe splashed and wiped with his hands until most of the mud dissolved off the tubes. Jose and Pepe pulled, pushed, and twisted the deflated dinghy until they finally freed it from the snag. It was a 10 or 11 foot Avon with a high pressure inflatable floor and a composite transom. With the proper size outboard, it could plane off with two average size men in it. The bow registration numbers were still intact on the starboard side and read: FL 2028 NP.

Pepe turned the dinghy over and exclaimed, "Look here, *Jefe*. The tubes have gashes in them, no wonder it's flat."

Jose looked at the torn Hypalon rubber coated fabric and recognized them as croc bites, but he also noticed that all the air valves on the tubes and floor were wide open.

"Good eye, Pepe, they look like croc bites to me. But look … all the air valves are unscrewed, a croc couldn't do that."

Jose wondered how the dinghy even got into this section of the river where the croc population was so concentrated by the tourist's continual bridge feeding. Most of the crocs submerged themselves on the bottom of the river and waited for a dead horse or steer to float by in the current. And occasionally, the crocs did nail a live steer or two when they waded into the river to cool themselves in the summer heat.

They would tow the muddy dinghy carcass back to his dock. There was no salvage value in it, but it appeared that someone discarded this dinghy, probably off the center of the bridge, and wanted it to sink and never be found. Actually, it was a good plan considering the croc population, but a drought of this magnitude had not been factored in. Like the Gringos would say, "Murphy's Law" was at work.

The first thing Jose would do tomorrow morning would be to call his cousin, Joaquin, who was a sergeant on the local police force in nearby Jaco. If there were any extenuating circumstances concerning this dinghy, like it had been reported stolen recently, the police might be interested.

Pepe secured the dinghy to the port side of the tour boat, and they started back to Tarcoles. Jose spotted two tiger herons, named for their orange and black striped appearance and aggressive nature, digging with their beaks in the exposed river bank. The tiger heron was the number one crocodile egg predator on the river, followed by the catfish and raccoon populations. Very few crocs (the large ones lived past one hundred years) made it to adulthood.

The sun was setting in the west and Jose headed right at it. As the sun slowly dipped below the tree line, hundreds of white marsh birds flew over the river on their way to their nocturnal roosts. The fading light of the sunset turned them all pink. Jose, who was born and raised on this river, never got tired of that beautiful sight.

***

When Jose pulled back in after his first tour the next morning, he saw Joaquin and Chief Rodriquez waiting on the dock. Joaquin was shorter and thinner than Jose, but he had the same jet black hair and light caramel complexion. Chief Rodriquez was a large swarthy man with a drooping black mustache. He towered over both of them and walked with a slight limp.

Jose thanked all the tourists as they left the tour boat and shook their hands. Every group tipped him handsomely, stuffing dollars and colones in his tip box. It was like this every day. They still couldn't quite believe what they had just seen, but they knew it was unique. Pepe appeared, tied up the boat, and began to refuel it for the next trip. Jose walked over to greet his cousin and the chief.

"Buenos dias, muchachos." said Jose.

"Hola, amigo," answered the chief. Switching to English the chief said, "Where is this dinghy that you dragged out of the river?"

"In the storage shed behind the tour office, follow me."

On the way to the shed, Jose said, "I didn't expect you to be interested enough to come out here to see this thrown away dinghy, Chief."

"There has been a rash of dinghy and tender thefts from Jaco, Los Suenos, and Herradura Bay in the last couple of years," said the chief while nervously fingering a purple scar on his left cheek. "The robbers get instant cash for the small outboard engines, and the inflatable dinghies and RIB's (a fiberglass hull with inflatable sides) are showing up in Flamingo, Quepos, and Golfito with the bow and serial numbers eradicated. They've been impossible to trace."

"All the numbers are still on this one."

"Joaquin told me, and that's why I'm here, amigo; the readable numbers and the fact that all the air valves were opened. It's obvious that the Avon was deflated before it was thrown off the bridge."

After examining the dinghy, the chief asked Joaquin and Jose to help load the dinghy in the police pick-up truck.

"Joaquin will send all the ID numbers to the Judicial Investigation Bureau. They will work through the U.S. Legal Attaché, FBI Office in Panama to find out who in Florida owns this dinghy, and also to try to identify from what yacht it might have been stolen. When we have that information we can match it with our robbery reports and see if anybody remembers anything that might lead us to the thieves. Thank you, Jose, for dragging this dinghy in, this might just be the break we need."

Jose watched the police truck creep up the narrow, dusty, road that wound thru the little town of Tarcoles back to the main highway. He hoped that his efforts would help the chief. Any crime that might keep visitors from returning to Costa Rica was bad for his business. He turned and waved to his second full tour boat of the day as it left the dock manned by two of his capable employees. Jose and Pepe would lunch at the local "tipico restaurante", Nambi, and then they would take the third boatload of tourists up the river to watch Jose hand feed the giant crocs. Again, the tourists would go back to their cruise ships and beach hotels not believing what they had just seen, and would hope that the likable and fearless Jose Eduardo Chaves's trust of the huge crocs would never be betrayed.

***

As soon as he got back to the police station in Jaco, Joaquin sent an email to his contact, Inspector Jorge Villa, at the JIB headquarters in San Jose. With that done, he turned his attention to the everyday occurrences that kept a police desk sergeant busy almost every moment: dispatching cars and emergency vehicles to car accidents, monitoring stolen cars, robberies, murders, frauds, assault and batteries, pedophiles, etcetera. He thought back to his days growing up on a farm as a boy, between Jaco and Tarcoles. Thirty years ago there was only commercial fishing, family and friends, farm work, school, and church. The boys played soccer when there was time. The girls were married with children by the time they were 15 or 16 years old. Back then there were only a few tourists, mostly trekker types, and a few visiting surfers. Jaco now had two 15 story condo buildings, 20-plus hotels, many upscale tourist restaurants, and even titty bars. The offshore fisherman came by the thousands each year, as did the surfers. There were discos, casinos, and three supermarkets. Jaco was built up with car rental agencies, an abundance of gift shops that all sold the exact same native trinkets, countless surf shops, and even some small strip shopping centers. There were plenty of Farmicias where you could buy any kind of prescription drugs, without a prescription, at bargain prices. The old slow paced way of life was a thing of the past. Now it was a fast paced life controlled in many ways by people and corporations that no one even knew, but the locals prospered financially. But, soon they realized that there was always a price to pay for the increased prosperity. The ever changing tourist population made sure that there was continual turmoil. An outside element brought in illegal drugs and worse. Wal-Mart bought Mas-y-Menos Supermarkets. The once self-sufficient agrarian, *Pura Vida*, way of life had been corrupted by progress and the all-mighty dollar. Ben Franklin had become the most admired American. Joaquin wondered, for a moment, whether it was all worth it. His rumination quickly ended as his radio crackled with a call for back-up at a domestic violence situation in nearby Playa Esterillos.

***

Sgt. Joaquin Chaves, Herradura Police Station, Jaco, C.R.: Below find a copy of the email we received from Agent Ricardo Bannon, FBI, U.S. Attaché Office, Panama City, Panama; Regards, Inspector Jorge Villa/C.R./JIB; Here is the info you requested from the State of Florida DMV, concerning U.S. / FL 2028 NP. The dinghy is a 1999 Avon 11 foot inflatable, ser# AV3287599, powered by a 1998 Johnson 8 hp. 2-stroke, outboard engine ser# JM548002298. The dinghy and engine are registered to Mr. Ronald Santos, P.O. Box 386, Fort Lauderdale, FL. 33311. We also requested a records search for any other Florida vessels registered to Mr. Santos. He also has a 1996 Bertram 54 Sportfish registered in his name. The U.S. Coast Guard is also listing this vessel as a U.S. Documented Vessel #958666; name: CHICA, hailing port Fort Lauderdale, FL. / Florida Documented Vessel registration # 673451. All registrations are expired at this time. If we can be of further assistance contact; Agent Ricardo Bannon/FBI/U.S. Attaché. Panama.

Joaquin read the email and started to pull up the local stolen boat report on his computer when a bell went off in his head. *Holy Shit! CHICA! Ronald Santos, Bertram 54! Of Course!!!* This dinghy belonged to the boat that exploded two years ago in Herradura Bay, while anchored just outside Los Suenos

Marina. The owner and captain of record, Ronald Santos, was presumed to have perished in the subsequent fire. The explosion blew the flybridge 50 feet in the air and the *CHICA* burned to the waterline before it sank to the bottom. Joaquin participated in the investigation. Ronald Santos had arrived in Los Suenos a couple of days before from Golfito, where he checked himself into the country at Banana Bay Marina. The next day he traveled up to Los Suenos and tried to rent a slip. The marina was temporarily full, so he was wait-listed and told he could anchor in the bay until a slip became available. In the meantime, he was given the run of the property and access to the dinghy dock. Employees reported that he had dinghyed in a few times to use the restaurants and the bars.

He had also paid a visit to the HMS Yacht Brokerage office and listed the Bertram for sale. He explained to Chip Caldwell, the head broker, that he wanted to retire on the Pacific coast of Costa Rica and wanted a smaller, more nimble, sportfishing boat. Chip also related that Mr. Santos was scheduled to travel the morning after the explosion, to San Jose to create some banking relationships. Chip had agreed to watch his yacht while he was gone, and to move it to the marina if a slip became available.

Joaquin remembered the dive he made a few days after the sinking with the three other officers in the department who were scuba divers. The water was only 30 feet deep in the bay and the visibility was reasonably good, but there wasn't much left of *CHICA*. The diesel fuel fed fire had burned so intensely that it melted the two large diesel engines and transmissions. They, understandably, had not found a body. The anchor and anchor chain were found intact, but what was left of the hull was unrecognizable. Chief Rodriquez made the decision to leave what little was left of her on the bottom of the bay. The dinghy was presumed to have been consumed in the fire. There was little information available about Mr. Santos. The Costa Rican Immigration Ministry turned over the final report to the U.S. Consulate in San Jose. They reported, out of courtesy, that no next of kin could be found.

Joaquin went to the chief's office, knocked on the open door and went inside. The chief was on the phone. When the chief hung up Joaquin said,

"The Avon belongs to the boat that blew up in Herradura Bay two years ago. Remember the *CHICA* and Ronald Santos?"

"How could I forget that," said the sheriff shaking his head. "I still think it was somehow drug related. I mean, nobody knows nothing about nothing! The owner of the boat runs the boat all the way here from Panama by himself. His crew, the Fernandez brothers, check out of Panama Immigration, but they do not arrive here or anywhere else in the world. No next of kin or address for the dead owner, just a P.O. Box in Ft. Lauderdale."

"That *is* strange, chief."

"Back in Miami, where the Fernandez brothers live, their cousin says they went to Mexico. None of that checks out. Next I hear from Agent Ricardo Bannon that the cousin disappeared from Miami a month later. *Carajo!*

'So now we have the *CHICA'S* dinghy, and the only thing we know for sure is that whoever crossed the Tarcoles Bridge and threw the dinghy in the river knows more than we do. I wonder if he kept the Johnson outboard."

"You've got a good point. Let's drag the river under the bridge and see if we can grapple hook the outboard."

"I'm glad you said grapple hook, Chief. I don't know anyone that would dive in that part of the river."

"Go ahead and send a crew down there tomorrow morning with two of our jon-boats and outboards, and rent one of your cousin's tour boats to tow any big logs or other debris that the jon-boats can't handle. We owe him for realizing the Avon might be important."

***

Chilly Willy was on his way to Los Suenos from the San Jose Airport, with a vanload of fisherman from Florida. Chilly had built up a thriving taxi, van, and tour business on the Pacific coast of Costa Rica over the past 15 years. The quick-witted Chilly was of average height and weight, and there was an ever-present smile on his pleasant face. Plaid board shorts and a white polo shirt set off Nike's latest creations on his feet. A pair of Costa Del Mar's crowned his close-cropped black hair. Chilly was Costa Rica's answer to Joe Cool. He lived in a house in San Jose with his wife and children, and he also owned a four unit apartment building in Herradura. He used one of the gated poolside units for layovers, and rented the other three to professional sportfish captains whose boats were located at the Los Suenos Marina. His tour business consisted of several vans, and he employed his extended family as his drivers. Like most Costa Ricans, they all spoke passable English, and if you had a problem in Costa Rica, Chilly could fix it.

Chilly Willy also had another job, one that only a few people knew about. He was the eyes and ears of the San Jose gambling cartel on the Pacific Coast. He reported any freelance or illegal gambling operations that he learned of to the cartel. They were dealt with harshly. Generally, a first offense got your building burned down; a second offense and you disappeared for good. Chilly knew that all the legal casinos, except the ones where the cartel was an actual partner, paid them protection money. Eliminating the illegal casinos from competition was one of the benefits. Having no employee union problems was another.

Chilly was happy with his position. He was anonymous, well paid, and didn't have to do any heavy lifting. He also managed a local informant's budget to insure that the information kept flowing. The word had gotten out that he was connected, so nobody dared to cross him. Chilly had even put sirens and blue flashing lights on his vans to enable them to run around the frequent mountain traffic jams. The police just smiled and waved when his vans went flashing by.

There are 35 legal casinos in Costa Rica, several international internet poker sites, and 250 sports books. The Tampa Mafia and their local partners run the show and have millions of dollars invested. The internet gambling and poker sites were ruled illegal in the United States, but they are still legal in the rest of the world. The use of credit cards on file to fund the international betting was also ruled illegal in the U.S., effectively cutting off the instantaneous international exchange of funds. The cartel made up for the lost poker revenues by buying into the larger casinos in San Jose. The casinos were not nearly as large as the ones in Las Vegas.

The casinos that the Mafia and their Costa Rican partners operated in San Jose were more important to them for laundering money from their illegal activities at home and abroad, than for the legal profits that the casinos earned. The Costa Rican government got a percentage of each casino's profits, but it was still a low cost way to launder the millions of dollars that they ran through them. Costa Rica did not belong to the AML/CFT World Organization that monitored casinos for money laundering activity. Actually, only half of the one hundred countries in the world that allowed and/or regulated casino gambling belonged.

Chilly Willy had received a phone call the night before that woke him from a deep sleep.

"Chilly, it's Pablo. I just got off my shift."

"Que pasa, Pablo?"

"*CHICA'S* dinghy has been found in the Tarcoles River near the Highway 34 Bridge. I remember that you were particularly interested in every piece of information that we uncovered concerning that case."

"*CHICA'S* dinghy ... Fuckin' A ... you were right to call, Pablo," answered Chilly, rubbing the sleep from his eyes.

"Chief Rodriquez said that the dinghy had been deflated and purposely thrown off the bridge into the river. He's ordered a crew to drag the river tomorrow ... to try to recover the dinghy's outboard."

"Good work, Pablo. Your envelope will be a little fatter when we meet next month. Call me, *pronto*, if you learn anything more about this matter."

Chilly immediately understood the importance of this development. At the request of his Mafia contact in San Jose, he had gathered as much information as possible after the Bertram exploded and sunk two years ago. All he was told at the time was that this boat had been involved in a heist of Mafia property in the United States. Chilly interviewed the waiters and waitresses at the Los Suenos restaurants that Ronald Santos had frequented. He extracted as much information from Chip Caldwell, the manager at the HMS Yacht Brokerage, as possible. He had known him for years because Chip used Chilly's service to shuttle his customers between the airport and Los Suenos. Chip told him that he was the first to dive on the *CHICA'S* remains and there was nothing recognizable left, not even the dinghy motor. He thought that maybe, somehow, the dinghy and motor had been entangled and finally engulfed by the raging inferno. Chilly had not been able to put much more information together than was in the copy of the original police report that his informant had supplied. The report surmised that Ronald Santos perished in the fire. The waiters, waitresses, and marina personnel remembered nothing but Ronald's dark good looks and his large tips. Chip related the same information to Chilly that he had given to the police. Chilly did not know why the San Jose cartel was so interested in the Bertram's explosion, but he learned early on not to ask too many questions. He just followed their instructions. Of course, Chilly knew that it was all yesterday's news now that the dinghy had been found, in the river, near the road to San Jose.

As his van approached the Tarcoles River Bridge, Chilly saw three police cars and a fire engine pulled off on the side of the highway. They all had their flashing lights on, and he could see a knot of traffic moving slowly across the narrow, two-lane bridge. He eased the van past the fire engine and started slowly across the bridge. He saw one of the crocodile tour boats anchored in the middle of the river with no tourists on it. Downriver, he spotted three policemen, with life jackets on, trailing two lines behind their jon-boat. He knew from his informant's phone call that there was another jon-boat under the bridge, but he couldn't see it.

One of his passengers wondered out loud, "What's going on down in the river, Chilly?"

"I do not know, Senor ... maybe a jumper?" He thought the police would probably find the outboard. As soon as Chilly dropped the fisherman off at Los Suenos he would head to his apartment in Herradura. Once he was there, he would call his cartel contact in San Jose and fill him in on this new development relating to the Bertram 54's explosion and sinking in Herradura Bay two years ago.

CHAPTER TWO

Seth Stone had been at the boatworks on Salt Creek in downtown St. Petersburg, Florida, since 8:15 that morning. Stone's Boatworks yard was double-stacked with yachts of all shapes and sizes: sailboats, trawlers, motor yachts, sportfishes, and a few center-consoles with three or four outboards hanging off their transoms. Business was coming back strong after a year's downturn following 9/11. Seth was still trying to retire, but was forced to pitch in more at the boatworks since the loss of his brother and partner, Beau, two years before.

Everyone, including Seth's son Jeb, who was now the boatwork's manager and his new partner, thought Beau had died amid mysterious circumstances in a shark tank in the Key West Aquarium. Only Seth and Beau's closest friend Gary Anderson, who lived in Cincinnati, knew that Beau was alive and living in Costa Rica. Seth had visited Beau twice in Tambor and fished with him in Playa Carillo, the last time on Beau's newly acquired Bertram 31. Beau seemed to have put his gambling and alcohol addictions behind him and was living the good life, called *Pura Vida* in Costa Rica. He was living under the radar since obtaining a new identity. If the Tampa Mafia ever found out that he was alive, Beau wouldn't last very long. Fortunately for Beau, as things worked out, he wound up with a lot of the Mob's money, which made it easier for him to stay dead.

Beau had Seth to thank for his last minute good fortune. Seth unexpectedly showed up on the deck of the Bertram in Costa Rica, and surprised Beau's Mafia captors just as were about to kill him. After turning the tables, *CHICA* was scuttled in a blaze of glory, and her dinghy was ditched off a bridge that spanned a broad crocodile infested river.

Seth was back home in St. Petersburg before the *CHICAS*'s charred and twisted wreck was surveyed on Herradura Bay's bottom. Beau, who had been using the bogus Ronald Santos passport since he staged his death in the Key

West shark tank, was still unidentified, but was presumed incinerated in the fire along with Cipriano's two enforcers. The Tampa Mafia continued to search for the turncoat Fernandez brothers and the stolen three million dollars, but they couldn't be found.

***

Seth and his son Jeb had recently hired a seasoned boatyard foreman from Ross Yacht in nearby Clearwater. Ross Yacht was going out of business after 40 years because their lease had run out and the land owner was selling the waterfront property to a condo developer. Seth hated to see good operators forced out and the working waterfront disappear. Courtney Ross had been good competition and had helped keep the standards high in the yacht repair and restoration business. Seth was happy though, to have been able to hire an experienced man to take Beau's place at Stone's Boatworks. Seth was looking forward to returning to being mostly retired, rather than semi-retired.

Seth looked at his watch and saw it was 11:00 a.m. He had a scheduled meeting with his long-time friend and customer, Charley Blevins. Charley owned a three year old 62 foot Huckins-built motor yacht, a Linwood model that had been stolen from the dock behind his Pinellas Point home about three months ago. The Huckins was equipped with twin Cummins diesel engines powering Hamilton waterjet drives and had an 18 foot RIB dinghy mounted behind the flybridge. It was a classic design, painted white, with lots of high-gloss varnished teak trim. The yacht would stand out no matter where it was. *ABOUT TIME* had not been found by the local or state police, the marine patrol, the U.S. Coast Guard, the U.S. Drug Enforcement Agency, the Bahamas Air Search and Rescue, or several private search firms employed by his insurance company. Neither had they found the two prime suspects, who had also vanished. During that thought, Charley walked into his office.

"Hey, Seth, nice to see you!"

"Good to see you too. Sit down and fill me in on what's happening."

"That's the problem, nothing is happening, and that's why I'm here. Nobody has any leads, but I am sure that the two owners of the boat maintenance company I use stole the boat."

"Peter and Randy?"

"Yeah, both of them disappeared from St. Pete at the same time *ABOUT TIME* did. I treated Peter and Randy like they were my friends. Now the adjustor is calling the robbery a 'mysterious disappearance'. Mysterious disappearance my ass! I know those two ungrateful bastards stole it."

"How does a mysterious disappearance affect your insurance claim?"

"It's an exclusion and I would have to fight them in court. Now the insurance company wants me to settle for 70% of the $2.5 million that I've got it insured for ... less my 1% deductible. There's no fucking way I'm going to do that!" said Charley, losing his normally cool demeanor and getting agitated.

"Take it easy, Charley ... don't blow a gasket. Let's run over the whole thing again and think it out. With the new Garmin electronics package you had installed last year, the Flir night vision camera, the Adiant remote GPS security system, sat-phone and satellite TV, AIS, three VHF radios, new flat screen TV's, and the hundred bottle refrigerated wine cellar we built in the galley, I would estimate you have three million dollars in her. It would take $3.5 million to replace her. So, do the math. The insurance company gets off the hook for $1.725 million, instead of $2.475 million.... I can see why you're upset."

Seth could testify that Charley had always kept the boat perfect ... "open checkbook" or "blank check", in boat yard lingo.

"What I really want Seth, is for you to hand-pick a crew and mount a search for my boat. I know who stole it, and my hunch is that it is being used to run cocaine into Florida from Mexico, Jamaica, or Columbia. I'll pay a fair per diem for you and your crew, all the expenses for boats, planes and whatever else you need. If you find the boat, you'll get a $100,000 bonus. If the boat's physical and cosmetic damage is $500,000 or less, it will be a good deal for everyone.

"That's a generous offer, Charley, but I don't know."

"Certainly, it will be money better spent than the money it will take to sue the Insurance Company. I send them the premium every month … and now the bastards want to cheap out on me."

"Let me think about it for a couple of days, Charley. I want to run it by some of the guys I might get for a crew, and I want to feel confident that I won't be wasting your money. After all, you are my friend, and you know I would spend your money like it was coming out of my own pocket."

"Fair enough, Seth. You've got my cell phone number," said Charley as he left Seth's office.

Seth had always liked Charley. He'd known him back when Charley first started in the environmental engineering business in Tampa, when they both were racing sailboats. He was 5' 9", slim and fit, with shaggy brown hair. Charley loved the water and boats, he was gregarious and unassuming, and related to people at all levels. Over the years he'd turned his small Tampa firm into an international hazmat and restoration contracting company employing thousands. Hurricane cleanup, flood remediation, natural or manmade disasters, no job seemed too big for them to handle.

After Charley left, Seth got on the telephone to his old friend and fishing buddy, Gene Johnson, a recently retired St. Petersburg Police detective. He explained the request Charley Blevins had made, and his take on the recovery possibilities and the probable suspects.

"Right now, I need to run background, arrest, and financial profiles on Peter Petcock, Randy Garrett, and their business ventures."

"I think I still have enough friends left at the police department that I can get that info."

If Gene's usual sources couldn't get everything they needed, Seth knew he could get his old football buddy from the University of Virginia, Bobby Thompson, to handle it. Bobby owned one of the largest security consulting companies in the world, headquartered in Washington D.C.

"I also would like you to take part in the two to three week search that I'm planning."

Gene said, "I'm all in, Seth."

Seth already knew a lot about Peter and Randy. They were both St. Petersburg natives and had grown up out on St. Pete Beach and Pass-a-Grille. Both had gone to Boca Ciega High School, "Bogie" to locals, during the same years that Seth went to St. Petersburg High. Seth was never friends with them but he knew Randy from hanging out at the Biff Burger, the old high school hangout drive-in on 49th street. Randy was into fast cars, drag racing, and street fighting in those days. Peter Petcock was a star football player at Bogie, and had played sports against Seth at all levels. Randy and Peter both had checkered pasts after graduating from high school. After working individually for several different yacht manufacturing companies, in a variety of jobs, they also did a couple of stints as commercial fisherman. Randy was arrested for smuggling cocaine, during his commercial fishing career, and did five years in federal prison. Seth had just graduated from the University of Virginia, and started work at the boatworks, when he witnessed Randy's arrest. Seth was tying up a customer's yacht at the boatwork's dock on Salt Creek when he heard a speeding car skid to a stop on top of the 3rd St. South, "Thrill Hill" Bridge, just up the creek 50 yards or so. A horde of police and DEA agents were in hot pursuit with sirens blaring. Randy Garrett jumped out with a large package in his arms and jumped off the bridge into the creek 15 feet below. The water at the bridge was about four feet deep at low tide. He dove under and stuffed the large package of cocaine into the soft mud bottom and headed for the creek bank. The cops plunged in after him, handcuffed, and hauled him away in a squad car. It took the police divers most of the next day to find the evidence in the soft mud of the creek bottom. When Randy returned to St. Pete after prison he worked as a boat detailer, diesel mechanic, fiberglass laminator, and a paint tech.

Peter had a hard luck story. At the end of his senior football season, he'd been named to the Florida High School All-State First Team at fullback. The University of Miami offered him a full scholarship. In the last game of the season Boca Ciega was playing its cross-town rival, St.Petersburg High, for the league championship. Peter suffered a career-ending knee injury as Seth Stone, who had also been named All-State at defensive back, tackled him on the sidelines. The Bogie pulling guard had missed his block on Seth then stumbled and fell on the back of Peter's left knee, just as Seth hit Peter and rolled him out of bounds. It was the start of a descent into bad luck for Peter. He never went to college. He bummed around the beach and worked as a cabana boy for a couple of seasons.

Peter was quite the physical specimen in those days and was popular with the beach bunnies and the older women at the Don CeSar Hotel. As time went on, he delivered new yachts long distances for the local boat builders like Irwin Yachts, Morgan Yachts, Endeavour, Watkins, and Gulfstar. Peter also became a periphery player with the Steinhatchee Seven marijuana drug ring. He was seen in the same Gulfport waterfront bars they frequented, hanging out with the smugglers and playing liar's poker with $100 bills. He was arrested a few times, but was never convicted of any crimes.

Peter and Randy rekindled their high school friendship in a Gulfport bar one night and soon decided to start a yacht bottom cleaning business called Bottom Boys Inc. The two losers got into the water and finally started building a real business. They dove under pleasure yachts once a month, wearing scuba gear, and brushed and scraped the boat bottoms clean. As their customer list grew, their customers asked them for more and more maintenance services. Their years working for the boat builders had given them a wide range of skill sets. They both were proficient in basic mechanical work, and started offering oil and filter changes, starter/alternator repair, and v-belt replacement. It wasn't long before they offered gel coat repair, waxing and detailing, touchup painting, varnish work, pump repair, cleaning a/c and water intake filters, and engine room/bilge cleaning.

Initially they did all the work themselves, diving, servicing, and detailing as the weather permitted. The business thrived, but the customer list basically stemmed from the once a month bottom cleanings. As the business, grew Randy and Peter stopped cleaning the boat bottoms themselves and hired two divers. The two owners worked on the detailing and the basic servicing. Soon they employed five divers and four detailers and an office manager to schedule it all. The two of them concentrated solely on the mechanical services. Their company became trusted and recommended. They had overcome their past indiscretions and were well on their way to becoming affluent, upright citizens. The business was renamed, Top to Bottom Inc.

Seth would wait for the reports from Gene Johnson before concluding that Randy and Peter were responsible for *ABOUT TIME*'s disappearance. They both had worked for Charley for over 15 years on all the boats he owned in those years, and he probably was their best customer. They knew where all the keys were hidden, and probably knew Charley's travel schedule. The neighbors saw a Top to Bottom truck there at least once a week or more.

Charley and his wife had been visiting their twin daughters in Cambridge, Massachusetts, where they were graduating from Harvard. They were gone for ten days. Charley had checked his boat through a cell phone link with *ABOUT TIME*'s Adiant security system several times and each time the screen read, "Systems OK". When they returned home, their yacht was gone. Their yacht's security system had been by-passed. The Adiant unit and all of its sensors had been reinstalled in Charley's dock box: door sensors, bilge pumps, emergency high water alarm, and GPS locator. The 50 amp shore power sensor was rigged and plugged into his shore power pedestal on the dock, then connected to a battery in the dock box with a trickle charger to fool the 12 volt sensor. No incriminating finger prints were found. No one in the neighborhood of large homes had seen or heard anything suspicious.

Seth was looking for a motive. There wasn't much more Seth could put together until Gene came through with his reports, so he headed over to the St. Pete Yacht Club for happy hour. He hoped his new friend, Lori Gudentite, would be there. She looked better to him each time he saw her, and he enjoyed their deepening conversations.

Lori was about 5'5" tall, had a slim athletic figure and her sandy hair was kissed by the sun. Her eyes were blue and her complexion flawless. If she'd had a facelift, it was undetectable. She was quick with a smile, compassionate, loved animals and nature, and always saw the positive side of people. Lori was a widow who had moved back to her hometown from Detroit. She was ten years younger than Seth, and liked all things about the water. Seth met her during a large mid-winters regatta where they were both part of the yacht club race committee. Seth and *TAR BABY* were a last minute replacement for a committee boat that had engine problems, and Lori was part of the race committee. They hit it off immediately. Since then, Seth had taken her grouper fishing twice with John Harvey and his wife, over to Tampa Yacht and Country Club for lunch once with a group of friends on the *TAR BABY*, and out to dinner several times … just the two of them. She was not needy, there was no drama, and she did not seem in any hurry to rush into a serious relationship. She just wanted to have fun with somebody that was thoughtful, kind, and interesting. Seth was all for that. It was during one of those dinners that Lori opened up about her personal life, "My marriage to Dieter was more than difficult. He was an abusive alcoholic and I left him several times."

"Why didn't you divorce him, Lori?"

"When I look back now, I probably should have, but I stayed because of the children. He tried rehab and alcoholics anonymous. I thought if I left for good with the children it would surely kill him. He was sick and each time he relapsed back into his nightmare, he got worse. Finally he died of a gastro-intestinal hemorrhage two years ago."

"Why did you move back to St. Pete?"

"I'm an only child, and my parents, Jack and Lois Dunn, were starting to need help, so I moved them into assisted living at Westminster, where a number of their friends live now. I need to be here for them and I guess I really didn't realize how much I missed St. Pete. So, I sold the house in Grosse Pointe and bought the condo on Beach Drive."

"I've known your parents for years, your dad always brought his boats to our boatworks."

"I knew that. I sort of remember your late brother Beau from high school but he was older than me. My son, Greg, and his wife live in Birmingham, Michigan. He runs our family business, Gudentite Tool and Die. Greg graduated from Georgia Tech three years ago. My daughter, Gladys, is a senior at Florida State. She's going to be a clinical psychologist."

"I'd like to meet them some time."

"Dieter left the business in trust to me and the children, it was one of the few things he did right. We have two hundred employees. I petitioned the court last week to legally reclaim my maiden name of Dunn."

Seth hadn't shared much with Lori about his marriage with Lisa, other than it had been a deeply loving relationship.

He had continued to see Annie Hart off and on since they became intimate on a boat delivery trip to Key West two years ago. But he and Annie were more like sex buddies. He had dated a few other women during the past two years, but none of them lasted once the initial physical attraction wore off. Seth hoped Lori might be different. She was the first woman since Lisa's sudden death, five years ago, for whom he was developing real feelings. He hoped she felt the same about him. He was moving slowly because he was sure that her rocky marriage must have damaged her psyche. He knew it would take some time for her to trust him or any man again. So he was letting her make the moves at her own pace. However, he noticed that her goodnight kisses were becoming more ardent during the last couple of weeks.

Seth drove over to the St. Petersburg Yacht Club which was 16 blocks from Stone's Boatworks. It was nice to be able to come and go as he pleased again. He and Jeb were fortunate to have finally found a competent yard foreman, so Jeb could just concentrate on customer contact and management.

Four months ago, Seth bought himself a second vehicle, a two year old BMW Z3 3.0i Roadster. He guessed he was going through some kind of a mid-life crisis, but he felt that his friend Annie Hart had helped him through the most difficult part of that. But, the car was a flat out hoot to drive. He particularly liked the step-tronic manual shift feature built into the automatic transmission. Two weeks ago Seth joined a few of his friends who raced with the local Porsche club at one of their outings at the Sebring Raceway. He was able to run in a couple of their half hour time trials, and also race with an instructor friend, Page Oben, who showed him how to max out his performance on the 17 turn racetrack. Between sportfishing, Lori, and his new car, retirement was agreeing with Seth.

He parked the convertible in the yacht club garage and walked into the Heritage Lounge, and there was Lori sitting at the bar with two of her "Salty Sister" friends. The way her eyes lit up when she saw him was a welcome giveaway that their relationship was approaching another level. The bar was packed, but they moved some chairs and made room for him as Seth greeted them all and kissed Lori on the cheek. Seth looked around the crowded bar and spotted Ken Carpenter sitting with a group of Seth's old sailing friends at a large round table across the room. Seth waved, and gave him the high sign.

The Salty Sisters were a dedicated group of St. Petersburg Yacht Club women, who loved to sail competitively. They had to pass a hands-on sailing proficiency test just to belong. Once accepted, they raced a number of different club boats against each other and other Florida yacht club teams, from prams to Sonars. They had weekly luncheon meetings and various other fun and charitable social functions. Many of them crewed and skippered on their own and other members' boats; and some of them served on race committees because of their racing experience. Seth's deceased wife, Lisa, had been an enthusiastic member and talented racing sailor in the "Salties".

Seth ordered a glass of "Sin Zin", one of his favorite Red Zinfandels, looked deeply into Lori's eyes and asked her how her day was going. They talked about their kids and his new grandson, Cullen Battle Stone, named after a famous Alabama Confederate General in the Stone Family tradition. Seth alluded to a fishing trip he might be taking in a week or so to the Keys. It depended on who could go and when. Seth had decided that if the search for Charley Blevins stolen Huckins happened, it would be under the guise of a Key's fishing trip.

As the preliminary chatter faded, Seth finally said, "Do you have any plans for dinner, Lori?"

"Well, actually I was ready for you to ask me to dinner about five minutes ago," said Lori laughing.

"Hmmm…what about Parkshore or Ceviche's, or … we could drive out to the beach to my favorite new restaurant, the Middle Grounds. Did your parents ever take you there when it was Robbie's Pancake House?"

"Lots of Sundays."

"Well, Rob has turned it into a great seafood and steak restaurant. They also have my new favorite red Zin, Klinker Brick, in their wine cellar."

"Let's save that for a special occasion, Seth. I'm not that hungry, but I'm up for a tapas plate at Ceviche's and a nightcap on my balcony."

Seth smiled and said, "That's works for me, Lori, let's go!" Seth had not gotten past her condo's lobby yet, so he left the Yacht Club with some anticipation.

The tapas went well at Ceviche's with more conversation and a little footsie under the table. Seth paid the bill and finished his glass of wine, a Spanish Rioja that did not stand up to the Sin Zin, but was otherwise smooth. They walked down Beach Drive for a block hand in hand not saying anything. Finally they turned into her condo's entrance, went past the concierge desk, and took the elevator to the 14th floor. The condo was tastefully furnished, had a large master suite, two small bedrooms sharing a bath, and a spacious kitchen/great room. The dining room was off to one side and had an alcove bar.

"Pick a bottle of wine from the cooler, Seth, and take two glasses out on the balcony. I'll join you out there after I freshen up."

Seth picked out a Smith and Hook Cab, opened it, and headed for the balcony. The balcony was really a small porch and the view of the bay and the city waterfront below was breathtaking. He set the wine and glasses on a table and sat on an outdoor rattan couch that was comfortably upholstered.

Seth laughed to himself, *Freshen up! That was definitely more serious than … Powder my nose.* Maybe that meant that she was going to change into something more comfortable. Well, he'd know at any moment. Seth heard the screen door slide open behind him and he turned his head in anticipation.

She did not disappoint him. Lori had changed into a flowing black negligee and she looked almost ethereal. She stepped through the door, and struck a curvaceous pose … and a mischievous smile crept onto her face.

Upon noticing Seth's rather visceral reaction she said, "Don't be shocked, Seth, I've been saving this for the right man and the right moment. I hope I haven't made a mistake."

Seth regained his composure, cleared his throat, and stood up. "There's no mistake, Lori, I think this is exactly the right moment."

With that said … he scooped her up and carried her into the master bedroom.

CHAPTER THREE

John "No Nose" Cipriano received a satellite phone call from his Tampa capo, Luigi "Wall to Wall" Scuzzi, as he sat on his second-story veranda overlooking Palma Ceia Country Club's golf course. He was smoking his customary after dinner Cuban cigar and enjoying some anisette.

"Hey, Luigi."

"Mr. C, I just got some important news about an old problem and I want to clue you in as soon as I can."

"Come over right away if you can, I just finished dinner."

"I'm on my way. I'll be there in 20 minutes."

Luigi, besides being No Nose's number one capo, also ran John Cipriano's multi-branched floor covering business, JC Carpet. Luigi's Mafia nickname, Wall to Wall, stemmed not only from his carpet background, but also from his physical size. He was as wide as he was tall.

No Nose owned many businesses in Tampa and St. Petersburg. He presented himself as a legitimate business man and had never been arrested or indicted for any crime. He acquired the patina of success in his speech, dress, and manners. His criminal empire laundered millions of dollars through his legal enterprises in the U.S and overseas. He paid corporate and personal taxes in the seven digit range every year. Yet, except for his mansion on Golf View Street, in a neighborhood of mansions, he did not live an outwardly ostentatious life. He played golf once a week at Palma Ceia Country Club, where he was known as John or Mr. C. His wife was active in Tampa charities, but No Nose might only attend one or two of those functions a year. If he dined out, it was always in a private room with his security nearby. When he traveled, he always booked the whole floor, which simplified security. His cousin, Pauly Castellucci, was president of No Nose's banks and owned a 72 foot captained sportfish plus a house on Scotland Key in the Bahamas. Pauly was also the owner, on paper, of a lakefront house on Lake Tahoe in Incline

Village, Nevada. A Falcon jet was registered to a Cipriano import/export company. All of his cars were registered to his various businesses. He made it a point to stay out of the public eye.

Cipriano came up the hard way in Tampa; he had been a Golden Gloves champ and a football star while at Robinson High in South Tampa. His distaste for authority got him expelled from high school and kicked out of his parents' house. Out on the streets and on his own, he soon fell in with the Trafficante crime family. His handsome good looks were only marred by a proboscis that had been broken so many times that it was splattered all over his face. Hence, his underworld nickname, No Nose. Besides being tough and street smart, John was also extremely intelligent. He rose quickly in the Tampa Mafia. He also had the good sense to marry one of Santo Trafficante's daughters. When the venerable old Don finally passed away leaving no family successor, No Nose was the logical choice. John set out to legitimize the Tampa Mafia. He also set up a communications system to prevent wiretaps and listening devices. He only used Iridium sat-phones that rotated fictitious sim cards daily. He used no cell phones or public utility phones. Nothing incriminating was kept on computers. All other communication was face to face with his capos. He never conversed with his soldiers. In fact, except for his bodyguards, most of them had never seen him. No Nose's low profile and attention to detail had switched the risk of jail to his rank and file operatives, who had never spoken to John Cipriano or even seen him in person.

No Nose loved to be outdoors, and when he built his Golf View house he commissioned a covered, 58 foot long, second story veranda that was furnished with upholstered rattan furniture. To make the veranda multi-seasonal he had piped in heat and air-conditioning all along it's curved open air length. Six ceiling fans delivered the controlled climate with balmy precision. The railings were 36" high and the bullet proof glass windscreen was designed to preserve the golf course view and also protect the occupants.

No Nose lit a second nine inch long cigar in anticipation of Wall to Wall's arrival.

***

Luigi drove down Golf View Street, turned into No Nose's driveway as the gate opened, and headed for the last garage door which was already automatically rising. The front of the mansion was walled, and all the windows and doors were covered with bullet and bomb proof Lexan panels. As Luigi came to a stop in the garage, the door started down behind his Escalade. One of No Nose's bodyguards, Anthony, was there to greet him. There were always two bodyguards with No Nose, 24/7.

"Workin' the graveyard shift, huh, Anthony?"

"Yeah, Wall to Wall, luck of the draw. Mr. C is out on the veranda smokin' a Cuban and waitin' for you. I'll follow you on up."

The mansion's garage had been designed so business visitors could come and go and remain unidentified by any surveillance. The car might be identified, but never the occupants. Luigi made his way up to the veranda. Anthony waited at the door as Luigi went out on the veranda.

"Down here, Luigi," called No Nose.

Luigi walked the length of the veranda and joined No Nose who was sitting in the dark with his cigar.

"You want a cigar, compadre?"

"Of course, I never pass up a real Cuban Corona y Corona." He lit it and took a long drag before exhaling. "I received some interestin' news from our partners in San Jose today. A couple of days ago, the Avon blow-up tender from Hector Fernandezes Bertram 54 *CHICA* was found in the Tarcoles River, close to the Highway 34 Bridge by a local river tour guide. It got like trapped in a tree snag on the river bottom."

"That's the road to San Jose from the Pacific coast, right?"

"Yeah, and this morning the local police dragged the river under the bridge and found the Johnson outboard. The Avon had all the air let out before it was thrown off the bridge."

No Nose took a long pull on his cigar and looked up at the ceiling as he slowly exhaled the smoke, "So, the worm turns again, Luigi. We need to find whoever threw that rubber boat in that river, because he must know something that we don't, and that's … WHO HAS MY FUCKING THREE MILLION DOLLARS???"

"Well … I thought about it comin' over and I think we should start right at Los Suenos Resort and in Jaco. Our San Jose operation has a good man down there who can bird dog some of the information we need. He also has a police informant in his pocket if he can't get the records we're lookin' for. I think we need to know who was stayin' in Jaco while the boat was anchored in Herradura Bay. That would include the Los Suenos rental condos and houses and the Marriott hotel. I already made a list of Jaco hotels: the Del Mar, Cocal, Clarita's, Best Western, Dolce Luna's, Hotel Nine, Tangrias, Morgan's Cove, Villas Calletas, Amapola, Daystar, Zephyr, and Blue Palms. It should be fairly easy because we're only lookin' at a four day window. We can have our information tech people check the airline passenger manifests around the same dates for any familiar names from Tampa, Orlando, Fort Lauderdale, and Miami. I wrote down the airlines that fly to Costa Rica: Jet Blue, Delta, American, Spirit, Copa, and Lacsa. We'll look for anybody related to, or friends with, the Fernandez brothers, Ricardo Cabeza, or Beau Stone. They'll check out that HMS boat broker, Chip Caldwell, for us again. Like to see if he bought a big house or condo, or has any bank accounts in the Caymans, Panama, or even Switzerland. Maybe he spotted the money when he looked over the boat before the brokerage contract was signed, or he might have run the whole end play. You know, with that Captain who called himself Jimmy Williams but was usin' Ronald Santos' passport. He coulda capped our two boys and blown up the fuckin' boat."

"You've certainly done your homework, Luigi," said No Nose finally calming down. "Call Cadillac down in Miami and brief him (Vincent Carlucci was Cipriano's Miami Capo and his underworld nickname was 'Cadillac'). You can lay-off some of this research on him. I still can't believe we haven't been able to find any trace of Hector and Luis Fernandez. I have to believe they were deep-sixed by the unknown Captain. How can anybody … hide out from us for that fucking long?"

"Fuck if I know, John?"

"One more thing. When you talk to Cadillac, tell him I want to kick the war we're waging on the Key West Russians up a couple of notches. Let's identify the bosses and determine how many men they have in Key West. I want him to wipe those fuckers out in one fell swoop if possible. We'll give him all the men and hardware he needs."

***

Back in his office at JC Carpet, Luigi contacted Cadillac by sat-phone and filled him in on No Nose's speed-up details concerning the Key West Russian Mafia situation. When that was understood, he explained the latest Costa Rican development and gave Cadillac the *CHICA* dates.

"Cadillac, Friday, August 3rd thru Monday, August 6th, 2001, are the dates that *CHICA* was at Los Suenos before she blew up. I'll fax you a list of airports and airlines that I want flight information both to and from San Jose."

"To and from?"

"Yeah, I wanna see if there's anyone we can connect to the Tampa money-drop robbery was in the Jaco/Herradura area on those dates. I'll call Felipe back, in Costa Rica, to check out the Jaco and Los Suenos hotels and rental condo guest manifests. Then we'll match 'em with the flights."

"OK, I'll hook my sat-phone to my fax."

Next, Luigi called his San Jose counterpart, Felipe "El Gato" Espinosa. Felipe was known in the Costa Rican underworld as El Gato, and it was said that he had nine lives as he had survived several attempts on his life.

"Felipe, this is Luigi in Tampa. I filled Mr. C in on the *CHICAS's* dinghy being found and we need you to perform a service for us in the Jaco area."

"Ah, Luigi, I figured I'd hear back from you soon, are you coming down?"

"Nah, we got a lot of business goin' on in Florida right now, Felipe. Right now, I need to fax you some dates from two years ago when *CHICA* was in Herradura Bay, and then have you get the guest manifests for those dates from a list of hotels and condos that will be in the fax."

"Fax them and I'll get my Pacific coast operative on your case right away. Chilly knows every front desk manager within 150 miles of Jaco."

"I'm also gonna need some more info on the HMS boat broker, Chip Caldwell. Like new houses, boats, real estate investments, and shit like new bank accounts or annuities."

"I'll put my man Chilly Willy on the hotels and he can also check out the condo and real estate ownership situation. The bank account and financial search will be handled by our casino controllers department. They'll request an international credit check on the broker based on a casino account credit request."

"Sounds good, Felipe, plug your sat-phone into your fax machine and I'll send you the lists."

***

Chilly Willy was on his way to Jaco the next morning, without any passengers. El Gato had given him a list of hotels that he wanted checked out, for the specific dates, leading up to the Bertram's explosion in Herradura Bay. There were 14 hotels on the list, plus the hotel and condos at Los Suenos. Luckily, Chilly knew every front desk clerk in Jaco. To make it even easier, Felipe had given him $3000 to spread around. The Tampa Mafia wanted this information quickly. Chilly thought he could do it for less than $2000, so that would mean at least an extra thousand for him. He drove through Jaco and went south to the Del Mar. He would start at the very southern most hotel and work his way north.

He parked his van in the turnaround and went to the Del Mar's front desk.

He spotted the head clerk and said, "Esteban, mi amigo, how is the family?"

"Everyone's OK Chilly. But, if you have a wife and four daughters, two of them are always pissed off about something."

Chilly Willy laughed and said, "I have a favor to ask. My friends in San Jose are trying to find someone, and I need your guest roster from August 3rd thru 6th from two years ago in 2001. If I can get it by tomorrow there's $100 in it for you. Also, this is on the tranquilo, mi amigo."

"No problem, Chilly, I won't say nothing. With the computers it will only take me a few minutes. I can't take your money, amigo. I don't forget when you rushed my daughter to the San Jose Hospital, in your van with the sirens, when she was sick with her appendix."

"Thank you, Esteban, but I insist that you take the $100. You would not want to offend the generosity of my friends in San Jose."

"Absolutely not, amigo. Come by later, and I will have it for you. If I am gone it will be in an envelope with your name on it."

And so it went as Chilly drove from hotel front desk to hotel front desk. Each one promised to have the information for him by the next morning.

Chilly drove to Herradura next and stopped at the *Stay in Costa Rica Inc.* office. They handled all the rentals for Los Suenos resort. Their office manager, Jose Frio, thought he could have it by noon the next day. Chilly drove into the resort and parked in the circle in front of the sprawling Marriott hotel. He hoped Alejandro Villegas would be manning the desk, and he was not disappointed. Chilly Willy explained his mission and Alejandro ran the report for him while he waited. Chilly slipped him a "Big Ben" and everybody was happy. He rode up to the Villa Calletas Hotel on top of the highest mountain in Herradura, where the view was indescribable. His wife's cousin, Mateo, was the night manager there. He treated Chilly to a vino tinto and dinner in the kitchen, while the desk clerk ran the report. Mateo wouldn't take the $100, under any circumstances, because he was never charged to ride back and forth to San Jose if Chilly had an extra seat in any of his vans.

Chilly drove down the mountain to Herradura and spent the night at his apartment. He took a swim in his pool, had another glass of red wine and turned in early. He would pick-up all his other reports tomorrow morning, and check out Chip Caldwell on his computer at the National Property Registry site on line. Chilly would return to San Jose in the afternoon, and meet with El Gato in the back offices of the Lucky Strike Casino. He was sure Felipe Espinosa would be pleased with his performance.

***

Chilly Willy rose early and made some strong Café Rey Tarrazu coffee. He powered up his computer and searched the Costa Rica National Property

Register site. Chip Caldwell didn't own any real estate in Costa Rica, according to the National Registry. Chilly made a few phone calls and found that Chip had been renting a two bedroom condo on the golf course in Los Suenos. He had no lease and was on a month to month basis at $1800 per month. He drove a six year old Ford Explorer, and the four year old 35 foot Contender with three, 250 hp. outboards belonged to the owner of HMS Boat Brokers in the United States.

Chilly drove down to the Del Mar to pick up his guest roster from Esteban. From there, he would pick one up at each hotel as he worked his way back north until he had them all. He should be sitting in El Gato's San Jose office no later than 3:00 that afternoon.

CHAPTER FOUR

Seth woke up the next morning with a smile on his face. Last night still seemed like a dream. It was the first time in five years that he had made love with real emotion. Lori had been beautiful in every way. She hadn't been self conscious and was both modest and passionate at the same time. Their first encounter didn't last long enough for either of them. But they whispered sweet nothings, and Seth started massaging her back. It didn't take too long before they were both discovering new territory.

In the afterglow of their second encounter of the night, Seth said, "I ought to be going now, Lori. I didn't come prepared to stay overnight, as much as I'd like to."

"You can stay, Seth, I have an extra toothbrush."

"Well, let's keep the doorman guessing for a little longer. On our next date we can plan to stay at one place or the other. But, I'm a happy man, Lori."

"That makes two of us, Seth. I can't wait to see you again."

"So, what's wrong with tomorrow? I'll call you from the boatworks around noon."

With that said, Seth got out of Lori's bed and got dressed. She wrapped the top sheet around her and headed to the bathroom. Seth went thru the living room and retrieved the open wine bottle and the two glasses from the balcony. He re-corked the Smith and Hook Cab and put it back in Lori's cooler. She met him at the front door and gave him a long goodnight kiss.

"Until tomorrow, Lori."

"Many, many, tomorrows, Seth."

They kissed again and Seth slipped out the door. The 20 minute drive home seemed like five minutes, and she was never off his mind for an instant.

***

Seth was up at 6:00 a.m., started the coffee, and headed for the shower. He started to think about Charley Blevin's project. He needed to get downtown to the boatyard to see if Gene had sent a report. Seth's three story townhouse was on the beach on Paradise Island, in Treasure Island. His porches overlooked the Intracoastal Waterway. Scores of boats passed by in both directions at all hours during the week, and hundreds went by on a good weather weekend. He could stand in his third floor shower and look thru its glass door, then thru the bathroom/porch access door window, and see the boats going by below. The thing he liked the best about it was watching the dolphin feed each morning and evening.

Seth moved out to Treasure Island after Lisa's death. There were too many memories in their old family house in the northeast section of St. Pete. He kept the house and rented it out. His son, Jeb, was married and had a baby. So when Jeb moved back to town to manage the boatyard, Seth gave the house to Jeb and his wife, Lynne rent free. He liked the fact that he could turn off the water and the water heater, set the a/c at 82 degrees, set the alarm, lock the front door, and leave the townhouse for as long as he wanted. The condo association took care of the townhouse's exterior and grounds. A neighbor, who was an old sailboat racing friend, had a key if something in the townhouse needed to be checked out. Seth had not participated in any condo meetings, boards, or committees. He was basically apolitical and knew he didn't have the patience to deal with the inevitable condo commandos. So far it had worked out fine.

After his shower, he made a light breakfast of coffee, a toasted bagel, and fresh fruit. He wondered what Lori was doing at this moment and smiled. He finished his breakfast and headed for Salt Creek and the boatworks in his Z3, with the top down. He still had his Yukon in the garage.

He parked in the lot across from the boatworks and was greeted by the shrill sound of grinders, sanders, and air compressors working. He loved those sounds because it meant the yard was busy and making money. After greeting Jeb and the office staff, he went straight to his desk and turned on his computer. There was an email from Gene Johnson sent four minutes ago. It read: *Call me.* Seth got a cup of coffee, sat back down, and called Gene.

"That was quick."

"Well, I just sat down at my desk."

"I've got all the information, but it's from a number of different sources. If you have time this morning, why don't I just come down there and give it to you rather than taking two hours to summarize it in an email. I'm only ten minutes away."

"Come on down, the coffee's free."

Gene walked in 15 minutes later and sat his tall, angular, frame in a chair across from Seth's desk. He looked tan, fit, and full of energy, even after 40 years of watching his back on the police force. Maybe that was what had turned his full head of hair snow white. He carried a file folder stuffed with paper.

"I see what you mean," said Seth.

"I'll read and you take notes. I'll start with their financial situations. Both Randy and Peter are divorced with no kids; they pay alimony, hefty alimony ... like $1500 a month. They both have a boat payment Randy pays $750 a month on a 42' Sea Ray and Peter pays $625 on a 38 Fountain."

"Nice boats."

"They both live in waterfront apartments with rents near $2000 a month."

"What do they drive?"

"They lease two, four door crew cab trucks through their business. With tax, the leases run $400 a month each."

"I know they run with a fast crowd, I've seen them around town, and out on the water. They have expensive girlfriends, big bar bills, big boat fuel bills, and who knows what they're blowing up their noses. What do you think they're spending a year?"

"I added all the known figures up, and estimated the rest. I'd say conservatively, $80K to $100K each."

"What else did you uncover?"

"You know about Randy's prison time, they both were arrested for assault and battery a couple of times but they got probation, and Peter had one DUI conviction."

"Par for the course."

"Neither one of them or their business has made any payments to their creditors or their landlords since *ABOUT TIME* disappeared. I obtained a 35 page deposition from the federal court house building, outlining their recent problems with OHSA and the federal lawsuit filed against Top to Bottom. I also included another report on the outcome and after effect of the federal lawsuit on their company."

"I heard about the OHSA problem through the grapevine a while back, but it was all hearsay. I'll read those reports this afternoon, and call you. So far it looks like these guys were digging themselves a deep hole. Thanks for all the info, Detective Johnson."

"Give me a call when you have digested the whole thing," said Gene smiling, as he got up to leave. "I'll be standing-by."

Gene's reports contained lawsuit information that Seth already knew about, however his report helped Seth separate fact from hearsay. Seth had heard, through his grapevine of suppliers and customers that Top to Bottom had been raided by OSHA and shut down by the Federal Marshals for violating federal commercial diving regulations. The federal court report corroborated those charges and provided the details. Apparently, a disgruntled diving employee had been fired for violating the companies non-compete regulations. The employee contacted OSHA and cited several commercial diving safety violations that were occurring during Top to Bottom's cleaning jobs. This employee was fired for moonlighting for some of Top to Bottom's customers at a lower cash price. A loyal customer turned him into Peter.

Bottom cleaning divers worked in six to eight feet of water and used a cart-mounted air tank connected to a 40 foot hose. The tank stayed on the dock while the diver cleaned the bottom. Commercial salvage and construction divers are required to have two divers in the water at all times with a third standing by on the dock or boat with a third air supply. Top to Bottom's divers worked alone driving from one location to another in a company van. OSHA shut their diving operation down and fined Top to Bottom $200,000. They hired a local lawyer to fight OSHA, but the lawyer informed them, after checking out the situation, that they were technically in the wrong. The rub was that one-man bottom cleaning dive companies (who numbered in the hundreds on the west coast of Florida) were allowed to continue their businesses because they had no employees.

Top to Bottom was forced to abandon bottom cleaning and dissolved the company to avoid the $200,000 fine. They sold the dive trucks to their former employees and let them divide up the bottom cleaning customers. The heartbeat of their business was gone. Peter and Randy were too old to get back in the water, so they set up a new detailing and yacht service company called Inside and Out Yacht Service and continued operating that portion of the business themselves, along with three detailers. Nobody could do anything for them. It was a classic case of Federal Government regulations putting the small business man out of business. Even the liberal *St. Petersburg Times* pointed out the unfairness by revealing that OSHA was no longer subsidized by Congress. OHSA existed on only the fines they collected; so more unfair interpretations of regulations could be expected in many more situations in the future.

Seth figured that it soon became evident to Peter and Randy that their cash flow had been cut in half, and they didn't have much chance of adding new customers regularly as in the past. They couldn't maintain their affluent life styles, even after downsizing their personnel and offices. Seth thought that they probably *had* reverted to their former lives. Charley was right. They very well could have stolen *ABOUT TIME* and used her to enter the drug trade. Seth thought that if that were the case they would have to disguise the Huckins in some manner. They certainly possessed the right skills to do that.

Seth started to pencil some facts about the Huckins Linwood 62 on a legal pad. The overall length of the vessel was 62 feet 3 inches, with a beam of 16 feet 6 inches, and because of the twin Hamilton water jet drives, her draft was a shallow 2 feet 6 inches. The entire vessel weighed 52,000 pounds; the boat had a stern mounted teak swim platform. The Huckins carried eight hundred gallons of diesel and two hundred gallons of water. At 9 knots, the Cummins QSM 11, 715 HP, diesels consumed 5.5 gallons of diesel per hour, and could cover 1400 miles. At 19 knots its range was 495 miles, and at its top speed of 35 knots the Huckins could travel 410 miles. The distance from Key West to Cancun, Mexico was approximately 404 miles. Seth thought that even with some added cargo weight and a 250 gallon auxiliary fuel tank, the Huckins could easily make it to Mexico, at high speeds, in decent weather. Traveling to Columbia would add another thousand miles or better, so Seth guessed Mexico would be the suspects' drug source.

Seth quickly came to the conclusion that it would be worth the time and effort to mount an organized effort to find *ABOUT TIME*. He would have to assume that Randy, Peter, and the Huckins all had new identities and were operating somewhere in plain sight based in the Florida Keys or in Mexico. Either way, the trip between the two had to take place fairly regularly. Seth hoped she was in the Keys. If they found the Huckins in the Keys and learned what the suspects' scam was, Seth could call in a host of authorities to take them down with little personal risk for his crew and himself. If the Huckins was based in Mexico, and was not coming into U.S. territorial waters to unload, it made things more difficult. The Coast Guard would be Seth's only choice and if the element of surprise was lost, the Huckins could run away from anything the Coast Guard had on the high seas, except their helicopters. Recovery of *ABOUT TIME* while in Mexico was futile unless Seth's team commandeered the Huckins and ran it back to Florida themselves. The Mexican authorities did not release stolen boats back to their owners. Nor did they extradite U.S. citizens or expats that had not already been charged with a specific crime committed inside U.S. territory.

Well, thought Seth, *first things first*. I've got to put a crew together and plan the logistics. He found Jeb alone in his office, went inside, and closed the door behind him. He briefed Jeb on the Charley Blevin's situation, suspects and all, and told him he would probably mount a search if he could get the right crew together. Jeb cautioned him not take unnecessary risks. Seth assured him he was planning to call the authorities if he located the boat.

Gene Johnson was the first person he called.

"Gene, based on the information you gave me about Peter and Randy, and several other factors I've considered, I think we have a good shot at finding the Huckins. We'll probably leave for the Keys in four or five days. If we don't find *ABOUT TIME* in two weeks time, we'll call it a day. Charley is going to pay all the expenses, plus $300 a day per man. If we find it, we'll divide a $100,000 bonus equally. Are you still in?"

"Shit fire! I already told you I'd do it for free. It sounds like a great adventure, and I've got nothing but time on my hands."

"The cover story will be that we're going on a two to three week fishing trip to the Keys in *TAR BABY*. That will let us move the boat around down there without suspicion and we will actually do a little fishing out in the Gulf Stream. It will also provide us with a cover if we happen to run into or get spotted by Randy Garrett or Peter Petcock somewhere. Even if they're disguised and we don't recognize them, they know some of us, and they'd recognize *TAR BABY*. You'll go with me on the Hatteras."

"Who else is going?"

"Well, I'm going to ask John Harvey to fly down in his airplane. He can fly back for a few days if he has to see patients, but maybe he can come full time. I know he's got a new dermatologist partner who's buying his practice. I'll figure it out with him. I'm going to ask Toby Warner and Billy Chandler from Boca Grande if they want to come. Toby is a good small plane pilot, besides being an excellent boat captain. He just retired and sold his charter boat a couple of months ago. I figure he can fly with John and fill in as pilot if John has to go back to St. Pete for a couple of days. Billy is semi-retired and is as good a fisherman, scuba diver, and blue water boatsman … as I know."

"Will Billy be coming with us on the *TAR BABY*?"

"Not initially, I'm going to charter a 40-foot trawler from Florida Charters over at the Vinoy Marina. I want Billy, Toby, and Freddy Buckley to bring that boat down to the Keys. We can use it as a dormitory, stake-out, and all around utility boat. We won't even berth the boats at the same marinas. You remember Freddy from hog hunting don't you? He's one of my old sailboat racing pals. He's a St. Pete Beach retired real estate developer and builder. There was just an article about him being the oldest finisher in the St. Pete to Key Largo beach catamaran race. He did it in a Hobie 18 catamaran, and he was also a judo champion when he was in the Army."

"I remember him, he's short and wiry, has a close trimmed beard, and he's a good shot. Sounds like you're putting together a Geezer all-star team, Seth. I liked fishing with Billy the last couple of years in the "Old Salts" tournaments out in the Gulf. Toby's the tall red-headed charter captain friend of yours from Boca Grande, right? Who else is going to be on *TAR BABY?*"

"I'm going to call Dino Vinocelli, a younger friend of mine, that I met hog hunting a couple of years ago. I've been doing a little grouper fishing and spearfishing with him, too. Dino is a high tech scuba instructor (nitrox etc.), and also has a black belt in karate. He's a big Italian guy, six feet, 250 lbs and he goes to the gym. He's single, in between scuba gigs now, and is negotiating to buy a dive business in the Keys. He might be receptive to the money and a chance at a share of the $100,000."

"Sounds like Dino can handle himself."

"He can. I'm hoping we can find that the boat and the suspects are based in the Keys. That way when we figure out what they're up to, we can call in the sheriff or local police and let them make the collar. I better get off the phone, Gene, and call the rest of the crew. I hope they all can go. I sure am glad you're going. Besides your law enforcement knowledge, you know more about my Hatteras than anybody but me."

Seth hung up and called John Harvey. He was seeing patients, but he called right back.

"Hey Seth, is everything OK?"

Seth asked if he had a few minutes and John said, "Sure, Seth, I just saw my last patient until after lunch."

Seth ran through the plan as fast as he could and asked John if he wanted in.

"Of course I do, I just closed my deal to sell the practice to my new partner two days ago. He has hired an additional P.A., and she starts Monday. I'm going to work three days a week by the hour, no salary. That way, I can leave whenever I want, on short notice. He can work straight thru the next two or three weeks. I did it for years."

"Sounds good to me, I need to call Toby and see if he can go. I know he can fly your airplane. The two of you would make a great aerial surveillance team. Remember to bring the telephoto lens for your good Nikon DF camera. I want you to take aerial photos through a parallax frame at a couple of different elevations to identify any vessels that are the same size as the Huckins."

"That might cause a problem around the Lower Keys where "Fat Albert" and the other tethered radar blimps are, and out over the Marquesas and Dry Tortugas National Parks. Since 9/11 the military has been enforcing the Air Defense Identification Zone-ADIZ down there. You have to file daily flight plans with crew information, exact course, times, and exact altitudes if you are going over the no fly boundaries. And you have to wait an hour for approval. If you fly in unidentified they put a fighter jet on your tail. "

"That's not going to work if we're tracking a vessel."

"There may be a simple solution to this. I know a photographer, who works for Florida Sportsman magazine, who got a special permit from John Timmons, the Coast Guard Commandant in St. Pete. He had no restrictions on altitudes, flight times, or landing locations. He just called in his tail numbers anytime he flew into the restricted zone."

"Well, John Timmons is a member of the Yacht Club and a neighbor of mine down in Bayboro Harbor. What are your Lance's tail numbers?

"9127Z."

"I'll explain that we're going to look for the Huckins and the robbery suspects by land, sea, and air. Then fill him in on our drug smuggling suspicions, and assure him that we intend to turn the evidence and the arrests over to the proper authorities, if we're successful. I think, under those circumstances, he'll grant us the special permit.

"I think you're right, Seth. Are we going to have a team meeting before we go?"

"Absolutely, I should know who's going to go by tomorrow. Then we'll have a meeting at my townhouse early next week. I'll call you as soon as I know."

Seth hung up and called Toby Warner in Boca Grande. Toby answered on the second ring.

"Hey, Toby, it's Seth Stone. How's retirement treating you, Buddy?"

"To tell you the truth, Alice is working me half to death around the house. She's getting even for all the years I didn't have the time because of the fishing charter business. To make matters worse, she tells me how to do everything, like I've forgotten how to fix a fucking toilet. I mean how many stopped up heads does she think I fixed on the charter boat? Anyhow, she's driving me freaking nuts."

Seth laughed and said, "How would you like to spend a couple of weeks in the Keys flying around in an airplane with John Harvey?"

"God Bless you, Seth Stone! Tell me more."

Seth laid out the whole plan for him, including Billy, Freddy, and Toby bringing the chartered trawler down from St. Petersburg. Toby was more than receptive.

"Have you seen Billy lately?" asked Seth.

"Saw him last week. We went out in his Bertram 31 and caught some grouper for the freezer."

"Do you think he's in town?"

"I think he is. He was talking about pulling his boat for some bottom painting over on Pine Island this week."

"I'll give him a call. I hope he'll join us."

"I don't think he would want to miss it, Seth. Call me when you have the team meeting set."

Seth dialed up Billy Chandler, and sure enough he was on Pine Island. He ran Billy through the plan, and Billy said he wouldn't miss it for the world. He was finished with his boat bottom and was launching it tomorrow on the high tide. He would call Toby and they would drive up for the team meeting together.

Seth called Freddy Buckley next. Freddy answered his cell phone after several rings, but Seth could hardly hear him.

"Freddy, where are you? I can hardly hear you."

"I'm down in the bilge of my boat, working on a generator, Seth. Can I call you back in five minutes?"

"Sure, I'll be waiting by the phone."

Freddy owned a 68 foot Irwin Ketch that he docked behind his waterfront house on St. Pete Beach. It was probably the last in a series of large sailboats that Freddy and his wife, Penelope, had sailed all over the world. Like most

Florida natives, he had grown up with boats and did most of the maintenance work on his boats when he had the time. It was good to know how to fix things when you were 350 miles from land and both your generators quit running. You only had about eight hours to get one fixed or you lost all your refrigerated food.

Seth's phone rang and it was Freddy, "Extricated yourself from the bilge, hey Freddy?"

"Yeah, I got the genset running … finally. Fuel problem as usual, air getting in thru the Racor. I put new seals in … so what's up?"

Seth filled Freddy in on everything. Then told him what crew members had committed to participate at this time, and who he had left to call.

"If you have the time, I would sure like to have you along, Freddy."

"You can count me in, Seth. Sounds like a great adventure. Call me when you set up the team meeting. I'll make sure I'm available for the whole trip."

Seth hung up and immediately dialed up Dino Vinocelli. He answered on the third ring, "Dino Vino!"

Seth laughed, "Where are you Dino, its Seth?"

"I'm in Key Largo at the dive shop I'm going to buy. I'm giving a certification class on Tri-mix/Helitrox for deep diving tonight and tomorrow. Classroom tonight, open water dive tomorrow. I've got to earn a little bread to pay the freaking bills."

"Do you have a minute to talk to me?"

"Sure, Seth, the classroom meeting doesn't start until 7:00 p.m."
Repeating the process, Seth ran Dino through the whole *ABOUT TIME* story, including profiles on the other crew members. Then Seth asked, "What do you think?"

"Well, I think you've got a good plan. It all sounds plausible. With the airplane, boats, and a couple of rental cars we should be able to check out a lot of territory, fairly quickly. You have a good cover story figured. I agree that the Huckins has got to have been altered. The boat probably *is* hiding in plain sight. They have to be making money to live, so they're doing what they know how to do, and I don't mean cleaning boat bottoms."

"Do you want to sign on?"

"I'm in. It sounds like a challenge, and I'd be lying if I said I can't use the money. I'm a good two months from closing on my dive shop deal here in Key Largo because of probate issues related to the owner's estate. Let me know when the team meeting is scheduled and I'll be there."

Seth called Charley on his cell phone, Charley answered and Seth said, "We're on Charley. I got the six guys I needed and we'll be leaving for the Keys the middle of next week."

"I've been waiting and hoping you would do this, Seth. I'll come down with some cash to the boatworks tomorrow. How much do you want?"

"Bring me $50,000 in $100 bills, in a duffle. If I need more, you can wire it to one of the banks in the Keys. Stay in St. Petersburg or wherever, Charley, and keep your cell phone with you 24/7, but ... **do not** ... come anywhere near the Keys unless I ask you to come."

"OK, you're the doctor. Thanks, Seth."

"Don't thank me yet, Charley. I'll see you at the boatworks tomorrow morning ... any time after 10:00."

Seth ended his call with Charley and speed-dialed Lori.

"Hi Seth," answered Lori, picking up on the first ring. "I was hoping you would call ... have you had a good day?"

"Yes, I have, and I'd like to tell you about it over dinner tonight."

"Well, that sounds good."

"How about coming out to the beach, and we'll go to the Middle Grounds ... and you can stay at the townhouse ... if you'd like."

"Sounds good to me, what time?"

"Come by about 6:30 for some wine on the porch, and I'll make reservations for 7:30. I don't have to be at the boatworks until 10:00 a.m. tomorrow."

"I'll see you at 6:30. Can I bring anything?"

"Don't forget your toothbrush."

CHAPTER FIVE

Wall to Wall turned in his chair and hooked his Iridium sat-phone to his FX2600 fax machine adaptor. Felipe had just called him from San Jose and already had all the information he had requested. El Gato's Pacific coast operative, Chilly Willy, had obtained and delivered the hotel guest lists, including the Chip Caldwell real estate information, in less than two days. Luigi was impressed by Chilly Willy's performance. It put him in a league with Luigi's best operative, "Fat John" Conte. The casino credit check showed that Chip had few assets. He hadn't gotten the airline manifests from Cadillac in Miami yet; he supposed that job might take a little longer since they were dealing with an FAA employee they had on their payroll. Luigi also knew that Cadillac was not bulldogging this task himself. He was busy planning the major move against the Russian Mafia in Key West that No Nose had ordered.

Over the past 18 months, the Cipriano family had eliminated the Russian street dealers and wise guys in South Miami and the Upper and Middle Keys. The strategy was to have them disappear slowly, one by one. John Cipriano didn't want to start an overt war on his own turf. Cadillac's soldiers would snatch the street dealers when they were alone. They were shot or garroted and dropped into the nearby Gulf Stream ten miles off of Miami packed in negative buoyancy 55 gallon drums. The drums had holes drilled in them and just enough Styrofoam was fastened inside to make them sink 20 or 30 feet below the surface, like a submarine. The Gulf Stream moved steadily offshore at 3 to 4 knots, on its way to 80 miles off New York City. There the stream moved the drums easterly off the coast towards Europe. Two of Cadillac's men had become quite proficient at rigging the drums, and to anyone's knowledge none had been found.

The Russians suspected the Tampa Mafia, but they had no proof. There were also the Latin, Haitian, and Black Miami street gangs to consider. All those gangs sold drugs, supplied by Cipriano, on Miami's streets. The Russians' presence in South Miami and the Upper Keys was not in Cipriano's original game plan. They fit in Key West because they controlled the cheap Baltic labor racket. But the Russians had gotten greedy. They had initially bought their drugs from the Cipriano family but were now obviously buying their cocaine elsewhere. It was evident that the Russians thought they had become strong enough in Key West to challenge the Cipriano Family. The turf war that started in Miami would move west to Key West and the lower Keys. Once the war started, it would take on a life of its own until it came to its bloody conclusion.

Luigi called his son, Giorgio, into the office and handed him the faxed pages from Costa Rica. Two years earlier, the college educated Giorgio had proven himself to be a computer wizard during the search for the Fernandezes Bertram 54. He now was developing a new cyber robbery division within the Cipriano family. John Cipriano recognized credit card and bank account hacking as another profit center for the Tampa family.

"Giorgio put these dates and hotel guest lists on a spread sheet. Later you can cross reference them against the airline manifests that I'm expectin' soon from Cadillac Carlucci in Miami."

"No problem, Dad. I'll set them up on an Excel spread sheet and program it to cross reference to the same names."

Luigi wished he was better with computers, but he had plenty of other things to worry about.

***

Cadillac had been down in the Key West area all day. He and his right hand man Pete "The Barber" Guggino were looking for a safe house to rent before he started the first phase of the family's war against the Russian Mafia. One of his informants, from the Key West Police Department, had given him a list of possible safe houses to rent. He thought he had finally found the perfect situation on the Atlantic side just below Big Coppitt Key on Geiger Key. The house was located in unincorporated Monroe County, and that area was not patrolled regularly by the sheriff's department. Monroe County stretched the whole 110 mile distance along Overseas Highway #1, from Key West to Key

Largo, then turned north towards Flamingo and occupied the western half of the Everglades almost up to Chokoloskee. The house was rented through an absentee owner who lived in Chicago. It was located in a sparsely built area off of Boca Chica Road just east of Boca Chica Air Force Base. Cadillac figured that the area was not built up like the surrounding Keys because of the constant noise from the jet fighters based on Boca Chica landing and taking off. The house was fairly secluded, and the rental sign advertised nine bedrooms. It was two stories, and was constructed of concrete block. There was a small swimming pool at the rear of the house that opened up to a nice size canal. The canal was deep enough to bring a boat that drew four feet to the dock at low tide. All of the land on the west side of Boundary Road was vacant. The road marked the Air Force Base boundary. There were no lots across the canal, just water and a reef. The whole compound had a six foot high concrete wall around it and there was ample room to park several vehicles behind the automatic wrought iron gate. The property had several mature palm trees, inside the wall, surrounding the main house and shading a large side yard. There was only low scrubby foliage on the vacant land across the road. It was located about a mile from Overseas Highway #1 and was about six miles from Key West.

Cadillac called the owner at the number that was on the sign fastened to the gate.

"I'm callin' about your house on Geiger Key."

"Great, my name is Martin, what can I tell you?"

"How much is it a week and can I get it for the next four or five weeks?"

"Let me look at my calendar ... It's available until the very end of July, and then it's rented for sportsman's lobster weekend ... all of August ... and September. I get $4,000 a week for it."

"Does the canal in back run out to the Atlantic?"

"You can carry four feet the whole way at low tide and there's no bridges.

"I wanna see the inside, Martin."

"You can get a gate opener and house key from Bobby Mongelli at the Geiger Key Marina and Smokehouse, a half mile back up the road. The food is good there and Bobby's wife runs the crew that cleans the house."

Cadillac and Pete, The Barber drove up to the marina, ate lunch, and got the gate opener and key from Bobby. The marina was surrounded by a trailer and RV park, and the food *was* good at the Smokehouse. The surroundings reminded Cadillac of the Keys back in the 60's and 70's.

They drove back, pulled thru the electric gate, and toured the house.

"It's not fancy but it looks clean and comfortable," said Pete as he sat down on one of the couches.

"I'm amazed at the amount of jet fighter traffic in and out of the Air Force base, like every five minutes. It's fuckin' deafenin'."

"Well, that's why it's remote and available I guess."

"There are two kitchens and three livin' rooms, and it can be divided into three separate apartments. We can probably sleep 14 or 15 guys in here easy."

They walked upstairs to the master bedroom and Pete looked out the window,

"Look here, Cadillac, you can look across the Boca Chica Airstrip and see Stock Island and Mount Trashmore (the old garbage dump). Nobody's gonna sneak up on us in this joint."

Cadillac called the owner back and leased it for six weeks.

"How about $3500 a week, cash, for six weeks with no housekeepin'?"

Martin said, "OK, pay the cash to Bobby Mongelli, at Geiger Key Marina. He'll take down your personal information and give you a receipt for the cash. Remember, Bobby's wife Michelle runs the cleaning crew from their office, just in case you change your mind and need a cleanup. Have fun!"

Cadillac gave Bobby a counterfeit driver's license, with his picture and a fictitious name on it, along with $21,000 in cash. He doubted the transaction would be reported in any case.

Pete drove Cadillac over to Key West, where they met four more of Cadillac's men at the Casa Marina Hotel's outside bar overlooking the Atlantic Ocean. There was a nice sea breeze cooling the afternoon heat. They drank at a private table out under the large, swaying palm trees that filled the spacious grounds and beachfront of the hotel. The plan was for Cadillac to fly back to Miami from the Key West Airport that night. Pete would stay at the safe house with the four soldiers and get the kitchen stocked. Tomorrow, four more of their men would arrive from Miami with two untraceable SUVs and an arsenal of guns, ammo, and explosives.

Cadillac discussed the plan with Pete and his top four soldiers.

"First, you'll case the Russians' daily movements for about a week. Our informants have identified the bosses, but we don't know where they live or what their daily habits and schedules are."

Pete commented, "Key West's not like Miami. It's less than eight square miles in size. First, we'll find the street drug dealers, and finally pinpoint the movements of the boss, the capo, his lieutenants, and their muscle."

"Yuly Yankovich is the big boss and he has offices in the back of three different T-shirt and beach clothing shops on Duval Street. He also owns a massage parlor and a restaurant-bar-strip club on southeast Duval Street, called the Southernmost Gulag. Our informer already got us pictures of most of the Russian bosses."

Cadillac further explained that the Russians were into supplying low wage, restaurant, bar, hotel cleaning, and strip club personnel on J-1 temporary visas. They had gotten their start in a legitimate way, but since the Russian Mafia had taken them over, they even used the J1 visas to bring in seasoned prostitutes and strippers. Key West restaurants, hotels, and titty bars were now almost exclusively staffed by eastern Europeans.

"I think we'll have a game plan in place pretty quick. Pete will be the field general, but I'll develop the plan from Miami and call the shots. Pete's arranged for a 38 foot Jupiter center console with three, 300 H.P., four stroke Yamaha outboards to arrive at The Geiger Key dock tomorrow afternoon. All calls to me in Miami will be by sat-phone. We'll give orders and keep in touch on prepaid cell phones that Pete will buy with cash at the local convenience stores."

"How are we gonna tail these guys in such a small place without them getting' wise," asked Frankie "Blue Eyes" Amaro.

"That's a good question Frankie. The surveillance teams will work in teams of two, so you can see if anyone is on to you. Forget about your Miami threads and wear t-shirts, shorts, flip-flops, sunglasses, and lots of different hats. You're gonna take photos of the targeted Russians with your cell phones.

Surveillance teams are gonna switch assignments and tourist duds every day so they won't be made. Every mornin' there will be a skull session and progress report, so everybody's up to speed."

Cadillac added, "Night surveillance will include goin' inta the titty bars and the Southernmost Gulag. But most important, we want to know where these fuckers sleep."

He reminded them that No Nose also wanted to know who was supplying the Russians with the drugs they were selling. Cadillac guessed it was one of the Mexican cartels. He didn't think it would be the same cartel that supplied the Tampa Mafia. After all, the Russians' volume was a drop in a bucket compared to Tampa's. If it was, however, No Nose would make sure there would be hell to pay.

Pete summed up the objectives by saying, "Once we can make a photo and name chart, me and Cadillac will put together a plan to eliminate all the Russians. We'll start with Yuly Yankovich and work down thru the capo, lieutenants, and muscle. We want to finish these dickwads off in one business day. The legitimate Key West J1 visa labor and bosses won't be touched, but they will pay us 'vig' to stay in place."

Nick "Pajama Boy" Bocci one of Cadillac's best operatives, said, "With all due respect, Boss, don't this plan sound a little ambitious?"

Pete reminded him, "Remember, we're only dealin' with an eight square mile island with one bridge and one road to get off. We think the Russians number 20 to 30 at most. No Nose told us that we can count on him to send down as many of his top men and all the other shit that it takes to do this job. But first, it's our job to figure the size and strength of the Russians."

***

Frankie Blue Eyes stood on the southeast corner of Front St. and Duval and watched the front door of the flagship of Yuly Yankovich's t-shirt empire, Southern Breeze 1. Pajama Boy Bocci sat at a sidewalk table, sipping an umbrella drink, at the Island Dog Bar on Front Street. He watched the blind alley that opened onto Front St. between the Two Friends Restaurant and

Southern Breeze 1. The alley was connected to a walled parking lot behind the t-shirt/clothing store. There had been foot traffic out of that alley approximately every 30 minutes. The same three Russians alternately exited every one and a half hours. Blue Eyes saw them enter the t-shirt shop five minutes before Pajama Boy saw each one of them leave by the back door alley. No one else used the alley except their employees and an occasional delivery truck. Frankie and Nick constantly changed positions, moved to opposite corners, sat in Two Friends Restaurant, and sat on a bench across the street from the Bagatelle Restaurant on Duval. Another surveillance crew picked the Russians up on Ann or Simonton Street and followed them to three different busy blocks further up Duval. They periodically called Blue Eyes on his cell to give him a progress report. There the Russians dealt the drugs they had to sell as they walked their blocks and popped in and out of the crowded outdoor restaurants and bars. They were carrying small amounts of drugs and money, which was a good precaution from all angles. Both Tampa crews took pictures of all three of the dealers with their cell phone cameras. The lieutenants were photographed coming and going at lunch and dinner time. Taking pictures in Key West did not attract any attention. The Tampa crews mixed it up so no one was anywhere more than four hours. Without the Hawaiian shirts, baggy shorts, flip flops, and floppy hats, the Italians would have stood out like sore thumbs wearing their black outfits and slicked back black hair. Actually the crews were beginning to like the comfortable casualness of it all.

Yuly's two other stores had much the same pattern. The Tampa crews ventured into the stores and cased the backrooms under the guise of needing a restroom. The lieutenant's offices were locked, but Blue Eyes saw one of the dealers fish a key out of his pocket as he walked through the store on his way to the back. Obviously the office was self service if the lieutenant was out or busy in the store. The central Duval store, Southern Breeze 2, serviced the projects, Truman Avenue, and the low rent district with three dealers. Southern Breeze 3 was down at the southeast end of Duval Street and serviced that end of the island with two dealers. The dealers who worked out of the other two stores followed the same pattern as Southern Breeze 1. They always went in the front door and exited out the back through a parking lot or alley.

The Tampa crew ran into a mobile operation over the bridge in Stock Island. Two dealers, on mopeds, worked two different shifts among the house trailers and lobster trap storage lots. Many of Key West's commercial fisherman and their families lived on Stock Island. A dealer could usually be found hanging out in the parking lot at Bone Island Liquors on the Overseas Highway or in the vicinity of the Hogfish Grille on Front Street, but never in it. The Stock island dealers worked out of Southern Breeze 3.

Pete called Henry, one of their police informers.

"What's goin' on at the Hogfish Grille? The Russian drug dealers don't go near it. They hang out by a dumpster down the road."

Henry laughed, "The Hogfish Bar and Grille and the Safe Harbor Marina complex is owned and operated by a bunch of hard cases that hit the *ATOCHA* mother lode with famous treasure hunter Mel Fisher back in the day. Drug dealers, grifters, deadbeats, and panhandlers are not welcome and they are dealt with harshly. The retired treasure hunters run a tight ship."

"Who are these guys?"

"There are nine or ten of them, the locals can tell them by the 'Key West dog tags' that they wear."

"Dog tags?"

"They all wear an 8 Reales silver coin that came from the Spanish Galleon *ATOCHA* around their neck and most have a gold and ruby dive flag ring. If you're up to no good, stay clear of them."

With the help of the informant, the photos yielded the names of all the dealers. The crews followed them home and to the Gulag in their off time. The Russian muscle also hung out at the Southernmost Gulag. They had motorbikes and small Mercedes for transportation. Pete sent two of his larger men, Joe "The Animal" DeLuca and Fredo "Big Fred" Langello into the Gulag late one night when Disney's "Big Red Boat" was docked downtown. They were disguised as inebriated tourists complete with Mickey Mouse nametags from the cruise ship. Big Fred reported that when they walked in, everyone in the bar section turned and looked at them like they were from Mars. They ordered a couple of beers and watched the titty dancers for 30 minutes and left. Joe The Animal reported that they were all speaking Russian, or something like it. The place was full of young eastern European waiters, waitresses, cooks, and shop clerks, mingling with the Russian muscle, drug dealers, lieutenants, and the captain. Big Fred came up with the idea of finding the Russians on whatever beach they hung at during the day and then photographing them there with a telephoto lens. There were only four beaches on Key West, Smathers, Fort Zachary Taylor, Higgs and Southernmost, so it shouldn't be that difficult.

The crews found that the Russians all hung out at Southernmost Beach right down the street from The Gulag. That beach had a restaurant and bar, lounge chairs, restrooms, and plenty of shady palm trees. Hundreds of tourists walked out to the southernmost point in the United States and took pictures every day. Pete bought a digital camera with a telephoto lens. In two days, the Tampa crews had pictures of all the muscle and two of the three lieutenants, Dimitry, and Ivan. Henry, the police informer put names with all the photos. The Capo or Kapitan, Nikolay Rutan, was photographed with his topless mistress, Svetlana, at the tiny beach at the Pier House Resort, courtesy of Henry.

Pete The Barber, put up a Russian photo and name chart at Geiger Central, and set up his crews to find out where the operatives lived and to confirm that they stayed there all night. The two lieutenants, who managed t-shirt shops 1 and 2, were tailed 24/7, as was the kapitan who managed the Gulag. The third lieutenant, at Southern Breeze 3, had not been identified yet. That store, except for the drug dealers, was totally staffed by women. For the next five days, their every movement was methodically cataloged.

Ivan made one trip off the island with three of the muscle boys to Sugarloaf Key in two of the Mercedes. Pajama Boy and Big Fred followed them in an Escalade. The Russians turned south at mile marker 17 and continued down two lane Sugarloaf Blvd., then turned left and drove to the end of Jamaica Lane. As the Mercedes approached the cul-de-sac, an electric gate slid open and they drove in. The foliage along the stockade fence was so high and thick that it concealed the entire house from the road. Pajama Boy was well back, and pulled into an open driveway, turned around, and headed back to the highway. He parked in a convenience store parking lot and waited it out.

Twenty minutes later the two Mercedes pulled back on the highway and drove past the convenience store. Pajama Boy followed them back to Key West with a two car buffer. The two Mercedes split up and Nick followed the second Mercedes to Southern Breeze 3. The Russian muscle took two wine cases out of the trunk and went into the back door of the shop. When Blue Eyes reported the incident, Pete thought it looked like a drug buy. They had probably stumbled onto the Russians new cocaine source.

Each morning the emerging patterns became stronger, criminals being creatures of habit just like the rest of the populace. Yuly Yankovich gave Pete the biggest headache. He lived in a private house on Sunset Key, which was owned by the Westin Hotel. Half of the little island, formally known as Tank Island, was an exclusive resort, with two story luxury condos for rent, and amenities like tennis, a five star restaurant, a cocktail lounge, and swimming pools with full bars and attendants. The island was accessible only by water, and a private ferry ran across Key West Channel to the Westin's dock near the Art Museum every half hour. The other half of the island was occupied by private residences. They were off limits to the paying guests, but the home owners had access to all of the islands amenities. The waterfront residences were permitted to moor a boat behind their houses. Most had boat lifts because there wasn't a no-wake zone in Key West Channel until you reached the Bight a few hundred yards further north. Pete rented a two bedroom condo on Sunset Key and installed one of his best soldiers, Vito "The Dancer" Pelosi, along with a trusted hooker who completed the picture of a vacationing couple. Yuly had a large waterfront house facing the naval base to the north. He also had a 37 foot Intrepid with three, 300 H.P. Verado outboards up on an electric lift behind the house. Vito observed that Yuly had two, bodyguards, 24/7. The bodyguards changed shifts using the Island's ferry. A replacement from the Russians' muscle group came over from Key West and the departing bodyguard caught the ferry's return trip. One bodyguard accompanied Yuly whenever he went in Key West. But he did not go often. Every other night between 8:00 and 9:00, a different young woman came over on the ferry. She stayed for an hour or so and took the ferry back to Key West. The same Hotel maids cleaned the house every day. Yuly used the Island Restaurant occasionally, always in the company of his bodyguards. Yuly did not use the ferry. He was taken in his boat by the two bodyguards, one of whom stayed with the Intrepid, at the Westin Marina, while Yuly was ashore. The only other Russian boat in evidence was a Yellowfin 31, powered by twin Yamaha 250 H.P. outboards, owned by Nikolay Rutan. He kept it in a high and dry on Stock Island.

Vito called Pete with an interesting observation, "A tall, stocky blonde, traveling on the ferry, visited Yuly's house this morning for about an hour. That makes three times in the space of four days she's come over."

"Did ya getta picture?"

"Yeah, she's tall, muscular, with a small potato lookin' nose, high cheekbones, and spiked hair … and she looks 'butch'. I'll email you her picture."

The crews identified her as an employee from Southern Breeze 3. Pete put Blue Eyes on her tail and she quickly led him into the gay side of town. He shed his tourist outfit and bought a pair of short shorts and a t-shirt a size to small. He was a naturally slim and handsome 35 year old Italian, with wavy black hair. Blue Eyes started hitting the gay bars and nightclubs she frequented and he noticed she had lunch at La Te Da's outside patio everyday with the same mix of gays. On his second night of surveillance he hit paydirt. Blue Eyes was sitting at the bar in the Aqua nightclub watching the mixed gay crowd "Boogay" to the music. He was beginning to understand how the girls he hit on in Miami must feel. A young blond lawyer from Coral Gables was hitting on him and buying the drinks. Blue Eyes said to his new friend, Tommy, "Who's that muscular blonde girl dancing with the little redhead?"

He winked and shouted in Frankie's ear above the deafening music, "That's Ivanna Yankovich. She runs the drug trade in the gay community."

Blue Eyes threw back the rest of his beer and shouted in Tommy's ear, "Order me another beer, sweetie, I've got to go drain my dragon."

Tommy giggled and pinched Blue Eye's butt as he walked away. Frankie walked past the men's room and out the back door. He couldn't get the fuck out of there fast enough.

Pete started to tally the numbers. There were ten street drug dealers, six full time muscle boys, three lieutenants, and one kapitan. Then add Yuly and his two bodyguards. The t-shirt shop girls, "masseuses", and Gulag titty dancers, bartenders, waiters, waitresses, cooks, and kitchen help wouldn't be counted. They would remain in Key West on their J1 visas and work until their visas expired. Twenty-three Russians would die in the purge. No Nose's plan was to eradicate the Key West Russian Mafia in one 24 hour day, but minimize collateral damage to civilians.

Cadillac came up with an idea to snatch almost all the Russians and kill them without firing a shot, and he also figured how to make their bodies disappear without a trace. It would take precise planning and execution. Pete had ten men in Key West, counting himself. He had four black SUVs and the Jupiter 38. They had an array of automatic weapons, grenade launchers, and explosive devices. They would not use those weapons unless they had too. He and Cadillac had been planning the nuts and bolts and also were working on an exit strategy. They would need ten or twelve more soldiers and additional vehicles on purge day. Cadillac would make sure the new men and equipment would arrive a few days early. These men would need some orientation. There was only one road out and it was 140 miles back to Miami, but they had access to boats, helicopters, and airplanes. They were not worried about retribution from the Russians. Even if something went wrong and a couple of Russians got away, they would not be strong enough to retaliate. The Russian Mafia differed in one respect from the Italian Mafia. The Russians would kill your family if it suited their purposes, the Italians would not. The key was to make sure they got all the bosses.

Pete was worried about getting his men out of town after the mayhem they would cause, should anything go wrong. It was the Key West Police, the Monroe County Sherriff's deputies, and the State Police in Marathon that worried him. Pete and Cadillac would insure their men's safe exit by going around the cops in boats and over them in airplanes. After the purge, No Nose would reestablish the political payoffs, and it would soon be business as usual.

CHAPTER SIX

Seth was putting together a cheese and cracker plate in the second floor kitchen when he heard Lori's car pull up in front of his garage. He finished putting the crackers on the plate and started down the stairs to let her in the front door.

He opened the door, and there she was getting an overnight bag out of the backseat of her black Mercedes sedan.

"Any trouble finding the townhouses, Lori?"

"No problem, I just followed my GPS right to your house, it took less than 20 minutes."

Seth walked over to the car, took the overnight bag, and gave her a kiss on the lips, "Well, welcome to my humble abode, come on upstairs ... but before we do let me show you the ground level."

They went through a side door in the entryway and entered the two car garage. Seth turned on the lights and said, "There's room for two cars in here, as you can see, and the washer, dryer, and utility tub are on the back wall. Now look through this door."

Seth opened the door and turned on the lights. They walked into a large wood paneled room with a leather couch and chair, a coffee table, a flat screen TV and audio console. In addition, there was a breakfront bar with three wine coolers under it. The bar top was high gloss varnished teak and holly yacht flooring with a teak fiddle around it. Overhead hung neat rows of deep sea fishing rods and reels of all sizes. Their gold reels shone in the light. There were many plastic bins of lures and tackle of all kinds, neatly stacked almost to the ceiling in one corner. At the other end of the room there was a work shop alcove complete with a butcher block workbench and peg boards hung with tools. Two pairs of varnished wood louvered doors stood ready to close the shop off from the rest of the room. In the corner next to the shop was a spiral staircase. The walls were hung with pictures of friends and family holding up impressive catches. There was a nice snook mount and a large sailfish mount on the back wall. In another corner a couple of fine mesh bait casting nets hung vertically from the ceiling. One wall was dedicated to sailboat racing trophies. Next to a storage closet door, stood an upright maple gun case. Lori could see through the locked glass door that it held a variety of shotguns and rifles. The room looked out through a sliding glass door at the water, across a terrazzo patio covered by the second floor porch. Seth had wicker seating around a copper bowl fire pit on the patio.

Lori was at a loss for words for only a moment. She looked around the room again, then looked at Seth and blurted out, "Quite a man cave, Seth!"

"It's been a great place to hang out and work on my fishing and hunting gear. I can keep all of it ship shape and still watch sports or listen to music."

"Well, I can't wait to see the rest of your townhouse. Where does the spiral stair case go?"

"It's another way up to the living room. Let me get a bottle of wine out of a cooler and we'll climb on up."

Seth pulled a bottle of Seghesio Zinfandel out of the third cooler and retrieved Lori's overnight bag. Lori wound up the spiral staircase and Seth followed. She stepped up into the living room and said, "What spacious and airy rooms! I like the corner fireplace with the big flat screen above the mantel, and I bet the leather sectional is great for watching football." She turned around and exclaimed with a hint of sarcasm, "Wow, a full size pool table on the other side of the living room! How wide is this room, Seth?"

"Its 24 feet, but you haven't seen the best feature, come out on the porch. The view of the Intracoastal Waterway is magnificent." Seth could tell she really didn't care for the bachelor living room set-up. She was smiling, but her scrunched up nose told the real tale.

Seth slid open the sliding glass doors and Lori stepped outside. He had a corner unit and the porch ran the width of the unit. Lori could see over a half mile in three directions.

"Now this *is* spectacular, and the boat channel is so close to your seawall. I bet it's just as pretty when it gets dark ... I mean with all the lights from the houses across the waterway."

"It's seldom boring out here with the lights and all the passing boats. It's a no-wake zone so you get to see them for awhile."

"How about upstairs, Seth?"

"Why don't we save that tour for after dinner? Let me show you the kitchen and dining room, and then we have just enough time for a leisurely glass of wine on the porch, before we head to the Middle Grounds."

"Sounds like a plan to me," said Lori as they walked thru the dining room. "Oh, a large round table and six chairs, and a granite topped bar alcove ... perfect for entertaining."

"Well, it comes in handy for my Thursday night poker games, too."

Seth opened the bottle of wine while Lori checked out the kitchen. She carried the cheese plate and two wine glasses out to the porch. They sat at a counter height bistro table and Seth poured the wine. They clinked their glasses together and Seth said, "To good beginnings."

Lori leaned over and gave him a kiss on the lips and they drank to it. A few yachts sailed by as they watched the sun set behind a beach condo to the southwest. Seth had the porch speakers on and Al Green was crooning about love, and feeling brand new, in the background.

Lori said, "I could get used to this view, and I like this wine."

"It is intoxicating isn't it? And the wine's not bad, either."

Night started to fall and Seth looked at his watch, "We better get started to the Middle Grounds; they'll only hold our reservation for fifteen minutes."

"Let me use the powder room and we'll be off."

They arrived at the Middle Grounds in the Z3 and the valet parked it. They were seated immediately and were soon drinking Klinker Brick Zin and looking at the menu.

"What do you like here, Seth?"

"I order the hogfish when they have it and the black grouper macadamia when they don't."

They both looked at the waiter, who said, "You're in luck."

When the waiter left, Lori asked about his upcoming fishing trip to the Keys. He explained that they would start off fishing in Marathon. They would most probably stay at the Marathon Yacht Club, or Burdine's Marina. The plan was to fish east and then west, until they found the fish. Then they'd move the boat to a marina closer to the fish. Dinner came and they both enjoyed the hogfish and vegetable medley immensely. Seth promised to call Lori a couple of times during the trip just so she wouldn't worry about him. She asked him how long he would be gone. He estimated two to three weeks, depending on the weather. Their conversation drifted off into talking about different people they both knew at the Yacht Club. Soon, they both realized that they wanted to be back at the townhouse, where they could be alone. Seth paid the bill, thanked the waiter for his good service, and headed for the valet. He put the top down and the ride home was cool and pleasant.

"How about a night-cap on the porch, there's still plenty of Seghesio."

"Can we sit out on the porch on the third floor?"

"Yes, it's off the master bedroom … would you rather sit up there?"

"Why don't you show me the third floor, then we can change and sit out there in the cool breeze."

Seth followed her up the stairs toting her overnight bag. All the ceilings on the third floor were cathedral, and Lori stopped on the landing and admired the art. Seth had paintings and prints hanging on all four walls, some ranging almost up to highest part of the ceiling.

"Well, I had no idea you were an art buff, Seth. You're just full of surprises. This is quite an eclectic collection you have hanging up here."

Seth looked for the telltale nose wrinkles, saw none, and said, "Its just art I've picked up in my travels around Florida, the Bahamas, and Central and South America over the years. A lot of them are originals, but some of them are prints. They all bring back memories of good times in exotic places."

"Some of them are hung way up high and out over the stairs. How did you hang them?"

"Very carefully. My brother, Beau, and I built some temporary scaffolds and somehow we got it done without falling."

"I heard about Beau from some of the girls at the Yacht Club. I'm sorry about his death, Seth."

"Thanks, Beau had a good life, on his own terms … But I do miss him. Let me put this bag in our room and I'll show you the rest of this floor."

He dropped the bag inside the master bedroom door and walked across the landing to an open door.

"This room is my office. I call it the computer room."

The computer room had a campaign style desk and chair, a pull-out couch against a side wall, and a floor to ceiling bookshelf on the back wall. Seth's personal computer and printers were at the desk.

"How cool is this," said Lori, "I notice that all your windows have these wood plantation shutters on them. It's very southern looking."

"Well, it lets the breeze thru whenever I can open up the house."

He showed her the guest bedroom with its twin beds and the full bathroom which opened off the center landing.

"Over here is the master bedroom and bath. What I like the best is the wood cathedral ceiling. The porch is out through those plantation shutters. They slide open just like the glass doors."

Seth walked past the king-size bed and pointed out the huge walk-in closet and then turned into the master bath. The bathroom had double granite sinks and a large walk in shower. To the left was a glass paned door that also led to the upper porch.

Seth opened the door, walked out on the porch, and said, "I had a full canvas awning put over this last year for two reasons. First, it keeps the bedroom cooler in the morning when the sun comes up, and secondly, I can sit out here in almost any kind of weather, in my skivvies, and read the newspaper and drink my coffee on Sundays."

"I noticed you have a coffee maker on one of the sink counters. That's not my sink is it?" said Lori laughing.

"I guess it's mine now," said Seth with a smile. "Make yourself comfortable and I'll go down and get the wine and glasses. When I come back up, I'm going to change into my sleeping shorts and shirt. I'll meet you out on the porch … the bathroom is all yours."

With that, Seth exited the porch through the bedroom sliding glass door and disappeared downstairs. When he came back he changed into his night clothes and noticed that the bathroom door was closed. He went out on the porch through the open sliding glass door and put the wine and glasses down on the teak bistro table. He lit the candle in the middle of the table, and having already retrieved his RF stereo controller, switched the music to the third floor porch. He poured the wine into the two large wine glasses, sat back, and waited for Lori to appear.

He didn't have to wait too long as she soon appeared from behind him through the open sliding glass door. She kissed him on the cheek as she made her way to the seat across from him.

"This is even more romantic than the other porch, Seth. Maybe it's the awning and the candle. If I stood back up I think I could almost see downtown from here."

She was wearing a black silk robe over a scoop neck, slinky, black nightgown.

Seth felt a major stirring in his loins as he said, "You look lovely, Lori."

"You're too sweet, thanks for dinner Seth, it was special ... I can see why you like that restaurant."

They sipped their wine, held hands, and kissed across the table. A few small boats glided by and finally Seth yawned and said, "Excuse the yawn, it's not the company, but it's been a long day and I figure I should get up around 7:00 in the morning."

"Well then, let's turn-in, I'm anxious to see how comfortable your bed is?"

Seth stood up and slid open the sliding glass door and said, "Ladies first."

Lori chuckled and moved into the bedroom. Seth followed her in and helped her take the bedspread off and pull down the covers. He tried not to stare, but her flawless visage held his gaze. They met at bedside where Seth took her in his arms and kissed her. Lori stepped back and dropped her robe to the floor. She smiled at Seth, then pulled her night gown slowly over her head and slipped into bed. The nipples on her sloping breasts stood at attention. Seth quickly shed his sleeping shorts and shirt and lay down next to Lori. He gently took her in his arms, and kissed her deeply.

Lori whispered, "I'm ready right now."

Seth rolled Lori on top of him and held her firm, round, bottom in his hands and guided her home. For a while, time stood still for the two lovers. But soon they were on their way to the Promised Land, and neither of them was disappointed. Only they existed for that brief moment, and nothing else mattered. When they were both spent, they stayed entwined not wanting to lose the intensity of the moment.

"It's been a long time since I felt like this, Seth," whispered Lori. "I'm so happy I found you."

"I glad we found each other too. I haven't felt at peace like this for quite awhile."

The happy couple fell asleep in each other's arms and slept until almost 8:00 the next morning. Seth woke with a start and almost leapt out of bed.

"Whoa, I'll have to hustle to get to the yard for my ten o'clock," said Seth to a startled Lori. "I was going to make you a nice breakfast, to eat out on the porch, before we left."

"Don't worry about me, Seth. I'll rustle something up for us. Go ahead and take your shower. I'll get the coffee going on your sink."

Seth padded into the bathroom, naked from the night before, and turned on the hot water in the shower. He looked out the window in the porch door and saw the wine glasses and empty wine bottle on the bistro table. The candle had burned down to nothing in the glass lantern holder. He turned and adjusted the now steaming water in the shower, tested the temperature with his hand, and moved his neck and shoulders under the therapeutic stream. As he turned to turn to find his bar of soap he felt something behind him. It was Lori … she had slipped in behind him and was starting to soap his back.

"I started the coffee, Seth, and I thought we could conserve some water and time by showering together."

One thing led to another and before long their soaped up bodies were at it again. Seth had Lori propped against the side wall and was lifting her off the shower floor with each gentle thrust. When they were finished they kissed under the steaming nozzle and laughed while they soaped each other's back.

"Let's promise to never act our age, Seth."

"I can say … I'm all for that, girl!"

Seth slapped her on her behind as she exited the shower and started to towel off.

Lori winced in mock pain and said, "Wipe that grin off your face, sailor!"

Seth just laughed and said, "What a great way to start a day!"

Once dressed, they poured their coffee into travel mugs, took along two hastily toasted bagels from the kitchen, and headed out. They kissed each other goodbye and were both on the road, with smiles on their faces, by 9:30.

***

Seth drove to the yard, smiling, and he made his mind start thinking about business. He would meet Charley in a few minutes and collect the cash for the trip. Then he would call each of the crew and invite them to the crew meeting at his town house Tuesday afternoon. Gene Johnson would help him provision for the first part of the trip. Once they were in the Keys, they'd have access to good supermarkets and pharmacies. He pulled in the boatwork's parking lot at 9:50, and hurried up to his office. Charley was already there sitting in his office with a dark blue duffel bag sitting on the chair beside him.

"Hey, Charley, you beat me in this morning," said Seth with a laugh.

"Well, I can't wait for you to start your search."

"We're going to start provisioning *TAR BABY* today and I'll charter a trawler over at the Vinoy and start getting it provisioned. The crew meeting is next Tuesday, and we'll shove off for the Keys the next day."

"I'm not going to pry and I will stay out of the Keys until the mission is over. If you need more money or logistics, call me on my cell. Right now I'm going to go for a brisk walk downtown. Then I'm going to the Yacht Club to have lunch at the bar. I like to get a little buzz on before my afternoon nap. Call me anytime you need me, Seth. Thanks again for taking the job."

With that said, Charley was gone.

Seth called Florida Charters and arranged to charter a 42 foot twin engine Grand Banks trawler, named *SIRENA,* for a month. He talked to the general manager, Patrick, who used to sailboat race with Jeb when they were youngsters. Stone's Boatworks did all the maintenance and repair on the bareboat charter fleet. The navigation was challenging on the west coast of Florida, as there were miles and miles of shallow bays that were just made for exploration and gunkholing. Running aground took its toll on the charter sailboats rudders and keels, and the trawlers running gear.

Seth called Gene and set him up for provisioning both boats, which would take the rest of the afternoon and most of the next couple of days. Then he called John Harvey, Dino Vino, Toby Warner, Billy Chandler, and Fred Buckley. The crew meeting was set for his townhouse at 3:00 P.M. next Tuesday. They would all leave the next morning for the Keys, with a couple of exceptions.

Jeb was on the phone when Seth walked into his office. He took a seat and waited for Jeb to finish his call. When Jeb hung up Seth said, "If you haven't guessed already, I decided to take on Charley's search project. Gene, John, Freddy, Billy, Toby, and Dino Vino are the crew. We'll search the Keys by land, water and air. We're taking *TAR BABY*, a couple of other boats, and John's airplane. We're not advertising that it's a search for the Huckins; we're billing it as a fishing trip to the Keys."

"When are you going to leave?"

"Next Wednesday."

"Well, be careful and call me if you need me."

Seth and Gene spent the next three days buying gear and provisioning *Tar Baby* and the trawler. Seth took time out on Sunday to take Lori to brunch at Cassis on Beach Drive. They spent a languid afternoon in her bed on the 14th floor and had a take-out dinner delivered from Gratzzi's Italian Grille in BayWalk. They finally showered and dressed, then walked out to Cha Cha Coconut's rooftop bar on the downtown pier for a nightcap.

***

Seth opened the man cave's sliding glass doors and brought in two of the wicker patio chairs. He would sit on the padded stool he used at his workbench. The other four crewmembers could sit on the leather couch and easy chair. It was still cool enough on this early summer day to leave the doors open and just turn on the overhead ceiling fan. Gene had been with Seth all morning while they finished provisioning the Grand Banks Trawler and *TAR BABY*. He was in the garage putting some beer and Diet Coke in a cooler for the meeting. Seth looked at his Rolex; the boys should start arriving any minute. Seth had told them all to park by the swimming pool, then walk around to the Intracoastal side, and come in through the patio doors. He got his notes, opened a cold Diet Coke, sat down on the wicker couch outside, and reviewed them.

Freddy and Dino arrived simultaneously. John Harvey ambled in, and Seth handed him a manila envelope with his Lance's 9127Z special ADIZ permit in it. John looked in the envelope, and emitted a low whistle. He smiled at Seth and said, "Good for a month. Wow, it's all about who you know, buddy!"

There were handshakes and greetings as each member strode into the cave. Toby and Billy were the last to arrive, and after they said their hellos Seth called the meeting to order.

"OK, guys, I'm going to explain our objectives and strategy on this operation to find Charley Blevins' *ABOUT TIME*. Gene and I have done some research on the two prime suspects Randy Garrett and Peter Petcock. We know that they were in financial trouble both personally and business-wise. They are both experienced boatwrights and boatsman. In their twenties and early thirties they both were involved in marijuana and cocaine smuggling. Randy served time in Federal prison. They finally straightened out and teamed up in their late 30's and built a successful boat service business. They've had some bad luck with women and alimony. Just lately they had a huge problem with the Federal Government, concerning commercial divers' safety regulations, which halved the size of their business. They both disappeared, along with Charley Blevin's Huckins, at precisely the same time. They were not authorized to move *ABOUT TIME*. A full array of insurance investigators, Local, County, and State Police, the Florida State Bureau of Investigation, the Florida Marine Patrol, BASRA, and the U.S Coast Guard have all failed to find the boat or the suspects. Charley and I believe that the suspects have purchased new identities in Miami; they've probably grown mustaches and beards and dyed their hair, or even had some plastic surgery. We also believe that they have altered the look of the Huckins radically, probably with plywood and paint. If they have reverted to their former drug smuggling ways, the uniqueness of *ABOUT TIME* could provide them with the combined advantages of speed, mobility, and stealth that are not available to other smugglers. Case in point, because of the Hamilton Jet drives, this vessel can operate at its full range of speeds in two and a half feet of water. The Huckins can run 40 miles per hour for four hundred miles with its stock fuel capacity of eight hundred gallons. At 62 feet long and 16.5 feet wide there is plenty of room for cocaine, crew, and extra fuel if needed. We think this boat and the two suspects are moving cocaine from Mexico to the Florida Keys. Any questions so far?"

Freddy raised his hand and asked, "How do you propose we find the Huckins, if its appearance has been so radically altered?"

"Good question, Fred. We are going to frame the Huckins "in a box". John and Toby are going to fly aerial reconnaissance and look at all the boats they fly over through the bottom of a 62' x 16.5' "box". First they'll establish a perspective. At different prescribed altitudes they will draw and cut out cardboard rectangular frames while flying over four orange 18" diameter Taylor fender ball floats that we'll set out for them in Florida Bay at 62' long x 16.5' wide. They will take a picture, follow, and get the name, hailing port, and numbers off every boat they fly over that fits in our proportional "box". They'll follow those boats to their dock or marina. John and Toby can eliminate all the sportfish and express boats, and all the production boats like Sea Ray, Azimuth, Viking, Meridian, etc. With our box and knowledge of production boats we can probably eliminate 90% of the boats that we fit in the box. Most of them that fit will probably be commercial fishing or work boats. If one looks promising we can run a couple of our guys in a car to check it out if it's moored in the Keys. If a good prospect runs west, the airplane will follow. Most boats that size will be running at or close to 8 knots. If we see one that size that is running up on plane, and we can't eliminate it as a sportfish or production boat, we will definitely want to follow it. If it runs up past Key Largo we will eliminate it. We won't search further west than the Dry

Tortugas or north of Everglades City. Now, I want you all to bring a couple of handguns and your hog or deer rifles, and plenty of ammo. I know we all have carry permits. We are not looking for trouble but, if trouble finds us I want to be ready. Like my Dad, Ol' Robert E. always said, 'Prepare for the worst, and hope for the best.' If we find the boat and the suspects in the Keys, I want to hand our evidence over to the Monroe County Sheriff's Department and let them make the collar. I don't want to put our crew in harm's way. Gene says they can be trusted, and Sheriff Billy Ray Stodgins is an old friend of his ...... Now, our cover story is that we're on a fishing trip. We will try not to have the two boats in the same marina. You guys on the Grand Banks are just cruising around. If we think we've found the Huckins, the Grand Banks will move in closer for surveillance. We'll rent a couple of cars when we get to Marathon. I also rented a 20 foot panga with a 115 H.P. Johnson on it for a utility boat. It will be towed down to the Keys behind the trawler ...... Each man will be paid $300 per day and all expenses are paid by Charley Blevins. I'll give Freddy a bank of cash for the Grand Banks. John, I'll do the same for you and your airplane. Anybody that spends money for the trip out of their pocket, give me a receipt and you'll be reimbursed. If you spend money out of the cash bank get a receipt, I'll need it for our final accounting. I'll settle the per diem up when we end the operation. If we find the Huckins we split $100,000 seven ways. I expect this operation to take two to three weeks. Have I forgotten anything?"

"Do you want me to bring my dive gear?" asked Dino.

"Absolutely, thanks for reminding me, and bring a couple of extra dive tanks. My dive gear is already on *TAR BABY.*"

"When do we leave, and who goes with who?" asked Toby.

"Thanks, Toby. I was just getting to that. But first I want you all to make sure that you have each other's cell phone numbers on your speed dials. Let's do that before we leave this room. I also have four sat-phones rented from International Satellite Service, for private communication between our boats, cars, and the airplane. John and Freddy pick yours up after the meeting. The trawler is going to leave tomorrow at 6:00 a.m. from the Vinoy. Dino and Freddy will be aboard. Freddy is the Captain. You will pick Billy and Toby up in Boca Grande about eight or nine hours later. The trawler will go straight thru to Marathon from there, and you will have a slip waiting at Burdine's on the way into Boot Key Harbor. Fuel up in Boca Grande when you pick up Billy and Toby. Gene and I will run down to Marathon Yacht Club tomorrow and rent two cars that night or the next morning. Call us when you get close to Burdine's. John will fly his plane down to Marathon the day after tomorrow. Now, somebody mentioned that I was putting together a "Geezer" all-star team for this operation. Well, that's exactly what I've done. We've all got a wealth of experience and expertise to bring to an operation of this nature. Any more questions ......?"

"OK, gentleman, next stop ...Marathon!"

CHAPTER SEVEN

Wall to Wall Scuzzi sat in his office at the St. Petersburg JC Carpet Store reviewing the previous month's sales figures. There would be room to slip in a substantial number of bogus sales invoices to help launder the family's money. The family owned two carpet manufacturing mills in Alabama that legitimately sold carpet. But, they also "sold" JC many thousands of dollars of carpet that did not exist to fill their bogus invoices. The money kept moving. JC paid sales tax, corporate income tax, and paid the mills they owned for the non-existent carpet and for shipment. It was still a cheap way to launder the family's illicit cash. Luigi would give Georgio a figure for each store every month and he would manufacture the bogus cash sale invoices, purchase orders, and phony receipt invoices from the mills. They had been investigated twice but the books added up and nobody could prove anything.

Luigi's sat-phone rang in his briefcase. He retrieved the phone and answered.

"Luigi, its Cadillac."

"Yo, Vinny."

"I've got the Costa Rica airline info for you. But, I also want you to tell No Nose that we're gonna make our move on the Russians in twelve days ... a week from this comin' Tuesday. I'm gonna need ten more men for that one day, but Pete needs to have 'em there no later than five days before hit day. He's rented another house on Geiger Key, for the extra men to stay, near the Boundary Road house. I'll send 'em down in four white cargo vans that you can't trace. We got plenty of assault weapons and explosives, if we need 'em. Make sure each man you send to Miami has a Glock 9mm with a silencer. We want 'em dressed in shorts, Hawaiian shirts, t-shirts, floppy hats, and flip-flops. You know, like a bunch of tourists from Ohio. Pete and I have worked out a step by step plan of attack. The new men will be briefed and we'll do a walk-through of each step of the plan with 'em, which should make sure we all get outta here safe. I need two six passenger airplanes to fly in and wait at the private plane FBO (Fixed Base Operators that provide aviation services) at the Key West Airport. It's down the other end from the terminal and the private jet port, where the seaplanes used to load to fly to Fort Jefferson. Then we can fly twelve of our men out to the grass strip airport we use up in the Everglades. We're gonna leave the four cargo vans, wiped clean, in a lobster trap yard on Stock Island. Nobody'll see 'em until the fisherman put the traps out in August. Today's Friday, so we got to get movin' on the extra men and supplies. There's too many people cloggin' up this little island to pull off a caper like this on a weekend. We've got four Escalades down here now and I'm worried that the State Police might set up checkpoints, if it gets messy."

"How you gonna to handle that?"

"We've got Pete looking for a rental house on Summerland Key that's got a two car garage or is walled. He'll rent it from Sunday to Sunday. Four of my men can drive the Escalades up there on Tuesday night. They'll hole up there the rest of the week, then drive off the Keys with the vacation traffic on Saturday and Sunday afternoon."

"What are you gonna do with the bodies?"

"Well, I thought I'd send a truck down to the Geiger Key house with two drums of heavy anchor chain, bolt cutters, a box of master links, and two dozen military body bags that one of my wiseguys stole durin' an explosives heist at Patrick Air Force Base. Next week I'm sendin' another Jupiter 38 down there. We got a straight shot out to the Gulf Stream from our dock. There are no houses across from us and we're the last house on our road. We're gonna snatch most of these people off the street on their early mornin' routes, like behind buildins' and in deserted alleys. Four vans with three man teams will grab them one by one. We'll use the Escalades when needed. We got Taser X26's to knock 'em out. Then we'll zip-cuff them inside the vans, garrote 'em, and put 'em inta body bags. Our men will drop 'em off at the safe house to be wrapped with chain. We should be able to shuttle most of them out to the Ups and Downs in the Jupiters to deep-six 'em durin' the afternoon. When it's over, four of our men will run the two boats up to Key Largo that night and anchor off of Rodriquez Key. Then they'll cruise into Miami on Wednesday mornin'."

"How deep are the Ups and Downs?"

"600 to 800 feet."

"Have you figured out how you gonna get to Yuly Yankovich yet?"

"Vito The Dancer is stayin' in a condo on Sunset Island with one of our Miami hookers. They don't look nothin' like June and Ward Cleaver, but they do look like a couple of tourists from New Jersey. They're watchin' his house 24/7; Yuly's only been off Sunset Island twice since we've been keepin' track him. Pete The Barber is thinkin' about plantin' a remote control bomb under the swim platform of Yuly's boat. Vito said that both times he rode over to Key West; a bodyguard lowered the boat into the water and started the engines first. Then Yuly and his second bodyguard came out of the house and got in the boat. All three motored over to the Westin Hotel Marina across the channel, where Yuly and one bodyguard got into a waitin' car while the second bodyguard waited in the boat. The bomb can be planted by a scuba diver in the middle of the night. We can whack Yuly and his two bodyguards with the push of a button, and it might look like an accident, the boat's gasoline powered, so it would trigger one hell of an explosion when the fuel tank blows. The next question is how to get Yuly in the boat on purge day. If that don't happen, we're lookin' at a frontal assault on an armed house."

"You and Vito will think of somethin'."

"Worst case … we take one of the boats over to Wisteria Island, which is just north of Sunset Island, on Tuesday night. Nobody lives there-the Fed's own it. There might be a few homeless campers on it, but they stay in the middle of the island. We'd stay in the boat and shoot a few incendiary grenades through Yuly's windows with our grenade launchers. If that don't kill him, it should at least flush him out of the burnin' house. When he takes off in the boat … Vito will hit the bomb remote. Vito and his "wife" will check out and leave with the tourists on Sunday. Their flyin' back to Miami on Continental."

"Where do you want me to send the reinforcements?"

"Send the extra men to the 'Pink Pony' in Miami next Thursday. They can leave their cars there and I'll send 'em down to Key West with one of my men in the four vans. So, just send me nine … You know, I just found out from Pete that Yuly has a daughter named Ivanna living in Key West. She's actually his third lieutenant, and here's the kicker … she's gay. She's a big, muscular, 'butch', carpet muncher. Ouch! No offense, Wall to Wall."

"No offense taken, Cadillac," said Luigi with a laugh. "Pretty fuckin' funny."

"Anyhow, we could snatch her, shit, *there I go again*, and maybe get Yuly to move to save her life. Like, 'Bring us a million dollars and you and your daughter get to leave Key West alive.' I know the Russians are not into gay rights and shit, but she *is* his daughter. I mean, we wouldn't let 'em go. We'd still blow Yuly and his two bodyguards up in the boat, and then we'd deep-six her."

"Yuly probably wouldn't fall for it. That kind of situation is how *they* always operate. They're ruthless, heartless, lyin' bastards. Families don't mean nothin' to them. I'd rather see you use the grenade launchers on the bastard. If you do, make sure that Vito is set up with an assault rifle, in case Yuly runs out the front door and tries to make it to that fancy restaurant near the ferry slip."

"Ok, I don't think we need to talk anymore about the purge, let's hang up and then both plug our sat-phones into our faxes. I'll scan the Florida/Costa Rica flight manifests and fax them over to you."

"I'll report to No Nose tonight and send down the men you need. The airplanes you need will be there on purge day. Keep me posted, Goomba."

The faxes came thru and Luigi gave the manifests to Giorgio in the next office.

"Run these Florida to San Jose, Costa Rica airline passenger manifests onto your hotel guest list spreadsheet, and let's see what matches up on the target dates."

"Ok Dad, I'll run it through as soon as I finish entering these bogus carpet sales invoices into the sales journal."

"What bogus sales invoices? I don't see no bogus invoices," said Luigi with a laugh.

***

Giorgio scanned and downloaded the airline passenger manifests into his computer page by page. Then he transferred the downloaded information onto his spreadsheet. In a matter of seconds the spread sheets began to appear. There were many pages and many matches. Each day there were approximately 30 flights out of the combined targeted cities of Orlando, Tampa, Fort Lauderdale, and Miami, to San Jose's Juan Santamaria Airport. There was the same number of departing flights from San Jose back to the four Florida cities each day. Those planes moved approximately 4,500 people each way, each day. The sixteen targeted hotels and condos in Jaco and Los Suenos had over a thousand available rooms. Giorgio programmed his spreadsheet to only print out matches. The print out was in alphabetical order and showed; Passenger Name, Airline flt#/departure, city/arrival, date/times. Hotel name, check-in/check-out dates, and Airline flt#/destination city/times. There were 626 names on the printed spread sheets.

Giorgio loaded more paper into his Brother Printer, set it to print both sides of the sheets, then clicked the print box. Several minutes later he had a finished product. He checked the collation, put the sheets in a file folder and dropped it on his father's desk. He looked at his watch and saw that it was 1:00 p.m. Luigi must have gone back to Tampa to have lunch at the Italian Club in Ybor City. On the infrequent days he visited his St. Pete office, he usually drove back to Tampa for lunch and spent the afternoon and evening at the Tampa store. Giorgio texted him on his cell phone: *The report is finished and on your desk.*

He left the office and drove across town to Mazzaro's Deli and Restaurant, in his new Jaguar XK convertible, to get an Italian Hoagie.

Luigi texted Giorgio: *Bring the report over to the Tampa store on Dale Mabry. I got a meeting tonight and I want to go over the report before I go.*

Giorgio texted his father back: *I'll drop it off as soon as I finish my lunch.*

It was a beautiful day and Giorgio looked forward to the ride across the bay with the Jaguar's top down. After lunch he would stop back by his office and pick up the report and get the floor manager, Mario, to cover for him the rest of the day. After he dropped off the report at the Tampa store he would head for Thee Dollhouse over on Westshore Boulevard, pick up one of the strippers, and make an afternoon of it.

***

Luigi came back from lunch and Giorgio's report was on his desk. He was surprised by the sheer volume of it. As he started to look through the report he noticed the sheets were printed on both sides. Wall to Wall had already scheduled a meeting with No Nose later that evening, to update him on the Key West Russian plan. He also hoped he would have the Costa Rica information that John had requested the week before. There was still time for him to research this report, if he wasn't interrupted and had dinner delivered.

He buzzed his secretary, told her to hold all his calls and asked her to call Donatello's, which was close to the carpet store on Dale Mabry, to order him a baked Ziti takeout dinner at 6:30. He told her to send one of the floor salesmen to pick it up, and tip Guido $20.

Luigi settled in and started to read over the lengthy report. He couldn't believe that 4500 people flew in and out of San Jose every day from four Florida cities. Giorgio's college boy programming skills had at least limited the report to those travelers that ended up in Jaco's hotels. He started through the pages and had yet to find a familiar name, when his dinner arrived. The baked Ziti and crisp salad were excellent, and Luigi enjoyed a glass of Barolo wine from the small wine cooler he kept in his office. He worked thru dinner and was in the R's by the time he finished eating. He lit up a Dominican Fuentes cigar and kept looking down the lists, his eyes growing tired of the seemingly endless list of names, hotels and airlines. He hadn't seen any familiar names; names that could be connected to the Fernandez brothers, Beau Stone, or Ricardo Cabeza. He began to wonder if all this work was leading nowhere. He moved into the S's and at the bottom of the second page he finally scored. He almost missed it, but his brain made his eyes go back and look again. There it was … Seth Stone, American Airlines, Sat. August 4th, Lv TPA 11:30; Arv SJO/12:35 p.m., Los Suenos Marriott Hotel, check in Sat, August 4th/checkout

Sun. August 5th, American Airlines Sun., August 5th, Lv SJO/1:30 ; Arv TPA/6:30p.m.

Seth Stone, the squeaky clean St. Pete boatyard owner. Brother of the deceased Beau Stone, the gambling addict and robbery accomplice of Mafia traitor Ricardo Cabeza and the turncoat Fernandez brothers. Beau and Ricardo found dead in the Key West Aquarium, eaten by sharks. Their deaths were both confirmed by the DNA testing of body parts recovered from the shark's stomachs. Seth arrived in San Jose and checked into the Marriott Los Suenos the afternoon before the Bertram blew up and sank. He checked out the next morning, traveled back to San Jose, and flew back to Tampa that same afternoon. Just a coincidence? ...... Luigi didn't think so.

Wall to Wall checked the rest of the spread sheet, and then skimmed the whole report to check for a traveling companion and any other passengers from Tampa that might have also checked into the Marriott or Los Suenos Condos that same night. He found three: Mr. and Mrs. David Degroot, and Richard Winning. Both parties had rented condos from Stay in Costa Rica, a local rental/concierge company. Luigi knew Richard Winning. He was one of the owners of the Derby Lane Dog Track and Poker Room in St.Petersburg. They met years ago at Arturo Fuente's cigar factory in Ybor City. Richard had always comped Luigi when he visited the Derby Lane Clubhouse Bar and Restaurant, and Richard had the same privileges at The Columbia Restaurant and Tampa's various Gentlemen's clubs. Luigi would get Giorgio to check out the Degroots. He looked at his watch; he still had 45 minutes until he was scheduled to meet at No Nose's Golf View Street house. He texted Giorgio, *Call me on your sat-phone now!*

Luigi's sat-phone rang almost immediately after he sent the text.

"Giorgio, your spread sheet was great! I found the lead we were lookin' for. Just one more thing, I need you to check out a married couple named Degroot. They live in St. Pete and might be involved, too. I need you to do it right now! I'm on my way to John's house in fifteen minutes"

"Can it wait until tomorrow morning, Dad?" whined Giorgio. "I'm a little tied up at the moment."

"Listen Giorgio, I don't care if you're fuckin' Eva Longoria right now, get your ass out of that bed and onto your computer and get me the Degroots' info now! I want you to check out Seth Stone's info too, but you can do that one tomorrow mornin'. You ran a profile on him two years ago. See if he's bought any real estate, boats, cars, or whatever. Call me about the Degroots on the sat-phone, I'll pick up even if I'm at John's house."

**

Luigi turned off of South Himes and onto South Golf View Street. As he turned into No Nose's driveway, the last garage door started up. He pulled in and waited until the garage door was all the way down before he got out of his Escalade. Anthony was waiting for him at the house end of the garage. He opened the door into the house and said, "Mr. C. is out on the second floor veranda, he seems like he's in a good mood tonight. The chef made Veal Saltimbocca with his special wine sauce ... Mr. C. had seconds."

"Thanks Anthony, I got mostly good news for him."

Luigi walked upstairs. Anthony followed him and stayed in the game room as Luigi went out on the veranda. John was sitting in his favorite spot overlooking the lit up swimming pool below.

"*Ciao*, John, how are you?"

"I'm good," said No Nose as he exhaled a puff of smoke from his ten inch custom Fuentes cigar. "Would you like a cigar?"

"Of course, I like the smell of the one you're smokin'."

"Your buddy, Arturo, made these. I like them as well as the real Cubans. Take one, the lighter is over there by the box."

Wall to Wall cut the end off of his cigar and lit it. He took a long puff and slowly exhaled. He held the cigar out, admired it, and said, "I heard a sayin' once about a cigar ... 'A woman ... is only a woman, but a good Cigar ... is a Smoke!'"

They both laughed and No Nose said, "A serious cigar lover named Rudyard Kipling said that, Luigi."

"Fuckin'A, John, Fuckin'A."

"Well, what have you got for me tonight?"

"Let me give you the skinny on the Key West, Russian situation first. Cadillac says he's ready to pull the trigger a week from Tuesday. He wants me to send down nine more men, a few days before, through Miami. They been casin' the Russians for over a week now, and Cadillac and Pete have a solid plan. They're gonna take out 23 Russians; includin' three lieutenants - one is Yuly Yankovich's daughter, a captain, and Yuly. The rest are muscle, bodyguards, and street dealers. There may be a few more, like girlfriends or shop girls, if they get in the way. Our boys have the Russians daily routines down pat and are going to snatch 'em off the streets and out of their offices, one by one usin' Tasers to stun them. They're going to grab the muscle first, on their way to a daily breakfast meetin' with Ivan, a lieutenant. The Key West Police make themselves scarce around the Gulag and the drug dealers' hangouts. They're sure 'the fix is in' with the coppers. Our guys'll get the other two lieutenants early and all the dealers durin' the first two hours. The kapo is married, but he visits his girlfriend at one of his condos every mornin' before lunch. They're lookin' at takin' him in the first floor parking garage, but need to do a little more thinkin' about it. He starts his day late and spends the afternoon and late night at the Gulag bar and restaurant. Yuly is the biggest problem because he stays holed up in his house on a little island just off of Key West with two bodyguards. Cadillac has two high speed boats down there and they will attack his house at the end of the day with some high tech firepower, if he stays put. They'll be done and gone before any enforcement can even get there. If Yuly gets wind of the purge earlier and tries to leave the island, we'll already have his boat rigged with a remote-controlled bomb. We are watchin' his house 24/7. Our men will kill all the Russians that they snatch off the streets and transport them to our ocean-side safe house. From there, the boats will take them offshore and deep-six them."

"How are our guys going to get out of Key West, Luigi?"

At that moment Luigi's sat-phone rang and he said, "Let me get this, John, I'm sure it's Giorgio with some more info." He answered and nodded a few times then said, "I thought they'd be clean ... just vacationin' ... Degroot owns a soft ware company. OK, good work, Giorgio."

"Sorry, for the interruption John …… Back to Cadillac, he asked for two, six passenger airplanes to fly the main body of men out. I'm sendin' two planes down the mornin' of the purge from our Everglades airstrip. The others will come out in the two boats. The four SUVs will be driven to Summerland Key to a rented house and will leave for Miami the followin' weekend. Vito and the hooker on Sunset Island will fly out with the tourists on Sunday. Four cargo vans will be hidden on Stock Island, and they're untraceable anyhow. Cadillac figures he'll pick'em up when we take back the drug trade down there."

"That raises a few questions in my mind," said No Nose. "The first is to make sure Cadillac has one of our Miami doctor associates on one of the planes, in case any of our men get hurt. Better safe than sorry. Second, Cadillac should have Pete The Barber question the Russian Kapo, or one of his lieutenants, about the police payoff schedule down there. I know Pete knew who was paid off before we turned the streets over to the Russians, but I'm sure that's changed some now. It would make the transition easier for everybody if we can get a current roster. Get that information and then deep-six him. Third, if the bastards hadn't gotten greedy and stopped buying their drugs from us we wouldn't have to do this. While we're down there, see if we can figure out where they've been buying their drugs. But, don't blow our element of surprise; we need that to make the purge work."

"Cadillac told me that they tailed a lieutenant and some muscle to a location up on Sugarloaf Key to what looked like a drug buy. We don't have enough men down there now to stake that house out. But if the Russians go back there for more drugs we will follow 'em again."

"We can deal with that after the purge since we know the address. It sounds like Cadillac and you have things under control in Key West, so far. What else have you got?"

"Well, our Costa Rican research project got a surprisin' result. You'll never guess who flew from Tampa and checked into the Los Suenos, Marriott Hotel the same day the Bertram blew up," said Luigi, smugly.

No Nose's head snapped to attention, "Who was it, Luigi, who?"

"Seth Stone."

No Nose ran it through his brain for a couple of seconds and finally shook his head, "Now, ain't that some shit! I'd have never guessed it. His brother died in Key West. So ... he had to be in it from the beginning. Why else would he be in Los Suenos? When did he fly back to Florida?"

"The next day."

"We definitely need to talk to Mr. Stone. He might have my three million dollars ... Does he still own the boatyard in St. Pete? We have a lot of questions for him to answer."

"Giorgio is going to run a new profile on him tomorrow mornin'. I want to see if he made any large purchases or investments in the past two years. I'm also gonna send Fat John Conte over to St. Pete to set up some surveillance at his boatworks and on Treasure Island where he lives. We need to snatch him and question him here in Tampa on our own terms."

"Good work, Luigi. He might be the key to the money and the identity of the unknown Captain." With that he sprang to his feet, pumped his fist in the air shouted, "We are back in the fucking ballgame!! They thought they could outsmart us ... but now the bastards are going to pay!!!"

CHAPTER EIGHT

SETH and Gene Johnson left Salt Creek at 7:00 a.m. in *TAR BABY*. They were traveling at 24 knots which would put them in Marathon at approximately 4:00 p.m., if the sea state remained on the calm side. Now the wind was 5-10 knots from the southeast and Tampa Bay had a light chop. Seth wanted the crew to get used to communicating on the sat-phones. They were all used to using VHF radios, but a significant drawback was that anybody that was tuned to the frequency they were using could hear their entire conversation. In addition, the VHF was limited to line of sight transmission, at best 14 to 18 miles. Most commercial vessels had scanners on their VHF's and listened to anything that sounded interesting. The sat-phones had none of these drawbacks.

Seth called Freddy Buckley on his sat-phone. He knew the Grand Banks had left the Vinoy Basin docks from downtown St. Petersburg at the crack of dawn, because Freddy had called, a few minutes later, to test his sat-phone.

Dino answered the sat-phone saying, "*M/V SIRENA* here, come back."

"Dino, it's not a radio," laughed Seth. "Talk on it just like you talk on a telephone. How's everything going so far?"

"We're making 9 knots and we just went under the Skyway Bridge. The trawler's engines are running fine. We're headed for Anna Maria Pass."

"We should pass you out in the Gulf, just after you turn south down the coast. Call us if you need any help, and please call when you have Toby and Billy aboard and are headed out of Boca Grande Pass."

"Will do, Seth."

Seth turned to Gene who was steering the Hatteras and said, "We should overtake them out at the end of Anna Maria Pass, when we turn south towards the Keys."

"What a beautiful morning to run down to the Keys, Seth. I wish Bobby Thompson was coming along."

"Bobby is a busy guy these days with his security business going worldwide after 9/11. I called him on my way to West Marine yesterday afternoon and filled him in on our investigation. He volunteered any of his investigative services, if we need any information. He's tuned into NSA and the FBI now that he has the Federal contract. He said he's got contracts with all of our country's allies now. If we need him, Bobby said he'd jet in for a few days from wherever he was. I just hope he doesn't get too busy to fish the tournaments with us later this summer."

"Me too, I'd like us to win the Old Salt's Gulf Loop Tournament this year and qualify to go to the IGFA Offshore World Championship in Costa Rica. It would be fun to meet the 60 or 70 teams that come from all over the world. Now that we're all pretty much retired we can take the time to pre-fish it, then kick back and relax down there for a couple of days when it's over. That beats rushing in and rushing back out to get back to work."

"Amen! I don't know if Bobby can cut that; but John, Billy, Toby, Freddy, and you and I can do it. Bobby and Dino will probably still be on tight schedules for the near future. But, they'll still want to fish the tournaments."

Seth could see the Grand Banks Trawler up ahead about two miles. It was just making the turn from west to south at the end of the Anna Maria Channel sand bar. Five minutes later they passed *SIRENA* with a hand wave and a blast of their bridge horn. Gene and Seth settled in for the long haul to Marathon, keeping watch for the lines of fish trap buoys they would encounter along the way. They would run two to three miles off the shoreline until they got down to Marco Island, then they'd angle around the numerous sand bores at Romano Shoals. Once around the shoals they'd reset their course across Florida Bay for the John Sawyer Bank which was about four miles north of Vaca Key, where the City of Marathon was located.

The voyage went smoothly and the wind didn't pick up until they reached Florida Bay. The afternoon sea breeze kicked in and a nasty little chop developed. At that point they had approximately 80 miles left to go. Seth was on the helm and trimmed the bow down, then pulled the throttles back until the 46 foot Hatteras was cruising at 22 kts. That speed would put them at Marathon Yacht club by 5:30 that afternoon. They were taking some intermittent spray on the Lexan windscreen up on the bridge, but the ride was still comfortable. Seth knew the bartender would check them in at the small yacht club marina that only had 20 docks. He had always stayed there when he brought a boat to Marathon. Actually, they didn't have an official dock master. Marathon Yacht Club was a small, but well- appointed, complex facing Florida Bay. The marina, like most marinas in the Keys, had been blasted out of the coral. Those pock-marked coral walls were loaded with lobsters. Seth liked the friendly, informal, atmosphere. It was located right behind a Florida State Police Headquarters and across from Fisherman's Hospital. The food was good and the club bar stayed open until 11:00 p.m., if there were any members or marina guests at the bar. The whole concept was refreshing to Seth, who belonged to a 2500 member club, with 75 slips, two bars, three dining rooms, and a formal ballroom. But of course, he understood that both yacht clubs had their place.

Even though Seth had made this trip countless times, he still continued to mark *TAR BABY's* position on his paper chart every half hour. He knew if he lost his GPS map, and didn't have his position marked on a paper chart; it could be the start of an unfortunate chain of events.

The radio and cell phone towers on Vaca Key finally came into view. West of their position several small, uninhabited, unnamed, mangrove keys popped up. Suddenly the day marker on the John Sawyer Bank loomed ahead. Seth skirted the bank and headed for the Intracoastal Waterway channel that ran on the north side of the Keys. He navigated between the Bethel Bank and the Rachel Bank markers, and headed for the three tallest radio beacons clustered above the Marathon Yacht Club's private "G1" day marker at the entrance to their channel. He called the bartender on channel 16, was switched to channel 68, and was given his slip assignment. Seth deftly backed *Tar Baby* into his front row slip as Gene lassoed the forward pilings and made the lines fast. Seth shifted into neutral and came down the flybridge ladder and tossed the aft cockpit lines to the waiting bartender, who he recognized as Scotty.

"Nice catch, Scotty, Gene will get the spring lines and I'll hook up the power. We'll see you inside shortly for a cold one and some dinner."

"It's nice to see you, Mr. Stone. We're still busy with happy hour so take your time!"

Seth shut down the Cummins diesels at the cockpit control station and stepped up on the dock with his shore cords and a 50 amp splitter. After plugging in and switching the power on at the pedestal he went into the Hatteras's salon, turned off the Onan gen-set, and switched the power from ship to shore at the main panel. He returned to the flybridge and turned off the radar and other electronics. As he started down the ladder, his sat-phone started to ring.

"Hey Seth, Freddy here. I topped off the fuel at Miller's Marina, picked up Billy and Toby, and we're headed back out Boca Grande Pass. We're looking at light wind and flat sea conditions tonight."

"Gene and I just pulled into Marathon. We had a good trip down. A little bumpy on Florida Bay, but at least the lobster traps are not out yet. You should have a nice ride tonight. Any problems towing the panga?"

"No, it tracks really well. We're going to do three hour watches, and split them with Toby and Billy. Dino's down in the galley cooking us up one of his gourmet dinners. We ought to get to Burdine's around noon tomorrow."

"Sounds like you guys are doing OK. Tomorrow morning, we're going to walk over to the Stuffed Pig for breakfast. After that, we'll catch a taxi to the Marathon Airport and rent a couple of vans."

"I like that place! I think I gained five pounds there the last time I fished out of Marathon," laughed Freddy.

"Call me when you get tied up at Burdine's and we'll shuttle your car over. Say 'hey' to Toby and Billy for me, and call us if you need us."

"Will do Seth, have a good night."

Gene was already hosing the boat off as Seth folded the sat-phone's antennae down.

"That was Freddy, they just left Boca Grande. Let's grab a quick shower and change. I'll meet you in the bar, and we'll have dinner here tonight," yelled Seth as he ducked into the cabin.

He made a quick call on his cell phone to Lori, she picked right up.

"Hi Seth, are you in the Keys?"

"Yes, we just got here and I wanted you to know we had a good trip down."

"I'm missing you already. Will you call me when you can?"

"I'll probably text with the guys being around all the time. You can do the same. I miss you too. I'll text in a few days."

Lori said, "I'll be waiting … good night Seth."

Seth and Gene sat down at the long horseshoe shaped bar inside the Yacht Club and ordered two glasses of Shiraz instead of cold beers. When Scotty brought their wine, Seth told him he had more friends coming in to fish, but they would be staying elsewhere on the island. He opened an account at the bar for the boat and gave Scotty a list of names who could charge to his account. He and Gene ate dinner right at the bar and each had another glass of Shiraz. By 9:00 p.m. they were the last two at the bar.

"Scotty, do you still play the ashtray game on the bar top? I'd like to show it to my friend Gene."

"Of course we do, Mr. Stone. Give me a second and I'll set it up." Scotty cleared the horseshoe bar's surface and pulled two large "Shooter" marbles out from under the bar. Seth and Gene were sitting at the apex of the horseshoe. The bar was built with a radiused polished wood armrest around its outer perimeter. Scotty turned a heavy square glass bar ashtray upside down at one end of the bar and propped the end facing the apex up with a cut piece of plastic soda straw in the center. He walked across to the other end of the horse shoe and rolled one of the marbles towards the horseshoe's apex. The marble banked off the inside of the arm rail and sped across the apex, hit the rail on the other side, and caromed down the middle of the opposite bar top. It hit the straw holding up the inverted ashtray, and the heavy glass ashtray fell flat capturing the marble.

"Unfucking believable," said Gene, as Seth just laughed. "You made that look easy, Scotty."

"I have lots of time to practice. I don't go home until 11:00."

"Don't ever play him," said Seth. "Why don't you and I play, Gene, say $5 a round?"

The two of them played until 10:30 and then turned in. As they walked out to the Hatteras, Gene said, "That was fun. I can't wait to get John Harvey in there some night. But, I definitely won't be playing you again, Seth."

"It cost me a few dollars to get the hang of it, Gene, the first couple times I played."

***

Seth and Gene rose early to a glorious Florida Keys' daybreak. The Keys were more famous for their spectacular sunsets. The sight of that flaming red ball of fire melting into the Gulf of Mexico had inspired artists, photographers, poets, and lovers for centuries. Some nights the disappearing sun almost made the water, which it appeared to sink into, look like it was boiling around it. Seth's favorite place to watch the sunset in Marathon was the Sunset Grille Tiki Bar. It was located at the west end of Vaca Key, near the base of the old Keys' Railroad Bridge, which was now a pedestrian bridge to Pigeon Key. Seth had seen the 'green flash' there, for the first time, in the late 1980's. But it was the sunrise that washed the Keys clean of its nightly hangover with pastel shades of pink and blue. It was a soft, dewy, unreal beauty that lasted for only about an hour. Everything looked brand new, and you were given a fresh start on another day in paradise.

Gene and Seth put six fishing rods up in the flybridge rod holders just to signal why they were there. When they finished moving the rods up, they walked east past the State Police building and the Fisherman's Hospital across the Highway. A block later they arrived at the Stuffed Pig. It was beginning to fill with locals as they took a seat in a back booth. After they finished their breakfast and coffee, Seth had the cashier call them a taxi to take them to the airport terminal.

Seth picked Enterprise and they rented two Dodge seven passenger Caravans. The vans had plenty of room for personnel and gear. Seth had copies of all the crews' driver licenses and signed them on as additional drivers. He and Gene drove back to the boat, checked the engine room over, and then motored *TAR* BABY over to the nearby Key's Fishery fuel dock and filled the tanks with diesel. After they were retied at the yacht club, they kicked back in the air conditioned salon to wait for the trawler boys to call.

The call came at 12:15 p.m. Billy called on the sat-phone and told Seth they were at Burdine's fuel dock taking on fuel.

"How was the ride across Florida Bay, Billy?"

"There was a light easterly breeze. Since the season doesn't start until August first, there weren't many lobster traps just a few old abandoned ones from last season. But bad luck, we managed to pick up one about 2:00 this morning. It wound the steel rebar line weight right onto the starboard shaft and stopped the engine. We turned off the port engine and I went under with a mask, dive light and serrated filet knife. I cut it all loose, but it took some time. It was definitely an old trap. The line and trap were all covered with barnacles. I'd figured it would be, so I went in with my gloves on. There was no damage to the running gear or cutlass bearing. Toby started both engines after I got out and we started back on course. It could have been worse, but it was just a normal Florida Bay pain in the ass."

"At least it wasn't rough. I always worry about the boat bottom or propellers hitting me in the head when the boat is lurching up and down."

"You've got that right, it's bad enough when you have to deal with the traps when its daylight."

"Well Billy, all of that gym time you put in every week pays off when you get in a situation like that. Gene and I will drive your van over in about a half an hour. You guys ought to be in your slip by that time. We can all drive to Herbie's and get a dolphin sandwich or eat right there at Burdine's on the second story deck."

"Ok, see you soon."

Seth wasn't surprised that Billy had handled the night time lobster trap without incident. He had boyish features, but the 175 lbs he packed on his six foot frame was all muscle. Seth had seen him pump up a couple of 200 lb jewfish off the bottom with a standard 30lb grouper rig ... just for fun.

Seth and Gene drove the two vans up 33rd St. and turned right on the Overseas Highway, drove about a mile, then turned left on 15th St. and traveled south thru endless rows of wooden lobster traps stacked 20 feet high. In the late spring and early summer, the staccato sound of pneumatic nail guns started at dawn and continued until dusk on Vaca Key in the Middle Keys and Stock Island in the Lower Keys. These two locations held the majority of the Key's commercial lobsterers. They were repairing the old traps and building new ones to replace the ones that they had lost. During the first week in August the hammering would suddenly stop, signaling the start of the commercial season. Seth saw Ocean View Dr. and turned right. A cluster of palm trees and a wrecked skiff with Burdine's Waterfront painted on it pointed the way. They parked the vans behind SIRENA'S slip as the crew finished washing her down.

They all decided to walk up to Burdine's restaurant for lunch. They sat at the east end of the thatched roof pavilion on the second level deck, overlooking undeveloped Boot Key, the Boot Key draw bridge, and the crowded bight anchorage past the bridge.

As they ordered lunch Freddy asked Seth, "When is John Harvey arriving in his airplane?"

"I'm expecting a call from him on the sat-phone any time now. I'll pick him up at the airport and bring him back here. John will bunk on the trawler with Toby, Dino, Billy, and you. You and Billy will run the trawler if it goes out while John and Toby are flying. Most of the time, you, Billy, and Dino will fish with us on the TAR BABY, when the two of them fly. If we need to get somewhere fast to see a boat that they have spotted from the plane, we want to be on the Hatteras."

"So, we start looking tomorrow?" asked Toby.

"The first thing we're going to do tomorrow is set the buoys out in Florida Bay to the Huckin's dimensions, and have you cut proportional frames out of cardboard at two or three different altitudes up in the airplane. For example, at 2000 feet, you'll have a small rectangular cardboard frame that the Huckins will fit in perfectly, when you look down thru it from the airplane. Then you're going to start looking, and we're going to go fishing out towards the Marathon Humps. The plane will start searching from here up to Key Largo and back."

Seth was in the midst of paying the lunch check when his sat-phone rang.

"Hey John, did you have a good flight?"

"Smooth as silk. Flight Base Operations is filling me up with fuel right now, and then I'll park her over by the FBO office."

"I'll be over to get you in about fifteen minutes; do you need something to eat? We just finished lunch here at Burdine's."

"No thanks, I had a sandwich in the plane on the way down."

"See you in a few."

Seth asked Toby to ride with him and they headed east towards the airport. John, all six foot two of him, was standing out in front of the FBO when they pulled up. Toby unwound his slender six foot four frame out of the van and shook John's hand as John threw his duffel in the van.

"Traveling light, hey?" said Seth, eyeing the small duffel.

Toby piped up, "Dino told me he brought John's guns and ammo down to the trawler the night before they left."

"That's right, I only have a few changes of clothes and a rain jacket. Freddy told me the trawler has a washer and dryer. But, I did bring my lightweight Ruger.380 with me in my pocket holster."

"How was the flight down?"

"Like I said, smooth as silk. There were some large thunderheads building in the middle of the state so I skirted around them, which put me out over the coast. I followed it down to Cape Sable and then cut across Florida Bay. I missed all the turbulence."

"Do you still cruise the plane at 150 mph and burn 16.5 gallons an hour?"

"Yes, that's fairly accurate depending on a headwind or tailwind."

"How many gallons of fuel can you carry?"

"About a hundred gallons usable."

"So you have about a nine hundred mile range."

"Yes, without stretching it."

"Then you can fly to Mexico, the Caymans, or even Jamaica, no sweat."

"No sweat."

They drove back to Burdine's and Seth went over the proportional box method of identifying boats from the air again. Toby and John decided to cut out two sets, one at a 1000', and another at 2000'. They felt they could fly over a suspect vessel two or three times at 2000' and not arouse any suspicion. If they had a low ceiling to deal with they'd drop down to 1000'. Seth dropped them off and picked up Gene. They all agreed to meet for dinner at one of Seth's top 10 best Cuban restaurants anywhere, Don Pedro's. Don Pedro and his wife had fled Cuba, and arrived in Marathon in the early 1970's on an inner-tube raft. The raft was displayed on one of the walls in the restaurant's main dining room. They were great people and the food was superb.

The next morning Seth was up at dawn. He had eaten too much roasted pork at Don Pedro's and settled for some coffee and a bagel for breakfast. He loaded the deflated buoys in the van and headed for the gas station near the Barracuda Grille, another one of his favorite restaurants in Marathon. The Barracuda's food was decidedly upscale and delicious, a real surprise in the Middle Keys. Seth fished in his pockets for his basketball inflation needle and put four quarters in the air station compressor and blew up the four buoys. Seth thought ... *whatever happened to free air at service stations?* Pumping your own gas was bad enough. Todd Muldoon, his service station buddy in St. Pete, told him he made no profit on gasoline. But he still had pump jockeys, who checked your tires, filled them with free air, cleaned your windshield, and checked under your hood. He made his profit with his mechanics shop, tire sales, and convenience/package store. The pump jockeys found enough mechanical work to keep the shop busy, and the extra service insured a high volume of customers. Seth figured if he had a service station in the Keys, he would emulate Todd's business plan, but he'd give away a free bag of ice with the purchase of every 12 pack of beer and maybe raise the gas price a little.

Seth checked *TAR BABY's* engine room; all the fluids were good and he found no water or fuel leaks. The Racor filters had no water in their bowls and a check of their paper cartridges showed little sediment. The crew was scheduled to show up at Marathon Yacht Club at 7:30, after dropping John and Toby at the airport. Dino and Billy pulled in a few minutes early, and they shoved off immediately. Freddy was waiting for them in the panga out at the green yacht club channel marker. Billy had two dozen fresh ballyhoos with him that he had picked up at Marathon Bait and Tackle, and he started to rig them before *TAR BABY* even left the dock.

Seth told the crew, "We're going to go north up into Florida Bay, about two miles past the John Sawyer Bank. We'll rendezvous with the airplane there. Dino will get in the panga with Freddy and set out the four buoys and mushroom anchors to match the length and beam of the Huckins. John and Toby will do a number of flyovers, while Toby cuts out a cardboard rectangular picture frame at each altitude that fit the buoy layout, down on the water, precisely. Then we'll pick up the buoys and deflate and store them below, while Freddy runs the panga back to Burdine's. The airplane will search up towards Key Largo over the open water and will also fly over the marinas and residential canals. We'll run through Channel Seven, pick up Freddy, then run out past the Sombrero Reef light, and troll towards the Marathon Humps. If the flyboys see something interesting in the airplane they'll take pictures and note the final position. We'll check it out tomorrow by land or sea."

Once in position, the crew deployed the buoys which were tied together with yellow floating polypropylene line precut to the exact dimensions of the Huckin's overall 62'3" length and 16'6" beam. Using the panga's maneuverability, the tide, and the wind to their advantage, Freddy and Dino launched the mushroom anchors with twelve feet of anchor line in eight feet of water. They tugged at each buoy with a boat hook until the lines were all taut, and the rectangle was symmetrical.

Seth called the airplane and gave John their position. Ten minutes later the plane appeared and took several passes over the buoys. Toby called back on the sat-phone and told Seth he had the boxes made for both altitudes. Everything had been checked and double-checked.

Seth said, "OK boys, pick up the buoys and let's go fishing."

CHAPTER NINE

Fat John Conte sat in his black Escalade in the parking lot across the street from Stone's Boatworks on the Coast Guard By-Pass in south Saint Petersburg. He had been there since 7:30 that morning. The road was actually 18th Ave. South but it was three lanes, had no on-the-street parking, or side streets entering it. The boatwork's parking lot surface was shell, with three foot hedges buffering the sidewalk and street. The back of the lot had a six foot grey wooden fence with oak trees shading most of the lot from the blazing afternoon summer sun. Fat John had a folder with three photos of Seth Stone in it, garnered from contacts at the *St. Petersburg Times* and the State of Florida Division of Motor Vehicles. There were newspaper pictures of Seth receiving sailing trophies several years ago, and a five year old driver's license mug shot. They were the most recent photos he could come up with. He also had one of his associates, Rico "Mo-Mo" Lestini, watching Seth Stone's Paradise Island townhouse out on Treasure Island Beach. People and cars had been coming and going all day, but Fat John saw no one that looked like Seth. Mo-Mo wasn't having any luck either. Fat John was beginning to think maybe Seth was out of town. The boatworks was busy, they had launched two boats that morning and hauled out a 65-footer just an hour ago. Fat John would stay put until quitting time, and if he didn't spot him by then, he'd get back to Wall to Wall with a new plan. In the meantime he felt secure in his SUV, behind the dark limo tint on the windows.

***

Luigi sat in his Tampa office reading Giorgio's latest report on Seth Stone. Nothing much had changed in the past two years. He lived in the same townhouse, had the same boat, and he drove the same GMC Yukon. The boatworks had not expanded physically, although they had collected more sales tax on increased sales this past year. Stone had purchased a used BMW roadster and had obtained a five year hunting lease on 259 acres near Brooksville, in Hernando County. His bank balances and investment accounts were virtually unchanged. Nothing indicated that he was spending the spoils from a three million dollar robbery. But Luigi knew in his bones that Seth Stone had the answers that they sought.

Fat John and his henchman, Mo-Mo, both had unproductive days at their stakeouts in St. Petersburg and Treasure Island. Luigi and Fat John concocted a more aggressive plan for the next day. If he or Mo-Mo did not see Stone before noon, Fat John was to impersonate an old customer who was moving back to Tampa after 15 years in Atlanta. He would question the yard foreman or manager about Seth's and Beau's whereabouts, stressing that he only wanted to deal with Seth or Beau, since they were who he had dealt with in the past. Of course, he would be told that Beau was dead, and that would lend credibility to Fat John's out of town story.

Luigi called No Nose's sportfish captain, Tony Fungello, in the Bahamas. "Tony, Luigi in Tampa, I need some information on a boat re-fit package that would get any boatyard owners attention."

"How big a boat?"

"Like an older 50 foot sportfish."

Thirty minutes later, Tony sent a fax to Luigi using their sat-phones.

Luigi called Fat John. "Come by my office in Tampa. I got a fax from Capt. Tony with the all boat information for the boat scam tomorrow. I'll put it in an envelope out front with the receptionist."

Wall to Wall knew Fat John could pull it off, if he hadn't been such an excellent criminal he probably could have been a professional actor.

***

The second day of surveillance at the boatworks went much the same as the first day. People and boats came and went, but Seth Stone was a no-show. Mo-Mo had the same luck at the townhouse out at the beach. He was parked under a large live oak tree near the swimming pool and watched the UPS, FedEx, and local mailman go by. A group of bikini-clad teen-aged girls swimming in the pool kept him from nodding off.

Fat John called Mo-Mo at 1:30 for a report and wasn't surprised that it was negative. "Listen, I'm going to check out the boatwork's office in a few minutes and see if I can find out where Stone is. You sit tight and I'll call you when I come out. If you see him out there before I call, text me on my cell phone with the word "yes". I'll hear the chime in my pocket and I'll exit as fast as I can. Either way I'll call you on my sat-phone when I'm back in my car."

"Standin'-by, John."

Fat John exited the Escalade and walked across the three lane road and through the gate. The whole yard was paved, and as he walked past the bunkered yachts that were being worked on, he found the sound from the air-driven grinders and sanders deafening. He was dressed casually in new khakis and a dark blue Tommy Hilfiger XXL, short-sleeved, knit shirt. He also had bought a pair of leather Sperry Top-sider boat shoes the night before at West Marine in Tampa, at Luigi's suggestion, and he wore a pair of aviator-style sunglasses. Luigi wanted him to look like an up-scale yachtsman. Fat John thought he probably looked more like "Tubby" Hilfiger in this preppy get-up than Tommy Hilfiger. He liked black clothes that somewhat hid his considerable bulk. By the time he got to the main building he was beginning to sweat from the afternoon heat. The sanding dust swirling around him in the air was starting to stick to him. As he walked through the open door he saw a sign that read, OFFICE UPSTAIRS. The bottom floor of the building housed a parts storeroom, and separate mechanic and carpenter shops. He found the stairs and was out of breath when he entered the office. There were two men sitting at desks in front of a row of file cabinets. Two open office doors opened off of the main office. The lights were off in the second one.

A large, affable looking man at the nearest desk said, "Hi, I'm Jeff, the office manager, can I help you?"

Fat John caught his breath and answered, "I'm here to see Seth."

"Seth's not here today, can I help you?"

"How about Beau, he usta to help me too."

"Beau passed away a couple of years ago, sir."

"Oh, I'm sorry to hear that. Well I guess you're gonna have to help me," said Fat John with a smile. "I usta bring my boats to Stone's when I lived in Tampa. I've been gone for 15 years, but I'm movin' back and I wanted to talk to Seth about a boat I'm thinkin' about refurbishin'.

"Well, I'm not sure when Seth will be coming back Mr..........?"

"Lombardo, John Lombardo."

"Mr. Lombardo. Why don't you talk to Jeb Stone, the boatwork's manager?"

"Ok, but I've always dealt with Seth or Beau."

"Jeb is Seth's son. Let me round him up for you."

Jeb was down in the yard somewhere, so Jeff called his cell phone and alerted him that there was a customer waiting in the office. Jeb arrived upstairs a few minutes later and Jeff said, "Jeb this is Mr. John Lombardo. Mr. Lombardo, meet Jeb Stone."

Fat John thought Jeb was a dead ringer for Seth, six feet tall, 200 lbs, same sandy brown hair and pleasant smile, just younger. They exchanged pleasantries, and Jeb invited John into his office.

"What can I do for you, sir?"

"I usta to bring my Bertram here, until I moved away from Tampa 15 years ago. I'm movin' back, from Atlanta, in about six months, and I've been lookin' at boats. I found one I like on the east coast, and I wanted to run the project by your dad, or your Uncle Beau, before I bought it and moved it over here. Your office manager told me that Beau passed away. I'm sorry to hear that, I liked him."

"Thank you."

"So that leaves your dad, and I really dealt with him more ... anyhow."

"What kind of boat are you interested in buying?"

"I've found a 1996 48' Ocean Super Sport at Florida Yachts in Fort Lauderdale. I wanna redo the interior, paint the whole exterior, put in two new gen-sets, all new electronics, and repower it."

"I think the Super Sport had twin Detroit 550 H.P. 6V-92's in it," said Jeb while taking some notes. "What do you want to repower her with?"

"I want Cummins QSM 11, 660's."

"How about the gen-sets?

"Northern Lights."

"Those are good choices. I'd be glad to work up a ballpark estimate for you, Mr. Lombardo. The materials, furniture, and appliances that you pick out will probably change the estimate the most, and there may be some structural problems that are discovered during hardware removal and prep for the paint job. But for the most part, my estimate should be accurate within 10 to 15%."

"Well, I really wanna do the job here and not on the other coast. I always felt I got first class work and a fair price from your dad. No offense Jeb, but I really wanna talk to him about it. Y'know ... face to face."

"OK, I don't know what your time frame is Mr. Lombardo, but he's off on a fishing trip right now and I don't expect him back for a couple of weeks."

"Ah, fishin'! That's what I want to start doin' when I move back down here. Did he go to the Bahamas?"

"No, he's somewhere in the Keys."

"I think it would be worth it for me to wait a coupla weeks. Can I leave my Atlanta number, so he can call me when he gets back? Then the three of us can work together on it."

"OK, Mr. Lombardo, jot your number down on this paper that I've been taking notes on, and I'll have him call you the day he gets back."

"Thanks Jeb and I can't tell you how helpful you've been."

Fat John wrote down a fictitious 404 area code phone number, shook hands with Jeb, and left the office.

***

Jeb had an uneasy feeling about John Lombardo, but he didn't get to think about it very long. Jeff handed him four call-back phone messages from current customers, so his mind went quickly back to all the work the boatworks had in hand.

***

Luigi was elated after he got Fat John's phone call. He and Mo-Mo were on their way back to Tampa, and once again Fat John had come through for him. It might be too much to ask Cadillac to find Seth Stone in the Keys right now, given the Russian situation. But it occurred to him that he could take a page out of an old playbook and have Captain Tony and Giorgio track him down. After all, Stone had to dock his 46' Hatteras, *TAR BABY*, somewhere each night, and he had to refuel it to keep fishing.

Luigi had sent down the extra nine men that Cadillac requested, early that morning. They should be on their way from Miami, to the Lower Keys by now. There were only five days left until the purge started. The airplanes were already fueled up and ready to go from their Everglades airstrip. Cadillac called in a favor and had a Miami emergency room surgeon flying down to Key West with the planes next Tuesday.

Two years ago the doctor had been pulled over late one night by the Miami Police, with his mistress in the car, and arrested for DUI and possession of cocaine. He knew Cadillac, because his mistress was one of Cadillac's dancers at the Pink Pony. His mistress had Cadillac's cell phone number. The doctor's life flashed before his eyes as he sat in the back of the paddy wagon on his way to the station. He was going to lose his driver's license, his medical license, his house in Coral Gables, his wife and kids, and half of his money in the impending divorce. He saw Cadillac as his only way out. He called Cadillac instead of his lawyer. Cadillac did the favor for the dancer, not the doctor; she was a big draw at his titty bar. Cadillac called a police captain and a county judge. Dr. Mendez walked free an hour later. There was no record of the traffic stop. The doctor had made his deal with the devil. He went straight. The mistress got a brand new BMW for a goodbye. But the doctor was called upon from time to time, to tend to wounds that could not be tended anywhere else.

Luigi called Captain Tony on his sat-phone and filled him in on Seth Stone and the *Tar Baby*. He told him he would have Giorgio provide him with lists of all the Key's marinas and fuel docks that could handle a Hatteras 46 Sportfish.

He said to Captain Tony, "Fat John said Seth's son took the bait on the Ocean 48 refit. He could tell that the kid was very interested in gettin' that work."

"Like I said, any good yard would like a project like that; it would run every bit of $400,000. Well, I'll wait to hear from Giorgio. It looks like I'll have that damn satellite telephone growing out of my fucking ear again."

Luigi dialed up Giorgio on his sat-phone at the St. Pete store and told him about Fat John's visit to Stone's Boatworks. "I need you to make a Key's marina and fuel dock list for Captain Tony. He will do the callin' from the Bahamas, like he did two years ago when we tracked the 54 Bertram to Costa Rica. It's Cadillac's territory, but he's got his hands full right now with the Russians. But really, I know Captain Tony has got the boating lingo to talk to the dock masters right. Start sendin' him lists as soon as you can."

Luigi called Cadillac on his sat-phone and he answered it on the third ring.

"What's up?"

"Well, Giorgio put the airline manifests and Jaco hotel guest list on a spread sheet, and Beau Stone's brother, Seth, flew from Tampa and checked into the Los Suenos Marriott the same day the Bertram blew up."

"No Shit!"

"Yeah, he checked out the next day and flew back to Tampa."

"I bet that's got No Nose all riled up again."

"That's a fuckin' understatement. We've had Seth Stone staked out for a couple a days, but we can't find him. This afternoon Fat John went into Stone's Boatworks office, scammed his son on a potential big boat job estimate, and found out Stone's down in the Keys fishin'. His boats not at his townhouse, the boatworks, or the St. Petersburg Yacht Club ... He must be usin' it. I figure you're too busy with the Russki's to look for him, so I got Giorgio and Captain Tony ham and eggin' it."

"Thanks, it all sounds good to me. I sent your guys down the Keys in the cargo vans; we'll start 'em on some dry runs and recon tomorrow. They'll all be paired up with my regulars."

"If we find Stone's location, I'll call you. Dependin' on the timin' maybe youse can snatch him for us. As you can imagine, Mr. C. wants to grill him up in Tampa. But, he doesn't want to jeopardize the purge in any way. I'm gonna try and see him tonight ... is there anythin' you want me to tell him?"

"Nope, I feel good about our situation down here. I think our plan will work because we're wired in and the Russians don't have a fuckin' clue. There may be a few surprises, but I'm sure we got enough people and hardware to whack them out."

"If you need anything Vinny, call me. I'll be standin' by on Tuesday."

Cadillac said, "Thanks, paisano."

Luigi called No Nose and set up a meeting after dinner.

***

John Cipriano sat on his porticoed veranda and watched the sun drop below the 80-year-old live oak trees that forested Palma Ceia's golf course. The sun flickered and danced through their long, outreaching, branches hung with Spanish moss. He enjoyed the mix along with the hundreds of stately palm trees that shared the rough and ringed the greens. He had the air conditioning on and the overhead fans set low. That combination made for a balmy breeze, while outside the porch Tampa's air was hot, humid and still. He had dined on peppered shrimp Alfredo, which were especially tasty since Chef Giovanni had scored some jumbo Key West Pinks. The wine was a surprise; the chef had passed up the traditional white wine with seafood rule and had chosen a bold red Italian Primativo from Puglia. It went perfectly with the spicy peppered shrimp. No Nose relaxed, as he sipped a 25 year old, small batch, single malt scotch and savored the aroma of his Cuban cigar, while he waited for Luigi to bring him the news of the day.

A few minutes later Luigi walked onto the veranda and sat down across from No Nose.

"Come stai, Luigi?"

"Molto bene."

"Would you like some scotch or a cigar?"

"I'll take a cigar, John. Thanks."

Luigi cut the end off the Habanos Fonseca cigar, lit it, and then blew some smoke in the air as he settled back in his chair.

"Fill me in on Key West first."

"The nine men I sent Cadillac should be down in the Keys by now. Cadillac's sure he's got all his bases covered. He thinks he's got enough men and firepower to kick ass this Tuesday."

"Good, good. Did we find Seth Stone yet?"

"Well, we couldn't find him in St.Pete. We staked out his townhouse and his boatworks for a coupla days and figured him and his 46' Hatteras were out of town. I sent Fat John into the boatwork's office posin' as an old customer from 15 years ago who was movin' back to Tampa and wanted to talk to Seth about a high dollar refit. Captain Tony told us what kind of renovations would ring their bell. Fat John made it clear that he wouldn't deal with nobody but Seth. He was told that Seth was fishin' down in the Keys and wouldn't be back for at least two weeks. John told them he would wait that long and left a fake Atlanta number for them to call when Seth got back. We should have him before that."

"I would hope so."

"I got Giorgio and Captain Tony checkin' out the Keys marinas and fuel docks, just like they did when we tracked the Bertram. They start tomorrow."

"If they find him before the Russian purge goes down, maybe some of Cadillac's muscle can snatch him. But, I don't want to endanger that operation at all. A couple of days one way or the other won't make any difference with Mr. Stone. Once we get him, it won't take us very long to find out what he knows. Either way, I hope he has fun on his last fishing trip," said No Nose sarcastically. "Keep me in the loop and call me when you have any new dope. Get some sleep Luigi, you look like shit."

"Good advice, Boss. I'll sleep better when this Russian thing is over," said Luigi on his way out.

CHAPTER TEN

Seth picked up Freddy at Burdine's, off the trawler's swim platform, and headed for Sombrero Light. Once through the reef, he ran southeast until he was in 650 feet of water then slowed to trolling speed. Once the outriggers were down, Dino and Billy put out the long rigger baits. Billy deployed a small blue and white Islander, in front of the ballyhoo, rigged with a #7 circle hook. Gene trailed back a right short outrigger naked ballyhoo, while Freddy ran a marlin lure out on the left flat line. All the rods were 30 lb. class with 30 lb. Hi-Viz mono and 80 lb. orange Capt. Harry's wind-on leaders. The exception was the marlin rod which was 50 lb. class with 50 lb. mono, with a 300 lb. wind- on leader. The marlin lure was rigged with a #11 J-hook. Dino splashed a neon blue, 5 squid, teaser rig on the right flat, and Freddy put a cedar plug all the way down the middle on the 30 lb. class shotgun rod, and let it way-back, about 250 feet. He handed the shotgun rod tip up to the bridge where Seth grabbed the line and clipped it into the center rigger. Freddy put the shotgun rod in the fighting chair rocket launcher. Billy had a 30 lb. spinning rod rigged with a naked ballyhoo ready to pitch to a white marlin should one make an appearance in the spread. All the drags were set on the light side. The crew was officially fishing.

Seth thought that during this time of year, they might catch dolphin, wahoo, sailfish, blackfin tuna, and white or blue marlin. This was a great time of year for a mixed bag. He kept his sat-phone right next to the helm, in case he got a call from John or Toby in the airplane. Seth could see the freighters on the horizon, plying the Gulf Stream, heading east or west. He zigzagged to the southeast towards the Marathon Humps.

They had no luck the first hour but as they got closer to the stream they started to raise small schools of flying fish. Finally, Seth saw what looked like debris ahead in the water, where there were a few birds diving and wheeling. As *TAR BABY* got closer, Seth identified the debris as wooden split fence rails. They likely had tumbled off an island coaster in a big sea. He squared up on a group and trolled past them. Seth yelled, "Get ready!", as he watched three dolphin come out from under the wooden rails and speed towards the baits. Both long riggers went off with a bang, and the clickers on those two reels screamed.

"Fish on!" yelled Billy as he jumped on the left rod. Dino grabbed the right one and they both started reeling as the dolphins ended their initial runs. Seth slowed down to idle as Gene pulled the blue squid chain teaser out, and reeled in the right short rigger ballyhoo. Freddy pulled the line out of the center rigger clip with a quick overhand flick and reeled in the shotgun while being careful not to cross either of the dolphin. They marlin lure remained in the water in case a marlin reacted to the commotion and came calling. Dino brought his dolphin to the boat and Gene gaffed her on the port side of the cockpit. It was a nice cow, about 25 lbs. Billy pumped and reeled as his dolphin turned sideways and tried to muscle himself away from the boat. Billy turned him and carefully thumbed the line while reeling with his other hand. Gene made a nice gaff shot to the fish's head and pulled him into the cockpit. The 35 lb. bull jumped off the gaff and rocketed airborne around the cockpit, as the crew looked for cover. Seth laughed up on the flybridge as the crew scrambled to avoid being slapped by the acrobatic fish. Gene slid across the slippery cockpit with a wet towel and threw it over the dolphin's head. The dolphin immediately calmed down. Then he knelt down and gently applied pressure to the dolphin's head and flank.

"Get me the dolphin calmer, Freddy, top drawer … tackle center." Freddy returned with a 30" length of 300 lb. mono with a large slip loop on one end and #12, big game, J-hook crimped to the other end. He carefully slipped the loop over the bull's tailfin and pulled the loop tight at the base of his tail. Next he moved the towel to expose the dolphin's mouth, being careful to keep the towel over the bull's eyes. Gene grasped the large hook in his right hand, while applying moderate pressure to the fish's gill plate with his left hand, and pulled the dolphin's tail toward its head so he could slip the hook in the corner of its mouth. The dolphin now looked like the letter C, and was completely immobilized. It certainly beat hitting him over the head with a billy club. He removed the original circle hook from his jaw and slid him into the fish box.

While Gene was calming the bull dolphin, Seth and the boys were resetting the spread. Billy rebaited the riggers with fresh ballyhoo, and within a matter of minutes, they were trolling again.

Seth called down to the crew, "Two nice fish guys, more than enough for a couple of dinners." He continued to fish the split rails for the rest of the afternoon catching four more dolphin in the 20 lb. range and a 32 lb. wahoo on the cedar plug. He hadn't heard from the fly boys, evidently they hadn't seen anything worth chasing down. The crew would look good at the cleaning table at the Marathon Yacht Club after they docked. Seth would send most of the filets over to the Grand Banks for tonight's crew dinner. The chef and the bartender at the club would get a couple of fish, for goodwill and to start a buzz about *TAR BABY's* success. He would not give away any of the wahoo. Seth had Dino cut a plate of paper thin pieces of the iced wahoo, along with Dino's own spicy bourbon soy sauce, for an appetizer on the way home. Seth liked fresh wahoo as much as he liked fresh caught yellowfin tuna. They would grill the rest of wahoo and dolphin for dinner.

He cut the throttles to idle and called down to the crew,

"That was a good day of fishing … Not bad for a bunch of old Geezers," he said laughing. "Get the lines out of the water, we're going to head for the dock. We'll clean the fish when we get in and have dinner on the Grand Banks tonight. Later, we'll have a skull session to see what the fly boys found. Right now, secure the rods and tackle, and let's have a cold one!"

Seth pulled in and secured the outriggers, then turned the Hatteras northwest towards Marathon, while setting his course on the autopilot. When the last line was in the boat he pushed up the throttles until they were running at 24 knots. He took a deep breath and sat back in his Murray Brothers helm chair, just as Gene handed him his first cold one of the day.

"Not a bad start, Seth! We were lucky to find those split rails."

"Absolutely, tomorrow I'd like to make it out to the humps and catch some blackfin tuna. That's out far enough to maybe get a shot at a billfish, too."

"Depends what we find out from John and Toby, we might be playing detective tomorrow."

"That's why we're here. But it was fun today with all the guys. It's a brilliant cover story, if I do say so myself. Will you take the helm? I need a head break before I settle in with this cerveza."

Seth climbed down the ladder and went below. The crew was rinsing off the rods and reels, lures, and teasers. They all had a cold one in their hands and they all were smiling. By the time Seth got back up the ladder, he could see the radio antennas on Vaca Key. He took the helm back and headed for Channel Seven and the Seven Mile Bridge.

A half hour later they idled past Pigeon Key which still had part the old Seven Mile Railroad Bridge running to it from Marathon. The old bridge still stood most of the way across, but it was missing three key spans between Pigeon Key and Bahia Honda to the west. The largest opening was at Channel 7, where TAR BABY was headed. Over the years, Pigeon Key had been a construction camp, and a private research center. It had been abandoned since the new highway bypassed it in 1982. For the past few years, the two mile stretch of old bridge was open to walkers, cyclers, fisherman, and golf cart traffic, but was closed to cars. The buildings had been restored and now housed a Keys' railroad museum. Visitors could get there by ferry and, for the price of admission, spend the day snorkeling with free equipment. Seth picked up the pace and ten minutes later was backing TAR BABY into her slip at the Marathon Yacht Club.

Once tied up, Dino and Billy headed for the cleaning table, over by the showers, with two coolers full of fish to clean. Freddy and Gene hosed the boat down, and Seth hooked up the shore power and turned off the gen-set. When the filets were all on ice, the crew headed for the air conditioned bar to wait for a sat-phone call from the fly boys.

Their drinks were soon interrupted by a call from the fly boys. Freddy and Dino got up to go to the airport.

Billy said, "I'm going to stay and rig some ballyhoo for tomorrow's fishing. I'll ride over to Burdine's with Seth and Gene later."

"OK, Dino and I will see you later."

Dino said, "I'll take a cooler full of filets back to the trawler now. What do you want me to grill tonight, Seth?"

"How about dolphin … and wahoo? You can make a fish salad for lunch tomorrow with the fish that's left over. I'll bring over a couple of bags of green beans; we'll do 'em in the microwave and season them with Everglades Seasoning."

"We've got three or four packages of frozen au gratin potatoes in the trawler's freezer, sounds like the makings of a good dinner."

Seth closed out the bar bill, and he and Gene headed for the showers. Billy headed for *TAR BABY* to rig a dozen ballyhoo.

***

Dinner was cleared off the table and the crew got their first look at the aerial surveillance photos that John and Toby had taken that day. Seth had set both the trawler and the Hatteras up with a Hewlett Packard photosmart printer. The unit could print, copy, and scan. It printed in color or black and white, and it used photo or regular print paper. He paired both printers with low cost HP laptops. The fly boys had taken scores of practice pictures since it was the first time the sizing box approach had been tried. The pictures from 1000' were the easiest to determine boat brand. After qualifying the boat's size with the sizing frame, Toby took a couple telephoto shots of each qualified boat. Boats that couldn't be easily identified as production boats got a second, closer look. Then John would fly closer to the water and Toby would take a profile shot. Toby downloaded all of that day's photos into the computer, then selected and printed one of each boat. The crew was having fun trying to identify them. With the high level of boat knowledge in the salon, the boats were quickly identified. The six boats that couldn't be identified were commercial fishing or work boats.

Seth said, "There's something to be learned from this. We suspect that the Huckin's appearance has been substantially altered. John's idea to fly down and take a profile shot, once a boat fits the box, is going to be the key."

117

Seth sat down at the computer and typed in 62' Huckins Linwood. He clicked on the Huckins brokerage site that came up, and scrolled down to a profile photo of a 62 Linwood model. He adjusted the photo's size to match Toby's profile shots and hit print.

Seth held up the profile of the Linwood, "We'll compare this with the commercial fishing and work boats, or any other likely candidates to see if it's possible to build off the Linwood's profile and end up with whatever we are looking at. If it is at all possible that the Linwood fits inside, we'll go to its home dock and check the vessel out closely. I don't see any candidates in today's photos, so tomorrow let's concentrate our aerial surveillance from Islamorada down thru Marathon."

***

The wind whistling through the outriggers was the first thing Seth heard when he woke up the next morning. He headed for the head and then the salon. The palm trees were swaying and Seth guessed the wind at 15 to 20 mph. Not a good day to go fishing. However, he had an alternate plan for the inevitable windy or rainy days. But first he started a pot of coffee and sat down at his computer in the salon. He Googled up Passage Weather, an internet site used by professional mariners worldwide. He zoned in on Florida and the Bahamas, animating the five day wind, wave height, and precipitation maps. It looked like a small low pressure system was moving thru the Keys today, but it would start to diminish that evening. There might be a few thunderstorms this afternoon. The wave height offshore would be four to five feet. The wind would blow 15 to 20 mph, today, and subside to 10 to 12 mph. tomorrow, with the wave height dropping to two to three feet, with no precipitation. Conditions would return to normal through the weekend as the Bermuda high pressure ridge moved south and became stationary.

Seth got on the sat-phone and called the *SIRENA* at Burdine's. Freddy answered. "Fred, the weather will be too bad today to go fishing, but there won't be any thunderstorms until about 4:00 this afternoon. Take John and Toby to the airport and then come over here with Dino and Billy. We're going to check all the marinas from Islamorada thru Marathon by car today. See you after breakfast."

Gene arrived in the galley during Seth's conversation and started to put a scrambled eggs and bacon breakfast together.

"So we're going to do some sleuthing today, Seth?"

Seth put the Linwood profile in the *TAR BABY's* printer scanner and ran off five copies, while saying, "Yeah, I figured we'd have a couple of bad weather days to do it. Doing it on a good day might tip our hand."

"Good thinking."

"I'll use the internet to compile a list of marinas from Islamorada to Key West. I can have that done and printed before the crew gets here …… It looks like there's eleven in Islamorada, twelve from there thru Marathon, and fourteen from Big Pine down to, and including Stock Island and Key West."

Seth also catalogued the commercial fishing companies that bought and sold seafood. Many provided permanent and temporary dockage for the commercial fishing boats that sold their catches to them. There were two in Islamorada, five in Marathon, three in the lower Keys, and seven on Stock Island, which was just above Key West. Seth thought they could check the marinas and commercial businesses out in two full days by splitting the crew in two. If more time was needed, he would just take Gene and Billy fishing and work Freddy and Dino in one of the vans another day or two.

The crew arrived 20 minutes later. Seth split the list in two and handed out the Linwood profiles and said, "If you see anything interesting, back off and call me. Gene and I will do the same thing. Otherwise, check out as much as you can and work your way back towards the airport by about 4:00 p.m. in case the thunderstorms materialize. We'll meet back at the trawler about 6:00 and recap the day."

Both vans drove east. Seth and Gene went all the way to Islamorada and started working the marinas and fish docks. He sent Freddy's crew to close-by Hawks Cay Marina first. They would stay in the Marathon area in case the flyboys came in early.

Gene drove up the hot black ribbon of asphalt and enjoyed the sight of continuous water and bridges. The water at each opening held a surprise of a hundred different shades of blue, green, yellow, and brown, depending on the depth. Each pass was laced with sand bars, underwater grass, and coral rock. Soon they drove onto the more populated Islamorada and started their search for the Huckins at Islamorada Marine. Seth quickly checked the 18 slips there and found nothing of interest. They stopped at mile marker 85 and Gene checked out Snake Creek Marina's 20 wet slips while Seth checked the small haul-out yard.

"Anything of interest at the docks? The yard has nothing."

"No, all sportfish boats."

They checked both the commercial fish houses with the same results. Bud N' Mary's, Smuggler's Cove, Tavernier Creek, and Caloosa Cove yielded more of the same. Seth pulled back into the large Plantation Yacht Harbor complex, again nothing of interest there.

"How about World Wide Sportsman for lunch? The Islamorada Fish Co. restaurant inside is always good."

"We can check their marina too. The Huckin's shallow draft would allow it to get through Blackwater Sound and dock back there."

They lunched on yellowtail snapper, french fried sweet potatoes, and coleslaw, and washed it down with sweet iced tea. After lunch, they checked out the marina behind the facility and found nothing that remotely resembled the Huckins.

"Let's walk back through the tackle store and take a look at the *PILAR* replica in the middle of the store. I can't pass this place without coming in to see it."

"It looks pretty authentic, Seth," said Gene as they walked up the boarding steps.

"It's very close, but the real *PILAR*, at Hemingway's estate down in Cuba, has a wooden roller across its transom gunnel. They used it to haul the big tuna up into the cockpit. That was before Rybovich started building a tuna door into their transoms. The galvanized pipe railing around the flybridge steering station is identical to *PILAR's*. It had to be one of the first sportfish boats with a flying bridge."

"Who built it?"

"It's a Wheeler, built in Brooklyn, New York. How about the custom writing table Hemingway had built below?"

"Well, we've gone for long periods between bites ourselves. I guess he used that time better than we do."

"Speaking of time, we better get our butts in gear. We need to check out a few more marinas."

They drove to Holiday Isle, Coral Bay, Matecumbe, and Whale Harbor with no results. Seth moved further south and pulled into Robbie's Marina at mm 77.5 on the bayside.

"When's the last time you were here?" said Seth.

"With my grandchildren, about five years ago, to feed the tarpon."

"It's a hoot, isn't it?"

They checked out Robbie's to no avail. A crowd of tourists were hand feeding the 150 to 200 pound tarpon off the end dock. They squealed with delight as the huge fish jumped three feet out of the water to snap a bait fish out of their hands. It looked more dangerous than it really was, tarpon don't have any teeth, just a boney maw.

"Let's head back to Marathon, Gene. We'll see how our other crew did with their list. They had six marinas, not including Hawk's Cay, the moorings in Boot Key Harbor, and five commercial operations to check."

Seth called Freddy to set up a meeting at the trawler at Burdine's.

"We're just finishing up at the Key's Fisheries Market and Marina. Billy checked out Boot Key Harbor and the Key Colony marinas in the panga, earlier." Freddy started laughing, "I can't wait to tell you about Dino and the dolphin up at Hawk's Cay, it cracked me up."

"You can tell me at dinner, I could use a laugh. Have you heard from Toby or John yet?"

"Not yet."

"OK, tell Dino to plan on us eating on the *SIRENA* again tonight."

CHAPTER ELEVEN

Georgio called Captain Tony to find out which end of the Keys he wanted him to start his marina list.

"Start in Key West and work east," said Tony. "Most fishermen, traveling down to the Keys to fish, go to Key West."

"I'll fax the marina and fuel dock lists to you as soon as I compile them. They'll cover Key West, the Middle Keys, Islamorada, and Key Largo. Don't forget to plug your sat-phone into your FX2600 adapter."

Giorgio got to work on his computer and an hour later faxed a list for Key West and Stock Island.

Captain Tony got right on his phone and called the Conch Harbor Marina and the Shell fuel dock in Key West Bight. He had called all of these marinas before, two years ago, while looking for the Bertram 54, *CHICA*. He knew that dock masters had unusually good memories. Remembering boats and boat owner's names helped make them bigger tips. He didn't know how many might recognize him as Captain Tony from his call two years ago, but one was too many.

"This is Captain Jack calling, is this the dock master?"

"No Sir, but he's standing right here, I'll put him on."

"This is Jason, can I help you?"

"Hey, Jason, this is Captain Jack up in St. Pete. I'm looking for a friend of mine who owns the *TAR BABY*, a 46' Hatteras. He's a day overdue calling me on his float plan, and he should be in Key West by now. Have you seen him?"

"I haven't. But let me check the fuel log." Jason picked the phone back up two minutes later and said, "I don't have that boat in the fuel log, and we have no reservation for *TAR BABY* on our marina schedule. Did he indicate a destination?"

"Just Key West, I'll keep on looking, thanks."

122

Captain Tony called The Galleon Marina, A&B Marina and fuel dock, The Conch Republic docks, Garrison Bight Marina, the Key West Yacht Club, The Key West City Marina, the Westin Hotel Marina, and even the remote Sunset Marina. No one had seen or had a reservation for *TAR BABY*. Tony went on to the Stock Island list and called Oceanside Marina. They had a full service operation that was on the Atlantic Ocean side. No one there had seen *TAR BABY*. Tony checked the new Florida Marine Club's marina that opened into Boca Chica channel, then the nearly finished, but open, Stock Island Marine Village across from the commercial shrimp docks, and finally, funky Safe Harbor Marina located behind the Hogfish Bar and Grille. All "no's." Tony could only figure that Seth Stone was fishing somewhere else in the Keys. He was done for this day, but would start on the Middle Keys tomorrow morning if he got the list.

***

Pete The Barber called Cadillac, up in Miami, on his sat-phone.

"Cadillac, I'm just callin' to give you an update."

"Go ahead. I'm hopin' we got this thing nailed by now."

"Well, the new men from Tampa are gettin' with the plan. They're all pros. We've been practicin' dry runs and have the travel times down pat from all the different pick-up locations. I've mixed up the SUVs and vans so no one sees the vans too much."

"What about the Russian muscle? We wanna get off to a good start, there's only three days left until the purge."

"Right, we'll get four of them in alleys or parkin' lots next to their various apartments. The other two, always walk out the front door together through a gate on a side street. Their motorbikes are parked on the street, and they're the only ones that live together."

"How are you gonna to handle them?"

"We'll have four men and a van parked in front of the motorbikes, which we'll disable. All six of the motorbike's ignition wires will be cut in the middle of the night."

"Good thinkin'."

"Two of our men will be sittin' on the sidewalk against the front yard fence, holdin' half-empty wine bottles, they'll look passed out and beat up. We see a lot of that shit down here, so it won't be no surprise. When the Russians try to start their bikes our two 'drunks' will Taser them. Our other two guys will jump out and help our 'derelicts' dump them in the van. It'll just take seconds."

"What if you get a passerby?"

"If they don't butt in, they won't get hurt. The license plates are untraceable. If they do they're goin' down the same road as the Russians. I've got several extra bogus plates if that happens."

"Well, shit happens. What about Ivan, the lieutenant?"

"He lives in a house on Passover Lane across from the cemetery. He parks on the street. We'll snatch him in an SUV usin' the derelict trick. Both his street side tires will be flat before mornin'. Once we got the others in the vehicles, we tie-wrap their hands and feet. Then we garrote 'em or stick an ice pick in their ear. We're gonna try and keep Ivan alive to see what he knows. He seems to be the go to guy in the Russki organization. We'll grill him about the payoff lineup, before we whack him."

"What about the Kapitan, Nicolay? Wouldn't he know who is being paid off?"

"I think we might have a problem takin' him alive. He closes the Gulag at 2:00 a.m., and the muscle escorts him home. He sleeps late and drives out of a condo parkin' garage that has a guard and a motorized roll-up door. He stops at the Galleon Condo/Hotel every mornin' about 10:30 and spends an hour with his bimbo. Then he goes to his office at the Gulag. The Galleon parkin' garage is on the ground floor, but it's always full of hotel guests. The west end of it's got the laundry and maintenance shops. We've rented the condo next to his for a month. It has a suite door between the condos. We jimmied and rigged the doors while his bimbo was at the pool workin' on her tan. The plan now is to shoot both of them, while they're doing the deed, with a silenced Glock. We'll hang a **Do Not Disturb** sign on the doorknob on our way out."

"Sounds like he's gonna go out with a bang," said Cadillac with a laugh.

"Fuckin' Don Rickles, right."

"Seriously now, I've been thinkin' about the vans sittin' in the parking lots and alleys of the Southern Breeze stores. They'll be there for at least two hours off and on."

"Right."

"I think we should make the vans look legit. I'll get some magnetic signs that say 'Keys Cable'. Everybody's used to seein' those trucks. We will look like a subcontractor for Comcast or AT&T. Go to the Home Depot up on North Roosevelt and get each truck a ladder, some tools … like shovels, wire cutters, crimpers, and a coupla big rolls of wire. Get some hardhats, tool belts, gloves, orange parking cones, and that yellow job site tape. I don't think nobody will question you. Also, a guy in a hard hat and tool belt walkin' up to a drug dealer won't look threatenin'. Our guys can get real close before they Taser 'em. They don't even have to look busy all day; those cable guys always look like they're on break anyway."

"Gotcha, Cadillac. That should help mess some minds up later in the day. We'll take the signs off when we're done at the stores."

"I'll have them made up here in Miami and have them delivered to the Geiger Key house tomorrow. Get the Home Depot stuff today and wear a disguise for their security cameras … What's happenin' with Yuly?"

"Nothin' has changed there. We haven't seen him outside at all. We're ready to attach a cell phone activated C4 bomb to his boat. Jackie "Frog Eyes" Salmi volunteered to swim it over tonight from one of our go-fast boats. I had his scuba gear sent down a couple of days ago. He's gonna use three of our big black handcuff tie-wraps to attach it behind the outboard trim tab cylinder. We got Vito a grenade launcher and a Remington Bushmaster semi-automatic with a scope, silencer, and flash suppressor. He's also got the boat bomb cell phone number. Maybe we'll get fuckin' lucky. If Yuly gets wind of the purge and tries to run to the Bahamas, Vito will trigger the boat bomb. If he runs for the Latitudes Restaurant or the hotel lobby in the reception center on the island, he'll cut Yuly and his bodyguards down from the second story window in his condo's master bedroom. Vito can see the entire front of Yuly's house and the boat lift at the end of his dock from that window. The path to the reception area passes right under him."

125

"With a little bit of luck it might not even be pinned on us, and worst case we gain some exit time. The biggest 'if' now is how aggressive we have to get to finish off Yuly."

"I think we got all the bases covered."

"One other thing, Pete. Luigi may need us to pick up Seth Stone, that's Beau Stone's older brother, when all the hub-bub calms down after the purge."

"Beau Stone bought it in the shark tank with Ricardo Cabeza, right?"

"You got it. Seth Stone just become a new suspect in the Hector Fernandez-Tampa money drop robbery from two years ago, and he is supposta be fishin' on his boat somewhere in the Keys. The Tampa boys are lookin' for him down there right now, but no luck yet. Dependin' when and where they find him and how the purge went, we might be able to have the guys we hide with the Escalades in Summerland Key pick him up for delivery to Miami later next week. It's all on the 'if-come', but I want it in the back of your mind."

"Ok, just let me know. Right now I'm gonna to put on a fake mustache, sun glasses, and my tourist duds. I'm headed for Home Depot."

"Keep me posted on purge day."

"You got it, Boss … goodnight."

***

Captain Tony was into his second cup of coffee when the fax machine spit out the second marina list. The weather in Marsh Harbor, in the Abacos, was perfect for fishing. The marlin were biting and most of the other sportfish boats were on their way out to the fishing grounds. Tony was tied to the dock. No Nose only came over two or three times a season to fish with his cousin Pauly Castellucci. Pauly was the president of No Nose's Florida banks. He also entertained different politicians, judges and government officials from time to time on the 72 foot Jim Smith sportfish. The famous tournament Captain, Tony Fungello, had been reduced to being a high priced bus driver and baby sitter. He did have a well paying job for life, but he knew this was his last job until he was put into the retirement home that No Nose owned in Brandon.

He regretted the choice he made three years ago, he missed fishing every day, but there was no turning back once you were on the dark side with those guys.

Little Palm Island Resort was first on the list. It's located at the entrance to Newfound Harbor and is a four mile boat ride from Looe Key. Captain Tony took the Jim Smith there a couple years ago with Pauly and his family and remembered it as being pretentious and very expensive. If Seth Stone had the robbery money he might be staying there. A call to the dock master confirmed that *TAR BABY* had never been there.

Tony looked back at the list with a yawn and started dialing. "Marathon Boat Yard and Marina, this is Johnny … can I help you?"

"Hey Johnny, Captain Jack here. I'm looking for a friend of mine on a Hatteras 46, called the *TAR BABY*. He's late calling me on his float plan, and he should have been in Marathon, yesterday. Have you seen him?"

"I was off yesterday; let me check with our cashier in the office …… No sir, he's not in the marina and hasn't been at our fuel dock."

Captain Tony called Boot Key Harbor City Marina, Pancho's Fuel Dock, Burdine's Marina, Key Colony Beach Marina, Sombrero Marina, and got a "this number has been disconnected" at Faro Blanco. Again, no one had seen *TAR BABY* or had fueled her. Hawk's Cay Resort and Marina were next and last on this list. Tony dialed them and was connected by the front desk to the dock master.

"This is Troy, how can I help you?"

"Troy, this is Captain Jack, I'm looking for a friend of mine, who's a day late calling me on his float plan. The vessel's name is *TAR BABY* out of St. Pete, his name is Seth Stone. Have you seen him?"

"Give me a second to check my guest and fuel logs……….No Sir, we have no record of him. Do you want to leave a number?"

"He's got it; if he wanders in please ask him to call Captain Jack. Thanks, Troy."

Well that pretty well shoots the morning, Captain Tony thought to himself, *I guess I'll get some exercise and walk down to Curly Tails for lunch. I might even check out Solomon's Mines, the duty free store, to see if Molly Mallory is working today. Maybe today is the day I'll get the courage to ask her out to dinner. There probably will be another list to call up in Islamorada and Key Largo when I get back.*

He got off the boat and nodded to the young Bahamian that was washing the boat. "Cedric, anybody that's looking for me, you can tell them I walked down to Curly Tails for lunch. I'll be back in a couple of hours. Put a little extra effort on the chrome on the fighting chair today, OK?"

"Dat's right Boss, I got dat!"

***

Pete, The Barber, and Cadillac set up two different venues for the two nights leading up to purge day. On Sunday, two nights before the purge, they laid on some R&R for their hardworking crew. Cadillac sent a tour bus down from Miami to the Geiger Key house. The bus came through the gate at 8:00 p.m., and delivered twelve handpicked working girls. Pete had a bar set up next to the pool and two of the boys had picked up a large food order from Antonia's Cucina on Duval Street. Pete still required continuous surveillance, but as the crews rotated off their shifts they had access to the ongoing swim party, for at least a couple of hours. They all understood they could not abuse the alcohol. The Tampa soldiers mixed well with the Miami soldiers. Some of the Miami boys had roots in Tampa. They all were in the same family and all lived under the strict code of the Mafia. There was honor among these thieves and murderers, and the penalty for breaking the code was death. In many ways, their code was very similar to the strict pirate's code two centuries before them. The swim party was designed to relieve any pre-purge stress and jitters, and to insure the crew was rested and relaxed before combat. There was much laughter, splashing, cannonball diving, and a no-swimsuit rule for the girls. A wet trail led from the pool deck, through the inside of the house, to its nine bedrooms. The party ended at 2:00 a.m. and the girls were on their way back to Miami before 2:30.

On Monday, the night before the purge, alcohol consumption was not allowed. The importance of corralling the Russian muscle and Ivan the lieutenant, before their daily breakfast, meeting was the key to Cadillac's plan.

Pete maintained around the clock monitoring to make sure where the Russians were sleeping Monday night. Two men were assigned to shadow each of the seven Russians. Once they were presumed in their beds, each location would still be watched all night in case one of them moved. The only way that a Russian on the list could survive purge day was to leave town on Monday.

That afternoon, Eddie "The Drummer" Gugliotta and Salvatore "Sally" Randazzo tailed the Russian muscle from Seabreeze 3 to the Sugarloaf Key drug depot. The same two car caravan traveled east to the turnoff at mm 17, and they watched the Russians drive down Sugarloaf Blvd. to Jamaica Lane. The return trip ended up back at Seabreeze 3, where four cases of presumed drugs were unloaded in wine bottle cases.

***

The Jupiter 38 had been anchored up off Wisteria Island for about ninety minutes. It was 10:00 p.m. and the Mallory Square crowd was long gone. It looked like Yuly had a bodyguard walk a lap around his house every 30 minutes. Jackie Frog Eyes, was suited up and ready to swim the five hundred feet across to Yuly's dock. The plan was to have him swim across submerged and come up under the lift, right at the swim platform. It would be easy to spot because of the sodium light illuminating the dock and lift area. Jackie strapped on his tank and slipped off the Gill bracket supporting the outboards. He submerged and went down 15 feet before starting across. The current was strong, but Frog Eyes had his long blade power fins on and was across quickly. He came up under the lift and stood on the frame. He reached up and fastened the bomb to the back of the port trim tab cylinder with three black zip-ties. Jackie slid back off the frame, cleared his mask, and swam back along the bottom to the Jupiter 38. Once back on board, they slowly idled across to the channel, picked up speed, and ran back to Geiger Central.

Late Monday night Nick Pajama Boy and Frankie Blue Eyes were tailing two of the muscle boys. Blue Eyes was sitting in the Gulag watching Vadim and Luka, the two muscle boys who lived together. Pajama Boy was sitting outside on a rented motor scooter watching the entrances. The two Russians

129

were at the crowded bar talking to each other over the loud music. They abruptly turned and walked out of the bar and onto the street. They started their motorbikes and headed northwest on Duval. Nick started his scooter and eased it out of the parking space. Frankie paid his tab, slipped out of the Gulag, and moved quickly to his rented scooter and sped down Duval. He caught up to Nick, and they followed the two motorbikes down Duval, trailing back a half of a block. The Russians stopped in front of the Bull and Whistle Bar and parked in a scooter parking spot. Nick eased in the other end of the scooter parking and Frankie went on to Greene St. and turned around at Sloppy Joes. He came back up Duval and parked around the corner on Caroline. They went into the Bull, but did not see the Russians. They continued up the stairs to the Whistle Bar and still didn't see them. So, they went up to the top floor and walked into the Garden of Eden Bar. The place was packed, the music was loud, and the mostly older crowd was fast dancing. Blue Eyes spotted the Russians at the bar. They were talking animatedly with a shaved head bartender who could have passed for a relative. Luka was wagging his finger in the bartenders face, and Vadim had himself all puffed up. They finally sat at the bar and were brought two beers while the bartender kept shaking his head, *yes*. Blue Eyes and Pajama Boy took a seat at a corner table.

Frankie looked around and surveyed the crowd on the dance floor. Most of the people, both young and old, were clothed, but some of the oldsters were in different stages of undress. One pensioner was stark naked and his wrinkled up tally-whacker and low hanging balls flapped in the breeze as he ponied across the dance floor. An older woman, covered only by an airbrushed bikini, was dancing in front of their table with a younger man wearing a butt floss speedo. Frankie hadn't seen flat, sagging boobs like that since he gave up his National Geographic subscription in favor of Playboy when he was twelve. Nobody in the room seemed a bit concerned with the bizarre scene. Nick leaned over to Frankie and said, "Do you believe this shit?"

"Frankie shrugged, and then shouted in Nick's ear, "After two weeks down here, nothin' surprises me. Key West is where the fuckin' weird turn pro."

The Russians finished their beers, wagged their fingers at the bartender one last time, and left. Frankie and Nick understood, since they were muscle too, that somebody owed somebody something. They followed the Russians down the street to Rick's. The Russians took a table up near the band stand. Frankie and Nick found a small table closer to the street. They could also see the side entrance of the Red Garter nude strip club that was part of Rick's complex. Luka and Vadim were joined by a couple of sallow complected Eastern European girls that came out of the Red Garter. They all settled in and listened to the rockin' tunes played by Jimmy "Bulldog" Byrne and the Vandals, an excellent live band fronted by Jimmy's wailing guitar. Frankie ordered two O'Doul's and asked the waitress where the men's room was.

"We use the Red Garter restrooms for the courtyard bar," said the waitress. "Do you want to run a tab?"

"No, we're gonna pay as we go; we're waitin' for a phone call and might have to leave fast."

"OK, that will be $10. Pay me when I bring 'em."

Frankie got up and walked through the saloon doors into the Red Garter. He asked the door bouncer where the men's room was.

"Turn left and it's down there past the lap dance booths."

"Thanks."

Frankie walked down the corridor. The right side had five small cubicles with identical louvered saloon doors on them. Inside each of them were nude dancers grinding on their patrons who were sitting on an upholstered bench. One girl had her head down in her customer's lap. She was not taking a nap. On his way back to the courtyard, Frankie passed by two middle aged women tourists, on their way to the ladies room. They were twittering and looked more than a bit uncomfortable.

Frankie sat back down and he and Nick nursed their O'Doul's. The Russians stayed for two sets and then left with the two girls, on their motorbikes. Frankie and Nick followed them to their apartment on Louisa Street where the two couples disappeared inside. Frankie called into Geiger Central, and reported their position. It was almost 2:00 a.m. and they were ready for a shift change.

Frankie suddenly realized ... purge day had already started!

CHAPTER TWELVE

The whole crew was on SIRENA and Seth was recapping the aerial surveillance of the day with Toby and John. They had covered Marathon, Spanish Channel, the Content Keys, Bahia Honda, Big Pine Island, Little Torch Key, Ramrod Key, and Summerland Key, in addition to the boat traffic in Hawk Channel, Channel 7, and Florida Bay outside of the Content Keys.

"We photographed 12 boats that fit in the box that were not production boats. Ten of them are commercial boats," said John Harvey.

The crew pored over the pictures while Dino and Freddy whipped up a grilled dolphin dinner, complete with steamed green beans, au gratin potatoes, and Cuban bread. Dino had scored a couple of bottles of Kim Crawford Sauvignon Blanc for the wine people, and had a cooler full of Michelob Ultra for the beer drinkers. The crew determined that none of the aerial photographed boats could have been the Huckins. The ground crews had come up empty too.

Dinner was served, and the whole crew was assembled in the main salon. Freddy stood up during dinner and proposed a toast, "Here's to Dino Vino's new boyfriend at Hawk's Cay." Dino got red in the face, and he shot Freddy the bird.

Freddy laughed and said, "Let me explain. When Dino and I were checking out Hawk's Cay, we walked by their Dolphin Encounter attraction. Two of the trainers knew Dino and called to him. They asked Dino to come into the lagoon with the dolphins so they could show him a new trick they had taught one of the dolphins. Dino said he was too busy, but they persisted and said, 'Come on in Dino. You've never seen anything like it.' Dino looks at me, and I said, 'Hey, five minutes won't make any difference, go ahead.' Dino gives me his wallet, peels down to his board shorts, and wades into the water. The trainers open a gate and let a new dolphin in the lagoon. The dolphin makes a bee-line for Dino and starts humping him from behind. So, Dino turns and pushes the dolphin away, and as he does the dolphin rolls over and reveals a 10 inch long, pink hard-on. Now the trainers are laughing hysterically. Dino exits the lagoon with the dolphin in hot pursuit. The trainers continue to roll with laughter. Finally, when everyone regains their composure, Dino says good-naturedly, 'OK, you no good bastards, you got me good. Where the hell did you get the gay dolphin?' His trainer friend says, 'we don't know what to do with him; he's actually bi-sexual. He'll fuck anything.' Then we all started laughing again, with tears rolling down our cheeks. It was funnier than shit."

The Geezer crew roared with laughter too, and they realized what a good sport Dino was. When the salon calmed down Dino acknowledged the whole thing with a shrug and a smile. Seth took that opportunity to address them all.

"Even though we've covered two thirds of the Keys and haven't found *ABOUT TIME,* we should not be discouraged. Tomorrow morning, we will move to the Key West area and thoroughly search that area, while maintaining our fishing cover. If the Huckins is in the Keys, and I still firmly believe it is, we've narrowed the search considerably. Between here and Stock Island there are no marinas that handle big boats, except for Little Palm Island, and there is virtually no commercial fishing presence. We have increased our odds of finding the Huckins immensely."

"I think you're right Seth," said John. "My hunch, after looking at all these photos, is that the Huckins is disguised as a commercial boat. A veritable wolf in sheep's clothing. There's not that many local commercial boats left in Key West and Stock Island. If it's in the Lower Keys we'll find it."

"OK, here's the plan for tomorrow," announced Seth. "Freddy, you call ahead to Oceanside Marina on Stock Island and make a reservation for the Grand Banks. It's about 30 miles from here to the marina. If you leave at 8:00 a.m., you should be there around noon. Take Billy with you on the trawler. Dino can drive the minivan down and be waiting for you on the dock. He'll have time to check out Key West Shellfish and Summerland Seafood on Summerland Key on his way down and Stock Island. I'll take *TAR BABY* around to A&B Marina in Key West Bight myself. It will take me less than two hours. Gene can drive the other van down, and he can catch me on the dock. I shouldn't have a problem getting a slip this time of year, especially on a

Sunday. We'll be about five miles from each other. Let's plan on fishing Monday morning."

"Where do you want us to fly tomorrow?" asked John.

"You and Toby will fly the back way out of here, west over the Content and Snipe Keys, then over Ibis Bay, out over the Lakes, Marquesas, Rebecca Shoals, and around the Dry Tortugas. That's about a hundred miles. Then come back over the edge of the Straits of Florida, to Key West, and up to Newfound Harbor. Then repeat it with some grid variation. At 150-plus knots you should be able to cover the grid with no problem. Oceanside and Stock Island are ten minutes from the Key West FBO. Gene and I can check out all the Key West Marinas tomorrow morning. Dino can check out the Stock Island marinas and commercial seafood companies like Bama, Fishbusterz, and The Stock Island Lobster Company, while he's waiting for the Grand Banks to arrive. Gentleman, I feel tomorrow will be a long day, let's have a night cap and call it a night."

***

Seth emerged from the engine room after checking the fluid levels in the engines, transmissions, and generator. All the bilge pumps were operational, and he hadn't noticed any leaks from the strainers or machinery. Gene had a toasted bagel and had a thermos of coffee ready for him up on the flybridge.

"I'll see you at A&B, Seth. Call me on my cell phone if there's a marina change or anything. I'm going to have one last breakfast at the Stuffed Pig, on the way out."

Seth started the engines and generator from the cockpit steering station, and went inside to change from shore power to the generator. Gene unplugged the shore power cords and stowed them in the cockpit. He threw the last stern line in the cockpit. Seth climbed up into the flybridge, put the engines in gear, and idled out the narrow channel to the Intracoastal Waterway. He turned and waved to his old friend Gene. He felt he was leading the crew in the right direction. He was a "seat of your pants" kind of guy and his butt felt comfortable. He ran past Pigeon Key, to Channel Seven, and then through

Moser Channel for about a mile. He turned west and set the autopilot to take him to Key West. The *TAR BABY was* throttled up to 24 knots, and Seth noted the time as 7:30 on his Submariner. He called A&B Marina on his cell phone and it connected on the third ring.

"This is Seth Stone calling. Is Don in?"

"No, Don went up to Miami this morning and won't be back until next Sunday. This is Travis, can I help you? "

"Sure, Travis, I need a slip for my 46 Hatteras sportfish for a week or so ... starting today."

"No problem, Mr. Stone, I have quite a few boats pulling out this morning. What is your ETA?"

"I'll be there before 9:30."

"No problem, give me a call when you get close on channel 69."

"Roger that."

Seth took a deep breath and looked around. He was approaching Bahia Honda and the water all around him was flushed with pinks and blues. The sky was bright blue and streaked with pink overtones created by the rising sun. The breeze was cool this time of the morning, but that would give way to hot and humid by the time he pulled into Key West Bight. He sipped his coffee, enjoyed his bagel, and the short-lived serenity of being alone. Sunday fisherman started coming out of the bridge cuts, headed south to fish the reefs and beyond. Soon the day boats, already tied up to the moorings at Looe Key, would loom from the southwest. Seth hoped that his instincts were good. He didn't want to let Charley Blevins down. He had another week to ten days to play it out. John and Toby should be flying up in Florida Bay, and the *SIRENA* should be on its way to Oceanside. Seth took a deep breath and cleared his head. He had almost been too busy this past week to think about Lori. His feelings for her tugged at him now. He would text her right now while he could see the cell phone tower on Big Pine Key: *Lori, fishing has been good, but not great. We are switching locations today, and hope the fishing is better tomorrow in Key West. I am missing you and hope to call you soon. I hope you're thinking about me too, Seth.* It was the truth. She just didn't know what they were really fishing for.

135

Seth ran down past Newfound Harbor and the new, posh, Little Palm Island Resort. He remembered 20 some years ago when he, Lisa, and Jeb anchored their 37 foot sloop behind where the resort now stood. Back then it was somebody's weekend fish camp, isolated, and reachable only by skiff. The lobstering inside and around the point was spectacular, as was the spearfishing on the coral heads just off the beach. Those days were over now, and only millionaires could afford to stay there. He knew the Huckins would not be there. Seth changed his course more southerly to round Loggerhead Key, then came up more westerly, and ran by Ramrod, Summerland, and the Sugarloaf Keys. Soon he was gliding by the Saddlebunch Keys and approaching Boca Chica, where the Air Force Base was located. He passed the Stock Island channels and could see the power plant stacks on the main channel into Stock Island. Seth angled closer to shore and ran by the palm tree laden Casa Marina property and Louie's Backyard Restaurant. He left the tripod mark at Fort Zachary Taylor to starboard and turned up into the ship's channel leading to Key West Harbor. There were no cruise ships moored at the harbor's docks. They usually came in during the late morning and left in the middle of the night. Seth pulled the throttles back to idle and moved slowly by the waterfront harbor hotels. Tourists were already swimming off the tiny sand beaches at the Pier House and the Galleon. Sunset Island sparkled in the morning sun, and Wisteria Island looked green and pristine. The Navy Base shimmered in the steadily building heat. He steered around the rock breakwater and noticed that the Conch Resort fuel dock was crowded. He continued towards A&B and called the assistant dock master on channel 69.

"A&B dock master, *TAR BABY* here, come back."

"This is A&B, *TAR BABY*."

"Permission to land at your fuel docks and take on fuel."

"Your friend Gene is on his way out, I'll be right behind him."

Seth maneuvered behind the big red harbor tug, C.O.JONES, that was perennially moored at the west end of the A&B fuel dock, and snuggled up to the fendered dock. Gene jumped aboard and threw a couple of lines to Travis. Seth turned off the diesels and came down the flybridge ladder as Gene started pumping fuel.

"Hey, Gene … Hey Travis, thanks. I hope nothing's wrong with Don. Why is he up in Miami all week?"

"He's mixing some R&R and some bridgework repair together. He likes to go up to his old dentist in Miami. He'll be back next Sunday."

"I'm glad that's all it is. Where do you want me?"

"Three slips down on the east side, you'll be able to watch the sunset from your flybridge."

Seth finished fueling and moved the Hatteras into the slip. Travis and Gene got him tied up and plugged into shore power. Seth went into the salon and turned off the gen-set and switched to shore power.

"Thanks Travis, and nice to meet you," said Seth as he handed him a $20 bill. "Do you still have night security on the dock?"

"Yes, sir! We can't keep the tourists off the docks and the boats otherwise. They open the gate, disregard the signs, and have no boating etiquette. So we have Bo Pinder and his German Shepard 'Fritz', patrolling all night. If you need anything, Mr. Stone, don't hesitate to call me."

"I won't."

"Hey Gene, let's take a walk around the Bight, stretch our legs, and look for the Huckins. Dino should be checking the marinas and commercial fish houses up on Stock Island right now. We ought to be hearing from the trawler boys in an hour or so."

They checked out the Galleon marina first, walked around past the Conch Republic docks, along the Municipal Marina in front of the waterfront super market, and finally down to the Conch Harbor Marina. Seth hadn't expected to see anything in the recreational marinas in Key West Bight and they didn't, but you never know.

"Let's sit under the thatched roof at Dante's while we're down here, Gene. We can order a cold one and check out the Ft. Myers Ferry talent in the pool."

"Sounds good to me, buddy!"

Dante's open air bar was located in the Conch Harbor complex. The Ft. Myers and Marco Island to Key West high speed catamaran ferries docked right next to the Conch Harbor Marina. The vessels are three stories high and 140 to 170 feet long. On most days they traveled at 25 knots. Most passengers sailed down Thursday or Friday and sailed back Sunday. The hotels had an 11:00 a.m. check out so the ferry travelers headed for Dante's and the spectacular Conch Harbor pool to bide their time. The weekend's fun and games continued in the pool, since the ferries didn't leave until about 5:00 p.m. The hard drinking persisted and Dante's line-up of Sunday Blues Bands kept them cranked up. By early afternoon, the pool was full of inebriated couples who thought they were invisible. Seth took a pull on his ice cold beer and grooved on the music. The pool was already getting crowded when two generously endowed, entrepreneurial, local strippers showed up and sold, then applied sequined pasties to a line-up of topless female revelers at poolside. It was just another day in paradise. Gene and Seth appeared relaxed and composed, but they both were glad they had their sunglasses on.

Seth's phone rang, he answered, said something that couldn't be heard above the loud music, and hung up.

Seth leaned toward Gene, "The trawler boys are docked at Oceanside. We're going to meet them for lunch at the Hogfish Bar and Grill on Stock Island in 30 minutes ... let's go."

They threw back their beers and started the walk back to A&B.

***

Billy, Dino, and Freddy were already seated around a large picnic table with two umbrellas over it out on the marina's edge. Billy had come over from Oceanside in the 20 foot panga, just to get the lay of the land. Dino and Freddy had arrived in the mini-van.

"Good trip down in the trawler, Freddy?"

"Everything was good but the generator; it flat out quit on us. The charter outfit must not have checked the filter, and it was all clogged up. Billy figured it out and luckily there was a spare filter. He filled up the little Racor filter with a Solo cup full of diesel that he got from opening and closing the petcocks on the main engines 500 Racor bowls, while they ran. The Onan 8 KW gen-set has an electric fuel pump so it was self bleeding."

"Good job, Billy. You saved all that food we have in the freezer."

"Dino, did you see anything interesting?"

"Nothing on the way down … There's lots of old shrimp and fishing boats scattered around this island, but they're not what we're looking for."

They all ordered hogfish sandwiches and cold beers.

"This marina is a funky place," said Billy. "I noticed that half the slips have floating cottages in them … not houseboats … but little floating houses. Then, there are a couple of shrimp boats and two big treasure salvage boats with prop wash "mailboxes" on the stern to move the sand. In between, there are a couple of big wooden sailboats in nice condition and some large motor yachts and sportfishes. The seawall is lined with marine trade shops."

"Charley owns a slip in this marina," added Seth. I think most of it was condoed out by Charley's friend, Joe O'Donald. Joe's a mover and shaker on Stock Island. He packaged all that old commercial warehouse land across the channel where the new mega-yacht marina is being finished. He lives in one of the warehouses right here in Safe Harbor. The inside of it looks like a Costa Rican rain forest. There are nook and cranny patios and gardens, here and there around the marina, and there is a small above ground pool next to the showers."

"Have you ever been in Joe's rainforest?" asked Freddy.

"Several years back, Charley let Lisa and me use his slip for a month, when we didn't go to the islands. You can't be here for more than a few days without meeting Joe."

Suddenly, Seth's sat-phone rang. He answered it, left the table, and walked up the dock out of ear shot of the other tables. When he came back he paid the check and calmly said, "That was Toby, they think they're on to something. Let's all go back to the Grand Banks and wait for the next call. I'll fill you all in when we get to the trawler."

Billy was tying up the panga alongside the *SIRENA* when Seth and the others pulled the vans into Oceanside. They boarded the trawler and gathered in the salon.

"Toby told me they were taking their third pass of the day out at the Tortugas, when they saw a commercial boat leaving the Fort Jefferson anchorage that fit in the box. They took a picture and started to drop down to take a profile shot. By then, they were half way out of the national park. Toby noticed three or four girls dancing on the foredeck buck naked. Of course, he took a picture. Now it gets interesting. John circled back because the profile looked like a possible. As they came up behind the boat, back up at 1000 feet, the clunky looking grouper boat with six electric Bandit reels mounted on the aft gunnels, got up on plane and took off east. John guessed they were making close to 35 knots. The name of the boat is the *GOFISH;* the hailing port is Key West. They're going to cut their air speed and climb to 2500 feet and follow them to their destination. If she keeps coming this way, she will pass Key West in about an hour and a half."

The sat-phone rang a half hour later and Seth answered, "Yeah, Toby we're sitting on pins and needles here. Due east, huh? You good with fuel ... great! Call again in a half hour, OK?"

"Partying on Sunday out at the Tortugas with the Dollies. That would be Randy's and Peter's style," said Seth. "*ABOUT TIME* can do 35 knots easy if it's not overloaded, it can do 30 even if it is ...... I'm getting myself all wound up ... I better take a walk before I blow a gasket."

"I'll go with you," said Freddy.

"We'll go too," chimed in the other three.

So they all got off the trawler and walked east down the road towards Boca Chica Channel. They walked a half mile along Peninsular Drive to the Florida Marina Club's new yacht basin and high and dry. A brand new facility with a hundred wet slips, three hundred dry slips, and a fancy restaurant and bar. Seth remembered when there was a working boat yard and marina there, along with the Peninsular Seafood Company. Back then, scores of shrimp boats were based there and also down in Key West Bight. Now there were only a few shrimp boats on Stock Island still trawling for Key West Pinks out by the Dry Tortugas and none left in Key West Bight. Key West Pinks are the best and the most expensive shrimp on the planet, and they are only found 70 miles from Key West. Seafood lovers should enjoy them while they can; the Pinks' days are numbered. As they started walking back to Oceanside the sat-phone rang again.

140

"Yeah, Toby... same course, same speed... you're just passing the Marquesas. With a Key West hailing port they'll probably go in around here somewhere... you really think it's the Huckins? Yeah, I know ... it's tough to tell... call me when they make a move."

The crew walked back to the trawler and went inside the cool interior. The walk had calmed everyone down, but they all were still edgy.

A half hour later the phone went off again. The minutes had gone by like hours.

"Toby ... Shitfire! ... well let's see what happens, circle around, but stay up high."

"OK, guys, as soon as the GOFISH got in sight of Sand Key Light, out on the reef, she slowed down to 9 knots. She's still headed east."

The crew made small talk and tried to make the time pass more quickly. Seth's phone rang, and they all jumped in unison.

Seth answered it saying, "Toby! ...... Really! OK ...well, wait until you're sure ... then call again. I'll send Gene to the FBO for you."

"The GOFISH turned north through the reef and is headed for the Stock Island, Safe Harbor Channel. When Toby calls back, we'll know for sure. We'll send Billy and Dino in the panga, and Freddy and I will take a van. Gene ... you'll go to the airport FBO and get the flyboys."

Toby called back. The GOFISH had come straight up the Stock island Channel and was docking on a western quayside, where two other commercial boats were tied up, just below the Old Island Boatyard. Seth sent Gene to the FBO. He decided not to send the panga. He didn't want the GOFISH crew to see any of his men. They all got in the van and rode up to the Hogfish Bar. Once there, they got a table and ordered four beers. Billy and Seth walked around to where the men's locker room was and continued out to the dock. They worked their way to a picnic area at the end of the quay and looked across the 350 foot wide channel, with their pocket binoculars.

"What do you think, Billy? Picture it without the aft cockpit hardtop and the squared off house with the little round portlights. It sure is hard to look at her painted gray."

"They've done a good job disguising her, Seth. The carpentry is pretty good. The helm bridge has been squared off, and they've put a full plywood extension on the hardtop. There's an overhang at the windshield, and then it carries all the way back to the stern."

With that, two Ford Expeditions pulled up, to pick up the crew and their women.

Seth said, "The third guy that got off, the one headed for the white Expedition, could be Peter. The dark hair and beard don't match him, but he's limping on the right knee. Let's leave Freddy here to watch the boat, and we'll meet Toby and John back at the trawler."

Seth arrived at the trawler to find the fly boys and Gene already there.

"Good job guys ... we just got a closer look, and I think it could be the Huckins."

"You could have knocked me over with a feather when that tubby looking grouper boat all of a sudden came out of the hole and went up on plane. Toby just wanted us to hang around so he could get another shot of the naked girls," said John laughing loudly. "I mean there's freaking Bandit reels hanging off that thing."

"Billy, take a van and go back to the Hogfish. Get Freddy and yourself a sandwich and a cold one and watch the *GOFISH* from the picnic spot. Call me on my cell phone if there's any more movement over there. Check in once an hour and someone will relieve you about 11:00 p.m."

Seth called Charley and said, "We haven't found the boat yet, and we're moving to the Key West area tomorrow morning. How about putting the trawler in the slip you own at Safe Harbor? It will save you from paying slip rent elsewhere, and the Hogfish is a good place for me to feed the crew."

"OK, Seth. I'll call Joe O'Donald on his cell tonight. He'll square it with the dock master. Any leads yet?"

"Nothing concrete, but I'm optimistic." He didn't want to take the chance that Charley might show up and complicate the situation.

Night had fallen and the crew made themselves sandwiches. As they ate, they discussed what to do from here.

Seth said, "Look, first we have to make a positive ID; second we have to build an open and shut case for the authorities. I want to find out what these guys are really up to so they're put away for a long time ... not just for stealing Charley's boat. Then we'll hand the case over to Gene's Monroe County Sheriff friend and the Commandant at the St. Petersburg Coast Guard Station. We have no idea what kind of loyalties the local police have."

Seth's cell phone rang ... it was Freddy.

"Seth, the last crewman looks like he's getting ready to leave. He's hosed off the boat and plugged in the shore power. He loaded two big trash bags in his pickup, and he looks like he's going back for more."

"You and Billy follow him off the Island. Hustle and get in the van. Wait at Fifth Street and MacDonald. He's got to go by there, tail him and keep me posted."

"Gene, take the other van and ride down to A&B and get my Spot GPS[3]. It's screwed to the back of the cabinet behind the bottom drawer in the cockpit tackle center. Also bring three or four of those big black zip-ties from the parts drawer in the engine room. Drop Toby and John off at the Hogfish. Take your cell phones. While you're gone, Dino and I are going to take a closer look at the GOFISH from the panga."

Dino and Seth pulled on their black neoprene wetsuits and each took a mask, snorkel, and fins from the dive gear locker in the aft deck lazarette. Dino retrieved a couple of underwater flashlights from his gear bag, and they were ready to go.

They climbed into the panga from the trawler's swim platform. Night had fallen and the marina dock lights danced on the still water. Seth started the outboard and idled out of the marina into the channel. He ran southwest until he reached the Safe Harbor Channel and then turned north and eased up the channel past the brightly lit power plant. Worst case scenario, they looked like a couple of night diving lobster poachers. Seth moored the panga in the shadows of the Marina Village mega-yacht quay, south of the GOFISH. He and Dino slipped into the water using the folding boarding ladder on the panga's transom. They swam silently across the canal to the darkened GOFISH. Seth took a breath and dove under the painted plywood swim platform. Dino saw

Seth's underwater flashlight came on for about ten seconds. Seth resurfaced and gave Dino, a thumbs up. Seth took off his fins and pulled himself up on the painted plywood swim platform and climbed the ladder to the aft deck. He looked into the salon and shined the light for just an instant. It was definitely Charley's Huckins; the salon was still recognizable, the aft cabin door had been painted gray, but it still had the Huckins lock and door knob. The high gloss teak transom had been painted over with gray paint and the carved and gold-leafed *ABOUT TIME* name board had been removed, but the screw holes were still there. Seth looked west a hundred yards towards Shrimp Road to check the boatyard's guard shack. There was a light on in it, but no movement. Seth got back on the swim platform and slipped silently into the water and put his fins back on. He motioned to Dino to swim back to the panga. They slowly swam across the canal through little ribbons of reflective light and finally reached the panga in the shadows. Seth idled back out of the canal past the power plant. He finally looked at Dino and said, "It's the Huckins, I can't believe we found it, but we did. I want you to bring the panga back here with my Spot^3 GPS unit and tie wrap the Spot^3 to the swim platform support frame between the two jet drives. The Spot^3 is waterproof to three feet and it will send my cell phone the Huckin's position every ten minutes whenever the boat is moving. I hide it on *TAR BABY* in case it's ever stolen."

"You got it Seth. Then we won't have to watch the boat every minute."
Gene was waiting for them with the Spot^3 when they tied up the panga behind the trawler.

"It's the Huckins, Gene, jet drives and all. They over-layed the teak swim platform with plywood so you can't see the jet drives ... I want you to go with Dino in the panga while he attaches the Spot^3 under the swim platform. He'll fill you in."

Dino and Gene left in the panga, along with a small tackle box and two light spinning rods that Seth had stashed aboard the trawler. The rods could give them an alibi. Seth peeled himself out of the wet suit and took a quick shower. His cell phone started ringing while he was drying off.

"Hey Seth ... Freddy. We followed the pickup truck up to Sugarloaf Key. We turned towards the Atlantic on Sugarloaf Blvd. and then east to the end of

Jamaica Lane. The house has a ten foot high vegetation fence all around it, and a big electric gate. It's dead ended on a cul-de-sac and the closest house is a block away. We parked the van near two houses and walked down there to take a look."

"Where are you now?

"About a half a block away, behind some big hibiscus bushes. I left Billy down there embedded in the fence foliage watching the pool area."

"What's going on at the house?"

"Basically, they've continued partying. They're having a freaking orgy in the pool area. Everybody's naked, the music is loud, the girls are dancing, and they're playing hide the weenie. The girls sound Polish or Bosnian. One of them has a tattoo of a flight of blue butterflies flying out of her ass and up her back. But, these girls are fine specimens, if I do say so myself."

"Well, I know you'd like to keep watching, Freddy, but how about getting your asses out of there and back here. Write down the address if there's a mailbox or it's on the gate. Pick up Toby and John at the Hogfish on the way back. Be careful, I've confirmed that *GOFISH* is the Huckins."

"Way to go, Seth! I'll see you in 20 minutes."

***

It was almost midnight before everybody was finally back at the *SIRENA*. Seth got the whole crew together in the main salon for a re-cap and a night-cap. "We had a great day today, boys. We found the Huckins (cheers), and we have a tracking device installed on it. We know where the perps live, and we're reasonably certain they are the St. Pete suspects. Now, we have to figure out how they are using the Huckins to finance their Keys' lifestyle. I doubt grouper fishing is paying for the big house, new trucks, and the dancing girls. I'd also like to thank the dancing girls for helping our two aerial aces find the Huckins (laughter)... Tomorrow, we move this boat into Charley's slip. Don't tell anybody there we know him, say we're friends of a friend. We can watch the *GOFISH* from the trawler's flybridge. Freddy will set up a surveillance schedule. First thing in the morning, Dino and Billy will visit the perp's house on Sugarloaf Key in the panga. They'll see if they have any other boats and how good their access is to the Atlantic. Take the spinning rods and tackle box and fish near their house. Let's all meet for lunch at the Hogfish tomorrow at one o'clock.

CHAPTER THIRTEEN

At 6:45, the sun started to rise over Key West. It promised to be a hot, clear day with seasonal late afternoon and evening thunder showers. The shift change at the five Russian muscle locations and Ivan's residence on Passover Lane, had all been completed by 6:00 a.m. Tuesday's action would start in 30 minutes, when the muscle made their way to their daily 7:30 morning meeting at the Gulag. Frankie Blue Eyes was dressed in his derelict outfit and had a half full bottle of wine in his left hand. He feigned sleep as he sat against the picket fence across from Vadim and Luka's disabled motorbikes. Rocco Guerra lay curled up next to Frankie pretending to be asleep. They both had X26 Tasers hidden in their right hands. Their van was parked along the curb next to the bikes. Inside the van were Emilio "The Mooch" Muccio and Big Fred Langello. Blue Eyes had worried about the two girls that Vadim and Luka had brought back to their apartment early that morning. He was relieved to hear from the second surveillance crew that a taxicab had picked them both up at 3:15 that morning. If they had stayed they would have probably been killed, unless they were late sleepers. No one was stirring much on Louisa Street. Only one car had driven past so far. Blue Eyes wanted to be long gone before the dog walkers got out. At 7:15, the front door opened and the two bleary eyed Russians came out. They walked through the gate and spotted the two drunks against the fence.

Vadim shouted in broken English, "*Focking* load-outs … get the *fock* out of here!"

It was the last thing Vadim would ever say. Blue Eyes shot him in the chest with his Taser, Vadim jerked violently from the massive electric shock and dropped to the sidewalk with the two Taser wires embedded in his chest. Rocco rolled over and shot an astonished Luka in the stomach with his Taser. Luka danced like a marionette and then collapsed like a ton of bricks. Blue Eyes gave Vadim a second pull of the trigger, making his body jump, as Big

Fred and The Mooch jumped out the back of the van. Just 30 seconds later the van was on its way to Geiger Central while Blue Eyes and Rocco zip-tied the Russians' hands and feet. Blue Eyes pulled the darts and wires out of both Russians, and they reloaded their Tasers with new cartridges. With that accomplished, they garotted both of them and zipped them up in the body bags. The Mafia boys were cold and efficient; it was strictly *business*. The quicker they got them in the body bags the less they had to smell the result of the Russians' sudden loss of sphincter control. The same scene played out at five different locations at approximately the same exact time. Ivan, the lieutenant, smelled a rat and turned to run down Passover Lane. But Pindaro "Slick Paul" Gagliano shot him in the back from ten feet away (the X26 Taser has a 15 foot range). He shivered and collapsed. His momentum caused him to face plant into the sidewalk. Slick Paul and his partner Johnny "The Gimp" Deo bundled the bleeding and unconscious Ivan into the rear space of their Escalade. He was zip-tied and his mouth duct taped. He would be interrogated at Geiger Central, if he recovered from his fall. Johnny retrieved Ivan's cell phone to give to Pete.

Vladimir Kronski walked out of his William Street apartment building and approached his motorbike parked next to the apartment's dumpster. As he swung his leg up to mount it, Joe The Animal, stepped from behind the dumpster and Tasered him in the back. Joe and his partner Jimmy "The Bull" Grattzi hustled him into their Escalade, and hogtied and garotted him. The Bull put Vladimir in a body bag and got into the front seat for the ride to the Geiger house. The other three Russian muscle boys fell for the derelict trick and were put in the vans without incident.

Only Sergei Romanov, the largest of the muscle boys, caused a problem. He fell for the derelict ruse and was Tasered in the chest by Pajama Boy. He and Angelo "Pepper" Abbotello had a tough time getting Sergei into the van because of his sheer size and weight. Once they got the side door closed and started to zip-tie his wrists behind him, Sergei suddenly surged back to life and started to struggle. The rear of the van turned into a tangle of asses and elbows. Pepper was thrown against the back doors and had the wind knocked out of him. Pajama Boy came up with the Taser and pulled the trigger just as

Sergei tried to pull the darts and wires out of his chest. Sergei shook from head to toe and screamed out loud, then fell silent and collapsed. Pajama Boy pulled an ice pick from a belt sheath and stuck it in Sergei's right ear, up to the hilt.

Pajama Boy looked over at Pepper, who was gasping for breath and said, "Fucker didn't wanna die, did he?"

"Truss him up good Nick," wheezed Pepper. "Just in case."

Pajama Boy zip-tied Sergei and quickly rolled him into a body bag. As he zipped up the bag he noticed a steady trickle of blood coming from Sergei's right ear. He helped Pepper into the front passenger seat and headed out. The ride back to Geiger Central took about 20 minutes. When they got to the end of Boundary Road, the gate opened as they approached. As they pulled in, two of the vans left. Pajama Boy noticed they had installed their magnetic, KEYS CABLE, signs.

Pete had organized a crew to take the body bags out of the vehicles and transport them, in wheelbarrows, to the pool area. There, the bags were wrapped in chains, which were secured by master links. Then the bodies were loaded into the boats three or four at a time. Sergei was the last body to be loaded. When Sergei was loaded into the second boat, both boats left the dock. They were headed for the "Ups and Downs", about 10 to 12 miles off shore, where the bottom undulated from 600 to 800 feet deep.

Each van was cleaned out, fitted with the magnetic signs, and loaded with wire, tools, a ladder, hard hats, tool belts, and orange parking cones. Three of the vans were headed for Sea Breeze 1, 2, and 3. The fourth headed for Stock Island. One of the Escalades was already staked out at Nikolay Rutan's condo in Truman Annex. Marco "Ace" Costagna would follow him to The Galleon Condo and alert Pajama Boy.

Pepper was placed on the disabled list. When the adrenaline wore off from his encounter with Sergei it was obvious that his right side collar bone was either dislocated or broken, and two ribs were possibly fractured. Pete sent Sally Randazzo, in an Escalade, to the Key West FBO to bring the Miami doctor back to Geiger Central from one of the Cessna Caravans that were waiting on the airport tarmac.

The Southern Breeze stores opened at 9:00 a.m. Pete wanted the vans in place before then, with traffic cones deployed, yellow tape strung, and some contrived work taking place. There were three workmen in each of the vans at the Southern Breeze stores. At each of those locations, a front door spotter had been dropped off dressed like a tourist. He alerted the crew leader by cell phone or text that the dealer was passing through the store. Once the progression started, if there was a delivery in progress or pedestrian traffic, they were instructed to be patient and wait for the next cycle. Big Fred pulled the van off Front Street into the Southern Breeze 1 rear parking lot. He turned around and parked facing the street in the driveway next to a telephone pole. The men exited the van, placed the orange cones, and ran yellow tape from the cones to the pole. They extended the ladder up the pole and quickly ran a length of cable wire from a junction box to the ground. Now it was break time. The Animal and Big Fred sat inside the rear doors, which were open, with their feet on the driveway, while Slick Paul sat in the driver's seat. Each man had a Taser in his tool pouch. Pete had provided a thermos of hot coffee and Styrofoam cups for each van.

Big Fred's phone vibrated in his pocket, with a call from Donato "Donny" Spicoli, their spotter on Duval Street. "The blond haired dealer just entered the store. His boss, Dimitry, went in about five minutes ago."

Ten minutes later, the blond dealer came out the back door and slowed down to look at the cable guys. Big Fred looked at him and said, "Do you work here?"

The dealer said, "Yeah."

Big Fred pulled out a map of Key West and asked, "Look at this for me, will ya? I want to make sure I'm in the right place."

The dealer walked over and looked at the map. The Animal stood up and Tasered him in the back. He fell forward into the rear of the van. Joe and Fredo pulled him all the way in and Slick Paul closed the rear doors. They zip-tied the Russian's hands and feet, and The Animal garotted him. Fredo emptied the dealer's pockets. He carried $600 in tens and twenties, ten 1 gram packets of cocaine worth $200 each, six small 1/2 ounce bags of marijuana worth $100 each, a switch blade knife, a cell phone, and a set of keys. Fredo zipped him up in a body bag, while Joe changed the cartridge in his Taser.

Fredo and Joe walked around to the back door of Southern Breeze 1 and quietly found the key that opened the door. They slipped in and found themselves in Dimitry's office. He was watching a porn movie on his computer, and said without looking up, "Did you forget something, Alexi?" Fredo Tasered him, at close range, in the back of his neck. Dimitry went instantly comatose and slumped in the chair. Joe locked the door that opened in from the store, then he texted Slick Paul to pull the van to the back door. They carried Dimitry out back and loaded him into the van. Joe zip-tied him and then Fredo garotted him. After relieving him of his cash, cell phone, and a diamond pinky ring, Fredo put him in a body bag. They left their traffic cones, and headed for Geiger Central. For them, it was two down and two to go.

Angelo "Poppy" Panzini was the oldest wise guy on this junket. He drove the van to Southern Breeze 2. There were only three dealers left to pick up since the early morning crew had already nailed Ivan. He was working with Rocco Guerra, and Eddie The Drummer. They backed into the narrow alleyway off of Walton Lane and set up on a telephone pole, which blocked off that alley. Their spotter was Johnny The Gimp. The "look at the map ploy" worked every time, and Poppy's crew was back at Geiger Central with three full body bags in less than three hours. The bodies were on their way out to sea in one of the Jupiters, 30 minutes after their arrival at Geiger Central.

The crew at Southern Breeze 3 had a tougher time. The third lieutenant, Ivanna, did not show up for work. Blue Eyes, the crew chief, called Pete at Geiger Central around 9:30 to report the AWOL. Pete sent Bobby Mancini in an Escalade to stake out Ivanna's apartment three blocks from the store. Blue Eyes, The Mooch, and Jimmy Grattzi worked the truck, with Tony Muzzio as their lookout. They scored both dealers within the first two hours. They would have been done sooner, but a dog walker passed by when the dealer walked out through the alley the first time. The second time around, the dealer made the fatal mistake by asking, "How's it going?" and stopped to look up at the pole. Pete told them to run their two bodies back to Geiger Central, unload, and then return. They left their lookout, Tony Muzzio, who would alert them if Ivanna showed up in the meantime.

Fredo's crew got back in place and bagged the other two dealers at Southern Breeze 1 before lunchtime.

Danny "Mango Man" Mangano and Johnny Martino worked Stock Island. They parked their KEYS CABLE van across the street, a half a block down from the Hogfish Grill, next to three large dumpsters. Behind them were dense mangrove trees and a shallow bay. They parked in front of a telephone pole just south of the dumpsters and set up their ladder, cones, and equipment. The two Russian dealers, who supplied Stock Island, worked from the south side of the last dumpster. It was as close as they could get to the Hogfish Bar and Grille without getting their ass kicked. Even the Russians didn't want to take on the "Mother Lode Gang", whose ties went deep in Key West.

The day shift dealer showed up about 11:00 in the morning on his motor scooter and parked it behind the dumpster. Both Stock Island dealers always got their drugs and money the previous day and kept their inventory in the fiberglass saddlebags on their scooters. Because of the distance back to Southern Breeze 3, they only came in during their shifts if they sold out. The dealer had two early customers, and kept looking down at the cable truck. Finally, Danny waved a map and motioned to him to come over. The dealer strode up and said, "How long are you guys going to be here?"

Danny said, "We're from Miami, and we're not sure we're in the right location. Take a look at this map for us, will ya?"

He was anxious to get them out of his territory so he came closer. He was Tasered, cuffed, garotted, and zipped in a body bag in less than five minutes. Johnny cleaned the drugs and money out of the saddlebags, then pushed the dealer's scooter out through the mangroves, and dumped it over in the water. Predictably, the same ploy worked on the second shift dealer, and Mango Man and Johnny were back at Geiger Central before sunset with the last two bodies.

***

Nick Pajama Boy Bocci sat in the rented Galleon Condo next to the suite door that opened into Nikolay's Rutan's unit. His unit's suite door was open, and he had a stethoscope pressed against Nicolay's door. Earlier that week, while Svetlana was down at the pool working on her tan, he had changed the lock. Now Nikolay's pass thru door had a deadbolt lever on both sides of the door. Pajama Boy could hear every word and sound that was made in their condo. They conversed mostly in Russian with some English mixed in. He could hear the toilet flush, and the king size bed creak. He gathered, from piecing together several of their broken English conversations, that Svetlana was an exotic dancer. Nicolay was paying her not to dance, and was also picking up all her expenses. Every visit started out the same, with her whining and working on him for a new bikini, new shoes, more spending money, etc. It was getting close to 10:30 and he expected a call from Ace Costagna at any moment. His phone finally vibrated and he read the text from Ace ... *the Kapo is on his way up.* He got up and walked around the unit to stretch his legs. He looked out the window at the pool below. The lounge chairs down at the pool were already filling up with tourists. Pajama Boy glanced across the harbor at Sunset Island and wondered how that whole scene was going down. There was a knock on the hall door in the next unit. He checked over his Glock 9mm and screwed the silencer on the end of the barrel, then sat back down and put the stethoscope probe back on the door. They were talking in the living room. Svetlana whined for money to send her mother. Nikolay gave her the money, and they retired to the bedroom. He heard the toilet flush twice, and then the bed creak a couple of times. A small rivulet of perspiration ran off his forehead. Five minutes later there was moaning, and soon the creaking bed was doing double time. Pajama Boy, wiped his brow, unbolted the door, and peered inside. The living room was empty. He slipped in silently, the Glock held with two hands out in front of him. The bedroom door was open and what he saw made him pause for a moment. Svetlana was straddling the kapo in the classic Cowgirl position and rode him facing the headboard. Nicolay was at the Bucking Bronco stage, and she was riding him like an old rodeo pro. Pajama Boy paused for a few more seconds to admire Svetlana's voluptuous ass and bouncing breasts. Then he stepped into the doorway and shot her in the small of her back. The silent bullet ripped through her arched back and lodged itself somewhere in Nicolay's chest cavity. Svetlana fell forward, her ample breasts suffocating a struggling and gasping Nicolay. Pajama Boy moved quickly forward and applied a coup de grace to each of their temples. Nick covered the two lovers with the top sheet and thought ... *what a waste of a truly spectacular piece of ass.* He retrieved Nicolay's cell phone and cash from his trousers, which were draped over a chair, then backtracked into the rented condo and took a screwdriver from his pocket. He changed the deadbolt back to the original, locked it from Nicolay's side, and let himself out their hall door while affixing the **Do Not Disturb** sign to the outside doorknob. He re-entered the rented condo and secured that unit's suite door. He was careful to wipe down all possible fingerprints, retrieved the temporary lockset and screwdriver, and left the condo. He walked down the fire stairs and exited through the parking garage. He got into the Black Escalade parked on Front Street.

Ace said, "How did it go?"

"Her topless picture didn't do her justice."

They drove in silence back to Geiger Central.

***

Captain Tony was just about finished calling the list of marinas and fuel docks in the Upper Keys, including Islamorada and Key Largo. He hadn't had any luck. He dialed up the largest marina in that area, Plantation Yacht Harbor Marina, and got the same reception. It didn't make any sense. Even if you anchored out or stayed at a private dock, if you went fishing, you had to burn fuel. Seth Stone had to be getting fuel somewhere. Tony checked J&S Diesel Service out of Marathon. They brought a tank truck to your dock. He told them he was a detective from the Tampa Police Department looking for *TAR BABY* and was following any and all leads. They checked their records and had not fueled the boat. He had even tried the tiny Marathon Yacht Club on Vaca Key. They would not reveal any information about their transient Council of Yacht Club members without authorization of the member's club manager.

That didn't surprise Captain Tony, but at least he gave it a try. Maybe he started too early. He would retrace his steps in a couple of days, concentrating on the fuel docks. Only one thing had gone right today. After lunch, he had scored a dinner date with Molly Mallory for that evening. He headed for the shower with a smile on his face.

***

Pete got a call from Bobby Mancini. Ivanna was on the move. She had walked out of her apartment on Whitehead St. five minutes ago, and was headed towards Duval via Catherine St. She stopped at La Te Da's for lunch with her regular lunch crowd. Bobby hung out across the street and would call when she moved again. Bobby called Pete 45 minutes later.

Pete immediately called Blue Eyes, "Ivanna is on the move again. Bobby says she's walking up Duval towards the store. Let me know how it goes."

Blue Eye's phone vibrated in his pocket. It was a text from Tony Muzzio; *Ivanna is outside the store.* Blue Eyes walked out to the front of the van, which was blocking the sidewalk and alley, and looked up the side street toward Duval Street. Ivanna looked down the street at the same time. She abruptly stopped and turned down the side walk and headed straight for Blue Eyes. She looked up the alley and looked at the truck blocking it. Then she glanced up at the cable hanging off the telephone pole, put her hands on her hips, and said, "You need to move this truck. I have deliveries coming in this afternoon."

"Lady, I'm sorry, but I gotta job to do."

With that said, Blue Eyes moved into the alley towards the back of the van.

Ivanna followed him saying, loudly, "Maybe you didn't hear me, *Jackoff.* I said … move this truck out of here now, or I'm going to move it for you."

Blue Eyes sized Ivanna up. She was bigger and taller than him, and she probably knew some martial arts, but she was still a girl. He backed off a couple more feet and said with a smile, "You can call me *Mr. Jackoff*, Lady."

Ivanna moved in closer, her face getting redder, and shouted, "Park the *focking* truck … in the *focking* street … or I'll kick your *focking ahss.*"

Blue Eyes looked over at The Mooch and nodded. Emilio drew his Taser from his tool pouch and shot Ivanna point blank in the chest. The darts hit her perfectly, one in each one of her large melon shaped breasts. She cocked her spikey-haired head and danced in place for a couple of seconds then collapsed on the asphalt. Blue Eyes and Mooch quickly lifted her into the van and cuffed her hands and feet. Blue Eyes retrieved her cell phone. The Mooch garotted her, and they started to zip her up in a body bag. The Mooch looked over at Blue Eyes and said, "Whew! I think the bitch shit herself when I Tasered her. We need to open the fuckin' windows in the van quick … before I start gaggin'."

They got the bag zipped and Jimmy threw the ladder, cones, and yellow tape in on top of her, and the KEYS CABLE boys headed for Geiger Central.

Pete The Barber sat at the dining room table at the Geiger house. He and Sally Randazzo had completed their interrogation of Ivan. They had picked the right man. He was the Russians' bag man. Once they cleaned up his bloody face and gave him a couple of shots of Jack Daniels, to ease the pain from his broken nose, he made them a list of the payoff recipients and the amounts. He asked not to be tortured and requested that he be dispatched with dignity with a pistol shot to his temple. He could see by the events that were swirling around him at Geiger Central that it was over for the Russians in Key West.

Pete heard the Jupiter 38's pull away from the Geiger dock on their way to deep-six Ivanna, Ivan, and the Stock Island dealers. The crew had packaged the magnetic signs, tools, cones, yellow tape, ladders, wheelbarrows, and leftover chain to dump overboard also. The rest of the crew was now in the process of sanitizing the vans and both Geiger houses. In front of Pete on the dining room table were four cell phones that had received a flurry of calls from the same number between 2:00 and 5:00 that afternoon. None of them were answered. Pete now had Yuly's cell phone number, and Yuly had to be certain that something was seriously wrong in Key West. Both Jupiters would run into Key West Harbor after dumping their last cargo. Frog Eye's boat would anchor off Wisteria Island just as night fell. The other Jupiter would take up station at the tripod marker off Fort Zachary Taylor. The plan was to force Yuly to make a move as soon as it got dark. Pete would send one flight of men out of Key West in about an hour. He would load the second plane and hold it at the airport until he could depart. He kept Cadillac advised throughout the day, and Cadillac was advising Luigi in Tampa.

The twelve men, including Pete, who were flying out were delivered to the planes. The four men, Fredo, Joe, Johnny, and Eddie, who would drive the Escalades up to the rented house in Summerland Key, moved the work vans in two shifts to the crab trap lot on Stock Island. They would stand by in the main airport parking lot in the Escalades. Pete was tying up all the loose ends that he could.

Frog Eyes called Pete, "I'm anchored up at Wisteria."

"If they make a break in the boat … I want *you* to trigger the bomb."

"OK, Boss."

Pete called Vito on Sunset Island from the Cessna Caravan while sitting on the tarmac. The other Caravan had just taken off with six soldiers, including Pepper who had a fractured clavicle and had his left arm immobilized in a sling. Vito kept the doctor on the last plane just in case.

"Vito, is there any movement at Yuly's house?"

"Well, it's just startin' to get dark here. About an hour ago one of the bodyguards came out and ran the boat lift down in the water and started the engines. I thought we were gonna get lucky, but he shut'em off and went back inside. Now I see one light upstairs and two lights on downstairs and the dock's lit up."

"Frog Eyes is on station in the Jupiter at Wisteria Island, he just called me. Let him blow the boat if they take it, he's only a couple hundred yards from it. If Yuly don't make a move in the next 30 minutes, we'll launch a couple of grenades into his second story. That oughta flush his ass out."

"OK, Boss, I've got my infrared sights, grenade launcher, and assault rifle. I'm sittin' in the dark lookin' out my bedroom window at Yuly's front door. The Mallory crowd should be totally gone in 30 minutes."

Pete took a deep breath, wiped his sweaty brow, and listened to his men chatting in the rear of the plane. He nervously checked his watch until 30 minutes had elapsed. It was time to make a decision. He called Frog Eyes and calmly said, "Launch two grenades into the second story in two minutes."

He texted Vito in the condo: *Two minutes to launch.*
Pete dialed Yuly's number on Nikolay's cell phone.

Yuly answered saying, "Nikolay, where the *fock* are you? I been …"

Pete cut him off and said, "Come Stai, Yuly? -- Y'all will sleep with the fish tonight!", and hung up. *That ought to put the fear of God in him,* thought Pete.

Frog Eyes and Rocco each launched a grenade into two of Yuly's upstairs windows. They both exploded as they broke through the windows and the second floor burst into flames. Frog Eyes looked over at Mallory Square and saw only a few stragglers standing in the dark. Five minutes later the back door opened, and the two bodyguards, with guns drawn, dragged Yuly out the back door and down the dock towards the boat.

"It looks like they're goin' to make a run for it, should I shoot them?"

"No, Rocco, The Barber wants it to look like an accident. I'll blow up the boat when they leave. It looks like Yuly's hurt."

The bodyguards stuffed Yuly in the cuddy cabin, started the boat, and moved out of the lift. As soon as they were clear, the helmsman buried the throttle and the boat leaped onto a plane. Frog Eyes calmly dialed the trigger code and the boat exploded in a huge ball of fire in the middle of Key West Harbor. Rocco pulled the anchor and Frog Eyes idled the Jupiter 38 around the west side of Sunset Island.

Frog Eyes called Pete and said, "Mission accomplished. The house is burnin', three of them ran out … Yuly looked hurt … and they tried to make a run for it in the boat. We blew it up. See you in Miami."

Then Frog Eyes called Mango Man and Donny Spicoli in the other Jupiter 38 and said, "See you guys at Rodriquez Key."

Vito saw the fireball and closed his second story window. He walked downstairs to have a celebratory glass of Pasqua Amarone red wine and maybe get a little "Choo Choo La La" going with Angela. He hadn't lived with a woman for quite awhile, and he was enjoying the familiarity and seemingly endless imagination of his new companion. He heard a helicopter go over the condo's roof. It sounded close. *Probably a police or TV news helicopter …* he thought. It sounded like it was landing right outside. An alarm went off in Vito's head. He put down his wine glass, told Angela to stay put, and ran back up the stairs. He opened the window and looked out at the helicopter landing in the middle of Yuly's cul de sac. The helicopter had no markings on it and the pilot flung open the passenger door from the inside.

The front door of Yuly's house flew open and smoke poured out. Suddenly, Yuly emerged out of the smoke, with a scuba tank strapped to his back and a scuba mask on his face. He was pulling a large roll-around suitcase with one hand. His Uzzi machine pistol was secured on a lanyard around his neck. Yuly headed for the helicopter on the run, shedding the scuba gear on the way. He threw his suitcase in the back of the copter, and climbed in after. Vito grabbed and aimed his grenade launcher out of the bedroom window. As the helicopter lifted off Vito launched the grenade directly at the front windshield. The helicopter blew up in the third spectacular explosion of the night. The flaming wreck came to rest back in the middle of the cul de sac.

Vito called Pete on his cell phone just as the Caravan was taxiing to the runway and filled him in on Yuly's final demise in the helicopter. Pete informed his crew on the plane and they celebrated Yuly's death a second time.

Pete called Cadillac on his sat-phone and filled him in on all the details. Cadillac said, "Mr. C will be pleased with your work."

Vito took the disassembled grenade launcher and assault rifle to the southern end of Sunset Island in a backpack and a beach bag. The police and fireman had left the island earlier, around 2:30 a.m. A Navy fireboat put the fire out at Yuly's house. Crime tape surrounded the house and the charred remains of the helicopter. Vito avoided the security guard doing his rounds in a golf cart, and dumped the guns off the rock seawall into the Northwest Channel.

CHAPTER FOURTEEN

All the Geezers, except Dino, were at lunch by 1:00 p.m. Dino was on watch in the flybridge of the *SIRENA* watching *GOFISH*. The day was moving by quickly. Billy and Dino had risen at first light, had breakfast, and were on their way to investigate the Jamaica Lane house on Sugarloaf Key by 7:30. They stopped for fuel and bought a bait bucket and two dozen shrimp at the Oceanside fuel dock on their way out. Dino drove and Billy navigated using a Garmin handheld GPS. The panga rode smoothly up Hawk Channel through the medium morning chop. Recreational fishing boats of all types were headed south out of Boca Chica Pass and Geiger Key further east. The Key's soft morning colors had a mellowing effect, making them feel cool and calm as they sped toward their reconnaissance mission. They turned and ran north up the narrow, mangrove lined Sugarloaf canal, and passed under the dilapidated Rte. 939 Bridge on their way to the Jamaica Lane house. Dino slowed the panga just before they got to the first cross canal. There were no other houses from the Atlantic to the Jamaica house. Then only a few houses were scattered up the cross canal and no houses were on the east side of main canal. Dino shifted the outboard into neutral and coasted to a stop. They eased a river anchor over the side, baited their hooks with a couple of live shrimp, and cast their baits into the canal junction. A seafoam green 37 Contender with triple 350 Yamaha's was moored to the Jamaica house's dock.

Dino said, "That Contender will do 70 miles per hour."

Billy nodded, but before he could comment his rod doubled over, and his reel started screaming. A 25 pound tarpon jumped clear of the water 30 feet up the channel. Billy fought and reeled the tarpon in, and then released him.

"Well, that was fun. Let's catch another one."

They caught three more and moved the panga up past the Jamaica house. They glimpsed two SUVs and a pickup truck that drove out while they fished. The World Cat 32 foot center console catamaran, with dual 300 Yamahas and a cuddy cabin, was docked behind the Contender. Dino and Billy figured the cat would do 50 miles per hour, and it only drew 16 inches of water. Dino caught a tarpon, another 20-plus pounder, before they pulled anchor and started back. Billy memorized the FL numbers on the World Cat and the Contender. He wrote them both in his day-timer log, along with the tarpon information, when they were out of sight. They figured somebody was probably watching them the whole time from inside the house.

Seth arrived at Safe Harbor Marina about 10:30. He and Gene slept late, had breakfast at Two Friends on Front Street, and then drove up to Stock Island. Freddy and Toby moved the trawler to Safe Harbor and had it secured in Charley's slip before 10:00 a.m. John drove the van to the airport and fueled up the Lance, for any eventuality.

Billy reported on the trip to the Jamaica Lane house, and gave the FL registration numbers of the two boats to Gene.

"I'll call these boat numbers in to the sheriff after lunch along with the Jamaica Lane address, the truck license plate numbers, and GOFISH's commercial fishing number," said Gene.

Freddy reported that the crew of the GOFISH had been busy since 9:00 a.m., provisioning the boat. They loaded scores of grocery bags from Publix along with ice, and 20 mixed cases of water, soft drinks, and beer. They also loaded several cases of frozen squid, Spanish sardines, and mullet. Dino had just texted Seth that the J&S diesel tank truck had just pulled in and was fueling GOFISH.

Seth responded, "We'll watch them until they leave and then we'll make sure the Spot[3] is tracking them. If it works like it should, we won't take off in the airplane until they're past the Dry Tortugas. That's when we'll see their real course. They may stay around the Tortugas and fish. We don't know yet."

At that moment the waitress arrived with their hogfish sandwiches and a to-go box for Dino.

"I'll take mine and run this out to Dino. I want to get a look at the GOFISH crew," said Seth. He left some cash with Gene to pay for lunch.

He walked out the dock and past Joe O'Donald's warehouse unit and sailboat. He would look Joe up when the case was closed. The fewer people who knew that there was something more happening here, than just a trawler full of friends having a good time in Key West, the better. He called up to Dino on the flybridge, "Dino, I've got your lunch down here, let me hand it up to you."

Dino left his post for a second and Seth handed up both sandwiches.

"What do you want to drink? I'll get it out of the fridge."

"Diet Coke."

Seth got two Diet Cokes and climbed up to the bridge. He and Dino observed five crew members loading the boat. The fuel truck had been there for 45 minutes. Dino said he saw a crew member, with a shaved head, and a full, close trimmed black beard and mustache, pay the J&S Diesel driver with cash. He also saw four five gallon pails of Shell Rotella oil carried aboard, along with a cardboard box full of boxed NAPA and Racor filters. Two hours later the five gallon pails were carried off, along with a box full of used oil and fuel filters. They were definitely getting ready for a long trip. Seth waited and got a good look at the whole crew.

"The shaved head crew member could be Randy Garrett. His beard color is probably natural. Randy had black curly hair, and he's the right size for Randy. The bearded one with long black hair has to be Peter Petcock, his limp gives him away. His hair used to be blond."

"This hogfish is great, Seth. Maybe we can dive a day out on the north side of the Marquesas. There are some patch reefs and rock piles along the side of the channel out there that hold hogfish. It wouldn't take me long to fill the cooler."

"We'll see how it goes, Dino."

By 4:30 p.m., the GOFISH crew was finished provisioning and doing maintenance. One by one, all their vehicles left the dusty boatyard. Seth guessed they might leave in the middle of the night or at first light. Visibility was not the issue because the Huckin's Flir night vision unit was still attached to the cabin top.

Seth's cell phone vibrated in his pocket. He took a look …it was a text from Lori: *Missing you Big Boy. I'm out at the Pass-a-Grille clubhouse for Happy Hour since the downtown Yacht Club is closed today. I'm sitting at the bar with Barbara Townsend and*

Carole Bardes, enjoying a Dirty Martini. I understand you've shot trap with Barbara, and used to lend Carole your racing sailboat for the Bikini Cup. I hope the fishing's improved. Love, Lori. Seth smiled and thought to himself, *Love, I haven't said that yet, but I'm starting to feel that way. When you say …Love … that's a commitment. I not sure if I'm ready … But I'll take a gut check when this is all over; it's not something to rush into. I certainly do miss her, though… and not just the good sex.* Seth texted Lori back: *Settled in Key West, but going fishing out in the Tortugas tomorrow for two or three days. We're getting good fishing reports from there. No cell phone service out there, I'll call you when we get back to Key West. I miss you too, and I think about you every day. Tell Barbara and Carole … Hey! Barbara is a really good shot and Carole won the Bikini Cup! …… Seth*

Gene climbed up on the bridge and told Seth, "I called Billy Ray an hour ago and told him about our private investigation. He said he would help us in any way he could, as long as we didn't try and make the collar. I assured him we had no intention of doing that and would share all the information with him if we found the Huckins. I didn't tell him we'd found the Huckins, I just told him we were following some promising leads and needed some boat ID numbers and a house address checked to confirm ownership. I gave him my email and he said he would fast track the research."

"Did you tell him we wanted to involve the Coast Guard?"

"First, I told him about the special month-long Adiz no fly zone permit that Commander Timmons gave us. Then I asked him if we found the boat in international waters, which agency had jurisdiction? He said the U.S Coast Guard or the DEA. I asked him who he preferred working with, and he said the Coast Guard."

"Good work, detective, you certainly know your way around law enforcement. Listen, if we find out that *GOFISH* is headed past the Tortugas to Cuba, Mexico, or wherever, I want to fly in the plane with Toby and John. And I'd like to take Dino and his diving gear with us. I want you to take Billy and Freddy fishing, weather permitting, while we're gone. We need to maintain our cover. I can check in with you, and vice versa, on our sat-phones, even if you're way offshore."

"Sounds good to me, what should I tell anyone that asks where you are?"

"Tell them I had to fly back to St. Pete for business reasons, and I should be back in a couple of days. I wanted to tell you this now because when *GOFISH* leaves, everything will happen quickly."

Gene's cell phone chimed and he looked at his email, "It's from Billy Ray."

"Let's go below and I'll read it to off your phone."

Gene handed Seth his phone when they got below: *The 37 foot Contender is titled to, Wayne D. Baxster, 1350 Jamaica Lane, Sugarloaf Key, FL 33042, FL6815MN. The World Cat 32 footer is titled to Chester J. Hawley at the same address, FL1486TD. Commercial Fishing Vessel 563487, GOFISH, FL DL#32561, Builder: Houma Fabricators, Houma La; Retitled to GOFISH LLC, 1350 Jamaica Lane, Fl 33042, US. Coast Guard Documentation, title and hailing port change, 2003: Houma, La. to Key West, FL. No Mortgage recorded. Both trucks are titled in Florida, one in Chester's name, and the other in Wayne's. Neither truck had a loan on it. The Jamaica Lane house was titled to Fish the Keys Rentals LLC, along with another house on Sugarloaf Key at 135 Wahoo Lane. No mortgage on either house. Wayne and Chester were listed on the LLC as officers and 50/50 stockholders.*

Background checks: Wayne Dennis Baxster, born March, 17, 1949, Forest Hills, N.Y. U.S. Army 1967-1971 Hon. Discharge, Soc. Sec # 289394704, no felonies, minor traffic offenses, NY,NY; vagrancy arrest 1999, Hallandale, Florida. Convicted, 30 days, Broward County jail. Chester James Hawley, born April 1, 1951, Secaucus, N.J., No military service, Soc. Sec # 316348901, automobile theft 1970, Clifton, N.J, probation, marijuana possession, Somers Point, N.J., 1973, probation.DUI, Miami, Fl. 1998, convicted, 6 months license suspension, 30 days in Dade County jail.

"Billy Ray sure didn't skimp on the info. It looks like these guys are building a vacation rental business and paying cash for everything. They've spent a lot of money in a short period of time, and it smells like drug money to me. How do you think they got these new identities, Gene?"

"We ran into this a few times when I was a detective in St. Petersburg. Especially in white collar crime. We'd book and fingerprint the suspect and then run a background check on his ID We would get back a basically clean or minor offense report. Then we'd send the prints to the national database, but that takes some time. In the meantime, the perp's lawyer would get him bail because of his basically clean record. By the time the prints came back with his real ID, he had skipped bail and town. We spent some time researching the origin of these stolen identities. All the trails led to Miami. Miami has more vagrants per square mile than any other city in America. There are criminal rings there that prey on the vagrants. They befriend the bums, ply them with drugs and alcohol, and then steal their personal information. If their records are fairly clean and they have no next of kin, they dump them offshore in the Gulf Stream. The criminals get $15,000 and more for a full set of ID. With a birth certificate, Social Security card, and no felony police record, anyone can get a new photo ID passport and drivers license. Their finger prints could trip them up later if the real person's fingerprints are in the database."

"Let's get the crew together for dinner here on the trawler. We'll update everyone on the new information and on the plan when the GOFISH pulls out."

Seth finished up dinner with the crew, minus Gene who took the watch, and filled the crew in on Billy Ray's information. Then he laid out their plan of action for when GOFISH departed. Freddy sent Billy to relieve Gene and he and Seth left for A&B.

As Seth left he looked back inside the cabin and said, "Whenever they leave, call me right away."

The call at came at 6:15 a.m. Seth was half awake from his last trip to the head and answered almost immediately. It was Freddy. "We've got liftoff! They pulled their trucks in 20 minutes ago, and they've started the generator and the engines. They are casting off the lines, right now!"

"The same five crew members, Freddy?"

"It's hard to be sure, even with your night scope. But I counted six. I think they brought a 'salad girl' with them."

Salad girl? …. thought Seth, then he remembered and laughed. A salad girl is a commercial fisherman's slang term for a girl who is brought along to keep the male crew happy, for a share of the catch. When one was asked if she could cook she replied, 'I can make a salad'. And from that moment on they were called … salad girls.

"Don't get the rest of our crew up until the GOFISH has left, and don't show yourself on the flybridge. Gene and I will be there in 20 minutes."

Seth woke Gene, and five minutes later they were in the van on their way to Stock Island. The sun would rise that Tuesday at 6:38. Seth His cell phone chimed, it was his Spot[3] sending him the GOFISH's position. The sunrise was just beginning as Seth drove thru the Safe Harbor Marina gate and headed for the parking area at the end of the Quay. SIRENA was moored, stern to, between a 70 foot long single story house built on a 20 foot wide steel barge, and a small two-story cottage built on a fiberglass barge. Such was the eclectic Safe Harbor Marina. Seth went aboard the trawler and into the main salon. The crew was in various stages of waking up, fixing coffee, making toast, and waiting to get into the forward and aft heads. Seth could feel the tension in the air.

Seth said, "John, get me the paper chart #411 of the Gulf of Mexico and the Straits of Florida chart. Maybe we ought to start with the Sombrero Key to the Dry Tortugas, to track them out of here. We'll take the whole chart kit with us on the airplane if we go."

Seth's cell phone was getting latitude/longitude texts from his Spot[3], every ten minutes. He and John planned on plotting them and then interpolating the time and distance into speed. If they took the airplane, they could enter GOFISH's positions as waypoints on the Lance's second Garmin GPS and track them that way too. John continued plotting on the Tortugas chart, while Dino and Freddy whipped up some breakfast for the assembling crew.

John plotted the first three lat/lon positions on the Key West to Tortugas chart and said, "The Huckins is thru the reef and has turned west. I calculate the speed at 9 knots. How long will the Spot[3]'s batteries hold out, Seth?"

"It only uses the batteries when the boat is moving. The batteries will last three weeks if the boat moves continuously, and longer if there are intermittent stops."

"Give me your cell phone while you eat breakfast and I'll continue to plot the lat/lon positions as they come in. How does this continue to work if the boat goes out of cell phone range?"

"The Spot[3] GPS works off the Globalstar satellite network. I can also get it sent to my sat-phone, but the air time is way more expensive."

Seth asked Toby, Dino, and John to pack light overnight bags so they could leave quickly if that was the decision. He also asked Dino to pack his scuba gear.

Seth asked John, "Is it OK to take a scuba tank full of compressed air?"

"I do it all the time, Seth. We'll just strap it in one of the empty seats."

"If we end up flying to a foreign country, where would be a good place to hide our weapons on the plane, or would it be better to declare them?"

"Let's only take two and we'll hide them in the life raft satchel, they never look there. If we declare them, they may arrest us on the spot depending on the country."

"I hope we don't have to use the guns, but I think we ought to have them … you know … just in case. Trying to break the tension, Seth added, "Like my old dad, Robert E. always said, 'Why do men have nipples? …… Just in case'."

The crew groaned as the joke fell flat, and pre-action nerves still hung in the air.

Seth said, "Take along the light spinning rods and the small tackle box. That will make us look like permit or bone fisherman, wherever we go."

"Let's pack a cooler with plenty of water and enough sandwiches for at least two lunches for everybody," said John.

Dino and Toby got busy in the galley making sandwiches and stocking the cooler.

"Seth, it looks like the GOFISH has picked up the pace, I estimate she's making better than 28 knots on a course a few degrees south of west."

"Freddy, do you know where my night scope is? I need to put that in my duffel."

"I'll get it. It's still up on the bridge."

The crew hung out in the main salon chatting and laughing distractedly at the different stories the Geezers told about their past adventures and fishing trips. Some went back for 30 years or more.

At about 9:00 a.m., the Huckins by-passed the Tortugas and struck a west by southwesterly course, still at a steady 28 knots. At that rate of speed

GOFISH could arrive in Cancun or Isla Mujeres by 7:30 p.m., Eastern Daylight Savings Time, as long as the sea conditions didn't deteriorate.

Seth said to John, "We don't know where the *GOFISH* is going to end up. They could run to Cancun, or further south in the Caribbean Sea to the Cayman Islands. They might continue more westerly and run to Progreso, Campeche, Veracruz, or Tampico on the western Gulf Coast. Cancun and nearby Isla Mujeres are 388 miles from Key West. Merida's inland airport is closer to Key West, but Campeche is the closest coastal airport on the Mexican Gulf Coast, but its 629 miles from here. We probably ought to fly to Cancun or Isla Mujeres and see which way they go and catch up with them early Wednesday morning."

"I prefer Isla Mujeres small airport (ISJ) to Cancun International (CUN), we can walk to a number of small hotels and restaurants from there. Do you remember when we flew in with our wives, after the 1986 St. Petersburg to Isla Mujeres sailboat race, to go sailfishing with Gene's cousin, Tony Johnson? We were in our 40's back then."

"How could I forget … We caught 17 sailfish in one day off the stern of Tony's sailboat, *EVOLUTION*. Lisa and Stacy each caught their first sailfish on that trip. That was before the rest of the world discovered the spring sailfish and white marlin bite, 24 miles off of Cancun."

"If we leave at 11:00, we can fly over the *GOFISH* and be in Isla Mujeres before 2:00 in the afternoon. We can monitor the Huckins position on your cell phone from a table at the Fenix Beach Bar. I stayed once at a nice, little, inexpensive hotel with a pool, called the Plaza Almendros. It's downtown, right at the end of the airport runway. We can Google them and call them from the airplane on your sat-phone."

"Sounds good, let's load up and go to the FBO. File your flight plan on your computer, John, so we can take off right away … Gene, will you drop us at the airport? Then start fishing with Billy and Freddy on *TAR BABY* until we get back. I'll keep you posted all along the way. Dino and I will take our pistols."

They arrived at the Key West Airport and loaded the Lance while John checked in at the FBO. They switched to the Gulf of Mexico chart and Toby plotted the lat/lons from Seth's phone while sitting in the co-pilots seat with the door open. Seth noticed two identical Cessna Caravans parked about 50 yards from the FBO. A Latino man carrying a doctor's bag stepped out of the Caravan and was whisked away in a black Cadillac Escalade. Seth thought … *probably a rich Miami Cuban's MDVIP doctor, flown down to treat a jellyfish rash or a stingray barb.* Seth only knew the planes were Caravans because all the float planes that flew tourists out to Fort Jefferson each day were Caravans fitted with floats.

John strode out of the FBO and said, "Has everybody got their passport?" The answer was affirmative. "Let's get going, *Muchachos.*"

Fifteen minutes later they were in the air. Dino and Seth put on their headsets and plugged them into the Lance's communication system. They could hear all the airplane/tower chatter, but they could also talk among themselves, with their voice activated microphones. The plane took off into an easterly wind and once aloft, John turned south and then west. Key West went by under the starboard wing. The pink art museum next to the Westin Hotel shone like a beacon in the rising sun. The Marquesas soon loomed off the starboard beam. They climbed up to 3000 ft. and settled in on a 265^0 course mirroring the Huckins course. Toby spotted her about 45 minutes after takeoff. She was up on plane and moving effortlessly through the light chop in the Straits of Florida.

The Lance flew on to Isla Mujeres. John flew along Cuba's coast and across the Straits of Yucatan and landed on the Isla Mujeres Airport's 3,437 foot runway. The FBO at ISJ did not offer fuel, but the Lance only used 35 gallons to get to Isla Mujeres and had 59 usable gallons left. John could easily fly to the Caymans, which were 384 miles away, or Campeche, which was 256 miles away. Anything further would require a quick fuel stop in Cancun or Merida. After they cleared customs, John made arrangements to leave the plane at the FBO. Seth had made reservations at the Plaza Alemendros with his sat-phone, as they flew along the Cuban coast. At $60 USD a night, Seth booked separate rooms because all of the Geezers snored like hibernating bears. If they had their own rooms they would all sleep better. They walked the two blocks to the hotel, checked in, and stowed their duffels. Seth rented a golf cart at the front desk and they rode three blocks to the Fenix Beach Bar for a late lunch. The streets and buildings looked like the Mexico of old, nothing like the modern, glitzy, resort city of Cancun, just 8 miles across the Bahia de Mujeres. The low-rise white stucco hotels and restaurants with their varnished hardwood doors, window frames, and balcony railings above, blended with native tile floors and the colorful Mexican accent tiles that served as moldings. They were a timeless contrast to the more modern hotels that had been built along the beaches. Isla Mujeres attracted Mexican tourists along with the more adventuresome Europeans and Americanos.

The boys settled in at a table under a thatched hut on the beach 30 yards from the water. They ordered lunch and kicked back with a foursome of ice cold Tecata cervezas. Their only interruption was the sound of Seth's cell phone chiming every ten minutes, and the constant swoosh of the gentle shore break. Toby marked the *GOFISH's* lat/lon position with each chime. The *GOFISH* had not deviated from its course or speed as it steadily moved along the coast of Cuba. There was nothing to do but enjoy the locally caught snapper, the vibrant beach scene, and the live music at the Fenix Beach Bar.

CHAPTER FIFTEEN

Seth was getting antsy, and John looked like he was going to nod off. The island band at Fenix was taking a break. The Huckins moved steadily westward. She was still at least three hours away from any possible landfall in Mexico. Toby and Dino had never been to Isla Mujeres, so Seth asked them if they were interested in seeing the ancient Mayan ruins at the south end of the island, or did they just want to take a nap? After being cooped up in a small plane all morning, they both opted to take a look around the six mile long by half-mile wide little island.

"Let's rent four mopeds at that place we passed near our hotel and ride out to the south end of the Island," said John.

They found the moped rental business on their way back to the hotel, Jose Maria's Rentadora. After getting checked out, the boys took off south following the road that ran along the west side of the airport runway. They pulled off the road at an overlook and surveyed the Garrafon reef, which was close to shore. There were several large dive catamarans from Cancun tied up to mooring balls and over a hundred snorkelers swam over the reef. The reef was breathtaking.

Dino said, "Are there any deeper reefs nearby to scuba dive on?"

"There's a series of reefs off the southern tip of the island in 25 to 75 feet of water. We dove on those reefs the last time we were here and speared some large grouper under the bottom ledges," replied John.

"Let's get out to the ruins," said Toby.

The boys jumped back on their mopeds and raced to the ruins, like 20 year olds. They might be growing old, but there was no chance of them growing up.

Not much was left of the ruins; the last couple of hurricanes had nearly flattened the small temple of the Mayan god of fertility, Ixchal. The southern point of the island was beautiful, though. There was a stone lighthouse there to help the local fisherman navigate home, and a landscaped park, called "The

Cliff of Dawn", overlooking the edge of a precipice where a 60 foot cliff fell into the sea and rocks below. They walked out to the edge and Seth and John pointed out the reefs where they had spearfished years ago. While following the road back north along the east side of the island, they stopped at a much larger Mayan ruin, built on the highest ground on the island. This one was also a temple to the same god, Ixchal. It was in better shape and had been incorporated into a large stone mansion built by the famous Carib Pirate, Muchada.

Seth said, "This mansion was later the headquarters of a wealthy French slave broker who supplied slaves to the sugar plantations in the New World. As old Robert E. would've said, 'The French ... there's no end to those pricks!'"

The last stop was the Turtle Farm, privately funded by a wealthy island resident. There, turtles were raised and released back into the wild to keep them from becoming extinct. Turtles were an important source of food on Isla Mujeres, and each year thousands of turtles were slaughtered by the natives when they came ashore to lay their eggs. The farm's employees and local volunteers gathered the eggs and took them to the farm. The farm nurtured the hatchlings and released them back to the sea.

The boys ran the mopeds back to town, avoiding the dangerous potholes and speed bumps called "topes". After dropping off their scooters they rode back to their hotel in their golf cart. They commandeered a poolside table with an umbrella by the hotel pool and ordered four cold ones. Toby started to plot the Huckins lat/lon positions that they missed while they were sight-seeing. When finished he said, "There's been no change in course or speed. I would have thought that they'd start angling north or south a bit, depending on where they're heading."

Seth said, "Maybe they're trying to get out of the north flowing current and are headed for Cancun or the Caymans. In another hour, they'll have to turn one way or the other, unless they're going into Holbox Island or Chiquila on the mainland."

"Where's Holbox Island? I've never even heard of it." said Toby.

"It's an exclusive tourist island about 42 miles from here by air. I drove up there from Cancun a few years back, to Chiquila, with Billy, Bobby Thompson, and Ricky Whirley. We were fishing for snook and tarpon around Contoy Island and staying at a hotel back in Cancun. Bobby heard it was remote and interesting. It is truly in the middle of nowhere. There's only one road in and out to Chiquila. You can only get to Holbox Island by a small plane or boat. There are about 30 small boutique hotels on the island, catering to wealthy Americans and Europeans who like low rise, quiet, and privacy. The island is famous for its large pink flamingo population, the opportunity to swim with 40 foot whale sharks, and a nearby fresh water spring that passing pirates used. There are no cars on Holbox's sand roads, just golf carts, mopeds, or bicycles. Chiquila, which is 8 miles away, supports a large local panga fishing fleet and has some services for commercial fishing boats. I almost died at Yalahau, the pirate's spring. It means 'eye in the water' in Mayan."

"What do you mean almost died?" asked Toby. "What happened?"

"We took a guided panga from Chiquila and looked around Holbox. Then we ran, about 25 minutes, across to Yalahau Lagoon and the spring on the Mexican mainland. It was low tide, so we couldn't get the panga to the long dock that juts out into the shallow lagoon. We had to wade to the dock which has five steps coming up out of the water. We climbed up the steps, put our flip-flops back on, and followed the boardwalk and trail thru the mangroves to the spring. The center of the spring is a super luminescent blue, where it flows up from far below. From there the spring flows, crystal clear and cold, into the Gulf of Mexico. On our way back to the panga the wind started to blow, and a fast moving thunder storm approached. I was leading and we decided to try and outrun the storm, back towards Chiquila, before it hit us. I started down the stairs and my foot slipped on the algae covered step. I went straight up in the air and landed, all crumpled up, on my back on the stairs. At that exact moment a lightning bolt hit the water between us and the panga. It was deafening and everyone's hair frizzed out and stood up on end. Bobby said, 'If you hadn't slipped, Seth, you would have stepped in the water and been electrocuted.' We decided to wait the storm out under the mangroves back on dry land."

John said, "Maybe it's a good thing Bobby couldn't make this trip, something always seems happen when he's around."

"I don't think he has anything to do with it, other than he just can't sit still."

An hour later, Toby said, "The Huckins has slowed down to about 9 knots, and it's still on the same course. It looks like they're going into Holbox."

Seth said. "They can only anchor in the lee off of Holbox because there is dockage there only for the ferry boat. But Chiquila has a small man-made harbor that can dock ten or twelve boats the size of the Huckins. They have diesel fuel, an ice plant, and a seafood processing plant. There is also an old marine railway and some repair sheds. The streets are just dirt and I remember a couple of dusty looking bars."

"Is there an airport close-by?" asked John.

"I recall seeing a sand and grass landing strip when we toured the island. I think most of the tourists get to Holbox on a jumper flight from Cancun. Look it up on your cell phone."

John looked it up on Google and said, "Listen to this. They have a small FBO, 24/7 aircraft mechanics shop, and fuel. It's an Aerosaab base, with 24 hour security. The 2100 foot runway is marked with hundreds of conch shells painted white."

"Let's wait and make sure that they dock in Chiquila overnight, and then we'll fly over to Holbox in the morning. It will only take us 30 or 40 minutes. We can rent a panga to get us over to Chiquila or take the ferry."

Forty-five minutes later Toby said, "The GOFISH has stopped moving, your phone has stopped chiming, and their position is static."

"OK, let's go out for dinner and be on deck at 7:00 a.m. tomorrow to check out the Huckins position and have breakfast. If she doesn't move by 9:00 a.m., we'll fly to Holbox. If she moves we'll track her awhile and try to figure out where she's headed."

Seth picked the Casa Rolandi restaurant for dinner. It was a fifteen minute golf cart ride, around some canals and over a little bridge, on the west side of the island. He remembered it as having a great view across the water of Cancun all lit up, plus great seafood. They all started off with a Mojito made with *Partida* Tequila. Seth and John had the Caribbean lobster. Dino and Toby had the sea bass. The food, drinks, and the atmosphere were all superb. They were in high spirits and looked forward to closing in on the boat thieves the next day. The dinner check came as they all had a forkful of a delicious slice of Tres Leche cake.

As they left, Dino looked across the room and said, "Y'all go ahead. I see somebody at the bar that looks interesting."

Seth said, "OK Dino, but be in good shape and be at the coffee shop in the hotel at 7:00 in the morning."

Toby, John, and Seth returned to the Plaza Alemendros and called it a night. For once, Seth's phone was silent.

***

The three amigos sat in the Alemendros coffee bar drinking café con leche while they waited for their breakfast order. Seth looked at his watch, it was 6:50. The question was … where is Dino? Seth knocked on Dino's door as he walked past his room on his way to the coffee shop, but didn't get a response. At precisely 7:00 Dino walked through the door and sat down at the table.

"About time, and you need to wipe that shit-eatin' grin off your face," laughed Toby.

Dino's face got red, and he said, "It's precisely 7:00, give me a fucking break."

John Harvey smiled and said, "Speaking of fucking, let's hear about it."

"A gentleman never reveals the physical information. But, she's from Chicago, vacationing down here with some girlfriends for a week. She's an operating room PA. She's the tall Polish blond who was watching us from the bar during dinner. Her name is Selenka Stupentaket."

"My place or yours?" said Seth.

"We heard you knock. I brought her back here in a taxi last night."

"You should have invited her to breakfast," said Seth.

"I did, but she said she'd be too embarrassed sitting around with all you old dogs leering at her. You might see her in St. Petersburg … she wants to fly down and visit me."

175

"Love at first sight," said Toby laughing.

"More like lust at first sight," said John, cracking up.

"Not to change the subject, but my phone hasn't chimed for twelve hours. Order some breakfast Dino, we need to get our butts in gear."

Seth checked them out of the hotel and arranged for a cab to the airport. Forty-five minutes later they were in the air flying over the north part of Cancun and Puerto Juarez, where the Isla Mujeres Ferry is based. The huge hotels along the sugar white beaches of Cancun shone like crown jewels in the morning sun. But in minutes, they were flying over the uninhabited desolate scrub jungle that covered the Yucatan peninsula. A single road reached out to the west towards Merida. Seth knew from his trip to Chiquila, years before, that you had to travel approximately 75 kilometers west on that road to reach the only road north which was another 80 kilometers from Chiquila. By plane, the trip was a shorter 70 kilometers as the crow flies. In less than a half an hour, they were over Holbox Island. Seth's phone had not yet chimed, so they followed the last known position to the man-made harbor in Chiquila eight miles away.

Toby spotted *GOFISH,* which was tied up inside the breakwater, with the help of his Steiner binoculars. John radioed the FBO for permission to land and buzzed the runway to get a better look. The runway was sand and grass, outlined by large conch shells, painted white, as advertised. "Bienvenido" was spelled out with the conch shells on the runway approach.

John made a smooth three-point landing and taxied to the neatly kept FBO and parked the Lance. It had a thatched roof and the native wood frame was varnished. A customs officer appeared, checked the crew's passports and visas, and then stamped them through. The FBO's manager personally welcomed them to Holbox.

"Bienvenido, Senors, welcome to our island. What can I do for you?"

"We need a hotel downtown for a couple of nights and a couple of golf carts," said Seth.

"No problem, Senor. My cousin, Ramon, owns the Hotel Amaite on the beach downtown. He has family rooms with two double beds to a room, a restaurant, and a beach bar. I can send you down there in a golf cart taxi, and Ramon will have two rooms and the golf carts waiting for you."

"How much are the rooms and the golf carts?"

"$106 USD per night for the room and $45 USD per day for the cart."

"Sounds reasonable, let's do it."

"OK, Senor ... anything else?"

John spoke up, "I'd like to have you top the fuel off in the Lance, Senor."

"No problem, did you know we have an airplane mechanic's shop here, too?"

"I did ... we Googled you before we flew over here from Isla Mujeres."

The six passenger gasoline-powered golf cart taxi arrived and the boys were on their way to downtown Holbox. The island was all sand roads and thatched roof houses, shops, restaurants, and hotels. Everything was well kept, neat, and brightly painted. It was obvious that the natives were proud of their little island. Chickens, goats, island dogs, and iguanas shared the sandy streets with the tourists and friendly islanders.

Ramon was waiting for them in the lobby of the Amaite Hotel. He helped get them checked in and sent their duffel bags and fishing rods up to their rooms. He asked Seth if there was anything else he could get for them.

"We need to rent a panga for a couple of days so we can fish the local waters."

"There are many excellent fishing guides who have pangas and bonefish skiffs. I would be glad to arrange it for you."

"Well, we are all professional fisherman and we would prefer to explore and fish these waters on our own. Can we just charter a bare boat?"

"The hotel has two pangas to pick-up guests at odd hours and to get supplies, and I have a personal one that I'm always too busy to use. How about $100 USD a day for my personal boat, and you return it with a full tank of gasoline?"

"More than fair, Ramon. Can you show me where you tie it up after we have some lunch at your restaurant?"

"It will be my pleasure, Senor."

After a nice lunch, washed down with cold Pacifico cervezas, the crew put their fishing poles in their golf carts and followed Ramon over to the ferry dock. His panga was docked at a small dock, a hundred feet from the large ferry dock. A small sign read, *Amaite Hotel-Private*. Ramon checked Dino out on the Suzuki four-stroke 70hp outboard. Then the boys cast off and idled east towards the bird preserve. As soon as Ramon's cart disappeared from sight, Dino put the panga up on a plane and headed south for Chiquila. They tied up behind the Flamingo Bar on the eastern side of town, among 50 or so commercial fishing pangas. A short walk to the large fountain in the center of town and gave them a vantage point. There were two large open air restaurant/bars across the main street from the fish processing plant and ice plant, both plants fronted on the man-made harbor on the west side of the quay. The ferry docked along the east side of the main rock jetty/quay. Seth did not want Randy Garrett or Peter Petcock to see him. He had on a large straw hat that he bought in the hotel's gift shop, and his sunglasses. He sent Dino and Toby out onto the quay to check the Huckins out.

While they did that, Seth and John skirted around the fish plant to check out the marine railroad on the western side of the little harbor. Being in the marine business, Seth liked to check out other marine repair facilities. Plus, he had a hunch. He and John walked through the back yard of the facility which was littered with old junked wooden shrimp boats, rotting hulls, decks, wheel houses, and piles of rusting engine blocks. One 60 foot hull that was lying on its side caught his eye. As Seth got closer he saw a large, ragged hole in the hull. The old boat had several stove-in planks where it had gone up on a reef. He walked around and looked at its weathered transom. It was almost completely covered by five foot weeds and leafy vines growing over it. Seth tilted his head to read the name … *Go Fish*, Houma, LA. He whispered, under his breath, *Fuckin'A*, and walked around to check out the listing wheelhouse. He could barely make out 563487 under a greenish coat of opaque algae. He motioned to John to come over and put a finger to his lips so he wouldn't speak.

"This is the original *GOFISH*," he whispered to John, as he took pictures of the transom and the wheelhouse with his cell phone. "Let's amble out front and take a look at the marine railway I saw from the air."

They walked around the west side of the shed and saw a 65 foot shrimp boat up on the railway getting its bottom prepped for painting. Two Mexicans in Tyvek suits and dust masks were working on the bottom with air powered sanders. Seth noted that, in the States, they would be wearing full face respirators. This boat was outside, but Seth saw that the rails continued inside the large rusting metal shed. The cable attached to the rail carriage under the boat ran into the shed, and disappeared into the darkness.

Seth shouted in John's ear over the din of the air powered sanders, "I'm going to take a look inside the shed. If anybody starts to walk in, take your hat off and intercept them. I'll be watching you from inside. Ask them how much they charge per foot for the railway and for bottom painting. Tell them you own two shrimp boats out of Houma, Louisiana."

John nodded and Seth slipped into the shed's darkness. Seth was comfortable with John at his back. John was 6'2"tall and weighed 215 lbs. He looked like John Wayne to these little Mexicans. He also had worked his way through the University of Florida's undergraduate school as a ranch foreman supervising migrant workers and spoke passable Spanish.

Seth's eyes quickly adjusted to the dark interior of the shed. There was about 75 feet of workspace from the overhead rollup door to the winch drum and motor. That workspace was empty now. Seth looked around and found a few pieces of stainless steel safety bow rail that could have come from the Huckins. There were piles of plywood cutoff pieces everywhere. The back wall was littered with empty cans of gray paint. Seth finally found what he was looking for. In a pile of cut up varnished teak, plywood, bulkheads and trim, he found *ABOUT TIME's* teak transom "name board". He blew off the dust and there were the gold leaf letters. He rooted around and found a pile of burlap sacks on a work bench. He put the name board in a sack and carried it to the overhead door. The two bottom sanders were still under the shrimp boat sanding up a storm. The only other humans in sight were some panga fisherman unloading their boats at an adjacent shallow water dock 150 feet away. Seth strode out of the shed opening, tapped John on the shoulder, and disappeared around the west side of the shed. They ducked behind *Go Fish* and Seth pulled the name board out of the bag and handed it to John.

John whistled softly and said, "Bingo, buddy!"

Seth had John hold up the name board while he took a quick picture of it next the original *Go Fish's* transom. He put it back in the burlap bag and stashed it under the tilted wheelhouse. Then he ambled out of the bone-yard with John in tow. They went back to the bar and waited for Dino and Toby to return.

"When I saw that railway and shed from the air this morning, I thought that might be where Randy and Peter stashed the Huckins to work on it. No wonder nobody could find the boat in Florida. They had a full week head start before Charley got back and found her gone. They already had her down here and were working on her in that shed."

"They probably knew about this place from their commercial fishing days."

"Absolutely, and they no doubt scouted it out and made arrangements beforehand. They knew that abandoned shrimp boat from Houma was back in that bone-yard."

Seth had heard his phone chime while he was in the shed, so he checked it. There was a new position indicated, but it was identical to the last one almost 24 hours ago.

Toby and Dino returned and Dino said, "They moved the boat to the fish plant dock and are almost finished taking on fish and ice right now. A fuel truck just showed up on the quay and it would be my guess that they'll fuel up next."

"How many pounds of fish did they take on Toby?" asked Seth.

"I'd guess 2000 to 2500 pounds of grouper and maybe 650 pounds of ice."

"Well, that will slow them down some if they leave tonight. I can't imagine they'd ice up and then not leave directly. I'm sure they'll run slower at night, anyhow, just for safety's sake. At any rate, we'd still catch up with them in the morning about half way back."

Seth filled Toby and Dino in on what they'd found in the marine railway's work shed.

Dino said, "You have to hand it to them. Their planning was certainly thorough. It's no wonder that the Coast Guard and Florida law enforcement couldn't find the Huckins. But there's more to it … like Seth says. The boat is uniquely suited for a high-speed three day round trip of eight hundred miles, in a boat that's disguised to look like a 9 knotter. It is operating in plain sight as a grouper digger that fishes around the Tortugas, which are only 70 miles from Key West. They don't fish; they buy their grouper here so it looks like they've had an average three day trip around the Tortugas. So, let's cut to the chase."

Seth smiled and said, "You're right Dino; the question is, how and where do they get the cocaine on board? ...... Certainly not in Chiquila. The docks here are busy with tourists coming and going every hour on the ferry ... There are other commercial fishing boats from the United States tied up in the harbor. The Mexican government has a customs and enforcement presence here. There are two to three hundred local panga fishermen that move in and out of this harbor every day. There are eyes everywhere. The drug cartels are not strong in Quintana Roo Province, because of Cancun. Cancun and Cabo San Lucas, on the Pacific coast, are the Mexican Government's cash cows. They can't afford to have any bad publicity in these locales."

"So we remain vigilant," said John.

"What's the plan, Seth?" asked Toby.

"Maybe they will meet another boat offshore on their way back to Key West? But, that would be unlikely, the way the Coast Guard and DEA track boats offshore with their sophisticated radar and drones. I mean, the cartels are using submarines to avoid that. I say we go back to Holbox and track them on the Spot[3]. We know it's still working, and at 9 knots it will take them at least two hours to get over the horizon."

CHAPTER SIXTEEN

Captain Tony sat up on the flybridge with a cup of coffee and smiled to himself. His dinner date with Molly had gone better than he could have ever imagined. Molly was a tall, cool, blue-eyed, beautifully proportioned blonde. She was an oddity in Marsh Harbor where she had grown up in the prominent, socially connected Mallory family. The Mallorys had lived in the Abacos since 1776 when crown loyalists Francis and Mary Mallory fled Charleston, South Carolina, a few days ahead of the hangman's noose. The Mallorys had tried their hand at farming on Great Abaco, but had failed to produce anything more than subsistence crops. Francis finally turned to the ship wrecking trade to support his growing family. He joined with other exiles on Great Abaco in moving the aids to navigation lights, on occasion, to produce shipwrecks which they subsequently salvaged. This enabled him to not only support his family, but made him a wealthy man. His ancestors now had large real estate holdings and investments in hotels, shops, and marinas. Molly looked nothing like the rest of the swarthy, dark haired, Mallory clan, and she revealed to Tony that she had been adopted at birth from the United States. Many of Abaco's original settlers had married their cousins out of necessity. Later generations began to suffer from the inevitable birth defects. Adopting children would add strength to their gene pool for the future.

They met for cocktails at the Jib Room, in the Harbor View Marina, near her house. Molly had on a little black dress that accentuated her pale white skin, and pair of rattan wedge sandals. Her hair was pulled back in a French twist and a pair of diamond earrings sparkled in her pierced earlobes. The scoop neck of her dress showed a faint trace of the very top of a hidden tattoo on her left breast. Captain Tony figured Molly to be in the early forties, making him about twenty years her senior. Tony's Italian heritage made him look ten years younger than his creaky bones made him feel. He was still trim and tanned because of his profession. Tony had black, curly, hair and people told him he looked like Tony Bennett. But he didn't dress like the east coast Italians. He wore a knee length pair of tan Tommy Bahama linen shorts, a Brighton belt, and a jet black collared Polo shirt. His leather Sperry billfish shoes were right out of the box and worn sockless. Tony had changed the heavy gold chain that he usually wore around his neck, to a thin link gold chain he bought from Molly earlier that day. He looked over at Molly sitting, ramrod straight, across from him sipping her vodka martini. She absolutely took his breath away.

Tony asked, "Did you go to school in the States, Molly?"

"No, actually I went to high school here and in Nassau. I graduated college in London."

"How did you like it over there?"

"I enjoyed traveling in Europe on holiday, but the weather in London was horrid."

"Have you lived here since graduating?"

"Yes."

"Why?"

She cocked her head, smiled, and said, "I'm an island girl."

They drove in Tony's golf cart from the Jib Room to Wally's, a quaint restaurant in a remodeled house. Wally's had very good food and an intimate atmosphere that was lacking at the other restaurants on the island. They talked about Tony's childhood in Fort Lauderdale, his love of big game fishing, and about Molly's love of the beautiful island that she grew up on. Tony started to realize that this woman, who looked so unapproachable because of her natural beauty, had just been waiting for someone to ask her to dinner. She had the same hopes and dreams, and wants and needs, as everyone else.

Tony asked her, "Have you ever been married or had a serious boyfriend?"

"Well, no ... I haven't been married. And there really isn't anyone on the island that I'm interested in romantically. The few men that I've met and liked ... always wanted me to go back to the States or Europe with them. I hope someone comes along someday, but until then I'm happy to live my life here with my family and work in the family business. What about you, Tony, do you have somebody, somewhere?"

"Actually, I don't. Living the life of a professional captain, I take the boat wherever the owner wants it to be. I live on his schedule, not mine. The trade off is, I get to big game fish all around the world, and that's always been my passion. I've met some interesting women along the way ... but just in passing."

"I grew up being told that the marlin fishing is very good here in the spring and early summer."

"That's true, but there are places its better, like Tortola in the Virgin Islands in August, and Cairns, Australia, on the Great Barrier Reef in January."

"We both seem to be living our lives on our own terms, but in some ways it can be a lonely existence."

"You're preaching to the choir, Molly, but ... we must want it this way or we would do something different."

Dinner was winding down; the local strawberry grouper had been cooked to perfection and topped with an excellent Nassau Royale rum reduction sauce. A bottle of Rombauer Chardonnay stood empty in its chiller. After dinner they enjoyed a glass of Vin Santo, a delicious Italian dessert wine that tasted like fresh apricots and caramel. Tony had already paid the check, and they were one table from being the last diners in the restaurant.

"Can I give you a lift home Molly? I've certainly enjoyed your company tonight."

"Sure, that would be great. I only live a few blocks from here."

They got in Tony's golf cart and made their way past the Boat Harbor Marina entrance and around the inner lagoon to Johnny Cake Lane. The breeze from the moving cart felt good on their faces in the heat of the tropical night.

"It's the little yellow cottage on the next corner."

Tony pulled into a small shell parking area between some queen palms and turned out the cart's lights.

Molly turned and said, "Thank you for the wonderful dinner and conversation, Tony. How about a nightcap?"

"I was hoping you'd ask."

He followed her inside. She turned on a light in the living room, and motioned for him to sit on the couch.

"A glass of red wine?"

"That would be perfect."

She opened the wine and poured it into two large Pinot Noir glasses.

"This is a California coastal Pinot called Meomi. I discovered it on my last buying trip to Miami. From what I've learned about your taste so far, I'm betting you'll like it."

She handed Tony his glass as she sat down next to him, then raised her glass towards him and said, "To kindred spirits passing in the night."

They clinked their glasses and took a sip of the sultry Pinot Noir.

"It's very, very, good", said Tony. "But I'm more attracted to you than the wine."

"Then let's do something about it," said Molly in a husky voice.

Tony set his wine on the end table and she did the same. They fell together in an embrace and kissed passionately. Tony slowly removed her little black dress as she tried to unbuckle his belt. In less than four minutes they lay naked in each other's arms. They caressed and kissed each other hungrily, unleashing their mutually pent-up passion. Tony admired the bottlenose dolphin that was leaping across Molly's generous left breast. The tip of its dorsal fin was what Tony had noticed earlier. Tony finally rolled on top and slowly entered the tunnel of love.

As in many first encounters, it was over to soon for both of them. So Tony joined her in her bedroom for Act Two, where she led him through her wants and needs, then her hopes and dreams, towards a most positive conclusion.

He finally pulled out … in his golf cart, as the sun came up over the Sea of Abaco. Everything seemed brighter in Marsh Harbor that morning as he rode back to Boat Harbor, and he looked forward to seeing more of Molly Mallory's indescribable body. Her dilemma was much the same as a rich heiress faces: Does a man want me for who I really am, or for my money … or, in Molly's case, exceptional beauty?

Tony finished his coffee and went down below to start calling his list of fuel docks and marinas for the second time. He called The Conch Harbor fuel dock in Key West Bight and asked if the Hatteras 46, *TAR BABY* had been there for fuel or dockage. The answer was still negative. He called A&B next and Travis answered the phone.

"This is Travis, how may I help you?"

"Travis, this is Captain Jack. Did Seth Stone and *TAR BABY* make it down there yet?"

"Why, yes sir, he did. He came in a couple days ago. They're out fishing right now; can I take a message or your phone number?"

"No, no, I'm an old friend from Miami … I heard he was fishing in the Keys and I want to come down and fish with him now that I know he's in Key West. I want it to be a surprise, though. We go way back. I talked to your dock master Don at the end of last week and he hadn't seen him yet. It'll be a nice surprise."

"OK, Captain Jack, my lips are sealed; I'll see you later in the week."

Tony called Giorgio in St. Petersburg, "Seth Stone and *TAR BABY* are fishing out of A&B Marina in Key West Bight. They didn't get there until this week."

"Good work, Tony. I'll tell Luigi. Everybody will be happy to hear you found him."

"OK, kiddo, I'm standing by if you need me."

Giorgio called Luigi, "Captain Tony located Seth Stone. His boat is docked at A&B Marina in Key West Bight. He arrived early this week. Tony said one of the dock masters told him they were out fishing today."

"Great. Mr. C is gonna be glad we finally tracked him down."

Luigi was happy he could finally tell that to No Nose. In the meantime, Cadillac had called and filled Luigi in on the Russian purge. Luigi got a "thumbs up" message from Cadillac Tuesday night, but he didn't get the details until Cadillac's call this morning. He had a sit-down scheduled with John, after dinner this evening, at the Golf View house. Now he could give him two positive reports.

***

Luigi watched the garage door close behind him in his rear view mirror, and he exited the car. Anthony followed him up to the second floor rear porch where No Nose sat smoking his customary after dinner Cuban cigar in his favorite chair at the end of the porch. The fans and the air conditioning were running full blast on this hot and humid July evening.

"Buonasera, John."

"Ciao, Luigi. Get yourself one of those Gran Corona Montecristo cigars and sit down. It was a fucking scorcher on the golf course today. I played eighteen holes this morning and was soaking wet from the third hole on."

"How'd ya hit it?"

"Thought I was going to break 90 today, but it was so hot I ran out of gas and double bogeyed the last two holes."

"You play with Sammy 'White Shoes', and the two Federal Judges?"

"Yeah, my regular foursome."

"Well, I got good news for you on two fronts."

"Tell me about Key West first. I know you told me last night it went well, but now tell me how well."

"Cadillac called this mornin' and gave me the blow by blow. We crushed it. All the Russians that we planned to ice were iced and deep-sixed. The Barber interrogated one of the Russian lieutenants, before he was wasted, and he coughed up a list of all the key payoff recipients and the amounts they got each week. The damage to civilians was almost nothin', only the mistress of Nikolay Rutan, the kapo, was killed. We had to shoot both of them in the condo where they shacked up every day. One of our men fractured his collar bone and ribs inna brawl with one of the Russian enforcers. Our Miami doctor gave him first aid in Key West, and operated on him this mornin' in Miami."

"I knew sending the doc would be smart."

"Right. The airplanes took off with 12 of our men early Tuesday evenin' with no problem. The use of the Tasers and Cadillac's idea to dress our men as tourists, bums, and cable installation installers was fuckin' brilliant. He even outfitted the four vans with ladders, tools, and magnetic signs that read KEYS CABLE. When they set-up outside residential and business locations nobody got wise to the set up. Our two Jupiter 38's were equipped with fishin' rods when they dumped the Russians bodies, wrapped in anchor chain, offshore in deep water. Those boats left Tuesday night and anchored off Key Largo for the night. On their way they threw all the weapons, tools, magnetic signs, ladders, and other shit overboard."

"So, everyone got out OK?"

"Yeah, the Jupiters arrived safely in Miami this mornin'. The four Escalades were driven to a rented house on Summerland Key, in case law enforcement put roadblocks on Highway 1. Four of our men will drive the cars up to Miami with the Sunday tourist traffic that leaves after the weekend. Only Vito The Dancer and the hooker are left in Key West. They'll fly out commercially on Sunday. Cadillac and Pete the Barber came up with a great plan, and they executed it perfect. There coulda been law enforcement hassles, but it didn't happen. The toughest part was Yuly … first they had to flush him out, and then they had to finish him and his two bodyguards off."

"Tell me how they got Yuly," said No Nose with anticipation.

"They planted a cell phone bomb on his boat behind his house the night before. On purge day there was no movement at Yuly's house until just before dark. Then one of his body guards lowered Yuly's boat in the water, test started it, and went back into the house. Pete was sure that Yuly knew somethin' was up. He had the Russian kapo's and the three lieutenant's cell phones on a table in the Geiger Key house. Yuly kept callin' throughout the afternoon and Pete just let 'em ring. So … now Pete had Yuly's cell phone number. Cadillac and Pete hoped Yuly would try to leave by boat and try to figure the whole thing out from another place. Then they'd just blow the boat up."

"So, what happened?"

"Pete had Vito watchin' Yuly's house from a two story condo 50 yards away, plus Frog Eyes was anchored in a Jupiter 38 next to Wisteria Island. They couldn't wait all fuckin' night, so Pete called Yuly on Nikolay Rutan's cell phone. When Yuly answered he said, '*Come Stai? -- Y'all will sleep with the fish tonight!*' Then he had Frog Eyes shoot a couple grenades thru the second story windows in the back of Yuly's house. The house immediately caught on fire and smoke started pourin' out. Ten minutes later the bodyguards came out the back door draggin' what Frog Eyes thought was Yuly between them. Frog Eyes waited until the boat started to get up on plane and triggered the bomb. It was a gasoline powered boat so you can imagine the fuckin' explosion. The Jupiter pulled anchor and idled around the back side of Sunset Island and took off for Key Largo. The other Jupiter was waitin' down near Fort Zachary to intercept Yuly in case the bomb didn't go off. Vito could see most of this from the condo and he got ready to ditch his weapons. When he got down to the first floor he heard a helicopter fly over and start to land. He went back upstairs to check it out, and saw Yuly come out of the front door of his house, in a big fuckin' cloud of smoke, with a scuba tank and mask on. Yuly tossed off the mask and tank on his way to the helicopter, and threw a suitcase in the back of the helicopter as he got in. Vito nailed the helicopter with his grenade launcher just as it lifted off. The bodyguards must have made a dummy with pillows and clothes to decoy us away from the house. Only 'cause Cadillac planted Vito on the island ... kept Yuly from gettin' away."

"You couldn't write any better stuff for a Hollywood movie, Luigi. Our men did a great job. History has taught us that the element of surprise is paramount to success in any war. The Russians never knew what fucking hit them."

"So far, the news reports today in the *Key West Citizen* and the *Miami Herald* only report: *A suspicious fire at the Sunset Island house of a wealthy Russian businessman and a fiery helicopter crash at the same location resulted in two deaths on Tuesday night. The victim's charred remains have yet to be identified*, and, *According to an eyewitness, a gasoline pleasure boat exploded in Key West Harbor Tuesday night, throwing a fireball 150 feet in the air. The boat and any remains have not been recovered at this time.*"

"Well, Luigi, I don't think we've left any loose ends down there. It will take the police some time just to figure out who died. They might figure that incendiary grenades started the house fire and shot the helicopter down. But, all those weapons are at the bottom of the Atlantic. Did Vito get rid of his weapons?"

"Yeah, Cadillac says he threw them in the Northwest Channel. All he has is a Glock 9mm, but he has a concealed carry permit. He'll ditch that gun before he gets to the airport."

"We'll have Cadillac up for a summit in the next week or two to plan our re-entry into the Key West drug market. They'll be a lot of addicts driving up to Key Largo, Homestead, and Miami until we're open for business down there again. I'd still like to find out who was supplying them. I want to know if our cartel was back-dooring us. Now, tell me about our other project."

"Captain Tony found Seth Stone. He showed up at A&B Marina earlier this week. He's fishin' with five or six of his friends on his Hatteras 46."

"I don't think there's going to be a lot of heat on us in Key West, unless we're missing something. Keep in touch with our news room informer at the *Key West Citizen*. Same with our police contacts. Why don't you get Vito to hang out around A&B and figure out where Seth goes when he's not fishing? I remember lots of restaurants and cafes right in that area. Maybe we can use some of the muscle Cadillac left at Summerland Key. We need to snatch him if we can. But, we don't want to hurt him. He's no good to us dead."

"I'll call Cadillac first thing in the mornin', John, and I'll keep you posted."

Wall to Wall knew Seth Stone had just become his number one priority. John was smiling and lighting a second Gran Corona as Luigi walked out.

CHAPTER SEVENTEEN

Seth and the crew rode back to the Amaite Hotel in their golf carts. They took a swim, had a cold one at the beach bar, and took showers before having a leisurely dinner at the hotel. Seth decided to stay at the hotel and wait for the Huckins to move. They could track it during dinner, or track it up in one of the rooms if it happened later that night. The panga was ten minutes away by golf cart if needed. The Huckins had to run eight and a half miles from Chiquila to reach the northwest end of Holbox. The opening out into the Gulf of Mexico between Holbox and the mainland was less than four miles across.

Seth arranged for a private table set on the pier in front of the Amaite Hotel that jutted out into the Gulf. He figured they could talk more freely and wouldn't arouse suspicion while they marked the chart when necessary.

After they were seated Toby laughed, "There isn't anybody eating inside this restaurant that doesn't think we're two gay couples from Atlanta."

Dino gave him a hard look, "Watch it big boy, or I'll unleash my dolphin buddy on you."

They cracked up laughing remembering Dino's horny friend at Hawks Cay. Dinner started with an appetizer of Octopus Pulpos ceviche for the table, followed by three grilled lobsters with tomato/mozzarella salads, and one local grilled snook with avocado and corn for John. The crew tried the Bohemia Lager cerveza at the recommendation of Ramon, who bought them a round. Hands down, it was the best Mexican cerveza they'd ever tasted.

As the sun was setting Dino remarked, "This Island is truly a little slice of Heaven. I'd like to come back here and dive with the whale sharks. This would be a great alternative dive trip after Cozumel or Providenciales. The whale shark, at 50 feet long, is the largest fish that swims in the ocean. They have no teeth, just ingest plankton, and they're docile. You can actually ride them.

When I take over the dive business in Key Largo, I'm going to market a trip here."

At that moment, Seth's sat-phone chimed. The crew sat up straight like they'd been zapped with a cattle prod.

"They're moving," said Seth. "Take it easy guys, let's enjoy our dinner. It will be almost an hour until the Huckins gets to the northwest end of the island, by that time it will be getting pitch dark. Then we'll go up to John's and my room, and see what happens."

Seth signed the bill and they all retired to his oceanfront room on the second floor. They lounged, but gathered around Toby and the chart every ten minutes when Seth's phone chimed.

After five more chimes, the Huckins rounded the point and headed on a more easterly course. Toby went out on the veranda with his binoculars, and saw the lit up Huckins motor by.

Seth said, "About five or six chimes from now, we might see a change in speed or she might just chug all night."

On the sixth chime the Huckins stopped dead in the water and turned around. The seventh chime revealed they were back tracking at double their previous speed. Their course was westerly about four miles offshore at 18 knots. Toby went back out on the veranda and swept the horizon with his binoculars.

After ten minutes he said, "I don't see them anywhere, they must be running with no lights."

The sat-phone chimed again and Seth said, "They'll be beam to us in another ten minutes. There's not enough moonlight tonight to see them with their lights out. Let's head for the panga. John, put the night scope, GPS, flashlight, and the sat-phone in duffel. Toby, take the chart and that red penlight. We'll wear our darkest shorts and t-shirts."

"Let's take our pistols, Seth," said Dino. "Better safe than sorry."

"OK, change your clothes and let's vamoose!"

After a brisk cart ride to the ferry dock, they jumped into Ramon's panga, started the outboard, and took off in the direction of the Huckins with their running lights off. Seth's phone chimed. He put the newest position in the back-lighted handheld GPS as a waypoint and hit "go to". The Huckins was northwest of them and moving at about the same speed. Seth expanded the parameters of his GPS chart a couple of clicks and said, "It looks like they're headed to Yalahau, the pirate's spring."

John said, "Didn't you say the water over there was really shallow?"

"I did, but remember, the Huckins can run in two and a half feet of water."

"Slow down, John, I can see the Huckins through the night scope ... it looks like ... they're slowing down," said Dino.

"We have to be careful," whispered Seth. "They have a Flir night vision system, but they will be looking forward. The four-stroke Suzuki will help us because it's so quiet at idle."

They slowed down, extinguished the phone and GPS back-lights, and idled after the Huckins. Seth put his phone on vibrate.

"She's stopping just short of the long dock with the stairs that go down into the water," said Dino, still using the night scope. "There are four men in the water next to the dock and they're pushing an inflatable towards the port side of the Huckins. The Huckins crew is manning the dinghy davit ... and they're winching a box the size of a medium suitcase aboard ... Someone is looking inside the box with a small red penlight. One of the GOFISH crew is handing a large suitcase down into the inflatable, I can see a red light down there ... now it's all dark and everyone in the water is moving back towards the dock, and the Huckins appears to be slowly backing away."

"Idle south, John. Let's give them a wide berth," said Seth.

John eased the boat away from the Huckins anticipated path.

A few minutes later Dino said, "I can see the Huckins, but it's her stern. She must be running almost due north."

"Keep watching her through the night scope, Dino, until you can't see her anymore," said Seth.

Five minutes later, Dino said, "I've lost her, when do you think she'll put her lights back on?"

"When she gets back on course and out where she should have been if she hadn't detoured. We can track her on the GPS now and calculate her speed."

John asked, "Can I speed up some now?"

"Yes, but take us over to Chiquila instead. Just aim for those lights to the southwest. Turn on our running lights and take her up to 15 knots. We'll get there in about 20 minutes."

"You're going back for the name board aren't you?"

"Yep, it's an irrefutable piece of evidence that I'd like to hand to Charley. There are enough other pieces of the Huckins strewn around that repair shed to prove it was altered there, and if the U.S. authorities need our testimony for the trial, I'll gladly testify. But, I seriously doubt the Mexican Government would do anything about it on their end."

"I'll testify too, Seth," said John.

They tied up the panga behind the Flamingo Bar and walked to the town fountain. Dino and Toby waited on a bench, while Seth and John walked west down the dimly lit street behind the fish plant. When they got to the boatyard's unfenced bone-yard, they ducked behind the wreckage of the old *Go Fish*. John was the lookout as Seth scrambled under the old wheel house and came out with the burlap bag. As he started back around the relic, he met John coming from the other direction.

"Two people are walking this way from town," whispered John.

They both hunkered down in the dark next to the wheel house until the two Mexicans went by, weaving and laughing as they walked. After they passed and disappeared into the night, he and John walked slowly back to the town square and collected Dino and Toby.

"I was worried when those two drunks came out of the bar and started towards you," said Toby.

"Yeah, John was looking out and saw them, so we just hid out behind the *Go Fish*."

The boat ride back went smoothly, and the hand held GPS put them right back at the Amaite dock. They rode the carts back to the hotel and went up to Seth's room.

"Dino would you mind going down to the bar and bringing up four of those beers we had with dinner? We're going to update the chart and see just where *GOFISH* is and how fast she's moving."

"Four Bohemia Lagers coming up, Chief," said Dino as he bounced out of the room.

"Just charge them to the room," Seth called after him.

Toby had the chart updated in a few minutes. It was clear that Randy and Peter were running a reciprocal course back to Key West. John got his cell phone out and calculated her speed from the time and distance information.

"They're traveling at 11 knots. If they maintain that speed for the next nine hours they will be about 120 miles from here. Holbox is 404 miles from Key West. Tomorrow morning dawn is at 6:44, and they will be about 275 miles from Key West. Even with the extra weight of 2500 to 3000 pounds of fish and ice, they can still cruise at 24 or 25 knots. That will put them back in Key West before 6:00 at night. They might go slower, so they can come in after the 8:16 sunset when it's getting dark."

"Let's talk about what we saw tonight," said Seth, as Dino entered the room with four ice cold Bohemia cervezas. "Dino saw them load a suitcase or crate of what we think are cocaine bricks. I did a little research back when I was considering taking on this investigation … A packaged brick is usually one kilo; its dimensions are 4"x 8"x 2"thick. A kilo weighs 2.2 pounds, so 50 kilos weighs 110 pounds. 50 bricks stacked and shrink wrapped measure approximately 16"x 20"x 10" thick, plus the shrink wrap. It could easily fit into a mid-sized metal suitcase. The approximate street value of 50 kilos is eight to ten million dollars, depending on how it's cut up. Wholesale, it's worth at least 1 million to 1.5 million dollars. Their cost from a Mexican cartel is probably, $500,000 to $600,000. I would guess Randy and Peter started with small buys and have reinvested the majority of their profits into larger and larger buys. You can see that you wouldn't have to smuggle cocaine for very long before you could make millions of dollars on each trip. They could easily smuggle 150 -200 kilos once their bankroll is big enough. They probably think they can smuggle for a year or two and continue to buy rental property for cash. Once they have enough cash flow from the houses and a few million in the bank, they'll sink the Huckins and retire to the good life."

"You've got it, Seth," said Toby. "Everybody in Chiquila thinks they chug in for fuel and top their catch off with the inexpensive Mexican grouper, then chug back to Key West. The people on Stock Island think they motor out to the Tortugas for a three or four day trip at 8 knots and motor back in with a couple thousand pounds of grouper every time . It's a hell of a cover."

"I think they'll use the 32 foot power cat to take the drugs off the Huckins before they get too near to Key West," said Dino. "A few miles from Sand Key Light would make sense. There's lots of pleasure boat traffic out there with the reef and sportfishing boats coming back in late in the day. It wouldn't take but a minute to transfer a 110 lb. crate or suitcase into that big cuddy cabin in the power cat."

Seth concluded the discussion. "Unless they speed up way before daylight, I don't think we have to rush out of here first thing in the morning. We can catch them in an hour and a half or so in the Lance. I'm going to call Gene on my sat-phone and fill him in so he can alert Billy Ray in the morning. Why don't you guys go down to the bar? I'll join you for a night cap in a few minutes."

The crew filed out and Seth headed for the veranda with his sat-phone and dialed Gene in Key West.

"Hey, Gene, its Seth … Can you talk?"

"Yeah, I just got back from dinner; Freddy and Billy are headed over to Schooner's for a nightcap."

Seth ran through the events of the day and earlier that evening. Gene took notes for his call to Billy Ray in the morning.

"I'm sure they have at least 50 kilos of cocaine on board. We think they'll transfer it to their 32 foot World Power Cat, before they dock or unload their fish at Bama or Fishbusterz Seafood. It depends on what time they dock. The earliest they can be there is 5:30 in the afternoon. But we'll be back and tracking them from the trawler in Safe Harbor way before that."

"I'll call Billy Ray at 8:00 in the morning, and get him ready to set up a task force. Do you want us to go fishing tomorrow?"

"How about going fishing for a half a day. Don't go further than the "Ups and Downs", so you can maintain cell phone contact with Billy Ray. The way I see it going down now is, the sheriff needs two unmarked center console fishing boats to watch the World Cat come out from the Sugarloaf Key canal, record the pickup, and then shadow it back to the Jamaica Lane house. Billy Ray and the DEA can make the drug pinch there simultaneously with the Huckins arrest. Depending on the time of day, the *GOFISH* will either go to Bama or Fishbusterz to unload the fish, or dock at Old Island Boatyard and unload the fish in the morning. Billy Ray can make the arrest wherever they land. I would suggest he get the Coast Guard to back him up just in case something goes wrong, and Randy and Peter try to make a run for it in the Huckins. The sheriff probably will have some helicopters standing by anyhow."

"Sounds like a good plan, Seth. You'd have made a good cop!"

"Bullshit, I've learned it all from you, Gene."

"Keep me posted with the Huckins locations."

"Ok, Gene, I'll start in the morning, so we should be back at the trawler at Safe Harbor around noon. Make sure there's a van at the FBO for us."

"We'll drop one off in the morning."

Seth went down to the bar and joined the boys for a nightcap.

"Well, I got Gene up to speed. He's going to get Billy Ray to organize a task force for tomorrow's *GOFISH* homecoming."

"It ought to be a doozy," said John.

"Have the fish been biting?" asked Toby.

"You know, I never asked," laughed Seth.

***

The Lance rolled down the Holbox Island runway and lifted off at 8:30 a.m., the next morning. The day was clear and bright and John flew low along the 42 mile long island to give the crew a final look at its unspoiled beauty. As they turned east towards the Keys, they flew over a pod of feeding whale sharks at the far end of the island. Toby snapped a few pictures with his telephoto for Dino. The whale sharks looked enormous even from the air, their jet black backs were speckled with white dots.

"No doubt about it, I'll be back," said Dino.

"Where's the Huckins, Toby?" asked Seth.

"Just about where we figured. They're about 230 miles from Key West right now. They've increased their speed to 24 knots."

"What are we making, John?"

"We've climbed to 2500 feet and our speed is 130 knots."

"So we should pass over them in an hour and a half or so."

"And we'll be in Key West in about two hours and forty-five minutes. I'll call in on the ADIZ flight permit with the sat-phone when we're close to the Tortugas; it looks like we're going to fly over it."

Seth called Gene on his sat-phone and he picked up on the third ring.

"Good morning, Seth."

"Hey, Gene, we're in the air, the Huckins ran all night at 11 knots and picked up the pace right at first light. They've cranked up to 24 knots. We should intercept them in about an hour and a half. Their ETA at Stock Island will be around 6:00 or 6:30 tonight, they'll likely slow down to 8 knots for the last 10 miles. It's during that chug period that we think they'll transfer the cocaine to the World Cat. We should be at the FBO in Key West around 11:30 this morning."

"Our crew dropped a van at the FBO at 6:30 a.m. and shoved off from A&B at 7:15. We ran out past the reef and started fishing. I called Billy Ray at 8:00 and let Freddy take the helm. Billy Ray's already putting a task force together--State Police, Marine Patrol, DEA, Coast Guard, and a couple of officers from the Florida Department of Law Enforcement. They're going to throw the book at these guys. He was full of questions, so I was glad I took notes last night. I explained the identity switch on the *ABOUT TIME* and the *GOFISH* and told him what you'd seen at the marine railway in Chiquila. I pointed out the high speed and range of the disguised Huckins 62. He understands the brilliant cover they created by buying and bringing back over two thousand pounds of Mexican grouper from a three or four day trip as if they had been fishing around the Tortugas. I also clued him in to the fake identities of Peter Petcock and Randy Garrett. He already had the alias info, and their residence and boat information from the ownership checks he did for us earlier. He said he'd have two unmarked, high speed sportfishing boats deployed with his men, trolling in that ten mile stretch where they always slow down and chug into Stock Island. Both boats will have telephoto/infrared video cameras along with their outriggers and fishing rods. He'll also have a Flir-night vision equipped chase boat and a helicopter standing by to track the World Cat if it takes a detour. He's really stoked about the possibility of a 50 kilo cocaine bust. He figures that these guys are the new source supplying the Russian Mafia in Key West. Billy Ray it heard from the DEA about a month ago, that there was an underworld rumor circulating that the Tampa Mafia was planning on retaliating because the Russians were not buying cocaine from them anymore. And, Billy Ray wants me to give him hour by hour lat/lon positions."

"No problem, I'll text you every hour. You catch any fish?"

"Yesterday, we landed some big dolphin and Billy caught a sailfish. So far, we've nailed two nice dolphin today. As soon as I gave the helm to Freddy, he found a weed line to troll down, and we picked up a bull and a cow. It was a fire drill since I was on the phone. Freddy steered away from the weed line, put *TAR* BABY on autopilot, and left the engines in gear at idle. Then he came down off the bridge and reeled in the cow."

"Sounds like you're having some fun, Gene. Come in early and bring the filets over to the trawler. We can grill them or eat at the Hogfish depending what's going down. I do have a favor to ask of Billy Ray. Ask him if he can clear me to inspect the Huckins once he makes the arrests. I feel I owe Charley, who made this all possible, an accurate preliminary assessment of the repair and refurbishment cost estimates as soon as possible. I'll wear latex gloves and whatever else I have to."

"I'll ask, but I'm sure it won't be a problem. Remember, text me every hour with the lat/lon. I'll be glad when these perps are collared. I'll see you soon, buddy. Oops ... *Fish On!*"

An hour later Toby spotted the Huckins moving east/northeast. Dino was sound asleep and Seth texted Gene the lat/lon position, and a message telling him that they had visual contact and the Huckins was still running at 24 knots. With that done, Seth decided to grab an hour's rest. He asked Toby to wake him in an hour, or right away if anything changed, and took off his headset.

Dino shook Seth awake, saying, "Toby told me to wake you. You've been asleep for an hour."

Seth put his headset back on and said, "Thanks, Dino, I've got to text Gene the Huckin's position. He's relaying it to Billy Ray and the task force."

"Toby, please give me the Huckin's latest lat/lon position."

Toby wrote it down and handed it and the sat-phone back to him. Seth texted it to Gene.

Soon, the Dry Tortugas came into view. They flew over Loggerhead Key and the lighthouse, affording them a spectacular view of the imposing red brick structure of Fort Jefferson. They all had fond memories of cruises to the Dry Tortugas that they had shared with friends and family. Next they passed Rebecca Shoals and its light tower. Seth remembered that it was a course marker in the annual S.O.R.C.--St. Petersburg to Fort Lauderdale sailboat race. He'd sailed around it many times. It's also where the south flowing Gulf Stream takes a left turn and then travels up the east coast of Florida. Straight ahead of them loomed a group of small, coral rock and mangrove laden islands called the Marquesas. The islands and the shallow Quicksands to the west were used during World War II as a practice bombing range. From an airplane you can still see the pock marks left in the bottom by the bombs. It was also the final resting place of the Spanish Treasure Galleon, *ATOCHA*, salvaged by Mel Fisher. Boca Grande Channel and the surrounding islands are excellent fishing areas for large permit and snook. Seth had fished the Marquesas just a year ago, and seeing them brought the memory back ……….. *He had trailered his 17' Scout flats boat down to Key West for a long weekend with Annie Hart. They stayed on Stock Island in a gated townhouse, on the Overseas Highway, across from the Key West Golf Club. Seth launched his boat four miles away on Key West at the Caroline Street ramp and drove it around to A&B in the Bight. Don, the dock master, had let him tie it up on the walkway ramp for $50 a day. Seth tipped Don $50. The slip included a pass for the A&B parking lot. He parked the empty trailer in the townhouse parking lot. They fished all morning, then swam in the pool, and relaxed at the townhouse during the late afternoon. After sunset they drove down and bar-hopped and dined in Key West. The first day they caught a few tarpon in the channel off the north point of Fleming Key. The second day they got up early and ran out through the Lakes Passage and Boca Grande Key, to the*

Marquesas. They fished with the tide in Boca Grande Channel and over the patch reefs and rocks south of Mooney Harbor. They were rewarded with two keeper snook and four 20-plus pound permit that they caught, out of a school, over a wreck. They released the last permit about mid-day, then eased the Scout up into secluded, mangrove ringed, Mooney Harbor and anchored for lunch and a swim in eight feet of water. There were no other boats in the anchorage, so Annie immediately took off her bikini and dove in. She didn't have to coax Seth to join her. After a few minutes of frolicking in the water, Annie climbed up the folding, gull-wing ladder that Seth had snapped in the Scout's transom bracket. She pulled a 16 oz. bottle of water out of the cooler, took a drink, and poured the rest over her head. The fresh water ran down over her voluptuous body as she toweled off. Seth came up the ladder, also "au natural", a moment later. Annie laughed and said, "I thought I got your red-necked friend quieted down last night, but I guess I was wrong." Seth just smiled, he couldn't hide it. She tossed him a bottle of water and the beach towel, then said, "Rinse off and come up here in the bow, Big'un." Annie spread a dry beach towel out on the forward casting deck and lay down on her back. The water felt cold running down Seth's body as he poured the bottled water over his head. As he toweled off in the small skiff he thought, 'Where's a guy's fighting chair when he really needs it?' The cold water cooled his head, but not his desire, and as he moved forward, Annie slowly spread her legs. Fishing was over for the day......

One of the things Seth liked about Annie was that she initiated a lot of their sexual encounters. The difference was that, even though they both respected each other, the sex was purely lust on both their parts. It had never been as satisfying as sex with love. After Lisa died Seth was lonely. He threw himself into his work to fill the void. As time passed, he spent more and more of his free time fishing and hunting with his friends. He enjoyed all the one and two week trips that might be extended a few days if the fishing was really good. After all, he was retired. Then, he finally started to enjoy the company of other women. He would give up the other women, but he did not want to give up his other interests. This whole commitment thing with Lori was far from over in his mind, and it just wasn't about sex. He also needed to find out if Lori expected marriage. Even with a pre-nup, Seth had no interest in that and he guessed she probably didn't either. He needed to spend more time with Lori to see if she would freely give him that time with his buddies. She had two children who lived out of town, and he knew how she'd feel when the grandbabies came along. He would give her the space she needed. But he had to be certain she would reciprocate. He wasn't going to rush into anything.

"I guess that kind of makes my mind up for right now," said Seth aloud, to no one but himself, forgetting that he had a live headset on.

"About what," asked John, snapping Seth back into reality.

"Aaaah …… yeah … Ah, let's have lunch at the Hogfish Bar when we get back instead of making sandwiches."

"Good call, Seth," said Dino, who had just been relieved of sandwich-making duty.

Fifteen minutes later, the Lance landed at Key West Airport.

***

Vito Pelosi missed the first ferry off Sunset Island Thursday morning because he got involved with Angela in a little early morning "Choo Choo La La", as she called it. He woke up with the sun, but when he rolled over there she was, sleepy-eyed, tousled, and naked. It was just too tempting, and he succumbed. He missed the ferry by five minutes, but what the fuck, it was worth it. He arrived at A&B an hour later armed with two pictures of Seth Stone and a description of the black hulled Hatteras 46, *TAR BABY*. The boat was gone. So, Vito spent the rest of that morning casing the bars and restaurants where he could sit in the shade, and watch the A&B docks. The Galleon Dock Deli was a good choice, as was The Conch Republic, and Alonzo's Oyster Bar's outdoor seating at A&B. He settled on The Galleon pool Tiki Bar overlooking Key West Harbor. *TAR BABY* had to run past it on the way back into Key West Bight, and he could also check out the bikini talent at the adjacent pool. Vito kept on the move from bar to bar so he wouldn't look conspicuous, but he was back at the Galleon Tiki Bar when *TAR BABY* went by about 1:00 p.m. Vito hurried around to The Galleon's Dock Deli and watched the crew dock her. There were only three men aboard. They tied her up and cleaned some fish on a large white cutting board on the transom gunnel. Finally they hosed the boat down and walked off the boat and down the dock carrying a large white Yeti cooler. None of the three men were Seth

Stone. Vito hustled out to the end of Front Street in time to see them drive out of the A&B parking lot in a white rental minivan. He wrote down the license number to report to Cadillac. Vito decided to go back to Sunset for some rest and food, and then come back at 5:00 p.m. to watch the boat that evening.

He picked up a copy of the *Key West Citizen* on the way back to the Westin's ferry dock. He read the front page as he waited for the ferry, which ran every half hour. Today's front page story read; *Dead Sunset Island Resident has suspected Russian Mafia ties …Yuly Yankovich was purported by the Key West Police to be an associate of Vladimir Ivankof, the head of the Russian Mafia, who is headquartered in Brighton Beach, New York City, in the Borough of Brooklyn. Yankovich was identified, by the Key West Police Chief Detective Troy Baggett, as the head of their Key West operation. Mr. Yankovich, described in an article Wednesday as "A wealthy Russian businessman", is also a suspected victim of a fiery helicopter crash in front of his burning Sunset Island home, last Tuesday. Neither he nor the pilot of the helicopter has been positively identified by authorities as yet.*

The local news page carried this story; *Eleven Russians living in Key West were reported missing to police on Wednesday by friends or their landlords. Their landlords reported in each case that all their belongings were left behind. In eight of the cases, the visas or green cards that had been presented to the landlords were found to be fictitious. The other three were admitted on J-1 visas, but their student status could not be confirmed. All these cases have been turned over to The U.S. Immigration Service for investigation.*

It seemed to Vito that the purge had worked to perfection. There were ten more victims who might be reported missing or found dead in the coming days, but Vito knew that Cadillac, and the other bosses, would be pleased with the press coverage so far. Vito vowed to himself that he would not miss the 5:00 o'clock ferry tonight.

CHAPTER EIGHTEEN

Seth hopped out of the van in front of the Hogfish Bar, went in, and ordered four hogfish sandwiches to go. He jumped back in the waiting van and Dino drove through Safe Harbor Marina's electronic gate. They drove down narrow Tropicana Avenue behind the warehouses and parked the van behind the Grand Banks 42 foot trawler at the western end of the marina.

"I'll walk back and pick up the sandwiches," said Dino as Seth handed him a $100 bill.

"Throw my duffel in the trawler, will you John?" asked Dino.

Toby carried his duffel, camera, and the tracking chart into the trawler and started to update the chart. Seth went inside right behind Toby, with his duffel and *ABOUT TIME's* name board in the burlap bag. He sat down and called Gene.

"Nice and cool in here, huh, Toby?" said Seth while he waited for Gene to pick up.

"Must be 95 degrees outside," answered Toby.

"Hey, Gene, time for the 1:00 o'clock lat/lon," said Seth while motioning to Toby to give him the numbers.

Seth gave the coordinates to Gene and added, "They're about a 120 miles from Stock Island and 50 miles from the Dry Tortugas ...... Yeah, it's getting closer to game time ... where are you? ...... OK, just approaching the Key West Bight ... and you've got some dolphin and a wahoo to clean? Great, we'll see you in about an hour or so. We're getting some take out from the Hogfish for lunch, stop there if you haven't had lunch already. Remember to bring the fresh fish out here for dinner, OK?"

"Toby, they caught two big dolphin and a 35 pound wahoo."

"I can already taste it. Fresh wahoo lightly grilled … wahoooo!"

Seth's cell phone rang just as Dino came aboard with the hogfish sandwiches. He sat down at the dinette table and answered his phone.

"It's Gene again," he mouthed to John who was sitting across from him.

"Yeah, Gene, I can go over as soon as you get here. You want me to get you guys' sandwiches? …… Ok, I'll see you in 20 minutes."

"The sheriff wants to meet with us over at his headquarters. He wants to be briefed on our entire investigation. It's a smart move. Things are going to happen awfully fast when this whole thing goes down. Dino, could you please call the bartender and order three more hogfish sandwiches, I'll go and get them when I finish mine."

Seth walked along the dock, past the row of craftsman shops and Joe O'Donald's indoor rainforest, and picked up the sandwiches at the bar. Going back, he ran into Hugh Spinner who lived in the houseboat next to Charley's slip. Seth had met Hugh about six summers ago when he and Lisa spent a month in Charley's slip. Hugh was an original "Mother Lode" member, certified by the Spanish silver coin he wore around his neck and his gold dive flag ring. Hugh had captained the salvage tug boat, was their best welder, and was a crack diver to boot. Now he operated the seaweed removal company contracted to keep Key West's beaches clean. That seemed like a simple business, but it was not. Many hundreds of thousands of dollars were invested in large mechanized equipment to quickly remove and load the seaweed, early in the morning, into trucks that drove it to a transfer station.

"Hey, Seth, what are you doing here?"

"Well I'll be … how are you, Hugh? I'm down here fishing with some friends and Charley let them use his slip. My Hatteras is down at A&B."

"I wondered whose boat it was, I just got back from visiting my farm up in Georgia. Has the fishing been any good?"

"Just dolphin and wahoo, but we did reel in a sailfish the other day."

"Not bad … well, I've got to run down west of the Seven Mile Bridge to my work yard and fix some of our equipment that broke down while I was gone. But, I'm going back up to the farm for a week during deer season, right after Fantasy Fest. Hey, ain't that something about Charley's Huckins being stolen?"

"Yeah, I've been keeping a weather eye out for it. It's nice to see you, Hugh."

"Same here, Seth."

Seth wanted to tell him about GOFISH. Hugh was one of the good guys, but one slip up could screw up the whole operation. Somebody who worked down at Hugh's shop might be okay in Hugh's eyes, but he might also have a connection with one of the GOFISH's crew. It was better not to tell anyone anything, until it was over. Seth got the sandwiches back to the boat just as Gene pulled in with Freddy and Billy.

"Hey guys, I've got your lunch, come on in the trawler and the boys will fill you in on Mexico." They went inside and everybody started talking at once. Seth gave Gene his sandwich and said, "Sit down and take your time, I'll get the latest position from Toby and we'll hand deliver it to Billy Ray."

"Gene took one bite and said, "Let's go now, I'll get a can of Diet Coke and eat this in the car. The Sheriff's Compound is only five minutes from here."

Seth got the lat/lon numbers from Toby, and he and Gene headed out the door to drive to headquarters. Seth put the burlap bag in the back seat.

"What's in the bag, Seth?"

"My trump card, if I need it."

"What do you think they'll do, Seth, come in before or after dark?"

"I've been thinking about it. If they come in right before sunset there will still be a lot of boat traffic around Sand Key Light. Boats will be coming in from fishing all day, and boats that were diving on the reef will be headed in every direction. The yellowtail fisherman will be setting up to night fish, and the large sunset cruise boats will be sailing out in the ship's channel. The Coast Guard's radar will be cluttered. It would be the safest time to make a low speed exchange of a 110 lb. crate. Then they can chug in as night falls, dock the boat, plug it in to shore power, and move it tomorrow morning to unload the grouper. After dark, two boats meeting up even for a moment would definitely draw the Coast Guard's attention."

"Makes sense to me, too," answered Gene.

They drove west on the Overseas Highway for about two minutes, then turned right on College Road at the end of the golf course. Two minutes later Seth said, "Wow, this facility is huge, and look at Mount Trashmore back there."

"It's almost brand new … just park in that lot in front of the four story office building. This complex houses the county jail, the court, and all the county administrative offices. The buildings are all 11 feet off the ground and were built to be hurricane proof. All the employees park under the buildings."

"Is that marina part of it?"

"No, that's Sunset Marina and Condos, but the sheriff does dock his enforcement boats there. He also has three helicopters and an airplane at his disposal."

"Wow … it's a bigger operation than I thought it would be."

"Wait until you see the Sheriff's Animal Farm."

"An animal farm?"

"Yeah," laughed Gene. "It started with some abandoned African tortoises and expanded to toucans, turkeys, horses, pythons, llamas, and whatever else you can imagine. The grounds keeper has turned it into a park and the inmates keep it clean and help care for the animals. They open it to the public twice a month."

Seth and Gene went through the metal detectors and continued to the reception desk. They were ushered into the sheriff's private office. Billy Ray, tall, stout, and affable looking, sat behind a large desk. Two other men sat off to his left. One was large, heavily muscled, and had a shaved head. He wore black paratrooper pants and a black t-shirt that read **SWAT** on the front. The other man was tall and trim, wore a dress shirt and tie, and reminded Seth of a local TV news anchorman. Billy Ray rose and shook Gene's and Seth's hands, and acknowledged each by name. Seth handed Billy Ray the Huckin's latest lat/lon position. The sheriff walked over to a chart pinned upon a large corkboard on the wall and put another red topped pin in it at the new location.

He turned back and said, "Gentlemen, meet Andy Arnold, our SWAT commander, and Douglas Roberts, our general counsel. We need you to brief us before we arrest the two perpetrators and their crew. Seth, will you explain how your investigation got started, and what you've done to get us this far? Doug will tape it."

Seth launched into a brief synopsis of how Charley Blevins had come to him, after being frustrated by the unsuccessful efforts of his insurance company and the authorities, and asked him to find his stolen boat. He outlined the checkered pasts and recent business problems of Randy Garrett and Peter Petcock. He pointed out the trusted access that Randy and Peter had to the Huckins after working for Charley for 15 years. He explained how they set up Charley's dock box with the Adiant security system. Seth stressed that their disappearance from St. Petersburg, at the exact same time the Huckins disappeared, was no coincidence. It was all part of a clever plan. He shared the theory that the boat had to be altered to elude all of the agencies that were searching for it. Seth laid out the pair's marine expertise and multiple skill-sets. He added the premise that the Huckins was probably being used in the drug trade. Then he tied that premise into Garrett's and Petcock's early backgrounds, their need for money and anonymity, and the financial mess that they left behind in St. Petersburg. He briefed them on the airplane "box-frame" search method, and the unsuccessful physical inspection of all the Key's marinas. He also filled them in on the use of the Spot[3] GPS, and the physical inspection that he and Dino made of the Huckins on Stock Island from the water at night. Next he recounted the tracking by plane to Mexico and the fresh fish loading in Chiquila. He described the marine railway and work shed at Chiquila, and recited what he and John Harvey had found there. Seth showed them dated pictures of the real *Go Fish*, in Chiquila, on his cell phone. He chronicled the double-back and the night scope visual surveillance at Yalahau Spring. He assured them that the perps loaded at least 50 kilos of cocaine, in exchange for a large suitcase full of money. Then, he informed them about the two go-fast boats tied up at the Jamaica Lane house on Sugarloaf Key, and his theory that they would transfer a hundred plus pounds of cocaine to the 32' World Cat, before they came through the reef at Stock Island. Seth was sure the cocaine was going to Jamaica Lane. He enumerated how they had built themselves an elaborate alibi by coming back after a three or four day trip with two to three thousand pounds of grouper, which is average for that trip duration, in local waters. The fact was they were traveling over eight hundred miles round-trip to and from Mexico at high speed. Further, the profit they made on the purchased grouper only covered half the fuel, and they never wetted a line on their own. Seth reiterated that the Huckins speed and altered appearance allowed them to operate without suspicion. He related the facts gathered concerning their present depraved lifestyle and hefty real estate investments. He concluded that they were definitely smuggling something.

When Seth was finished he asked, "Any questions, gentlemen?"

Douglas Roberts said, "Great briefing, Mr. Stone, but the cocaine smuggling and vessel identification issues both seem circumstantial at this point, and there is no hard evidence that the vessel is *ABOUT TIME*. I think we might have enough probable cause to get a warrant. But that's up to a Judge."

"Well, you're right, Mr. Roberts, it is circumstantial at this time. I am hoping that you can get that warrant, and have your surveillance boats get some daytime or infrared video of the cocaine transfer. But the beauty of this situation is this … we should be able to arrest them for stealing the Huckins on what we have now. Two eyewitnesses have already identified it, hands on, and … I have this!"

Seth handed the burlap bag to Billy Ray and sat back down next to Gene. Billy Ray looked into the bag, reached in, and pulled out *ABOUT TIME's* 48 inch long teak and gold leaf name board out. He looked at Seth and grinned ear to ear.

"Well, Doug, I guess with this and a deposition from Seth, we should be able to get our warrants. If not, we'll let the Coast Guard and DEA interdict. But, Doug … I'd like us to make this whole bust ourselves, and have the Coast Guard back us up if they run, OK?"

"Yes, Sir."

"Okay then, you haul ass over to Judicial and get a Judge to issue those warrants. Seth, send a copy of the bone-yard pictures to Doug's phone … here's his number. Doug, take a picture of this name board with your cell phone. I'm not letting it out of my sight."

Douglas left and Billy Ray said, "Seth, you would have made a hell of a detective."

"Thanks, Billy Ray, but Gene is the real man."

Billy Ray added, "We pay Doug a handsome salary to challenge the legality of what we do here, and it pays off in the long run. He made his bones right out of Stetson Law School, defending one of the famous "Steinhatchee Seven" defendants. So, Doug's been on both sides of the line of scrimmage.

Andy Arnold spoke up, "I have two questions for you, Seth: Did you see any display of weapons while you've had the Huckins under surveillance, and how many perps are we dealing with on the Huckins?"

"No Andy, none at all, but my guess is with the large amounts of cash they were carrying and the value of the drugs, they're probably heavily armed. The answer to the second question is; we counted six total, five males and a salad girl."

"That would be my guess about the weapons, as well. We have plenty of firepower planned for them in any case."

"Gene told me you think they'll come in right before dark, say around 8:30 to 9:00." said Billy Ray. We've also had the Jamaica Lane house staked out since Gene's last phone call. There are two male perps there along with some occasional female visitors. The latest reports state that apparently they're not into wearing swimsuits."

Seth chuckled, and said, "I think Peter and Randy will take advantage of all the boat traffic around Sand Key and fading light to offload the cocaine. Remember, in sight of Key West they'll travel at only 8 or 9 knots. Then they'll go to their dock on Stock Island, at the Old Island Boatyard, and plan on offloading the fish the next morning. The cocaine will get to the Sugarloaf house about the same time. I don't think they'll run the World Cat faster than 20 miles an hour, so they don't attract any attention. The Huckins will slow down sometime soon if that's their plan."

Billy Ray responded, "Let me tell you the task force plan. We're five minutes from their dock. Andy and his twelve man Swat team will be deployed as they start up the channel. We will have an armored assault vehicle on site. Two of our police boats will make a high speed approach toward the GOFISH dock from the Oceanside Marina channel, where they'll be hiding. Our decoy sportfishing/video boats will close on the channel, and stand-by. We will have two plainclothes detectives stationed at both Bama Seafood and Fishbusterz. If they decide to unload, we will drive the SWAT team around. It will take five minutes. I have a helicopter standing by and the Coast Guard will be backing us up, but they will be invisible to the Huckins. I have a second assault group ready to swoop down on the Jamaica Lane house, but they are out of sight and will only move on my command. Two DEA agents will be assisting them, but we will retain control of the cocaine. I included them as a professional courtesy. I have two unmarked police boats that will block that canal when the arrest begins. The head of the FDLE, Dwight Mileman, sent us two of his best forensic men to do the post-mortem on the Huckins."

"Sounds like you've got it together, Billy Ray," said Gene.

"Well, there is one more thing. I have four deputies who will secure the quays north and south of Old Island Boatyard and a couple more up on the east side above Safe Harbor Marina. I thought, because your crew has been so involved in making this arrest possible, you could secure Safe Harbor in case the Huckins runs over there or someone tries to swim across after the fireworks start. Stranger things have happened in a task force operation. I plan on putting one of my men over there with you. You can say no if you want to."

"What are the ground rules?" asked Gene.

"If the perp is armed, yell *Stop or I'll shoot!* If he doesn't stop, shoot him. If he isn't armed and runs, try to detain him."

"We all have CCW permits and handguns."

"In that case if you feel physically threatened, shoot. Now all seven of you "Geezers", as Gene likes to call you, are deputized, and I have official T-shirts for you that say SHERIFF on the front and back and official ball caps. Gene, you can get the sizes you need out of those two boxes in the corner. I'm also going to equip each of you with a walkie-talkie, so you can hear the whole operation go down. If you need help, state your position and situation. Go back to Safe Harbor Marina now and keep sending the lat/lons, but please send them every 20 minutes. That way we'll know when they slow down. My decoy boats are all trolling on the Huckins rhumb line. I'll send Deputy Sheriff Bill Pearce over to your trawler in about an hour to help deploy y'all."

"Sheriff, please don't let that name board out of your sight. I want to give it to Charley Blevin's when this is all over."

"I'll make sure you get it, Seth. It's the least I can do."

Seth and Gene rode back to Safe Harbor.

"Well, Deputy Johnson, You are now officially unretired from law enforcement for the rest of today."

"I told you you'd make a good cop, Deputy Stone. The guys are going to go fucking bananas when we get back to the trawler with the t-shirts and hats."

"So far, it's been all good," laughed Seth.

"I liked the way you reasoned with their lawyer. Billy Ray saw your point of view, too. The name board, and pictures of the 'real' *Go Fish* in that Mexican bone-yard, clinched the deal."

"Well Robert's is not your typical prosecutor. Usually they want their cases to be open and shut. If they didn't take a chance, now and then, a lot more bad guys would still be on the street. I guess they think a loss will ruin their future political aspirations. Like Billy Ray said, Doug has worked both sides of the street. I'll think he'll get us both the robbery and the drug trafficking warrants."

They opened the gate with their remote at the Marina and drove down the palm tree lined gravel lane along the south seawall, boats moored on the left, warehouse back doors to the right. They rounded the corner at the metal sculpture garden, and pulled in behind *SIRENA*. Once aboard, Seth and Gene struggled into the main salon with two armfuls of t-shirts, hats, and police radios.

Seth instructed Toby to text a new position update to Billy Ray, every 20 minutes. Toby texted him *GOFISH's* current position and set his cell phone alarm app. to beep at 20 minute intervals. With that done, Seth filled the crew in on the meeting with Billy Ray. They were all impressed by the thoroughness of the task force plan, and pumped to be included in the bust.

The Geezers broke into cheers when Seth announced they were deputized for the operation. "Don't put on the t-shirts and hats until the Huckins docks across the channel or down at Bama's. We don't want to compromise the surprise element of this arrest. I suspect the sheriff included us as a gesture of courtesy and respect for our efforts, we should take it seriously. From this point on, carry your concealed weapon until the operation is over. If something goes awry during the arrest and someone tries to escape through Safe Harbor Marina, communicate on your police radio and remember Billy Ray's rules of engagement. More importantly, don't do anything to endanger your life."

The crew settled in to wait for the Huckins to show. John, Billy, and Freddy caught a quick nap; Dino took a walk around the marina. Seth, Gene, and Toby set up a little command central and continued to mark the chart and text Billy Ray every 20 minutes. At 4:00 p.m., the Huckins was about 40 miles from Stock Island. Ten minutes later the Huckins cut her speed. Toby figured they were moving at 7 knots and were 38 miles from Stock Island. Sunset was at 8:15. It looked like the Huckins would go past Sand Key Light just before sunset and would arrive at her dock just as darkness fell. All the current information was texted to Billy Ray.

Seth observed, "It looks like we've got this one figured. Low light will work to the task force's advantage as far as setting up their men for the arrest at the dock. There isn't much cover around the west side quays since Joe O'Donald razed all the warehouses and trees for development. The darkness could help the World Cat if they suspect anything, but if the Huckins runs they're still toast because of the Spot[3]. The Coast Guard helicopters would run them down, but that might prove interesting if the Huckins is well armed. See if you can find Dino, Gene, and let's organize an early dinner, say grilled dolphin and whatever vegetables we have in the freezer. We should plan on being on deck by 7:00."

Dinner was served, and the whole crew hovered around Toby and the chart. Seth listened to the weather report up on the bridge. It was like it was every day in July: scattered thunder storms, 95⁰, humidity 98%, wind 5 to10 knots from the S.E. Seth could see some big towering cumulus clouds building out over the Atlantic, but that happened every afternoon this time of the year. An unmarked car pulled in the parking lot and a man dressed in dark green fatigues got out. He spotted *SIRENA'S* transom and headed for the trawler. Seth climbed down from the flybridge to intercept him.

"Bill Pearce? C'mon aboard."

The large, pleasant looking, ruddy complected, man stepped aboard.

"Are you Seth Stone?"

"That's me."

"Billy Ray wants you to know the two suspects at the Jamaica Lane house have been checking the oil, and test starting the outboards on the World Cat. They pulled out fifteen minutes ago headed for Hawk Channel."

"Looks like things are falling into place, come on inside deputy," said Seth as he opened the salon door. "Gentlemen, this is Deputy Bill Pearce."

Deputy Pearce met the whole crew, went over the guidelines again, and handed out a map of Safe Haven Marina to each crewmember with his position assignment noted.

"Keep this in your pocket, along with these red pencil lights, in case you need to alert any of your crew to a problem. Now that I've met you guys, I don't really understand why they call you the 'Geezers'. You don't look that old to me."

John told the deputy, "We're always the oldest guys at the billfish tournaments. We don't have any hired mates and or hired captains; we're just a bunch of old grouper diggers from Florida's left coast."

Gene added, "At one of the marlin tournaments we won a couple of years ago, we overheard one of the two young mates on the second place boat say to the other during the trophy presentation, 'The fucking Geezers got us!' That incident and remark was repeated many times, by many people, and the name stuck. We all thought it was hilarious."

Toby interrupted, "The Huckins is about seven miles from Sand Key light."

Deputy Pearce said, "Let's get ready, gentlemen!"

The crew all put on their official green hats and t-shirts with the word SHERIFF emblazoned on the front and back in reflective gold.

Seth went up on the flybridge, turned on the radar, and adjusted the range to 12 miles. There was a lot of boat traffic coming in off the Atlantic, and the ship's channel was cluttered with boats sailing out of Key West Harbor. He couldn't figure out exactly where the Huckins was, but he knew it was among ten or twelve vessels moving towards the Sand Key Light. He looked across the Safe Harbor Channel and saw the sun getting closer to the horizon. It wouldn't be long now. He held his hand up and counted the horizontal fingers he could fit between the sun and the horizon. Three fingers, which was about 45 minutes to sunset; his Submariner read 7:30 pm.

CHAPTER NINETEEN

At 8:15, Billy Ray called on his cell phone, "Seth, I wanted you to know they just made the cocaine switch. The World Cat came along side the Huckins and two of the crew lowered the crate into their fishing cockpit, using a couple of dock lines. My men got telephoto videos from two different angles. The decoy boats kept their outriggers out and caught a couple of dolphin while they were trolling at dusk. It looks like a little weather might blow in … soon."

"Catching fish, you couldn't ask for a better cover. They don't suspect a thing, and 10-4 on that weather. I've been watching the clouds build out over the Gulf Stream. Maybe it will hold off for awhile. Deputy Pearce has us all organized, we'll deploy here when it gets a little darker."

The sun went down in its usual Key West blaze of glory, signaling its residents and guests that it was party time. Seth put his green and gold Sheriff's shirt on and adjusted his "one size fits all" hat.

Deputy Pearce pulled on his bullet proof vest. "OK, Geezers, its show time. I didn't want to deploy you until it was dark so we wouldn't worry the residents or restaurant guests. If anybody asks what's going on, just tell them it's a Homeland Security drill for the Power Plant. Ask them to stay inside the restaurant or on their boats until they see us leave. Now let's get out there and I'll run through a radio check with each one of you after we're in position. After that, no one talks on the radio unless it's an emergency. Plug the earpiece wire jack in the side of the radio, then put the earpiece in your ear, and you'll hear all the chatter from the task force across the channel. The task force leader is Andy Arnold, from the SWAT team. His code name is 'Big Dog'. Good luck, and let's go!"

Seth was assigned to the palm tree lined marina entrance road on the south side of the quay. He walked thru the metal sculpture park and down the backside of the metal warehouse that housed all of the craft shops. There were seven back doors and a few parked cars. He counted 20 boats moored, stern-to, along the south sea wall. He took up his position at the electronic gate, between two of the outboard queen palms that lined the narrow lane. He gazed out over the electric light-streaked water. Bama Seafood's quay was 350 feet south, and he could see a large slice of the Stock Island Channel to the southwest. The Key West power plant and its stacks were lit up and visible just south of Bama's seawall and buildings. The police radio crackled from time to time as the sheriff's task force assembled on the other side of the channel.

He tensed when he heard a message to Andy Arnold, the task force leader, "Big Dog, Big Dog, subject vessel *GOFISH*, entering the Stock Island Channel. ETA ten minutes."

"Big Dog copies, 10-4."

The hair stood up on the back of Seth's neck, the dragnet was closing and the arrests were minutes away. His heart raced, and he forced himself to breathe deeply to calm down. He strained his eyes, trying to see the approaching Huckins. First, he saw the green running light, then the wheelhouse lights and the steaming light. The boat glided through the water like a gray ghost, and then it was gone from his sight ... blocked by the buildings and trees. He could hear the Huckin's engines revving to turn and maneuver the boat towards its dock. Then everything went silent ...... Big Dog's voice exploded from his bullhorn.

"This is the Monroe County Sheriff's Department, you are under arrest! You are surrounded, put up your hands, and come ashore." A few shots rang out, and the crackle of gunfire filled the air.

Big Dog radioed, "Put the spotlights on them, Jackson, and shoot their VHF antennas down."

Seth could see the glare of the spotlights from his position. Three police boats, sirens blaring, blasted up the channel at top speed and closed in on the Huckins. Seth heard rapid gunfire and a helicopter beating overhead.

"Bring in the assault vehicle, Deputy Rogers, and return fire. They're shooting up our squad cars with their automatic weapons."

There was a barrage of larger caliber gunfire, and the shooting stopped.

"This is Big Dog ... they've got out the white flag boys ... cease fire and let them deploy their gangplank and walk off their boat. SWAT team members close in and cuff them ... Deputy Catlin, give me a perp head count."

"Big Dog, we've got four men and one very scared, hysterical woman in custody ... Two of the men have gunshot wounds."

"Deputy Jackson, get two ambulances down here for the wounded perps. Deputy Catlin, we're one perp short ... Take two men and search the boat."

"Deputy Derrick reports he hit one perp during the firefight ... He saw him fall overboard near the bow."

"This is Big Dog to the harbor police boats and helicopter, start searching the harbor for the missing male perp. Jackson, I need some divers over here, pronto. NOW HEAR THIS, NOW HEAR THIS! All shore-based backup, you are now on full alert."

The police boat's spotlights scanned the channel across the surface and the helicopter searched from above. Another police boat was sweeping the surface of the water with their spotlight between Seth and the Bama quay, to no avail. Seth could hear thunder to the south, and the wind was starting to pick up velocity as it was pulled into the approaching storm.

"Jackson, Big Dog here, have headquarters send over a paddy wagon to haul the perps we've got to the detention center ... They shot up these squad cars so badly I don't know if any of them are drivable. Try to get the wagon here before it starts to rain"

A new voice crackled on the radio, "Deputy Pearce, this is Dino Vino, I just saw somebody run down the rear gangplank of that big motor yacht north of you. The lightning flash lit him up. He's headed towards you on the seawall. I'm in hot pursuit ... over!"

Seth looked up the 85 yard long road towards the southwest corner of the seawall where Deputy Pearce had stationed himself. There were only two back door light fixtures lighting the road. He saw a muzzle flash near the far corner, and heard a loud ... **Bang**! He hoped Deputy Pearce had gotten the perp.

"This is Dino, Officer down! Officer down! ... at the southwest corner! John Harvey, get over here, quick ... call an ambulance! ... over."

Seth could see some movement at the top of the road. The perp moved quickly through the first back door light and then was lost, as the palms on each side of the road started swaying wildly in the rising wind. He looked large and ran with a galloping gait. Seth moved up a couple of palm trees closer to the second back door light and pulled his Ruger .380 LCP from his pocket. He crouched down as the rain started pelting his face with large stinging drops. As the perp galloped past the second light, Seth recognized that it was Peter Petcock. Peter held his pistol with both hands as if his right shoulder had been injured. He was breathing heavily, his face contorted with pain. Seth made a quick decision; he couldn't hear any pursuit coming his way or cries of, "Stop or I'll Shoot!" It was up to him. He slipped the Ruger back into his right pocket and sprang from his crouched position. Seth took two quick steps and buried his shoulder into Peter's exposed solar plexus. He wrapped his arms around Peter's legs and drove him into the back wall of the warehouse. Seth could hear the air exit from Peter's lungs with a loud *whoosh*, and he heard Peter's pistol clatter harmlessly on the gravel road behind him. Peter's head hit the metal warehouse wall and it knocked him cold. As he stood over him catching his breath, Seth thought this tackle might have been even better than the one he put on Peter 40 years before … on the St. Pete High sidelines. Dino was twenty seconds behind Peter and pulled up with his gun drawn.

"You flattened his ass, Seth!"

"Well, practice makes perfect," gasped Seth. "Is Deputy Pearce ……?"

"No, his bulletproof vest saved him. The bullet knocked the wind out of him … but he's OK."

"Keep your gun on Peter, Dino, he may wake up soon."

"I know this guy used to be a hell of an athlete, like All State Football, but how in the world did he swim across that canal underwater with a bullet in his shoulder."

"I forgot to tell you he was an All State Swimmer, too."

"I guess all that pussy went to his head," said Dino. "Now look how he's ended up."

"Call Big Dog on your radio and ask him to come collect Peter. I'm going back to the trawler, to get out of this rain, and to put some ice on my shoulder."

It started to rain even harder as Seth walked back to the trawler. He could hear the sirens from the sheriff's cars and the ambulances racing to pick up the wounded. He climbed up on the flybridge and viewed the confluence of red, white, and blue flashing lights on the Old Island Boatyard quay across the channel. He wondered how badly ABOUT *TIME* had been shot up.

Seth had put on some borrowed dry clothes and was icing his left shoulder, when Gene walked into the trawler's salon with Billy Ray.

Billy Ray said, "Seth, the collar at the Jamaica Lane house went off with no hitches. They walked into a trap, and all they could do was throw their hands up. We waited until they unloaded the cocaine, and then we brought the police boats up the canal and stepped out of the bushes. But, the question is … how are you Seth? We heard about your heroics."

"Hey, there were no heroics and I'm fine, I should have just shot him, but I just couldn't help myself. It was like a flashback."

"Yeah, Gene told me about the high school rivalry. You saved me a lot of paper work by not shooting him. Glad we had you guys over here. Listen … Gene told me you want to take a look at the Huckins in the morning. I'm going to go you one better than that. I don't have anybody who can run those jet drives, and we need to get Charley's fish off the boat at Bama's tomorrow morning."

"Charley's fish?"

"I don't reckon I know who else owns them … it's his boat. It will get him some expense money back. You'll have full sheriff's department credentials and the run of the boat. I'll also let you check the name board out of the evidence room, if you promise to bring it back for the trial. My bet is these guys will cop a plea, if they can get one. They're looking at a lot of time."

"There sure was a lot of shooting going on over there. How bad is the Huckins shot up?"

"Not as bad as my squad cars. Their automatics took their toll on my Crown Vics. The Huckin's plywood façade caught most of our bullets."

"Well, we're going to celebrate, and fish some, and celebrate some more. I would sure like to take you, Bill Pearce, and Big Dog fishing with us."

"I would sure like to do that. I'll see if we can break away. Deputy Pearce is having his ribs checked at the Lower Keys' Medical Center near our complex, right now. I'm hoping nothing was fractured. We are keeping the press off the premises for the time being."

"We don't want any publicity. We're just a bunch of guys that came down here to fish, if you know what I mean. It's your bust, Billy Ray."

"I hear you loud and clear, Seth, and I'll take care of it. Gene, your guys can keep the t-shirts and hats, but let's put them away before the press sees them."

The crew straggled in one by one and changed into dry clothes, then gathered in the main salon. Everybody popped a cold one. There was a continuous undercurrent as they rehashed the night's events. Finally, Gene stood up. "Gentlemen, I propose a toast to the "Geezers" and our leader ... Seth."

Beer bottles clinked all around, and a chant broke out, "Geezers! Geezers! Geezers! Geezers!" ...... until they all broke up laughing at themselves and started pounding each other on the back.

John Harvey said to Seth, "Well, we might be growing old, but we'll definitely never grow up."

"Why would we ... we're actually getting paid for it now," chuckled Seth.

Dino was over in the corner of the galley recounting his version of tonight's action with the rest of the crew, "It was just lucky that the lightning flashed when it did, or I wouldn't have seen him run down the gangplank. John ran down the length of the seawall in like ten seconds when I called him. I was impressed."

"You can do a lot of things when the adrenaline is pumping, that you can't do normally," said John.

"Talk about a front row seat to a major firefight," said Toby to Billy.

"I thought I was back in fucking 'Nam'," said Freddy with a grin.

Seth spoke, "Listen up guys ... I want to thank all of you for an outstanding effort. It's because of all of you that we found *ABOUT TIME*. Charley figured out who stole it and also figured the drug angle. Gene got me the bottom boys' financial and personal rap sheets. I knew about their business problems. It all added up. The authorities were looking for something and somebody that no longer existed. I picked each one of you because of your courage, experience, skills, intellect, and proven mental stamina. Young guys have skills, strength, and intellect, but most lack experience and mental stamina (snickers). We laugh, but the Geezers have something called synergy. There are no prima donnas in the Geezers. We look at each situation from our individual perspectives and give our input to the group. We distill all the ideas and come up with a better one. My hat's off to you guys! … Let's have another beer and call it a night. The sheriff asked me to move the Huckins to Bama Seafood first thing in the morning to unload the fish, which now belong to Charley (cheers). I guess that'll help pay our way, and I also want to do a quick damage survey while I'm on board. All of you guys sleep late tomorrow and have a big breakfast on Charley. My plan is for us to fish the rest of the day tomorrow and the next day. I've invited Billy Ray, Big Dog, and Bill Pearce to fish tomorrow … if they can get loose. We'll do some celebrating on Duval Street. Then we'll go home. We've finished this job in just over ten days, so we're under budget. You all are on the payroll until we get the boats and the airplane home. If anybody wants to go home early, raise your hand …… no takers? … OK, Geezers, we've got a plan."

Seth and Gene finished their last beer and went back to A&B. They walked in from the parking lot and started past the outside tables at Alonzo's. A black haired, dapper looking tourist took a flash picture of his female companion sitting at their table, just as Seth walked past. The flash momentarily blinded Seth, and he stopped short.

The tourist said, "Hey, sorry about that."

Seth blinked a couple of times, "That's OK, I'm sure you didn't do it on purpose. How about I take a shot of the two of you?"

"Oh … that'd be great." He handed Seth his cell phone and said, "Move around here, Angela."

Seth took the picture and handed the cell phone back to the tourist. They both thanked Seth, and he continued around the corner and down the ramp to the dock. Seth smiled to himself as he walked down the dock. Angela certainly was sporting a spectacular pair of milk dispensers in her halter top.

He caught up to Gene, "What a day, *amigo*, I'm looking forward to a good night's sleep and a little R & R the next two days." He looked at his watch and said, "But first, I need to send a couple of texts."

Seth climbed up in the flybridge and pulled out his cell phone. He sent a text to Jeb, who probably wouldn't read it until tomorrow morning: *Jeb, Huckins recovered, arrests made by the sheriff's department, long story that will require a bottle of Caymus Cab and your undivided attention. The boat will be impounded for two or three weeks, and then delivered to our yard by the insurance company. We won't see it for a month. Big job, probably $500K … I'll be your project manager. We're going to fish and R&R for a while, and then I'll be home. We're keeping the story quiet until we get back. I'll call soon.*

My love to you, Lynne, and little Cullen

Seth sent a short text to Charley: *ABOUT TIME recovered in Key West, tonight. You were right, Peter and Randy are in custody, both were wounded. Running cocaine from Mexico, 50 kilo bust. Boat altered and perps had disguised appearance and identities. Boat impounded by the Monroe County Sheriff. Local and FDLE forensic personnel will be on it at least two to three weeks. Notify your insurance company. They should arrange to deliver the boat to the yard. I will assess damages in the a.m., special pass. Keep this info confidential, we're flying under the radar here. I will call you tomorrow. Then I'm going fishing! …….Seth*

Next he sent Lori a text: *Lori, back in Key West, fishing was excellent in the Tortugas, going to fish here in Key West for a while. It's good to be retired and not on a schedule. I'll be back in St. Petersburg when the boys are fished-out. I hope all is well, and I miss you! ……. Seth*

***

Billy Ray was already waiting, inside the yellow crime tape draped off the dock pilings at Old Island Boatyard, when Gene dropped Seth off at 8:00 a.m. the next morning. From there Gene was headed to the trawler to take the crew to Blue Heaven for breakfast. Seth had picked up a 96 oz. box of hot Starbucks coffee, 12 cups and a dozen assorted pastries, for himself and the forensic crew.

Billy Ray smiled when Seth came aboard, and said, "Well, look at everybody's new best friend. This isn't your first rodeo is it?"

"Well, you have to break the ice somehow, right Billy Ray? Let's get the show on the road."

Seth set up the coffee and donuts in the galley, and Billy Ray introduced him all around. Billy issued Seth a pair of latex gloves and followed him down into the engine room. Seth checked all the fluid levels and checked the bilge for water and contaminants. He started the Cummins engines and the smaller of two generators, and then switched from shore power to the ship's generator. Billy Ray unplugged the shore cords from the dock pedestal and Seth activated the Glendenning retractable reel system. Two deputies handled the dock lines as Seth maneuvered the Huckins away from the dock.

"All the finger prints have been lifted from the wheel house area, Seth. But be careful what you touch, any other place around the boat. I called Bama early this morning so they're expecting us. Their personnel will unload us and clean the hold. Courtesy of Monroe County."

"Charley will thank you. It shouldn't take but a few minutes to get over there and get tied up. It sure is nice and cool in here with the air running."

"I left two guards on the boat last night and instructed them to leave it on. I had them put a couple hundred more pounds of ice on the fish in the hold. It's the least I could do after you dropped this bust in my lap."

Seth maneuvered the Huckins tight to the Bama dock, and their efficient crew started to unload the hold. Seth started to systematically survey the Huckins from stem to stern. The plywood facade had stopped most of the bullets. Actually, the screws holding the plywood on the cabin top and sides had done more damage to the mix of gelcoat and high gloss teak that was under and behind the painted plywood. The starboard hull side had sustained some bullet damage. The large original windows were still in place behind the plywood siding and the small circular commercial bronze port holes that had been installed by the thieves. The fiberglass and gelcoat could be repaired and repainted, but the teak facia boards would have to be replaced. The full length plywood hard top could be removed and the shorter, original cabin roof underneath looked restorable. The solid teak caprail had been painted gray, and could be sanded back and revarnished with 20 new coats. The same held true with the painted aft salon doors and teak transom. The entire boat would have to be repainted; hull, nonskid deck, and cabin/aft fan deck. The aft fan deck coaming, where the bandit reels had been installed, would be replaced. The interior was another story. The aft salon was structurally intact, as was the galley, but they both would have to be redecorated and refurbished. The forward owner's cabin had been converted to an insulated fish hold, with access thru a large deck hatch. That cabin would be gutted and rebuilt from scratch. The guest cabin queen size berth had also been removed and replaced with one double wide and one single wide bunk bed set for the crew. There was already a pilot's berth in the wheelhouse, and a pull out couch in the aft salon. The forward berth had been gutted and replaced with a 250 gallon auxiliary fuel tank and built in gear lockers with false bottoms. They were large enough to store hundreds of cocaine bricks. Seth noted all this in his pocket spiral note pad. The RIB inflatable launch and outboard motor were missing, probably sold in Mexico. The electronics package was intact. Wear and tear on the mechanicals had to be added into the estimate, and the teak swim platform was beyond repair. The Hamilton jets had to be checked out and serviced when the Huckins was hauled. Seth's many years of experience told him that they were in the ballpark at the $500,000 figure, if there weren't any surprises on the mechanical end.

Billy Ray found Seth up on the bow writing some notes about the missing bow pulpit and checking the operation of the anchor windlass.

"We are unloaded, cleaned up, and paid … for 2800 pounds of fresh grouper. I'll keep this check in escrow for Charley Blevins."

"You might have to mail it to him at some point. He's up in Nantucket with his family for a couple of weeks at his family's compound. I texted him the news late last night, and he answered me about ten minutes ago. I bet he had a grin on his face a mile wide when he was texting me back. You'll be hearing from his insurance company, they will take responsibility to transport *ABOUT TIME* to my boatyard in St. Pete. Can you write me an evidence ticket on the teak name board? I want to hand it to Charley when I see him in a couple of weeks."

"I'll bring the name board and the ticket down to your boat when we go fishing later, OK? We're still on aren't we?"

"Absolutely, we'll leave A&B at the crack of noon."

"It will only be Andy and me fishing. The bullet fractured two of Deputy Pearce's ribs and his chest is all wrapped up, but he said he wouldn't miss the ride for the world."

Seth put the Huckins back alongside the south side quay at the Old Island Boatyard, and said his goodbyes to the forensic crew. He asked Billy Ray if one of his men could retrieve his Spot[3] from under the swim platform.

"I'd like to put it back on my Hatteras. My phone dinged on our way over to Bama, and reminded me it was still there."

"No problem, I've got a diver standing by to check the whole bottom now that we're tied up again. I'll bring it down along with the name board."

Seth called Gene, and Freddy picked him up ten minutes later.

Freddy said, "The crew's looking forward to taking the sheriff, Big Dog, and Deputy Bill out fishing. Sorry you missed a great breakfast at Blue Heaven."

"When it ends like this, Fred, it's all good!"

***

Vito finally had something positive to tell Cadillac. After a whole day of staking out TAR BABY, he had finally seen Seth Stone. Better than that, he had taken a picture of him. He was sitting at a table, outside at Alonzo's, eating clams on the half shell with Angela. There hadn't been anyone at the boat since the three guys came in from fishing around lunchtime. He was checking his personal email when he saw one of the men, who got off the Hatteras earlier, walking out of the darkness towards them from Front Street. The man walking behind him, he recognized immediately as Seth. He hit his camera button and told Angela to smile. She looked up in surprise. When Stone walked behind her, Vito snapped the picture. The flash momentarily blinded him, and he stopped. Vito apologized. Stone smiled and asked if they'd like him to take their picture together. Well, it was a touristy thing to do, so they did it. Then he walked out to his boat. He seemed like a real nice guy. But that was not Vito's call.

Vito emailed the picture of Seth Stone to Cadillac, and then followed up on his sat-phone.

"Good work, Vito, that's him. Keep your eye on him and try and figure a way to get him off alone ... away from the boat and his buddies. If you see a way, I'll send a SUV with some the muscle that we've got hidin' out on Summerland Key until Sunday, to pick him up. We want him alive. They're only 20 miles away, so call me. Our contact on the police desk at the *Key West Citizen* called to tell me there was a big drug bust up on Stock Island tonight. They could be the people that were supplyin' the Russians. Talk about good luck. Also, he told me a maid found the Russian kapo and his girlfriend shot dead in his Galleon condo this mornin'. They'll link him to Yuly in the newspaper story tomorrow. Somebody has to figure we coulda had somethin' to do with what went down Tuesday, but I bet they investigate Nicolay's wife. There's just no evidence linkin' us to being there. The police have also hadda few more missin' persons reports filed by girlfriends and landlords this afternoon, imagine that. He said that most of the Russians had forged paperwork ... that helps us too."

"I've been hangin' out all day around the Galleon watchin' the Hatteras, and I did see some police cars and an ambulance with their lights flashin' this morning out front. I figured it was a heart attack. I didn't get too close ... They didn't need to see me."

"Right, let's see if you can get us a shot at snatchin' Stone. Keep me posted."

CHAPTER TWENTY

Seth pulled *TAR BABY* out of the slip at A&B at noon. There were ten men aboard, and their spirits were running high. Sheriff Stodgins, Big Dog, Gene, John, and Seth sat up in the flybridge. Freddy, Dino, Billy, Toby, and Deputy Pearce, were scattered in the cockpit below. A climb up a flybridge ladder was not in Deputy Bill's near future. They were still chattering about the arrests and all the shooting that had taken place, while enjoying a cold one.

Big Dog said, "It could have been a bad scene if we hadn't had the intelligence we had, and been ready for their firepower. The assault vehicle took the fight out of them. We wounded three of them in the initial volley. Really, we're lucky that all they took out were four of our squad cars."

"Well, they did do a job on our vehicles, but we'll recoup that from the spoils of war," stated Billy Ray.

"How does that work, Sheriff?" asked John.

"Well, we were the lead agency in the arrest ... so we confiscated the 32 foot World Cat and the 37 foot Contender. We also seized the Ford Expeditions, a couple of pickup trucks, and the Jamaica Lane house. There are no mortgages or liens on any of the property so we'll sell it all at a sheriff's auction. We found a large sum of money at the house this morning, and we'll appropriate that along with the TV's, and furniture. The 50 kilos of cocaine will be shared with the DEA for our informer/undercover agent programs. So, this arrest will help us maintain our budget, and it would be hard to put a number on the publicity and political value for the upcoming election in November. The DEA agents think Peter and Randy's smuggling operation may have been supplying cocaine to the local Russian Mafia drug trade."

"That makes sense ... Just curious, so what happens to the rental house they own on Geiger Key?" asked Seth.

"We've got Douglas Roberts checking that out right now. If it was bought with illegal drug profits, we'll get that house too. Hey, enough about business, let's talk about fishin'. Where are we headed, Seth?"

"To the east crack in Wood's Wall. I hope there will be some hot blackfin tuna action there, and you never know what else might come up and bite you. We're running at 24 knots, so we'll be there in about an hour."

"That sounds good, how about another cold one? I am enjoying this nice riding boat."

As they got close to the east crack, they spotted clouds of birds working bait on the surface. Seth slowed down and dropped the outriggers, and the crew put out three tuna feather jet-heads and a naked ballyhoo off the shotgun ... way back. Groups of porpoise were also working throughout the large bait schools. Seth worked the leading edges of the schools and ten minutes later they had three fish on. Billy Ray and Andy came down off the bridge and fought two of them. Freddy wound the third one to the boat. Dino and Billy gaffed them at boat side and they slid three beautiful 20-plus pound blackfin tuna into the fish box. Seth started to troll again, but the bait school had left the surface and gone down. The wheeling birds landed on the water to rest and await their return. The fishing slowed down for a time, and Toby came out of the cabin with a large funnel and a silver dollar.

"Who's up for the funnel game?"

"I am, I am," yelled Billy and Dino.

"Alright, $10 a try."

Billy took the funnel and stuck the snout down the front of his fishing shorts. Toby gave him the silver dollar. Billy took off his hat and tilted his head way back, then set the silver dollar flat on his forehead. He clasped his hands behind his waist, and slowly tilted his head forward until the coin slid off and fell into the funnel. Everybody cheered and Toby handed Billy $10. Freddy tried next and the coin hit the edge of the funnel and clattered to the deck. Freddy gave $10 to Toby. Dino was next, his coin fell into the funnel, and Toby handed him $10.

"Anybody else want to try? If not it's back to Freddy."

"I'll try," said Big Dog. "I think I can do it."

229

Big Dog stuffed the funnel snout down the front of his shorts and Toby handed him the silver dollar. Big Dog tilted his head back and started to place the coin on his forehead ... Freddy twisted the top off an ice cold bottle of water and poured the whole bottle into the funnel. Big Dog yelped and jerked the funnel out of his pants. He grimaced and his face turned bright red. He looked around the cockpit at all the guys cracking up ... then started to laugh himself.

"You guys really got me good!!!" he said good-naturedly. "I never saw that coming."

Deputy Pearce groaned with pain, from the corner of the cockpit, trying not to laugh because of his fractured ribs. There was no ice left to break with the sheriff's group now, and ten minutes later they had another blackfin tuna on. They continued fishing for an hour and put seven more tuna in the fish box.

Seth spotted a weed line and broke off from the bait schools to follow it. The crew brought in the tuna feathers and put out four Islander saillures with ballyhoo behind them. Billy wound in the shotgun and put a fresh ballyhoo on it. Fifteen minutes later the left long and short riggers went off. It was two nice sized dolphins. Andy took the long rigger, Billy Ray handled the short. Billy Ray wound the cow to the boat in a few minutes, but the bull was giving Andy a hard go of it.

Dino yelled, "C'mon, Big Dog, put your back in it. That's a bad fish!" Andy wound the reel against the drag in frustration.

Billy eased over, "Take your time Andy ... Let him run, the drag will wear him out."

A few minutes later Big Dog brought the bull dolphin to the boat. Billy gaffed him and Freddy helped pull it aboard. He was too big to fit in the cooler, so Billy immediately threw a wet towel over the big dolphin's head and put the "dolphin calmer" on him. He carefully slipped the 300 lb. mono lariat loop over his tail and slowly bent the dolphin's tail towards its head, while tightening the tail loop. Billy hooked the #12 J-hook that was crimped to the other end in the corner of the big bull's mouth. Then he pulled the wet towel off the dolphin's head to reveal a 40 lb. immobilized dolphin.

"That's really slick," said Billy Ray. "I've had some big ones get loose and start jumping around, what a fire drill."

Seth yelled down from the bridge, "We first saw that done down in Panama, years ago, Billy Ray ...... Andy, that's a nice fish ... we're going thru the weeds at that thin spot up ahead, and then we'll fish back towards the tuna bite."

They caught two more dolphin on the way back to the tuna bite, and Seth started working the edge of the ever-moving bait school. Seth told them to leave the Islander spread out, and they picked up two more nice sized tuna. Seth throttled up some and got a little in front of the bait school. He turned in front of the school and pulled the way-back shotgun bait across the school diagonally; he continued the turn and slowed down some. The bait sank a little and Seth throttled back up. As the bait rose it was hit hard and snapped out of the center rigger with a loud pop. The reel screamed and within seconds a white marlin jumped 50 yards behind *TAR BABY*.

Billy took the rod from the holder and handed it to Billy Ray.

"Don't tighten the drag, and reel only when he stops taking line. When he jumps, point the rod at him and reel hard," said Billy as John put a Bimini belt on the sheriff. "He looks like he's about 90-100 lbs."

The rest of the crew pulled in the teasers and wound in the other baits. Billy Ray played the fish just the way he was told, he wasn't a rookie. The white marlin put on quite a show jumping and somersaulting, drawing whoops and hollers from the crew. Ten minutes later the sheriff had him at boat side. Dino grabbed the leader and handled his bill. John got the hook out and Gene took a picture before they released it. Billy Ray grinned, from ear to ear.

Seth called down to the crew, "Let's get the outriggers up and head for home. That was a perfect ending to a perfect afternoon." When the outriggers were secure, Seth throttled the Hatteras up to planing speed and leveled off at 24 knots.

Billy Ray came back up onto the flybridge and said, "What a great afternoon, Seth, 13 tuna and four big dolphin ... the white marlin was just icing on the cake. That's only the second one I ever caught ... and the biggest."

"We're going to grill these fish back at Safe Harbor tonight. Why don't you guys call your significant others and have them come over for grilled tuna and dolphin. We'd love to have y'all come, Billy Ray."

Andy nodded *yes*, and Billy Ray called down to Deputy Bill in the cockpit and got a thumbs up.

"We'll call the girls as soon as we get in cell phone range."

"Gene, will you go down and clue Dino in on the dinner plans. Oh, and make sure everybody has a fresh cold one."

TAR BABY was tied up, hosed off, and the trawler boys were on their way to Publix and then back to Safe Harbor to shower. The sheriff's contingent was planning to meet them at Safe Harbor at 7:00. Seth and Gene showered, dressed, and pulled into Safe Harbor at 6:30. Billy and Toby had the coolers full of fish filets and tuna steaks set out next to the grills in the picnic area and were already setting the picnic tables and filling the beer coolers. Freddy had the charcoal in the grills lit, and Gene took a bushel of white corn over to the grill area. Dino headed for the *SIRENA'S* galley to mix up copious amounts of salad. John pulled back in from a trip to the package store with paper plates, bags of potato chips, pretzels, cheeses and crackers, an assorted case of fine wine, and more beer and ice.

Seth walked over to Hugh Spinner's floating house and knocked on the door. Hugh answered and Seth invited him and his wife to their impromptu shindig. Hugh accepted with a smile. Seth proceeded down artisan's row and knocked on Joe O'Donald's door, Joe answered, cocktail in hand.

"Joe, Seth Stone, do you remember me?"

"Of course I do, Seth, you and your wife went to the opening of the new Peninsular Marina with me a few years back. How could I forget? Charley told me last week that you were down here fishing. But, I've been hearing stories around town about you finding his Huckins. I guess it was right under our noses the whole time. What's up?"

"Well, we did go fishing today with the sheriff and some of his personnel and caught a bunch of tuna and dolphin. We're having a grilled fish dinner out in your picnic area, and I'd like to invite you and whoever you'd like to bring. It would give me a chance to fill you in about Charley's boat. You probably already know Billy Ray."

"I do, and I'd love to come. What time?"

"Around 7:00, it will give me a chance to fill you in on the details. We are trying to minimize publicity concerning our part in this bust. We want the sheriff to get the credit. But, I know Charley would want you to hear the real story."

Billy Ray, Andy, and Bill Pearce pulled in with their wives and the party began. Hugh Spinner put two big speakers on the top of his floating house and streamed in some 70's and 80's rock music from Pandora. The beer and wine flowed, the snacks were consumed, laughter ensued, and the conversation grew animated.

Joe O'Donald arrived with two women in tow. One was a tall, thin, tan, attractive blonde named Vanessa. She was dressed in light blue Capri pants, a white spandex top, and Miami style raffia high-heeled wedge sandals. The other woman was named Blanca. She was a sultry Cuban with a gymnast's build. Her tight black short shorts, and handkerchief halter top, accentuated the positive. Whatever her clothes didn't cover, was covered by Technicolor tattoos. A rattlesnake was coiled around her left leg, the snake's head disappearing up under her shorts. Her left leg was etched with a spider's web, with a large black widow spider poised on the back of her calf. Her right arm had a bright yellow lightning bolt shooting from storm clouds on her shoulder down to her right hand's middle finger. A red, white, and blue barber pole spiral tattoo covered her left arm. Angel wings adorned her muscular back, and a bouquet of daisies bloomed out of her ample cleavage. It was hard to imagine what scenes might lurk behind the clothed portions of her body. She moved like a cat, her electric blue eyes constantly moving. Joe's ladies quickly assimilated into the growing throng. He acknowledged the sheriff and then sought out Seth.

"Have you talked to Charley? I'm surprised he's not down here, hugging his long lost boat," said Joe with a chuckle.

"I talked to him, and he's up in Nantucket with his whole family. Billy Ray will keep it impounded for a few weeks until the forensic studies are all completed. Then the insurance company will have a crew deliver it up to St. Petersburg."

"Well, he missed a good party. The grilled tuna and roasted corn on the cob is delicious, Seth. So, how did you figure out that *ABOUT TIME* was here?"

"Actually, Charley figured it out. He was sure that Petcock and Garrett stole her, and he figured they were using her to run cocaine. I guessed that they had changed the Huckins and their own appearances, radically, to have eluded detection by all the experienced agencies that were searching for them. I figured they couldn't alter her overall size much, so that became the key."

Seth filled Joe in on the aerial "box" method, the background checks, Holbox, the skills and experience of his crew, and the perp's Sugarloaf Key properties.

"What a great cover those guys figured out for themselves. Without Charley's persistence they might have made it to retirement."

"It's hard to say, Joe. They had four or five other partners in crime. It's always hard to end a thing like they had going. But, hey … we're happy we got Charley's boat back for him, and Billy Ray made a big bust. Now tell me about your property across the canal. It looks like it's starting to pay off for you."

"Yeah, the marina is about half done, and the artisan shops are being built. The mega-yachts are starting to use it. Robbie's Boat Yard is getting more yacht service business, now that he's cleaned the yard up and put in a one hundred ton travelift."

"You may need to build that twelve story lighthouse replica building, with the car storage elevators, you told me about, before you know it."

"Believe it or not, some of the mega-yacht guys are already looking for a safe place to store their toys. Thanks for dinner, Seth. I hate to eat and run. If I can ever do anything for you in Key West, you know where I live. I've got to collect the girls and head down to Truman Annex and make an appearance at a county commissioner's fundraiser. I'd rather stay right here, but opportunity knocks … if you know what I mean."

"Thanks for coming, Joe."

Seth moved across the picnic area and joined Billy Ray and the deputies group. Dinner was winding down, and they were getting ready to leave.

"Thanks again for a great day," said Billy Ray, echoed by Andy and Deputy Bill. "The girls enjoyed meeting your crew, and getting out of their kitchens for a night."

"The pleasure was all ours, Sheriff, and thanks for keeping us out of the limelight."

"I had our press spokesman refer to y'all as, 'a crew of alert fisherman, who wish to remain anonymous.' I wish you'd take more credit than that, though."

"No, that's perfect, Billy Ray. You are everything Gene told us you'd be."

Everyone said their goodbyes, and Seth gathered the crew together.

"Well boys, let's clean this area up, then we'll take the two vans down to Sloppy Joes and blow off some more steam. *TAR BABY* leaves the dock for our last fishing trip of this campaign tomorrow morning at 10:00 sharp. We'll have a farewell dinner tomorrow night at Seven Fish up on Elizabeth St., and head for home on Sunday morning. I'll settle up the per diems and bonus when Charley and I settle up accounts in a couple of weeks. Everybody gets paid for 14 days through Tuesday. That's $4200, per man, plus any out of pocket receipts that you turn in. The bonus will be $14,285, each, for a total of $18,485. Not bad for two weeks work! If anybody needs an advance let me know."

They took in the band at Sloppy Joes and moved over to the Hog's Breath Saloon for another cold one. Then walked up Duval to the Bull and Whistle for the live blues band playing at the second floor Whistle Bar. Dino checked out the third floor Garden of Eden dance bar and pronounced it not worth the walk upstairs. They backtracked to Rick's and finally called it a night. They all walked back to the vans parked on Greene Street, and the trawler boys returned to Stock Island. Gene and Seth headed for A&B.

***

"Fish on," yelled Billy as they approached a group of wheeling birds near the west crack of Wood's Wall. Billy grabbed the rod as a sailfish popped the

235

outrigger clip on the left long rigger. He free-spooled the reel for a few seconds and then slowly applied some drag with the lever. The fish came tight.

Seth called down to the crew, "Leave the lines in, and man the rods. I see another fish behind the right long!"

He kept the boat moving forward for a few seconds, and then turned the boat into a gradual turn towards the hooked fish. Billy's reel screamed as the sailfish sped away. As TAR BABY came out of the turn, the second sailfish made a move on the right long rigger. The line popped out of the rigger, and John dropped the bait back in free spool for a four count. He eased the drag lever up and that fish came tight.

"We've got the second one on Seth," shouted John.

Seth throttled back as the crew brought in the other lines. When everything was clear, Seth settled in and began slowly backing towards the hooked fish. Billy fought a stalemate with the first fish. He bobbed and weaved with John at the cockpit transom to keep the lines from tangling, as both sailfish jumped and surged. John put the heat on the second fish and had it to the boat in three minutes. Toby released the fish cleanly, and Seth backed the boat quickly towards Billy's tiring fish. A few minutes later, Freddy released Billy's sailfish and the crew celebrated their double header. Seth went back to working the feeding birds, and by the early afternoon they had two dolphin and a wahoo for their efforts.

Seth called down to the cockpit, "Pull the lines out boys, I want to go in a little early to top off the fuel tanks so I don't have to stop in the morning."

The lines were pulled out, and the outriggers were pulled up and secured. TAR BABY started her journey back to A&B in the Bight. They returned to the Hatteras's slip after fueling up. The crew hosed off the boat, cleaned the dolphin and the wahoo, and put them on ice.

"We'll meet at Seven Fish at 7:30 tonight, so we can get an early start tomorrow. Unfortunately, Gene got some bad news this morning and has a family funeral to attend. He'll be staying on the trawler tonight and will fly home with John in the morning. Toby and Billy will rent a one-way Enterpise car in St. Pete to get back to Boca Grande. Dino will stay on TAR BABY tonight and help me run her back to Salt Creek tomorrow. You guys on the trawler will take both vans from the restaurant tonight and Gene and John will drop them at the airport tomorrow morning. Seven Fish is only six blocks from the Key West Bight, so Dino and I will walk back to *TAR BABY*. We'll see you guys at 7:30. I made reservations."

Locals jammed Seven Fish, but Seth's table for seven was ready and waiting. The food was superb, and Seth and Dino shared a bottle of Seghesio Old Vines Red Zinfandel. The other boys drank their favorite beers. There were a few toasts shared, and the crew's admiration for one another was apparent. Not only had their mission been successful, but they all had enjoyed each other's company.

When dinner was over Seth stood up and gave the last toast, "To the Geezer's, and our next adventure, whatever it may be." There were cheers and *hear- hears* all around.

Seth paid the check and the crew spilled out onto Elizabeth Street.

"Get in our van," said Freddy. "We'll run you down to A&B."

"Thanks, Freddy, but Dino and I will walk back. It's only six blocks, and it's all downhill. After that big dinner, we can use the exercise. We'll see you guys back in St. Pete, have a safe trip."

There were fist bumps and handshakes. Seth and Dino crossed Olivia Street, and disappeared into the dark down Elizabeth's north sidewalk.

***

Vito The Dancer, called Cadillac on his sat-phone, "I've been trackin' Stone, night and day. I rented a moped and followed him out to Stock Island after they went fishin' yesterday. He took the sheriff with him … I mean this guy is fuckin' connected. A&B was crawlin' with sheriff's cars around noon, and then they all went fishin' until about 5:00 in the afternoon. I asked the car park attendant what the sheriff was doin' there, after they left on Stone's boat. He said the sheriff and a couple of his deputies went fishin' with some friends."

"What happened on Stock Island?"

"I followed them to the Hogfish Bar and Grille. I bought a beer and walked out into the marina where I saw them go. They were grillin' fish out behind a boat that some of his friends are stayin' on. The sheriff's group showed up later with their wives and girlfriends. There was lots of people at the cook out. I figured there was no chance to collar him there. All seven of them went down to Duval Street about 9:30 to party, and they stuck together like glue."

"What about today?"

"The regular bunch went fishin'. When they came back in they cleaned up the boat, then five of them drove back to Stock Island. About an hour later Stone and the big Italian guy drove up to the Seven Fish Restaurant on Elizabeth. The five guys stayin' on the trawler in Stock Island arrived, in the other van, a few minutes later. They just got seated. There might be a chance tonight, if they don't all hang out together after dinner. Once he's back on the A&B dock, there's a guard and a watchdog."

"I'll send down an Escalade with Big Fred and Joe The Animal. Meet them at Duval and Olivia Streets. You get in and drive since you know the streets. Since he's in the van with just one friend, maybe you'll get a chance to snatch him if they stop somewhere else, or after they park at A&B, or maybe near the marina bathrooms, behind the restaurant later. I'm pullin' the Escalades out of Summerland Key tomorrow. If we don't get Stone tonight, No Nose is gonna have to wait until he gets back to St. Petersburg. I'll have them there in less than 25 minutes. But remember, don't kill him, we need to question him."

"We'll be on his tail when he comes out of the restaurant, Boss."

CHAPTER TWENTY-ONE

Dino and Seth walked west down Elizabeth Street in the dark. It was one-way, so an occasional car passing from behind lit their way. As they crossed Windsor Lane, which angled into Elizabeth from the northeast, Seth heard a car start up across the irregular intersection on Angela Street and saw the headlights come on. He and Dino stepped up over the curb and continued down the sidewalk. The car turned down Elizabeth behind them and slowly accelerated. As it passed, Seth recognized it as a black Cadillac Escalade. Suddenly, the driver slammed on the brakes and the two right passenger doors flew open. Two large men dressed in black jumped out wielding pistols and yelled, "Hands up and get your asses in the truck!"

Seth and Dino were startled and turned to run. The two big men were on them in an instant. Dino grabbed the largest one by his gun arm, pivoted, and broke his wrist. Seth could hear the big man's wrist bone snap. He screamed in pain as his gun fell to the sidewalk. The other assailant grabbed Seth by the shoulder, and he turned back into him with a cross body block. They landed in a heap on the sidewalk struggling for the gun. Seth got him in a bear hug, but the big man rolled on top of him. Dino spun his injured attacker around and kicked the man's left foot and ankle out from under him, fracturing both in the process. Then he bounded over and grabbed Seth's attacker by his long black hair. He tilted his head back and karate chopped him in the throat. The big man dropped his weapon and clasped his shattered larynx with both hands, gasping for air. Seth jumped up and grabbed him by the back of his heavy link gold neck chain and the back of his belt and ran his head into a nearby tree trunk, knocking him unconscious. The Escalade's driver jumped out in the street and fired two pistol shots in the air. Dino and Seth looked at each other, and hauled ass down Angela Street towards Duval. Angela Street was one-way going north so they both stopped running when they crossed Simonton. Both of them were out of breath, but charged with adrenaline. They continued to walk quickly towards Duval Street to lose themselves in the weekend crowd.

As they approached Duval, Dino asked, "What the fuck was that all about?"

"I'm not sure," answered Seth, whose mind was on overload at this point. "Maybe it was retribution from the Russian Mafia, pissed off that we cut off their drug source. Billy Ray told me that the DEA suspected Randy and Peter might be supplying them."

"That would make sense. I'm glad we're getting out of town in the morning."

Seth's mind was still processing what had just happened, and it did not add up. The huge man who he had bear-hugged was an Italian, not a Russian, with long, greasy, black hair. The Russians he had seen around Key West all had their heads shaved. His attacker's breath also reeked of garlic. The other assailant had wavy black hair and also had a gold chain around his neck. The medium built driver who fired the shots in the air also had slicked back black hair, and looked vaguely familiar to Seth. They were Goombas, not Russians. If they had been Russians they would have shot and killed both of them, and the driver certainly would not have fired shots in the air after Dino took out the two hit men. The Tampa Mafia wanted him for something, and they wanted him alive. It had to be related to his Brother Beau's escapade. Maybe they had somehow … finally … added one plus one together.

Seth and Dino continued to walk northwest down Duval street hidden in the crowd. They passed by DJ's Clam Shack; then they ducked into Willie T's and ordered a couple of beers. The whole time Seth was weighing alternative actions in his mind. If he did nothing, he would eventually be kidnapped by the Tampa Mafia. He would never be seen again, no matter if he gave up Beau or not. A shiver went up his spine as he wondered if Jeb and his family were in danger. Normally the Italian Mafia did not involve innocent family members in their retribution. Everything with them was strictly business. But Dino and Seth had just destroyed two of their soldiers. He decided he had better become proactive and go on the offense.

Dino took a long pull on his beer and said, "Maybe we ought to get out of town tonight, Seth? We're like sitting ducks at A&B. You've got a full load of fuel. Let's just slip the lines and go."

"Not a bad idea, Dino. But I think I have an even a better idea. Let me call Gene at the trawler and see if they've had any trouble."

Seth called Gene on his cell and asked if they had been harassed by the Russian Mafia. The answer was no. He recounted what had happened to Dino and him on the way down Elizabeth Street, and Dino's idea to leave early. Gene agreed that might be a prudent decision.

"Ask John Harvey if he's comfortable with flying out at this time of night."

Gene came back on the line and said, "John says no problem. He thinks discretion would be the better part of valor at this point. Freddy is also ready to start the trip back to St. Pete in the trawler right now."

"I'm going to throw in one more hitch, Gene. I don't want to take TAR BABY back to St. Pete right now. The Russians have obviously been watching it. I'm going to make it hard for them to find me. I'll drop Dino off on my way past Stock Island and he can go back with Freddy on the trawler. That way they can drop Billy and Toby off in Boca Grande on the way back to St. Pete. I'm going to take the Hatteras back up to Marathon Yacht Club and stash it for a few weeks. I'll rent a car and drive up into the North Georgia Mountains to my sister's cabin for awhile. If they want to find me, they'll have to look hard. We should be back at A&B in ten minutes or so, and it won't take another ten to cast off. You and John can take the two vans out to the airport. You can leave right now, but do me a favor first and call Billy Ray. Explain that we had a possible retribution problem with the Russian Mafia. Ask him to send a couple of deputies to A&B and out to Safe Harbor until we all get clear of Key West."

"You're not going to run all the way to Marathon tonight are, you Seth?"

"No, I'll anchor up in Newfound Harbor, and run the rest of the way tomorrow morning."

As Seth paid the tab at Willy T's, the blues band started playing Dickey Betts' "Back to Daytona". He and Dino hurried back to A&B, and as they walked briskly down Front Street two sheriff's cars sped past them and stopped at the marina/restaurant entrance. They got out and gave Seth the high sign as he strode past them. He jumped aboard and started the boat engines, as Dino collected the lines, shore cord, and fenders. Seth pulled *TAR BABY* out of the slip and idled out of the marina. He put the Hatteras up on plane in front of a darkened Mallory Square and headed for Hawk Channel.

Things were starting to fall in place in Seth's mind. He would actually run the boat up to Stuart and hide it there at an old fishing buddy's house on the south fork of the St. Lucie River. He would ask his friend to rent a car for him so he couldn't be traced. At least that was plan A. He was reasonably certain that everything he owned in St. Petersburg was being watched. Tomorrow morning, he would make calls to his son Jeb, Bill Tilley in Stuart, his sister Scarlett in Atlanta, the A&B dock master in Key West, and his brother Beau in Costa Rica. He would text Lori. Seth ran the Hatteras east past Louie's Backyard, the Casa Marina, and Key West Airport. He soon saw the loom of the Key West power plant and finally turned up into the Stock Island Channel. He slowed down at the power plant, idled up into Safe Harbor Marina, and eased in next to the trawler's bow to let Dino off with his duffel.

Gene and Freddy were waiting on the trawler's bow. Freddy helped get Dino and his duffel off *TAR BABY* while Gene said, "Billy Ray was really surprised that the Russian Mafia retaliated. He said in the last few days it has become apparent that most of the Key West Russian Mafia personnel are either dead or missing. His intelligence unit suspects that the Tampa Mafia is responsible for the Russians' demise, but nothing concrete has been uncovered. He speculated that any retribution would come from the Russians in New York City. But he sent us police protection immediately. He also said his department and the FDLE would monitor any Russian activity closely and try to make some arrests."

Seth could see two sheriff's cars with their lights blinking in the parking lot behind the trawler's stern.

"Well, better safe than sorry."

"John and I are headed for the airport. The squad cars are going to escort us."

Seth waved to all of them, backed away from *SIRENA*, and maneuvered out the cut. He ran at 10 knots up Hawk Channel and two hours later was anchored up in Newfound Harbor. He switched on his anchor light, locked the Hatteras's salon door, and put his Ruger .380 LCP under his pillow. Seth tossed and turned for about an hour and finally fell into a totally exhausted, sound sleep. A passing late night thunderstorm didn't even wake him up.

***

Seth awakened as the sun came up. His back felt a little tender on the left side, where his assailant's huge bulk had pinned him to the concrete sidewalk the night before. He took a long, hot, shower. The hot, pulsating, water made his body feel relaxed and re-energized. Seth knew that feeling of well-being really came from the negative ion charge the water left behind on his skin, as the positive ions ran off and went down the drain. A little lesson he had learned back in college Physics 101. He shaved, and put on fresh shorts and a t-shirt. After checking the engine room, he made coffee and popped a Jimmy Dean breakfast sandwich in the microwave oven. He took took a second cup up on the flybridge in a Styrofoam cup with a lid. Seth pulled a notebook and pen from under the steering console to take notes during his upcoming phone calls. He started the engines, climbed down, and walked out on the foredeck to weigh the anchor. The 12 volt Ideal windlass helped him make short work of that. He fastened a safety line from the anchor shank to the port bow cleat and returned to the flybridge. Seth idled out of Newfound Harbor and made his first call.

It was 7:00 a.m. He called A&B first, knowing that the dock master got there at 6:00 a.m.

"A&B marina, this is Don ... how can I help you?"

"Hey, Don ... Seth Stone, sorry I missed you. How did the dentistry go?"

"Oh ...Travis must have told you. Everything went fine; my teeth are in great shape now. He told me you've been fishing and he figured you went out really early today since you were gone before we got here this morning."

"Well, something came up and we started out for home early this morning, and I just wanted to clue you in. Just run any charges on the credit card imprint you have. Travis did a good job in your absence."

"That's good to hear! Something you should know, before I left for Miami, a Captain Jack was looking for you. He said you were late calling in on your float plan. We had no reservation for you and he said he would keep looking."

Seth immediately remembered the ubiquitous Captain Tony, from his inquiries into the movements of CHICA two years before. This could be the same m.o. with Captain Tony using a different name; only the Mafia was looking for Seth now. Every step seemed to lead in the same direction. The Tampa Mafia had made the Costa Rican connection.

"Well, some people knew I was coming down to the Keys to fish, but I didn't specifically tell anyone where. Thanks, Don."

"See you next time, Seth."

Seth called Jeb on his cell phone. He answered on the second ring.

"Hey, Dad, how's it going?"

"Where are you, Jeb?"

"I'm just pulling into the parking lot at the boatworks."

"OK, stay in your truck until I fill you in on the latest ... We all left Key West last night. We had a run-in with the Russian Mafia. It was probably retribution for the drug bust, but nobody on our side got hurt. We advised the sheriff, and both boats and John Harvey's plane left Key West just before midnight."

"Smart move."

"I don't know if they'll follow us back to St. Petersburg, so I'm going to stash the boat up in Stuart, then drive up to Aunt Scarlett's mountain house in Hiawassee for a week or so. The Monroe County Sheriff and FDLE are monitoring the Key West Russians' activities and will try to make some indictments. I would like you to take your family to the Bahamas for a week as soon as you can arrange it. Go to Atlantis on Paradise Island, and put the whole thing on the company Visa card and use the card's rewards air miles. I know Lynne and Cullen will enjoy it. I'm probably overreacting, but like your Grandaddy Robert E. would have said, 'An ounce of prevention is worth a pound of cure'. Don't alarm Lynne; just tell her it's some R&R before the

Huckins job starts. You won't have time for a vacation for at least six months once that job starts. We'll be working a six day week. Make a good list of what you want the yard to accomplish while you're away. Between Jeff and your new foreman, things should go smoothly."

"I won't argue, Dad, but we probably need to have a little talk about your retirement hobbies, if this blows over. Fishing and hunting is one thing, but maybe this amateur sleuthing is not such a good idea."

"All right … I'll listen. Text me with your trip itinerary, and we'll stay in touch."

"One more thing Dad, I had a heavy-set, Italian-looking guy, come in about a week and a half ago, asking for you. He said his name was John Lombardo, and he was a former customer of yours. He said that some years ago he had a Bertram that we worked on, before he moved to Atlanta. He's moving back to Tampa, and he's buying a 46 Ocean sportfish. He wants some high dollar work done to it; new engines, generators, paint, electronics, and interior refurb. I gave him a ballpark, and he said he only wanted to deal with you. I told him you were fishing in the Keys and would be back in two to three weeks. He said he could wait and left a number to call. It didn't sit right with me, so Jeff looked back in the records, and we couldn't find him. We called the contact number he left, but it was disconnected."

"I don't remember anybody by that name either. I don't know if he is connected with the Russians or what."

Seth thought that was just additional proof that the Tampa Mafia was trying to find him. The information, innocently shared by Jeb, probably got Captain Tony/Jack zeroed in on the Keys. Seth was glad that Jeb didn't protest about leaving town. The Italian Mafia was known for its business-like policies. They normally never brought any harm to innocent family members. But he still didn't want to take a chance that they would kidnap Jeb, out of frustration, and use him as a bargaining chip. The recovery of three million dollars might be reason enough to bend the rules. The Russian angle was a convenient way to avoid telling Jeb the truth about Beau, and his own Costa Rican involvement in the Mafia money drop robbery. Giving up Beau was not an option. And

Seth knew if the Tampa Mafia got him he was a dead man, whether he gave up Beau or not.

Bill Tilley was his next call. Seth found him out on his dock in the Palm City section of Stuart. Seth explained the situation using the Russian Mafia angle, and asked Bill if he could borrow the spare slip behind his house on Riverside Drive for a few weeks.

"Sure, Seth, you can keep it here all summer if you want. Your bow will face the Okeechobee Waterway, so nobody can see *TAR BABY's* name on the transom."

"I need a car or truck to drive up to the mountains. Will you rent one for me, using your name, and put me on the contract as an additional driver?"

"I can do better than that. I have a five year old Ford F-150 pickup truck from a commercial fishing company that I used to own. You can use it if you don't mind the faint odor of fish."

"Does it have air conditioning?"

"Ice cold."

"I'll see you tonight or tomorrow morning ... and thanks Bill."

Next he called his sister Scarlett, in Atlanta. She didn't pick up so he left her a message. She called back five minutes later as *TAR BABY* idled eastward.

"Hey Sis, how is the family? .... That's good to hear ... You're out in Rockford, Illinois ... at a soccer tournament ... he's in the semi-finals. Would you mind if I used your mountain house for a week or so? I need to get away from the saltwater for awhile ... no, everything's all right ... Thanks, and tell my nephew Rhett I said hello and good luck ... anything up there need fixing? OK ... call me when it's over and let me know who won. Love you, Scarlett, and say 'Hey' to Lon for me."

Seth activated his sat-phone and dialed Beau's cell phone in Costa Rica. Beau answered on the fifth ring.

"What's up 'Bro', you coming down to fish with me?"

"I wish ... we've got a situation developing up here that requires our attention." He filled Beau in on the whole story, beginning to end. Seth explained the need for them to be proactive.

"This is not going to go away, Beau. Somehow, something has clued them into discovering that I was in Costa Rica when the Bertram blew up. They probably think I have the money. They want to question me, so they won't kill me until they find out where the money is. But, eventually it will lead to you … sooner or later. I think our only way out is to take the offensive …… We have to eliminate No Nose Cipriano."

"Whoa! … How do you propose that we do that? Normally these Mafia Dons have a lot of protection and limit their exposure."

"Everyone has a weak spot. We just have to find it. We'll have to put him under surveillance and figure it out. He lives on a golf course, doesn't he? That might give us a great viewing opportunity. I figure we can use the sniper skills you developed with the Rangers in Vietnam to take him out."

"What about the blow back? His capo is going to know about you."

"Well, right now the Tampa Mafia is at war with a Russian Mafia faction in Key West. The Sheriff of Monroe County believes that the Tampa mob has eliminated most of the Key West Russians. The Russians are still strong in New York City, and that's where he thinks any retribution might come from. Any attempt on No Nose's life would be viewed as Russian retribution, both inside and outside of the Tampa Mafia. Once we get Cipriano, we can deal with his capo. I'm sure I can get us a profile and photographs of all the higher up Florida-based Mafia members on the internet."

"Those Cuban boys, who snatched me at Los Suenos, called him Wall to Wall. More important, though, do you have the necessary rifles and shooting equipment, like flash suppressors, night scopes, and silencers to handle an urban covert operation like this?"

"I have it all from the night hog hunting that I've been doing up at my Brooksville hunting lease."

"How about Jeb? Does he know I'm alive?"

"No, he thinks this is all fallout from the Russian related drug bust in Key West. I don't want to re-open your chapter with anyone. I'm concerned that Cipriano might grab Jeb in frustration, if he doesn't get me."

"Well, I agree. I can't see any solution other than to go for broke. I wonder how they figured out you were there? I guess it wouldn't be too hard to check the hotel records and airline manifests if you had the right connections, but why would they? But it doesn't matter … that's all academic now. When do you want me stateside?"

"I'm on my way to Stuart right now, and I'll probably get there tonight. I called Bill Tilley and I'm going to dock at his house on the St. Lucie River. He's lending me a truck and I'm going to drive up to Scarlett's mountain house … I used the Russian angle as an explanation. I want to give Jeb and his family some time to get out of town; I'm sending them to the Bahamas for ten days. I'll drive down from the mountains to Orlando and pick you up. So let's plan on Friday. We'll start our surveillance that same night."

"Where are the guns located?"

"Everything is on the boat with me. I thought we might need them since I didn't know what kind of hornet's nest we might walk into on the Huckins operation."

"I'll make an airplane reservation when we hang up. Sorry for this second shit storm, 'Bro', I'll try my best to make it right."

"I'll call you tomorrow or the next day to get your travel information."

"OK … and Seth … keep your eyes open."

Seth feared he might be stretching his relationship with Lori a little thin. Just when they finally got serious and became intimate, he takes off with the boys on an open-ended fishing trip. Of course he hadn't counted on this complication with the Tampa Mafia, and really, everything had to be put on hold until it was settled.

He sent Lori a text: *Lori, We're finished fishing in Key West and are now going to fish the sea-mounts (humps) off Marathon and Islamorada for tuna and then finally end up in Stuart. I'll either leave the boat in Stuart at my friend Bill Tilley's dock and drive home, or motor across the Okeechobee waterway to Fort Myers. Maybe you can join me for all or part of the trip home, whenever I bring TAR BABY across. I'll keep you posted. I miss you and I'm looking forward to seeing you soon…… Seth*

Seth wouldn't blame her if she moved on, but there wasn't anything he could do about it right now. If she gave him the chance, he would explain the Huckins operation and the Russian retribution that resulted from their success. But only after he and Beau settled the Tampa Mafia thing.

Seth put *TAR BABY* up on plane and throttled her up to 24 knots. At that speed, according to his GPS, he was eight hours from St. Lucie Inlet. That would put him at Bill Tilley's dock around 6:00 p.m.

***

Cadillac called Luigi with the bad news.

"Vito called ... and we missed our chance to snatch Stone in Key West."

"What went wrong?"

"Well, we caught a break when the main group left the Seven Fish restaurant in both of their rental vans. Stone and the big Italian guy walked down Elizabeth Street towards his boat at A&B Marina by themselves. I had already sent Joe The Animal and Big Fred down because it looked like our last chance to snatch him down here. I had Vito meet them and drive the Escalade since he knew the area better. They drove past them on that dark street and cut them off with the SUV. Joe and Fredo jumped out and pulled their guns. Stone and his buddy turned tail and took off. Our guys ran 'em down and that's when it all went to shit."

"Whadda ya mean ... it went to shit?"

"Well, Vito said that Stone turned back around and tackled Joe, knockin' the wind out of him. Stone's buddy turned out to be some kind of Kung Fu, fuckin' hero. He took Fredo's gun away and broke his wrist. Then he whirled around and broke Fredo's ankle with one of those Bruce Lee kicks. Next he pulled Joe offa Stone and crushed his throat with a karate chop. Stone jumped up and grabbed Joe, who could hardly breathe, and ran his head into a fuckin' tree trunk, knockin' him cold. Vito jumped out of the SUV and fired a couple of shots in the air, and the two of them ran off. Vito got our guys back in the Escalade and took them back to Summerland Key. He called me from there. I told him to have Johnny The Gimp drive Fredo and Joe up here tonight and I'd have Doctor Mendez waitin'. Vito and Angela will cancel their flight to Miami tomorrow, and take a cab to Summerland Key to help Eddie The Drummer bring back the other three Escalades. Luigi ... I got a call comin' in from Vito … hold on a minute, I'll be right back ………… OK, I'm back. Vito just checked A&B, and Stone's boat is gone."

"It looks like we have underestimated Mr. Stone. You take care of your guys, and let me know at the end of the week how your payoffs and everythin' else is going in Key West."

Luigi set up an immediate meeting with No Nose, and was there in 30 minutes.

"Sorry to come over so late John, but this couldn't wait."

"Light up one of these Nicaraguans and pull up a chair, Luigi."

Wall to Wall related that night's events and suggested that they pull all the stops out on Seth Stone, short of killing him.

"I agree we need to turn the heat up. I see in Giorgio's updated profile that Stone has a hunting lease outside of Brooksville. Put a team up there to watch that place. Keep Fat John and Mo-Mo watching the boatworks and his townhouse. But he might not come this way for awhile. Keep Giorgio and Captain Tony looking at the marinas and fuel docks on both coasts. Also have his boat and vehicles checked through the DOT for bridges and tolls. Have our information techs find and hack his credit cards, and report the location of any charges. I also want his sister's houses in Atlanta and in North Georgia watched. Call Jo-Jo Sabatini at the Cheetah lounge in Atlanta and Chief Johnny Peckerwood up at the Cherokee Casino in North Carolina. They both owe us a few favors. I hate to do it … but if we don't get him in a week or so we may have to snatch his son and trade him."

"Consider it all done, John," said Wall to Wall as he walked off the veranda.

CHAPTER TWENTY-TWO

Seth enjoyed the brisk and scenic ride up the Middle and Upper Keys. He followed Hawk Channel past Rodriquez Key, just off of Key Largo, to unspoiled Elliott Key. The only discordant sight was the two huge red and white stacks at the Turkey Point Nuclear Plant across lower Biscayne Bay. A reactor accident there could wipe out a large part of the Everglades eco-system, not to mention Homestead, and South Miami. He moved closer to shore and soon spied the remaining stilt houses south of Key Biscayne. Old Florida was slowly fading away. At that point the "Great Wall of Florida" started in Miami Beach. The ride became monotonous as he passed one high rise condo or resort hotel after another. Passing by at 26 knots blended them together and the shore line took on the appearance of a solid concrete and glass wall with an erratic parapet. He gazed mostly offshore for the next four hours thinking about the perfect hurricane that would level all the offending condos. But, Seth was not naïve. He knew the developers would build them all back even bigger, on a beach reclaimed from the sea, for the insatiable refugees from the frozen north.

As he neared Palm Beach, the wall started to melt away into single family homes and low-rise town homes. He ran by Jupiter and along uninhabited Long Island, part of St. Lucie State Park. There was a light east wind and an outgoing tide when Seth arrived at St. Lucie Inlet. The inlet was a bit lumpy and the inside marks were in different locations than the last time he had come through. But that was par for the course in this inlet, as the ever present dredging barges attested. If the wind had been 15-20 knots he would have come in at Lake Worth or Jupiter, as St. Lucie Inlet could be dangerous in those conditions. Once past Manatee Pocket and closer to the three bridge congregation at Roosevelt Highway, he took *Tar Baby* off plane and pulled the throttles back to idle. He motored slightly out of the channel and shifted into neutral. He went hustled below and retrieved a roll of masking tape and a piece of bed sheet he had cut up earlier. He hosed off the transom with fresh water and dried it with a towel, leaning over from the fishing cockpit. Next he taped the sheet over the name and hailing port. The old blue Roosevelt Bridge was a drawbridge with a bridge tender. The bridge tender logged the name and hailing port of every boat that passed thru his bridge into his state DOT computer. It was the only way that anybody could track Seth on this particular trip. He returned to the flybridge and passed thru the railroad and draw bridges and started under the new 65 foot high Roosevelt Bridge. Suddenly, *TAR BABY's* VHF radio crackled with, "Hatteras sportfish, Hatteras sportfish, this is the Roosevelt Bridge tender. Please identify your yacht's name and hailing port."

Seth figured that might happen, if the bridge tender was alert. He radioed back, "The MV, *REEL TIGHT,* Tampa, Florida, sustained transom damage … standing by on channel 16."

"Thank you, captain, have a safe trip home."

Seth throttled up and headed for Bill Tilley's house, in Stuart's Palm City suburb. The actual Hatteras 46 *REEL TIGHT* belonged to Tim Gripe, a long time customer at the boatworks and Tampa's unofficial titty bar king. Seth didn't think Tim would mind.

As he neared the Martin Downs Boulevard Bridge, Seth angled to starboard towards Bill Tilley's dock on the west side of the St. Lucie's River south fork. He turned the Hatteras all the way around and backed in next to the empty side of the dock. Tilley's 35 Cabo Express was tied up on the other side. Seth didn't want the name on the transom to be visible from the waterway channel. Bill walked out to the dock to help him tie up; Bill was 5'9" tall, sandy haired, with a medium build, and a disarming smile. It was 6:15 and he had his customary nightly martini in his left hand.

"Hey, Seth, you made good time. I wasn't sure if you'd make it today."

"It was pretty flat out there, and I ran up here at a little over 24 knots. Is Trudy in the house?"

"Trudy's been up in Atlanta all week with the grandkids, and I was just fixin' to go to dinner."

"Well, help me tie her up and plug her in, and I'll buy you dinner."

"Throw me your stern lines and a spring."

Seth got tied up, shut down, and plugged in. He gave the boat a quick hosing. He cleaned himself up, changed into a fresh shirt, and joined Bill on the dock.

"Where to, amigo?"

"The Riverwalk Café and Oyster Bar, downtown. I like the bronzed wahoo, but all the fish and steaks are good … and they have a great wine list."

"Sounds good to me, Bill, let's go, I'm hungry."

The bronzed wahoo was outstanding and Seth found a Ridge, Geyersville, Red Zinfandel blend on the wine list. After Bill was sworn to secrecy, he asked question after question about the Stock Island bust and the Huckins recovery. He made Seth promise to consider him for the next Geezer's caper if there was one. They had a nightcap on his dock and Bill gave him the keys to the Ford-150 pickup. Seth was glad to see that the fish company's name had been removed from the doors. Bill was reluctant to talk about the company's demise.

"I chalked it up to experience. It was like a hobby, I learned a lot, and it was fun while it lasted. It helped me stay busy my first two years of retirement … now I'm just going to concentrate on recreational fishing and being a professional witness."

"Well, it certainly was a change from 40 years in forensic accounting," said Seth. "Thanks for lending me your truck. I should be back in a couple of weeks or so. The keys are in the baitwell. I'm going to load up and head out early, it'll take me ten or eleven hours to get up to Hiawassee. In case you're not up … I'll say goodbye now."

"I'll be up. Do you want me to fuel her up while you're gone? I'm going to fill mine sometime this week, I have a tanker truck coming … You can pay me when you get back."

"That would be great; you're a good friend, Bill."

***

Seth loaded up his duffel, pistols, rifles, cash, computer and printer, ammo and other gear, locked the boat and left Palm City at first light. He didn't wake Bill Tilley and headed for Interstate 95 north after back-tracking to a Starbucks on Rte. 1, for a breakfast sandwich and two venti coffees to go. The Florida Turnpike was risky because of the cameras at the toll plazas. He turned north on I-95 from SW Martin Hwy. and was on his way to the mountains at 7:15. It was a great morning to drive, as it was overcast and not as hot as usual.

As he mulled over different options, his cell phone chimed. It was a text message from Jeb: *Leaving this coming Thursday for Nassau, Atlantis, and the Bahamas. Lynne's looking forward to the change of scenery and the kiddie activities that are available at Atlantis. We'll all have some quality time together. I also booked a three day side trip to Valentine's on Harbor Island, in Eleuthera. We're going by high speed ferry, three hours, with a stop in Spanish Wells. Busy making work lists for Jerry and Jeff. Bookings are steady at the yard. Be back in St. Pete a week from Saturday … Thanks, and be careful, JEB*

Seth smiled to himself; he knew they would enjoy the amenities at Atlantis, and Jeb had added a little adventure with the ferry ride to Spanish Wells and Harbor Island. Lynne would love Valentine's Boutique Resort, its three mile pink sand beach, and quaint little Dunmore Town. They probably would be able to go scuba diving, since the hotel offered babysitting services. Seth knew because he and Lisa had taken Jeb there when he was four years old and had done that very same thing.

Soon, Seth was driving west on I-10, headed towards I-75. The persistent fish smell in the pickup cab was only bearable with the air conditioning on full blast. Once on I-75 he would drive north to the south side of Macon, Georgia and pickup Rte. 129 to Athens.

He stopped for gas in Perry, and grabbed a Chick-fil-A chicken sandwich for lunch. He bought two large sugar-free lemonades for the road. When he arrived in Athens, at about 5:00 in the afternoon, he took Rte. 441 north to Clayton, about an hour north. When he got to Clayton he topped off his tank, and had a Big Mac for dinner. He turned west on Hwy. 76 and drove over the mountain to Hiawassee, Georgia.

It was 7:00 p.m. when Seth drove through the little town of Hiawassee. After a brief stop at Ingles Supermarket for some essential groceries and beverages, he crossed the bridge over the south part of Lake Chatuge, and passed the Fieldstone Marina Resort. He drove another half-mile to Rte. 515/69 and turned right towards Hayesville, North Carolina. The road to Scarlett's cabin was a mile down this road at the bottom of the hill. Seth yawned and thought about just jumping in bed when he got there. The last bank sign he passed had the temperature at 78°, by 11:00 tonight it would be 65°. The overcast start to the day had faded out to partly cloudy. As Seth slowed down to make a right turn, he noticed a black Escalade EXT parked on the county highway's berm on the other side of the road. It looked occupied. As he turned up the access road the alarm in his head went off. After his Key West experience, the Escalade was too much of a coincidence. He needed to make damn sure there wasn't something suspicious going on here.

Seth drove up the hill from the highway and tucked the pickup into Scarlett's detached garage behind the cabin. He stowed the groceries in the cabin's kitchen refrigerator and stowed his duffel, guns, and other equipment in a guest bedroom. He shucked his shorts and flip flops, put on blue jeans, a black long sleeve t-shirt, and his leather boat shoes. As the sun slowly faded over the mountains, Seth slipped his Ruger LCP in his pocket, grabbed his binoculars, and slithered down through the woods at the rear of Scarlett's property. The Escalade was still sitting there on the berm; Seth trained his binoculars on the front windshield from his hidden vantage point. There were two large American Indians sitting in the front seat. The driver had on a black cowboy hat, and his slightly smaller passenger wore a tan cowboy hat. Seth thought; *maybe the gambling interests in the Cherokee tribe in North Carolina and the Tampa Mafia wash each other's hands. After all there is a Seminole Casino right in the middle of Tampa.* Seth changed his location to get a rear view of the Escalade from a different vantage point. The truck had North Carolina, Swain County, license plates on it--the county where the Cherokee reservation and casino are located. Seth's instincts told him it was indeed too much of a coincidence. He climbed back up to the cabin and decided he better be more safe than sorry. Setting himself up in the detached garage for the night would probably be the safest alternative. He thought: *Better paranoid than kidnapped or worse.* As the sun went down, he went back into the house and constructed a dummy out of pillows and some of his clothes. He sat the dummy on the couch in front of the television in the great room, put his hat on the dummy's head, and turned on the TV and a few lights.

In the event of an altercation, Seth did not want to attract any attention from the neighbors. The size of the acre-plus lots and the amount of foliage and trees blocked out any sight of each other, but sound carried in the hollows and across the lake below. As Seth considered his next move, he remembered that his brother-in-law, Lon, had some trouble here with aggressive bears. They had to take their bird feeders in at night or the bears would rip them off the porches and empty the birdseed down their throats. On occasion, the frustrated bears would try to break down the cabin doors. Scarlett would not let Lon shoot them with a shotgun, so he took the counsel of the county animal trapper and bought a tranquilizer/dart pistol. Lon had already tranquilized two offending bears and the trapper had picked them up and relocated them. Lon had told Seth that the veterinarian who sold him the M99 tranquilizing chemical informed him the bear dose was strong enough to kill a man, so he had to be careful when he filled the darts. The vet supplied Lon with a vial of the antidote Naloxone in case he accidentally got pricked by the dart. He cautioned him that he had about 20 minutes to administer the antidote. Lon kept the tranquilizing gun and supplies in a locked drawer in the master bedroom.

Seth retrieved the key from the house's master key ring, hidden in the pantry. He opened the wooden case containing the Teledart RD206 CO_2 pistol, assembled it, and screwed on the barrel rated for a hundred feet. He removed three Teledarts with their red woolen stabilizing feathers, two syringes, a fill adapter, and two chemical vials. First, though, he filled a syringe with a dose of Naloxone. Then he carefully filled the three darts with M99, two-thirds of the way to the prescribed bear mark. He didn't want to kill anyone, and he felt that his life was not in immediate danger. Next, he inserted a CO_2 cartridge in the pistol grip and pressurized it until the gauge read max. After clicking on the safety he opened the breech and loaded the dart. It took two trips for him to carry the darts and gun, a loaded rifle, a pillow and blanket, two bottles of water, his night scope, and his tactical flashlight to the garage. He left the lights and TV on and locked the cabin door as he left.

Out in the garage, Seth found a blow-up water raft that his nephews used in the lake below the cabin. He blew it up, and put it in the empty bed of the pick-up truck. Then he lowered the tailgate and placed the dart pistol, rifle, and other gear into the pickup's bed. He opened the garage's side and rear windows, which were screened, and closed the overhead garage door. It would be pitch dark in about an hour.

Scarlett's cabin was equipped with outdoor motion sensor spotlights to discourage burglars. There was a double spotlight under each of the eaves on all four corners of the cabin. The garage also had a double motion spot up at the roof peak above the overhead garage door. When tripped, they stayed lit for five minutes. Seth could see the back of the cabin out of the horizontal row of small windows in the closed overhead door. He should be able to hear anybody coming up through the dense woods behind the cabin and garage.

Seth settled in and looped his night scope around his neck. He sipped some water as he waited for something to happen. He heard a few cars go up and down the steep road in front of the cabin. He fought off sleep by drinking a 5 hour energy drink that came in a little red bottle. He had used the product during long boat deliveries, and liked it because it had no sugar or caffeine crash.

About 1:00 a.m., Seth heard a twig break, and then noticed a slight rustling of the leaves on the forest floor. He didn't move a muscle. Next, he heard the crunch of cowboy boots as they crossed the gravel driveway turn-around up by the cabin. Seth moved quietly to the overhead door windows and took the dart gun and extra darts with him. He watched thru the night scope as two silhouettes crept up the eight steps to the rear deck and stood on the landing. It was the two Indians from the Escalade. Seth lowered the night scope and silently slipped out of the garage's side door and stood motionless, next to the trunk of an 80 foot high white oak. As Tan Hat moved forward towards the rear deck, the motion spotlight came on above them. They both recoiled in surprise and started to run down the narrow walkway deck on the side of the house, only to set off the spotlights at the other end. They jumped over the railing, fell to the ground, and started to scramble across the driveway for the safety of the woods. Black Hat struggled up first and Seth stepped away from the tree trunk and shot him in the right thigh. The Indian yelped and swatted at the dart in his leg. Seth calmly opened the breech of the Teledart pistol and reloaded. Black Hat took two more steps and started to stagger. Tan Hat rolled up off the driveway and headed for the woods. As he sprinted past his faltering comrade he yelled, "Come on, Red Bird!" When he passed the garage he set off the double spotlight there, and saw Seth standing in the shadows. Seth crouched, aimed, and squeezed the trigger as Tan Hat turned on his afterburner. The dart flew true and hit the fast moving redskin in the left buttock. Seth could hear him exhale as he disappeared into the thick underbrush. Seth was glad that Tan Hat had run straight away from him, so he didn't have to lead him. The Indian was as fast as any deer that Seth had ever shot.

Seth checked the now unconscious "Red Bird" who was lying in the middle of the driveway. He was breathing and had a pulse. Seth pulled his tactical flashlight from his rear pocket, drew his Ruger from his pocket holster, and eased down into the woods to find the second Indian. He found him about 100 feet downhill from the cabin in a twisted heap. Tan Hat had managed to pull the tranquilizing dart out of his butt cheek and still had it clasped in his hand. His vital signs were OK. Seth slowly dragged him by the feet back up the hill to the driveway. He duct taped their hands, arms, legs, feet, and mouths. Then he hogtied them with clothesline, and blindfolded each one of them. Finally, Seth pulled, pushed, and slid them up a 4'x 8' piece of plywood that he found in the garage, into the pickup's bed, aided by wrapping a plastic drop cloth around them. At that point, he administered a Naloxone antidote shot to both of them. He found the Escalade's keys in Red Bird's jeans pocket, confiscated two Glock 9mm pistol's, and collected their cell phones. Seth took both their wallets, which had all their IDs, cash, and credit cards. They needed to be engaged with the local sheriff for a long time.

After tidying-up the cabin, he loaded all his gear in the front seat of the Ford. Then he put the tranquilizing pistol and supplies away, turned off the cabin's water and water heater, and reset the AC at 82^0. He borrowed a cooler from the garage for his drinks and groceries, and stowed it in the pickup bed with the Indians. Seth took a bottle of Canadian whiskey from his brother-in-law's bar, found a Sharpie pen, an empty cardboard box, then turned out the lights and locked the door. He took a brown tarp out of the garage, checked the Indians' breathing, and covered them up. They were both breathing OK, but were still unconscious. Seth drove down the hill to the Indians' Escalade, rifled thru the backseat area, and came up with a Remington 870 tactical 12 gauge shotgun and a Winchester 30.06 deer rifle with a scope. He put everything in his truck and moved the Escalade about a half a mile up the road to a small crossroads strip shopping mall where there were several businesses: Mary's Southern Grill, Verizon, Spike's Vacuums, a consignment shop, a candy store, and some vacancies. Then he walked back down the hill, put an Ingles plastic grocery bag over his license plate, and drove north about a mile to the sheriff's headquarters on Crooked Creek Road. He stopped the truck in front of the large TOWNS COUNTY JAIL sign in front of the concertina wire topped, 12 foot high, chain link fence that surrounded the complex. Seth rolled the two hog-tied Indians out of the pick-up bed onto the lawn in front of the sign. Neither one of them stirred. The large sign blocked the surveillance cameras mounted on the office and jail buildings, from recording Seth's movements. He sprinkled the contents of the Canadian whiskey bottle over both Indians. Next, he tore a flap off the cardboard box, wrote a message on it with the Sharpie, and duct-taped it to Red Bird's chest.

The sign read: **These here drunk, thieving, injuns ..... Courtesy of the KKK.**

Seth drove back thru Hiawassee and headed south, over a different mountain, for Helen, Georgia. Once through Helen, he rode down into Nacoochee and turned left on Rte. 384, and drove the narrow, winding, unlit, road through the pitch dark night until he crossed the Chattahoochee River on the Duncan Bridge. Only one car had passed him in the last 20 minutes, so he pulled off the road at the far side of the bridge and turned off his lights. He gathered up the Indians' rifle, shotgun, pistols, cell phones, keys, IDs, and wallets and bundled them all in the brown tarp. Walking quickly to the center of the span, he threw the bundle into the river, 75 feet below.

As Seth walked back to his truck a chill ran up his spine. He suddenly recalled the vision of *CHICA'S* inflatable dinghy plunging into the Tarcoles River, and it made his asshole pucker. *That was it!* Someone had found the dinghy or the outboard near that bridge. Both were registered to the *CHICA* in Florida. The discovery of the dinghy made it obvious that someone had gotten off the Bertram before it blew up that night. The hotel and airline records would place him there. But who would be crazy enough to ply a river full of hungry 25 foot crocodiles? His mind couldn't answer that question.

Seth finally found a mom and pop motel in Gainesville, Georgia, The Guest House Inn and Suites, which was not part of a chain. It was just off Rte. 129 and close to the top of Lake Lanier. He paid cash, and slept for the next 12 hours.

CHAPTER TWENTY-THREE

Seth liked his location in Gainesville. It was off the beaten path, only seven to eight hours from Orlando or Tampa. He needed some time to research the Tampa Mafia. Researching and chronicling their hierarchy was critical, and he also wanted pictures of John Cipriano and his capos. He couldn't just call Gene Johnson or Bobby Thompson to get the information, that would require an explanation. Seth did not want to reveal the truth about Beau to anyone. He had the computer and printer from *TAR BABY* to work with, and had plenty of photographic and regular copy paper left over from the Huckins project.

He called Beau and got his flight information; Friday: arrive 5:11 p.m.-Jet Blue flt. 1692, Orlando International Airport, (MCO). He wrote it down and said, "Wait until you hear this!" and launched into a monologue describing the Indian attack in Hiawassee.

"The tranquilizer gun was brilliant, Seth, then dropping them off at the Towns County Jail in the middle of the night ... way cool. They'll be in there for a few days at least, even after they call the tribe's mouthpiece. I think you're right about the dinghy or engine being found ... that would definitely get the Tampa boys looking again. Where's Scarlett?"

"She's in Rockford, Illinois, at a soccer tournament with the whole family. So they're not in any danger."

"Where are you?"

"I'm in Gainesville, Ga. in a nice old motel by Lake Lanier. I'm paying cash and I'm pretty much incognito. I'm planning on doing some internet research here on the Tampa Mafia today and tonight. I'm going to catch up on my sleep, and then I'll leave tomorrow to get us set up in Brandon. I might start some surveillance tomorrow night and get comfortable with the Tampa streets. Cipriano lives on South Golf View, in Palma Ceia, right?"

"Last time I checked he did, and remember to check out the Tampa capo, the one the Cubans called Wall to Wall."

"OK, see you Friday, Beau. But first, give me a credit card so I can book us a room. They're probably monitoring my credit cards, but they don't know Robert Cornett."

Seth jotted the card number down, and hung up. Beau's new identity was Robert Jonathon Cornett, Toronto, Canada. The real Robert Cornett had retired early, moved to Costa Rica, and died of natural causes a couple years back at 58 years of age. He had no next of kin so a coroner's assistant in San Jose neglected to file his death certificate and sold his papers to an underworld identity broker. Beau laid out some serious cash for this ID, but it came with a Canadian pension and health benefits. He was free to travel the world with his Canadian passport, although he probably would not chance a trip to Canada.

Seth went the front desk, re-upped for another night, and asked for the Wi-Fi code. He spent the rest of the afternoon, interrupted only for lunch and a swim in the motel's pool, compiling information on the Tampa Mafia. He found Cipriano's address in Hillsborough County's public records. He scoured articles in the *Tampa Tribune*, *St. Times Petersburg*, and *The Miami Herald*. He found articles and family charts produced by Mario Machi and Scott Deitche, two Florida West Coast investigative reporters. Information surfaced on Luigi "Wall to Wall" Scuzzi, Cipriano's top capo. He found indictments against Luigi and Giorgio Scuzzi for money laundering through JC Carpet, and the various carpet manufacturers that JC owned. They had no convictions. Vincent "Cadillac" Carlucci was listed on the family chart as the Miami capo. He had indictments for human trafficking, assault and battery, and running a house of prostitution. Also no convictions. Public records revealed their residence and business addresses. The newspapers provided several pictures of John Cipriano, Luigi Scuzzi, and Vincent Carlucci. Seth printed the pictures and public record information, and printed a few articles for Beau to read. He took another swim and drove up the parkway for dinner at an Outback Steakhouse. After dinner, Seth went back to his room and used Google Earth to familiarize himself with the Palma Ceia area of South Tampa, and JC Carpet located on Dale Mabry Avenue. Seth also located a non-chain motel in Brandon on Rte. 60, The Brandon Motor Lodge, where they could park their vehicles out of site of the highway. He called on his sat-phone and made a reservation for a first floor suite, facing the outside, with two beds, for a week starting Thursday. Seth and Beau could be in downtown or South Tampa in 20 minutes using a number of different routes. Seth slept soundly and requested a 6:00 a.m. wake-up call.

Seth was on I-985 south at 6:30 after a quick stop at a Dunkin' Donuts for two large coffees and a bagel to go. He drove the Ford pickup south to I-85, and then took I-285 west, then I-675 south, and finally I-75 south at Stockbridge. He stopped for gas along the I-475 Macon by-pass and continued down to Florida, stopping only for a Chick-fil-A sandwich near Valdosta. Seth pulled into the Brandon Motor Lodge at 2:30 p.m. He checked in, prepaid with cash, and stowed most of his gear in the room's closet. He looked at his watch; *Jeb, Lynne, and Cullen should be safely in Nassau by now, and just getting their first look at the spectacular setting at Atlantis.*

Golf View Street was exactly 20 minutes from the Brandon Motel. The homes were stately and the surrounding streets were dotted with parked service trucks and vans—mostly white: air conditioning service trucks, landscapers, painting contractors, lawn services, window washers, and carpet cleaner trucks and vans. The neighborhood streets were lined with live oak trees, their branches draped with Spanish moss. Every house had extensive landscaping. All the driveways had pavers, and John Cipriano's mansion had a six car garage behind a wrought iron gate and a formidable stuccoed wall. It backed up to the Palma Ceia Country Club golf course. Seth drove by it twice, and on his second trip he noticed a narrow cart path that led to the golf course between the second and third house east of Cipriano's. There was a chain with a spring clip strung across the paved path, attached to two waist-high black iron posts. It was probably there so the neighborhood club members could drive their personal golf carts to the clubhouse. He drove out to Himes Avenue and turned left, then took a right on Neptune, then a quick left on Frankland and drove along the golf course. The course had hundreds of queen palm trees and stately old southern live oaks. There was a low wall on the Himes Ave. section, and large homes further south on Frankland. The wall could easily be scaled, and several of the large homes had no fences or walls around them. It looked like easy access to the golf course from that direction.

Seth explored the streets west towards South Dale Mabry. A plan started forming in his head. Dale Mabry was four blocks from Cipriano's mansion. He scoured the area for a low traffic, non-monitored, parking lot. One block north was Watrous Avenue. Wright's Gourmet House Supermarket was located on the southeast side of Dale Mabry and Watrous. There were two large unsupervised parking lots that were accessible only from an alley behind the store, and no evidence of any surveillance cameras. It looked like a good place to park a small truck. Seth figured that a bicyclist would not attract any attention, day or night, in that neighborhood. There was constant bicycle traffic in that area. He would buy a bicycle back in Brandon, and try out this theory later this evening.

Driving south again on Frankland, Seth turned west at Plant High School and drove towards Luigi Scuzzi's residence in Beach Park. He turned right when he got to Westshore, then left on West Bay Way Drive. Luigi Scuzzi's house was a two-story Mediterranean "McMansion" with a six foot iron fence around it. There were two black cars parked outside the attached garage. Seth could see the top of a two story pool screen enclosure behind the garage. His house backed up to a canal that led to Tampa Bay.

Next Seth drove to West Kennedy which would take him back to Dale Mabry and the Tampa location of JC Carpets. He was there in ten minutes. He parked across the street in an automated BP gas station and observed JC's operation through its glass-fronted showroom with his binoculars. He could see the small, glass sales cubicles along the back wall, and a door marked **Executive Offices** in the middle. The rest of the showroom was filled with carpet, tile, and wooden floor samples. Seth studied his Tampa street map on his cell phone and figured Luigi was fifteen minutes from Cipriano's house, from either his house or office.

Back in Brandon Seth found a bike store a few blocks east of his motel. He walked in Brandon Bike and Mower at 5:00 and bought a used black mountain bike for $400 cash. He asked the proprietor, "How did you come up with the Lawnmower/Bike combination?"

"Well," said Jack, the owner. "I'm a certified small engine mechanic, and mountain and cross-country biking is my hobby."

At West Marine, a few blocks away on Rte. 60, and bought one hundred feet of ½" black nylon rope.

Next, he headed for a nearby Lowes. There he bought a brown tarp, four 1 ½"x 4' wooden dowels, a Ryobi 18 volt rechargeable hand drill and two drill bit kits, two lag-in metal bicycle hangers, a box of assorted Velcro wraps, a roll of black electrical tape, a dark green canvas tool satchel, a box of black contractor garbage bags, a butane grill lighter, a package of bungee cord straps, and a hack saw. He drove back to the motel and took his purchases, including the bike, into his suite. He plugged in the Ryobi charger, and while the drill battery charged, he used the electrical tape to black out the chrome on the mountain bike. He cut the dowels into 12" pieces with the hack saw. When the battery was charged he inserted a 9/16" spade bit into the drill chuck, snapped the battery in place, and drilled parallel holes at each end of the cut dowels. Seth did all this work in the bathtub over a wastebasket lined with a garbage bag. With that done, he cut two 25' pieces of ½"rope, and started threading the pre-drilled dowels on it to make a rope ladder. He spaced the rungs at 16" intervals and tied an overhand knot on each side of the drilled hole. When completed, he had a 20 foot ladder. Seth tied the remaining 50 feet of line into a bridle loop he had fashioned at the top of the ladder, using a bowline knot. Next he crafted a monkey fist knot at the other end, burned all the cut ends with the grill lighter, and stowed the ladder in the tool satchel. He also put the charged drill, a ¼" drill bit, the lag bicycle hangars, binoculars, night scope, and Velcro wraps in the satchel. He used two of the Velcro straps to secure the satchel under the bike's crossbar above the pedal chain sprocket.

Seth was ready for some dinner, but first changed into a black long sleeved performance t-shirt and blue jeans. He took his navy blue fishing cap, and wore his leather boat shoes. After a light dinner at Chili's he returned to the motel as darkness fell. He loaded the bike and the gear into the white Ford F-150 pickup's bed and covered the bed with the tarp and secured it with bungee cords.

Seth drove west on Rte. 60 towards South Tampa and Palma Ceia. He had his tactical flashlight in his back pocket and his Ruger LCP.380 in his right front pocket. He stayed on Rte. 60, drove down through Channelside and downtown Tampa, and finally turned left on Dale Mabry. He took another left, at Watrous, and then drove into the alley behind the gourmet supermarket. There were only two cars parked in the back lot. After parking, he locked the truck and pulled the bike from under the tarp through the tailgate. In less than 30 seconds he was pedaling, eastbound on West Watrous. Seth turned south on Himes, left on Jean Circle, and then he took a sharp right at the east end of South Golf View Street. He pedaled down Golf View to the cart path, threaded the bike around the outside of the black pipe and chain barrier, and headed for the golf course. Suddenly, he was in the middle of a fairway and it was pitch dark. He stopped and retrieved his night scope. The backs of the houses behind him were lit up in various stages, and in front of him was a large yawning sand trap. Behind the sand trap was a stand of 80 year old, moss draped, live oak trees. Seth put the night scope's lanyard around his neck and let his eyes adjust. He maneuvered around the sand trap and eased into the stand of live oaks. To his surprise, a paved cart path wound its way thru the live oaks. He hid his bike in a cluster of large oleander bushes and covered the reflectors with some Spanish moss. He surveyed the back of Cipriano's house with his binoculars. It appeared that the underwater pool light was on from the glow on the house and foliage. There was some candle-like light coming from a very wide second story veranda, and one pair of spotlights shone down from a roof eave high-up on the house.

Seth decided to see what was on the south side of the live oak trees. As he moved across the cart path and into the open he could see a pond and a cluster of low buildings with two spotlights shining straight down. They looked like course maintenance buildings. The abundance of large hardwood trees led Seth to believe he could find a vantage point up in one of the huge trees to watch the Cipriano house at night.

He returned to the oleander bushes and retrieved his tool satchel, and walked over to the base of the largest oak on the north side of the cart path. Seth removed the rope ladder, and uncoiled the 50 foot line. He twirled the heavy monkey fist knot around his head like a lariat, and threw it up and over a large branch about 15 feet up. The monkey fist fell back to the ground, pulling the line behind it. He hoisted the rope ladder up to the limb with the line, and pulled it next to the tree's trunk. He quickly retrieved the Ryobi drill from the bag and drilled a ¼" pilot hole in the tree trunk. Next he hand-turned the bicycle storage lag into the tree. It would serve as a cleat to secure the ladder line. Seth tied the tool satchel to the bottom rung of the rope ladder and then climbed up the ladder to the branch. Once he was straddling the branch, he pulled the ladder and bag up and secured them to the branch with a bungee cord tie down. Seth surveyed the tree's branches above him. Several were reachable and afforded a clear view of Cipriano's house. He worked his way up about six feet higher and straddled that branch with his back against the trunk.

Suddenly, he heard an engine noise and saw headlights coming down the cart path from the west. It was a groundskeeper in a gasoline powered cart, probably on his way to water a green. He drove almost under Seth, and then disappeared into the darkness. Seth heard the cart stop about 150 yards to the east and start up ten minutes later. Seth trained his binoculars on the back of Cipriano's house. He could clearly see the swimming pool across the fairway, 90 yards away. He could also see the entire second floor veranda and into the lit-up rooms behind it. There was a tall man standing by a lighted door, and further down the veranda someone sat in the dark smoking a cigar. Seth could see the cigar's glowing red tip and watched the smoke waft up through the spotlights that lit the yard below. A shorter, heavier man, probably another bodyguard, patrolled the backyard systematically.

Seth looked at his Submariner and the luminous dial read 9:36. The darker it got the more Seth could see with his nightscope, by then there was almost no twilight left in the sky above the horizon. At 9:45, the man standing at the lighted door went inside, walked by a billiards table, and out of sight. Five minutes later a short, rotund man stepped onto the veranda. The tall man, following him, stopped at the door. The rotund man kept moving towards the still-seated cigar smoker. He sat down next to the cigar smoker and within a minute, lit his own cigar. Seth couldn't see their faces, but he guessed, from the visitors build, and the fact that Cipriano did not stand up to acknowledge his visitor, that he was watching Luigi Scuzzi paying a visit to John Cipriano. They sat in the candle-lit shadows and talked for about 30 minutes. Seth rearranged some of the Spanish moss that hung from the tree limbs around him, to get a better view. Even with his night scope, Seth could only make out silhouettes … the most visible thing was the glowing red ash on the end of their cigars. The glass windscreen, below the veranda's polished stainless steel railing, looked too thick to be regular window glass. Seth figured it had to be bulletproof. But, from his elevation in the oak tree, he had a clear downward angle over the railing. Finally, Luigi got up and was escorted through the billiards room by the tall man, who returned five minutes later. At 10:30, Cipriano extinguished his cigar and left the veranda. The tall man snuffed out the candles, and then turned the lights out in the billiards room. A light came on at the west end of the second floor, illuminating a large drape-covered window.

At almost the same moment, a light snapped on and a set of French doors opened in the neighbor's house directly to the east of Cipriano's. A tall blonde woman dressed in a white robe walked out towards a darkened pool. She bent over and switched on the pool's underwater lights. She slowly dropped her robe, and walked down a set of stairs in the shallow end, stark naked. She started to swim laps, and Seth grudgingly turned his attention back to Cipriano's backyard. Cipriano's stocky bodyguard had pulled a bar stool over to the wall, was standing on it, and was watching the naked neighbor swim. Seth had to chuckle; *well, boys will be boys, won't they?* He wondered if this was a nightly ritual.

Soon the bodyguard lost interest and the woman retired back into her house. Seth had seen enough for one night. He climbed back down to the lower branch and dropped the rope ladder. After descending to the ground, he stowed the ladder in the satchel, and unscrewed the bicycle hangar lag. He broke a small branch off an oleander, stripped off the flowers, but left a couple of leaves. He carefully fitted the twig into the drilled hole. He would have no trouble finding it the next night.

With the satchel stowed back on the bike's crossbar, he exited the oleanders. Seth rode quickly across the fairway and down the cart path. He pedaled out of the neighborhood the same way he had entered, not riding past Cipriano's mansion. The parking lot behind Wright's was deserted and he was loaded and gone in under a minute.

Seth thought about what he had seen and wondered if Luigi had a meeting there every night or was just on call. He also wondered how Luigi got there-- from his residence or JC Carpet. They would find all this out when Beau arrived. Beau would rent a van at the airport and Seth would buy two prepaid cell phones for communication, at the Super Wal-Mart a block from the motel. Seth would get the phones tomorrow morning since Beau's flight didn't land until 5:11 p.m.

***

On Thursday afternoon, Luigi got a long-distance call on his sat-phone from Jack Standing Bear, Chief Peckerwood's General Counsel.

"Luigi, I'm in Towns County, Georgia. I'm trying to bail two of the Chief's operatives out of the county jail here. They called me from the jail on Wednesday after they requested a lawyer. I just talked to them and am waiting for a bail hearing. But, Chief Peckerwood thought you should know what went on here as soon as possible."

"I appreciate the call, but it don't sound good already."

"Our two braves, Red Bird and Blue Fox have been charged with public drunkenness and disturbing the peace. The Sheriff's Department could not connect them to any crimes committed that night. The sheriff's deputies found them early Wednesday morning, totally incoherent and reeking of whiskey. They had been duct-taped, hog-tied, and then dumped on the front lawn of the jail. A sign indicated that they had been delivered there by the local KKK. They had no identification, had lost their truck keys, and their truck was not where they said they'd left it. They claimed they did not remember what happened to them. During their private lawyer/client interview with me, they said that they had seen the person they were sent to kidnap arrive at the Hiawassee house, early Tuesday night. They drove by the house a couple times later that night and saw lights inside the cabin and the subject watching television. They waited until after midnight, then crept up through the backwoods to surprise and kidnap him. Red Bird said the subject had an ambush set up and shot them both with tranquilizing darts. They don't remember anything after that, until they woke up in jail."

"I'm sorry it turned out like this, Standin' Bear. Please give Chief Peckerwood our thanks for tryin'."

"I will, and I'm sure I can get them off with a fine, but it looks like you might have your hands full with this Seth Stone character."

"It would be lots easier just to whack him, but that's not gonna happen, just yet."

Luigi couldn't believe the headache Seth Stone had become. He was making them look foolish. Thankfully, he had some good news for No Nose about the Key West Russian transition from Cadillac. His Key West Police informant related that since the political and police payoffs had been reinstated by Cadillac's man, there was little interest in pursuing the Russian disappearances and murders. But, he knew tonight's meeting with No Nose still would not be pleasant. He set it up for 9:45 p.m.

***

Luigi lit the cigar that No Nose offered. It was a Cuban Bolivar Coronas Gigantes. He filled him in on the progress in Key West and No Nose said, "The payoff money always helps, but society views the murder of a criminal as a victimless crime. Nobody will miss the Russians ... except their families."

Luigi took a deep breath and launched into the Seth Stone Indian massacre. No Nose was not happy.

"I think we are finished playing nice with Mr. Stone, Luigi. If we don't have him in our custody by Monday morning, instruct Fat John and Mo-Mo to pick up Jeb Stone after work on Monday, or as soon as they can after that. Fat John's report says that Jeb always works late and leaves after all the other employees are gone. Don't touch his wife or little boy and don't explain anything to him once you get him. Just blindfold him, and keep him comfortable. When his father comes in ... we'll let him go."

"OK, John, I'll set it up Monday mornin'."

CHAPTER TWENTY-FOUR

Seth was up early Friday morning, and ate breakfast at the Waffle House a few blocks from the motel. He back-tracked to the Super Wal-Mart and purchased a couple of prepaid cell phones for $20 each and loaded each of them with $30 worth of minutes and text. While he was there, he picked up six black long sleeved XL t-shirts, two pairs of 36R black jeans, a black and gray backpack, and a black adjustable ball cap. He also bought a couple of inexpensive tactical flashlights, a box of twelve--5 hour energy drinks, a case of Fiji water, and a 15-pak of PowerBar/Protein and Recovery bars. After stowing the purchases at the motel, Seth drove into Tampa and set up surveillance across from JC Carpets. He saw a young, tall, good looking Italian man come in about 10:30 a.m. in a Jaguar XK with the top down. Seth figured, from his Cipriano family chart, that he was probably Giorgio, Luigi's son. He took Giorgio's picture with his telephoto Nikon. Luigi pulled in about 11:00 a.m. in a black Escalade, and Seth was sure he was the same person he had seen meeting with Cipriano the night before, he took a snap-shot of the 5'5", 350 lb capo. Luigi was dressed in black clothes and his black hair was slicked-back. A half hour later Giorgio left in his Jaguar, probably for their St. Petersburg location in Tyrone. Seth looked up JC Carpet's hours on his cell phone: 10:00 a.m. to 9:00 p.m. Mon-Sat., and closed on Sunday. While he watched and waited, he cross-programmed the disposable cell phones, and familiarized himself with their operation. Seth stayed there until 2:00 in the afternoon. That's when the second pizza delivery man arrived and went inside the carpet store. He figured Luigi wasn't going out for lunch. He drove over to Golf View and wended his way through the same service truck maze that he had traversed the day before. It took fifteen minutes to get to Cipriano's house from the carpet store. Seth headed out Dale Mabry towards I-275 north and I-4 "malfunction junction". He didn't expect to encounter any delays before 3:00

in the afternoon, but with Tampa's poorly designed traffic pattern, you never knew. Soon he was on his way past the Fairgrounds and The Seminole Hardrock Casino. He smiled and wondered how his two Indian assailants were making out at the county jail in Towns County. When he passed the metal Mickey Mouse ears, "hidden" in the power substation near Disney World at exit 25, he knew he was close to the airport exit. Seth took the Central Florida Greenway South, Rte. 417 and entered the airport on Jeff Fuqua Boulevard. He parked in the short term parking garage, and took the elevator down to ground transportation outside of customs and immigration.

Seth sat on a bench and thought about how things were shaping up. They'd gotten a huge break with Cipriano's residence location. The accessibility of the golf course behind his house and the presence of the venerable old live oaks were more than beneficial. He figured it would be an easy shot for someone of Beau's considerable skill and experience. Beau had sniped out of the top of palm trees in Vietnam. He had killed many high ranking North Vietnamese military officers and politicians for the U.S. Government. Special-ops had trained him to kill with no remorse, and Beau had a hefty bounty on his head by the time he left "Nam". After the war, Beau struggled with the fact that he had started to like the killing. Rather than join a mercenary force like most of his sniper compatriots, he opted to return to his life at the boatworks. It had been a tough transition, marked by his drinking and gambling. But, Seth knew that Beau would not have a moral problem with this new situation. He would not enjoy killing Cipriano or his minions, but he would kill them because this was truly ...... *kill or be killed.*

Seth was sure they could have found a way to get Beau up in a palm tree if they had to, but the current situation was ideal. He hoped that Cipriano's cigar smoking was a nightly routine. No Nose's wife probably called the shots inside the residence and didn't allow him to stink up the interior beyond the billiards room. The next couple days of surveillance would confirm or deny it.

Passengers with luggage started pouring out the U.S. Customs exit. Beau appeared, carrying his duffel and pulling a small roll-around suitcase. His face broke into a big smile when he spotted Seth.

"Here I am, Bro, right on time … how are you?" asked Beau as he was greeted with a hug.

"Good to see you Beau … you don't look any worse for the wear." Beau looked tan, fit, and had maintained a close cropped full beard. His hair was still jet black, but his beard now revealed a little salt and pepper in places. Seth got right to cases. "I've got a lot to tell you, but it will have to wait until we get back to our motel in Brandon. I want you to rent a white van, with navigation, so we can be in two different places at the same time. Here's a prepaid cell phone, my number is the only number that's in contacts. Get the van and you can follow me back to the motel. If we lose each other, call me. I'm going to bring the pickup truck that Bill Tilley lent me, down from short-term parking while you sign up. It's a white, Ford F-150 … Rent the van for a week."

Beau followed Seth out of the airport and they drove in tandem, on I-4, to I-75 south which they took for a few miles, then exited at the Brandon Rte. 60 exit and drove east to the motel.

Beau walked into the suite and looked around. "This place has seen better days."

"I didn't want a chain motel, I only used your card to guarantee the reservation, and I paid cash in advance. Also, I wanted to be on the first floor with two exits. The back one opens to the pool. No one will screw with our vehicles since they're right outside of our door. It's twice as big as a Hampton Inn room and it has a kitchenette."

"Whoooa … don't take it personally, I know we're hiding out. This must have been a classy place back in its day."

Beau got comfortable and Seth started at the beginning. He showed Beau the Mafia family charts, the newspaper pictures, mug shots, and the sketches of the rear of the house. He put Google Earth 3D on the computer and reviewed the aerial shots of the house, neighborhood, golf course, and trees. He showed him the Remington 700, .308, 26" barrel, bolt action, outfitted for night time hog hunting. It was fitted with a Yukon 2.5 to 50 night vision scope, and Weaver side mounted red dot/infrared tactical lasers. Seth had also equipped it with a Surefire silencer and suppressor. Because of the silencer/suppressor, Seth explained, he was able to aim and shoot a hog, work the bolt rapidly, and shoot a second hog before the first one fell. It took about an hour for them to get on the same page.

"So the venue is perfect to take Cipriano out if he doesn't quit smoking. The access and large trees sound good."

"I'm hoping that enough shit is hitting the Mafia's fan that Luigi has to go over there every night with a report … even if it's just the cash flow numbers for the day or about trying to find me. I know these Mafia guys are paranoid about cell phones, wiretaps, bugs, eavesdropping, and keeping a low public profile, especially after the Gotti mess in New York. So … this is probably how the hierarchy communicates."

"OK, I can see that we need to take Luigi out, too. If we don't, we're not that far from square one. If we don't get him at the same time we get Cipriano, Luigi will go underground, thinking the Russians are coming."

"I agree, now let's get something to eat and then I'll take you to the venue and you can see it all first hand."

They went over to Chili's, sat at a remote table in the uncrowded restaurant. Seth explained, again, about the Russian connection. "The sheriff down in Key West told us that his chief intelligence deputy had informed him that the Tampa Mafia had eliminated the Russian Mafia in Key West, in a single day. However, there is no solid evidence it was them. All they had were few dead bodies that were vaporized in explosions and bombings, and one love triangle murder. The rest of the twenty-some Russians just disappeared. It happened right about the same time we were busy busting their new drug source. The Tampa mob let the Russians sell drugs in the Keys because they were already there, with our government's blessing, recruiting and supplying cheap green card labor to the hotels, restaurants, titty bars, and massage parlors. Once established in the drug trade, the Russians got greedy and started buying their cocaine cheaper from the freelancers who stole the Huckins. Sheriff Billy Ray Stodgins thought there would be retribution from the Russian Mafia in New York, directed at the Tampa mob. That just plays into our hand, if we take out Cipriano and Luigi Scuzzi. The Russian Mafia will get blamed and more shit hits the fan. Cadillac Carlucci, in Miami, will be the new boss. He'll be spread so thin he'll forget all about me. He will have to retaliate against the Russians to save face and the whole thing will feed upon itself until they call a truce or the major New York Italian families step in and end it."

Beau nodded and added, "Like I said, if we only get Cipriano, Luigi will figure it's the Russians, but he will eventually snatch you. We need to figure a way to get the two of them on that veranda together, to insure our safety."

They finished dinner, drove back, and loaded the bicycle and gear in Beau's rental van. They dressed in black. Beau emptied the satchel and packed the tree gear in the backpack Seth had bought. He strapped the Remington 700's black canvas case to the bike's crossbar, slipped the rifle in it, and zipped it up. He was more comfortable with a backpack, than with the satchel, from his days in Vietnam. They both went in the rental van so Seth could show Beau the area firsthand. They drove over using the Channelside route, but Seth would bring them back on the freeway route, so Beau would see the alternative. He eased the van down Golf View and showed Beau the cart path. Beau checked the site map and noted the relationship it had with Cipriano's residence, the golf course, and the oak trees. They drove the route along Watrous, turned up Dale Mabry and parked in the BP station across from JC's, just long enough for Seth to point out Luigi's black Escalade. Then they drove back down Dale Mabry and parked behind Wright's Gourmet.

"Do you remember the route to the cart path? I can drive the van in front of you if you want."

"No, I got it … east on Watrous, south on Himes, cut up Jean Circle, go right on Golf View. Then I zig-zag around the golf cart path chain pole … hang the night scope around my neck … pedal across the fairway to the stand of live oaks … hide the bike in the oleanders and cover the reflectors with Spanish moss … then find the biggest oak and feel for the twig sticking out of the drilled hole about waist high … deploy the rope ladder, lag in the hanger … climb up and pull the ladder up after me. Oh… and watch out for the night green keepers in the gasoline carts. How'd I do?"

"You got it, smartass. Here are the van keys. Give me a ten minute head start. I'm going to walk over to Frankland and up a block and a half. There are a few houses there, with no fences, that back up to the golf course. This time of the year, half the people in this neighborhood are up in the North Carolina

Mountains. I'll just ease out onto the course, and walk about three hundred yards to your tree."

Thirty minutes later they were both sitting 26 feet up in the live oak watching an empty veranda. Beau fiddled with the Remington's laser sights and infrared scope. He inched out further on the long horizontal limb into a branch cluster. He motioned for Seth to join him. Seth shimmied out there and Beau whispered, "This is a great angle, and the cross branches make a good armrest."

The lights in the backyard pool area were the same as they were the night before. The same stocky bodyguard made his rounds.

At 9:30 the lights snapped on in the billiards room and No Nose Cipriano strode past the table. His tall bodyguard opened the door to the veranda and he stepped through it. He made his way to the east end of the veranda and sat in an overstuffed chair. His bodyguard turned on the fans, lit some candles on a low table in front of Cipriano, and lit No Nose's king-size cigar. Beau took some test sightings on No Nose with the Remington and then lowered it.

"We need to sight-in this rifle tomorrow," whispered Beau with his hand covering his mouth.

"Can do," whispered Seth.

They sat up in the tree watching Cipriano smoke his cigar. Suddenly, the bodyguard appeared next to No Nose with a large lit up phone which had a long, thick antenna. No Nose conversed with the caller and then handed a dark phone back to the tall bodyguard. At precisely 10:30 p.m. Cipriano stood up, made his way down the dark veranda, entered the billiards room door, and disappeared into the interior of the house. The bodyguard came out, blew out the candles, turned off the fans, closed the door, and turned off the lights.

Beau started to shimmy back on the branch he was straddling, but Seth whispered, "Hold on a couple of minutes."

Cipriano's bedroom light went on at the west end of the second floor. Then a light suddenly went on behind two French doors on the first floor of the house to the east of Cipriano's. The doors were flung open and the tall blonde in a white bathrobe walked toward a darkened pool. She bent down and turned on the pool's underwater lights. She took off her robe and carefully folded it, then turned, bent over, and placed it on the edge of the pool deck, affording Seth and Beau with a marvelous view of her spectacular bare derrière. Seth tapped Beau on the shoulder and whispered, "Look at the wall!"

Beau at once saw the stocky bodyguard, standing on his toes on top of the bar stool, looking over the wall. Beau stifled a laugh with his hand as Seth whispered; "Now I know this happens ... every night. She's driving that poor bastard crazy."

They waited patiently until the naked blonde tease finished her laps and re-entered her house. The outside bodyguard returned the bar stool to the pool bar and resumed his rounds. Seth and Beau exited the tree and made their separate ways back to the van.

Seth slipped into the passenger seat of the waiting van and said, "Pull out of the alley and turn left. Then take a right on Dale Mabry. We'll go back to the motel on the freeways."

"So that whole thing went well ... except Luigi didn't show."

"I would bet that sat-phone call was him checking-in."

"Good guess. I wish we could be sure when he was coming."

"Slow down, we're going to pass the carpet store at the end of this block." JC Carpet's building was dark and the parking lot was empty.

"Looks like Luigi went home. So, where are we going to sight-in the rifle tomorrow?"

"Take a right on 275 up ahead and head for I-4 ...... Tomorrow, we'll go to the Shoot Straight range up on Rte. 301 near Lake Orient Park ... the rifle range is 110 yards long. It's ten minutes from the motel and opens at 10:00 a.m."

"Cool, this will be the shortest sniper shot I've ever taken. Your infrared telescopic sight and those lasers should make it pretty easy ... if it's all zeroed-in. What got you interested in high-tech hog hunting?"

"Well, our old buddy Dixie invited me up to Crystal River for a deer and hog hunt a couple of years ago, and I shot a hog up there during the day."

"Dogs running it?"

"Yeah, but at dusk they come out to the feeders he had set up, and you basically got one shot and the rest hauled ass. I had fun and liked being in the woods, so I bought a lease up near Brooksville for deer and hogs and started hunting with my fishing buddies. At night I can shoot two at each of my feeders, using the silencer and suppressor system. They don't run until the first one falls. Then we change locations in an electric golf cart and have another feeder go off a half an hour later. There are so many nuisance feral hogs in Florida that there's always an open season with no limits. I would have liked to show you the lease and zeroed the rifle in up there, but I'm sure at this point the Goombas are watching it ... turn south on 75, and then east on route 60."

"So how are things at the boatworks? I miss it."

"Well, we miss you. We hired a foreman from Ross Marine when they closed."

"They closed?"

"Yeah, a developer bought the yard to build waterfront condos. Courtney still has the boat brokerage, though. The foreman's working out and Jeb is doing great. I don't really need to be there, unless we have a bunch of big projects."

"I guess you'll be going back to work when Charley's boat arrives?"

"I'm actually looking forward to it, I've got a lady that I'm interested in right now, and the Huckins will be a challenging project. It will give me a chance to show Jeb how critical path project planning works."

"Critical path planning, Ol' Robert E. taught us that skill. You can cut a project's timeline in half if you stick to it. I can hear him now, 'If you two don't finish this today, the two carpenters can't start on that tomorrow!' So we wouldn't go home until we were caught up on the plan."

"Right, and he always had the materials and equipment on hand ahead of time so you couldn't argue with him."

"Well, here's the motel ... it took 20 minutes that way too."

CHAPTER TWENTY-FIVE

Seth was up first the next morning, figuring Beau was probably tired from traveling and the two hour time-zone change.

"Rise and shine, Beau, We've got some things to do and I want you to see the whole venue in the daylight."

Beau rolled out of bed, took a shower, and put on some fresh shorts and a Polo shirt. They drove to the Waffle House for breakfast in the Ford pickup. Half way there Beau said, "Excuse me … is there a dead mullet under your freaking seat?"

Seth snorted and replied, "Tilley was in the fish business over in Stuart for a couple of years after he retired. You won't notice it as much when the AC starts cranking."

They ordered breakfast and Beau asked, "So what about this lady you're interested in? You and Annie were sort of an item the last time I saw you."

"Annie and I had some good times. But it wasn't going anywhere. This woman is different; I think I could live with her. Her name is Lori and she's widowed with two grown children. She moved back to St. Pete after her husband died. You know her parents, the Dunn's, from the Yacht Club and the boatworks."

"I remember her, she's almost my age."

"What's going on with you and Fonda Johnson?"

"Well, her ailing mother's still alive, so I fly over to Panama City and see her every other month. I haven't told her the truth, yet. I think I'd need a commitment from her to move to Costa Rica and marry me first. I think she would understand."

"Did you buy any more real estate in Tambor?"

"I did. I bought two more rental houses, but I'm not in a hurry to buy any more unless they're really good deal and have a strong rental history."

"What have you done with the three million?"

"I have three $500,000 guaranteed annuities. They're separately located in the Caymans, Bermuda, and the Bahamas. I own my house and the three rental properties. I bought the Bertram 31 you've been fishing in, and put two new Yanmar 315's in her a few months ago. And I have some gold and $200,000 cash in a safe place."

"Sounds like you're in good shape."

"Yeah, I get a little pension and my healthcare from Canada. The rental properties generate a good rental income, and I can easily live off of that. I have two three-bedroom houses and one four-bedroom. They all have swimming pools, and ocean views. Depending on the season they rent for $1500 to $2,500 a week. I can fix most anything myself, and I pay a reasonable booking fee by renting them on the internet. Two maids and a gardener-pool man only run me $10,000 a year. Costa Rica's low taxes help, too."

"So you're going to stay in Tambor?"

"I like it. I've made some friends among the locals and the ex-pats. They go fishing with me and we socialize. Nobody asks too many questions, we just enjoy the moment."

Seth picked up the breakfast check and they headed for Shoot Straight to zero-in the Remington. They pulled into the range as it was opening and an hour later they were back at the motel.

"Now that the rifle is sighted in, let's load the bike and all your gear in the rental van and take a ride to south Tampa."

Beau drove in using the Channelside route and passed the docked cruise ships that were disembarking their passengers. Sunday the ships would fill back up and head back to the Caribbean. They drove past Cipriano's Golf View house, weaving among the service vans parked on the narrow brick street. Seth directed Beau around the perimeter of the entire golf course all the way over to S. MacDill Avenue, just in case he had to find a different escape route off the course. They drove west across West Swann Avenue and Seth showed Beau where Wall to Wall lived on Tampa Bay. They drove back to Palma Ceia and he showed Beau how he could throw off a tail by cutting through Plant High School south of the golf course. They ended up parking in the BP automated gas station a half a block north of Donatello's Restaurant, and across the divided section of South Dale Mabry from JC Carpet. Luigi's black Escalade was parked in the back of JC's lot.

At 1:30, Luigi and two other men came out of JC's and walked down to Donatello's for lunch.

"No wonder they call him Wall to Wall," said Beau, as he watched Luigi navigate the sidewalk. "He waddles like a damn penguin."

"Don't underestimate him, Beau. He may look like a penguin, but he's as smart as a fox."

They waited about an hour, and watched Luigi and his two companions walk back into the carpet store.

"Let's head back to Brandon, have a late lunch, and then take a short nap. You know, just sitting here thinking, I believe I've figured out how to ensure that Luigi will be at Cipriano's tonight."

"Really ... tell me all about it, Seth."

***

Beau rode the mountain bike across West Watrous Avenue and turned down South Himes. He turned back left when he reached Jean Circle and rode northwest the long way to South Golf View. He rode south on Golf View and made the zig-zag onto the cart path. It was 8:45 p.m. and the twilight was just beginning to wane. The western sky was overcast with the building cumulus clouds making it darker than normal. The wind was light and from the east. Beau made his way to the live oak stand. He hid the bike and positioned himself at the base of the chosen tree. The monkey fist flew over the horizontal limb, and ten minutes later Beau was straddling the limb behind the cross cluster of branches. He snapped a magazine into the Remington and took a test sight on Cipriano's empty chair. His angle was perfect. The laser sight's carried over the railing and bulletproof glass producing tiny red dots on the chair's headrest. He had his prepaid cell phone in his pocket on vibrate and dark. He took a deep breath and relaxed. At 9:00, Cipriano's stocky bodyguard walked the perimeter of the walled yard below. The billiards room light snapped on at 9:15 and No Nose walked out on the veranda. Three minutes later Beau saw the tall bodyguard light Cipriano's 9 inch long cigar and watched his target settle into his easy chair.

***

Seth Stone sat across Dale Mabry from JC Carpet, in a small strip shopping mall next to the BP station. The engine of the Ford F-150 was running, and the air conditioning was on high. No matter how cold he made it, he could still smell the fish. Two different pizza delivery men arrived at JC between 7:45 and 8:00. Seth figured that car salesman, flooring salesman, and all other big box store employees probably consumed the unhealthiest diet in the country. A few carpet customers pulled in and out. Seth nervously checked his Rolex, it was 8:45. He opened his pre-paid cell phone and dialed 813-555-1234.

"JC Carpet, this is Rhonda. How can I help you?"

"Rhonda, this is Seth Stone, Luigi Scuzzi is expecting my call."

"Hold one moment, Mr. Stone, and I'll see if Mr. Scuzzi is in his office."..............................

.........."Ahhh, the elusive Mr. Stone, this is Luigi Scuzzi, you've obviously figured out we want to talk to you."

"Yes, Mr. Scuzzi ... I am very willing to talk to your boss, John Cipriano, but only on my own terms."

"Which are?"

"I think he wants to ask me what I was doing at the Los Suenos Marriott the night that the Bertram 54, *CHICA,* blew up and burned. There is a very logical reason why I was there, and I will be happy to explain it to him. I know he is a man that understands family. I will meet him in a public place with two of my associates nearby, if he will do the same. Say, home plate at Al Lang Field in St., Petersburg. He can name the time. My two associates will stay in the home dugout and his two will stay in the visitors. A friend of mine, who runs the St. Pete Parks Department, will give us exclusive and confidential access."

"I can ask him ... where can I get back to you?"

"You have caller ID?"

"Yeah."

"Then you've got my number. It's a prepaid, untraceable, cell phone. Call me as soon as possible."

Seth ended the call, took a deep breath, and wiped the sweat off his forehead.

Fifteen minutes later Luigi scurried across JC's parking lot, got in his Escalade, and took off south on Dale Mabry. If he took the bait, Wall to Wall was on his way to meet with No Nose and provide Beau with a "two-fer".

Seth pulled quickly out of the strip mall, crossed the median at Fig Street, and headed south two cars behind him. Luigi crossed West Kennedy, West Swann, and turned left on West Watrous. Seth followed him, but turned right into the alley behind Wright's Gourmet and parked next to the rental van.

He speed-dialed Beau ...... Seth whispered, "The penguin is on his way."

"Cipriano is puffing on his cigar," whispered Beau.

"Good luck, I'm waiting at the van."

***

Beau double checked his equipment and then remained motionless in the live oak. Ten minutes later the tall bodyguard left his post on the veranda and walked through the billiards room. In less than five minutes, Luigi walked past the billiards table and the bodyguard took up his post at the door. Luigi walked down the veranda, shook hands with No Nose and sat down next to him. Beau could see a small table between their chairs. Cipriano handed Luigi a long cigar. Luigi cut the tip, and lit it. Soon two plumes of cigar smoke wafted gently through the spot lights in the roof eaves above them. Their conversation was animated. Luigi shook his head *yes* as Cipriano gesticulated with his hands and arms. Cipriano finally calmed down and poured them both a drink from a decanter into two heavy old-fashioned glasses, neat. They clinked their glasses, took a sip, and sat back in their chairs to savor it. As No Nose raised his cigar to his lips, Beau's middle finger pressed the laser sight switch on his rifle grip. He had the cigar's red glowing tip in his scope's cross hairs. The red laser dot settled in on No Nose's forehead. Beau squeezed the trigger. There was no flash and no bang, just a whoosh. As No Nose's forehead exploded, Beau quickly worked the Remington's bolt action, and chambered another round. He moved the laser dot smoothly onto the right temple of Luigi Scuzzi, who had turned his head towards the sound of No Nose's old-fashioned glass shattering on the tile floor. Beau squeezed off a second round. The top of Luigi's head erupted. Beau looked through the scope for the tall bodyguard, but he had apparently taken cover. The stocky bodyguard was standing near the pool, shouting up to the veranda. Beau slung the rifle over his shoulder and shimmied back to the tree trunk. He dropped the rope ladder, climbed down, and quickly repacked his backpack ... remembering to remove the bicycle lag from the tree trunk. He walked over to the oleander bushes, sheathed the rifle, slung on his backpack, and pedaled across the fairway and out the cart path onto Golf View Street. He sped north to West Morrison to put some distance between himself and Cipriano's neighborhood, turned left and pedaled normally to South Sterling, where he turned south to Watrous.

Seth was waiting behind Wright's and helped him load the bike.

"How did it go?"

"It's finished, let's get the fuck out of here ... now!"

"Drive back on the expressway, go north on Dale Mabry," said Seth, as the sound of sirens started to fill the air.

***

Beau arrived back at the Brandon motel just in front of Seth. There wasn't much traffic once they got off of I-275. When they were safely inside their suite, they cracked two Negra Modelos and started a post mortem.

"I wish we had been able to retrieve the shell casing from the first shot," said Seth.

"I don't think it makes any difference. The ballistic people will recover both the bullets and identify the caliber. They also will determine the angle of entry, and that will lead them right to the tree. The main thing you have to do is get rid of the rifle. It can be identified by its barrel markings on the slugs. I'd also ditch the silencer, but you can reuse the infrared scope, laser sights, and gun case. There also may be some bicycle tire tracks on the cart path. The fairway was a little squishy from the automatic sprinklers night watering when I left."

"We also need to disassemble and get rid of the rope ladder. I'll wipe the prints off the rungs. Will you do the same on the bicycle lag hangars? Where do you think we should dump the evidence?"

"First, I'd disassemble the gun and take the lag hangers and throw them all in the Alafia River near the mouth. The river is polluted regularly by U.S. Phosphoric, Cargill/Monsanto, Virginia-Carolina Chemical, and others, with acid and fluoride. The water there looks like tomato soup sometimes. The metal won't last long and nobody's going to swim or dive there. Second, I think we can just drop a print-free bike off by the West Union Street projects, along I-275, and nobody will ever see it again. Third, put the black rope in one garbage bag, and the rungs in another, and we'll find a couple of remote dumpsters. Put the drill and other tools and supplies in that tool satchel and take it with you to Stuart. I'll take the backpack and a set of those black clothes to Costa Rica with me in my suitcase."

Seth disassembled the rifle, wiped the pieces clean, and put them in a garbage bag along with the bike hangars. Beau bagged the rungs and rope in two separate bags. He brought the mountain bike in and wiped it clean. They loaded it all in the rental van and headed for the Alafia River, taking Rte. 60 to Rte 41. They took four trips over the bridge to Gibsonton, with Seth in the back seat throwing in one piece at a time. Then they headed north to the projects and dropped the bike off on a deserted corner on West Union. They drove back to Brandon and found remote dumpsters in Seffner and Dover. As they pulled back into the Brandon Motor Lodge Beau turned to Seth and said, "I hope throwing evidence off a bridge works better this time than it did two years ago."

"I knew it ... I knew you were going to ... **FUCKING** ... say that. How did you wait that long?"

"It wasn't easy, Bro," said Beau cracking up.

***

285

Seth woke up to a rainy overcast day. Beau woke a few minutes later, and he immediately hit the shower. Seth threw on his shorts, a t-shirt, and his flip-flops, and walked to the office to settle their final bill and get a Sunday *Tampa Tribune*. When he came back, Beau was sitting in the living room watching the local news.

"The shooting is all over the local TV stations," said Beau. "They call Cipriano a prominent local businessman and philanthropist, and in the next breath say he has suspected Mafia ties. They cite Luigi as his longtime employee and associate. So far they say law enforcement have no leads."

"*The Tribune* has both their pictures on the front page, and pictures of the Golf View mansion on the inside page. Listen to this … *As police try to piece together a motive for the killings, an undisclosed source at the FDLE suspects retaliation by the Russian Mafia, for a recent Tampa Mafia purge of Russian Mafia members operating in the Key West area* … I knew that's where this would go, because of Billy Ray."

"If it's all right with you Bro, I think I'm going to head back to Costa Rica … by way of Panama. I might as well drop in on Fonda for a couple of days. I'll call Copa and see if I can get a reservation."

"I think it would be wise if we vacate Tampa. I'm going to head to Stuart. But first, I need to take a shower."

When Seth came out of the bathroom, Beau was packing his duffel and carry-on suitcase.

"Did you get a flight?"

"Copa 479, to Panama City from Orlando, at 2:54 this afternoon."

"I'll pack my stuff and we'll split for the airport. Let's have a late breakfast off the Lakeland exit at Rte. 98, there's a Bob Evans there. I'll follow you to the airport in case you have any trouble. I'll keep going on the Beeline Expressway when you turn in at the airport."

They pulled out 20 minutes later and ate their breakfast up I-4 in Lakeland, the Bob Evans was busy with Sunday church families coming and going. Seth promised to call Beau in a couple of weeks to update him on the Tampa/Russian Mafia situation. They said their goodbyes in the parking lot.

"Thanks, Beau. I couldn't have done this by myself."

"Hey, I owe you … big time, or have you forgotten? I wouldn't even be here today if it weren't for you."

"Well, I guess we can call it even now?"

"There's no even, Seth, you're my brother."

The brothers hugged and headed for the airport. Beau waved out the window as he coasted off the Beeline at the airport. Seth tooted his horn and settled in for the ride over to I-95. He could hardly wait to rid himself of the fishy smelling Ford pickup.

Two hours and fifteen minutes later Seth pulled into Bill Tilley's drive way in Palm City. He found Bill cleaning up his Cabo 35 at the dock.

"Hey, Seth, how were the mountains?"

"Peaceful, for the most part. The whole Russian Mafia thing with "The Geezers" has blown over, although from what I read in the *Tampa Tribune's* Sunday paper on the internet this morning, it looks like they're at war with the Tampa Mafia."

"That's good news! What are your plans now?"

"I'm going to call a friend of mine in St. Pete and see if she wants to cruise through the Okeechobee and back up the west coast with me."

"She? … Is it someone special?"

"She may be … is Trudy back yet?"

"No, one of the grandkids got strep throat, so she's helping out."

"I'm sure she's worried, strep can turn into all kinds of problems if it isn't taken care of quickly."

"Amen … Hey, you're all fueled up, and I had my detailer give *TAR BABY* a wash on Friday."

"Thanks, Bill, what do I owe you?"

"The fuel was $1135 and the wash $55. How about dinner tonight? We can go over the bridge to Wahoo's."

"Sounds good, I'll buy dinner and give you cash for the fuel and boat wash. Right now I want to reload my gear on the boat and make that phone call. Thanks again for lending me your truck, and that reminds me … would you mind if we went to a steak restaurant tonight? For some reason … I'm just not up for fish tonight."

Seth got situated on the Hatteras, sat down in the air conditioned salon, took a deep breath, and dialed Lori. She picked up on the third ring.

"Well, if it isn't my prodigal fisherman."

"Yes it is. I'm in Stuart and I'm all fished-out for awhile."

"Well … that's good news, because I've been missing you!"

"How would you like to see me tomorrow?"

"I'd like that."

"Well, do you think you could rent a car and drive over tomorrow? We can spend the night in Stuart, and you can meet my friend Bill Tilley. Then we'll discuss a leisurely cruise home through the waterway or the longer route down the east coast and through the Keys."

"I already like the longer route."

"Call me when you get to the rental car office in Stuart, and I'll come pick you up. Pack casual … but bring a slinky black dress. I'll take you to a couple places, along the way, where I can show you off."

"I'll be there before lunch, Seth."

EPILOGUE

Vincent "Cadillac" Carlucci became the new boss of the Tampa Mafia. He chose to run it out of Miami, much like Santos Trafficante had back in the mid-1950s, when he owned the Capri Hotel and Casino in Havana. His first order of business, after seeing that "No Nose" and Luigi had proper gangland funerals, was to send "Fat John" Conte to Brighton Beach, in New York City, to assassinate Vladimir Ivankof with a cell phone car bomb. Unfortunately, for Fat John, the bomb went off as he activated it under Vladimir's BMW sedan.

Six weeks later, after going missing for two weeks, Pete "The Barber" Guggino washed up on Miami Beach, in front of the Fontainebleau Hotel, in a 55 gallon drum which had been purposely rigged to float.

Three weeks after The Barber was found; Aleksey Radoslav, Vladimir's consigliore, was gunned down in front of the Skovorodka Restaurant on Brighton Beach Avenue, in New York.

Ten days later, Giorgio Scuzzi was found dead in his Bayshore Boulevard penthouse condo, stark naked, with an ice pick in his left ear. The forensic pathologist detected a strong scent of Chanel No.5 on his body.

A month later, Cadillac Carlucci and his two bodyguards, "Big Fred" and "The Animal" were killed by a bomb attached to a remote controlled DJI Phantom-2, four-rotor, helicopter mini-drone, as they were putting the top down on his Cadillac Eldorado convertible, behind the Pink Pony in Miami. This scheme ushered in a whole new, high-tech chapter in gangland murder methods.

At this point, the five major Mafia families in New York City stepped in and negotiated a truce with the Russians. They split up Florida, assimilated the remaining Tampa Mafia members, and gave Key West back to the Russians.

Captain Tony Fungello found a new ride and went Big Game fishing.

www.ingramcontent.com/pod-product-compliance
Lightning Source LLC
Chambersburg PA
CBHW070840250626

47159CB00003B/856